RUN, RIVER, RUN

THE JAMES GANG

C. F. FRANCIS

To all the medical professionals.
Bless you and thank you.

RUN, RIVER, RUN

By

C. F. Francis

PROLOGUE

*S*ummer, *North Carolina Mountains*

A LOW-GROWING branch whipped across River Chandler's cheek. She didn't think it was possible, but her heart ratcheted up another notch. Ignoring the pounding in her chest and the sting from the cut, she kept up her frantic pace as she dodged and weaved a convoluted path through the thick forest. Invisible ants scurried over her skin as she continued on legs that were less than steady. There were moments when she was fourteen years old again, sprinting through this same forest desperately seeking a place to hide. She hadn't died that day. Would today be her day?

River pushed the debilitating thoughts aside. They would do her no good.

Her eyes flicked from the decayed leaves carpeting the forest floor to the web of trees and shrubs in front of her. She'd already tripped over one exposed root. The stumble had cost her seconds—precious seconds she might not have to spare. Her pursuer could be right behind her or nowhere nearby. She couldn't hear over the sound of her lungs gushing air like bellows fanning a flame.

Reaching up to deflect another branch, the morning sun caught the wet, crimson blood on the back of her hand. The slash across her arm from the hunting knife was deep, but she'd been too busy running to deal with it or to think about the consequences. Now she saw the wound was bleeding freely. Blood trickled down her forearm and dripped off the tip of her finger onto a discarded leaf. Her stomach twisted. She'd been leaving a trail a toddler could follow.

Weighing her odds, River ducked behind a large rhododendron and yanked off her shirt. Despite her trembling hands, she ripped a sleeve from the old flannel garment and wrapped it tightly around her arm. Her fingers fumbled with the fabric. It took two tries to secure the knot. She slipped on what was left of her shirt, then wiped her bloody arm on the back of her jeans. With the flow of blood stopped, she took a bigger risk and poked her head from her hiding place, forcing her breathing to slow so she could hear as well as see.

No creatures stirred. No birds sang. Other than the rustling of leaves from the cool mountain breeze, the forest was silent—not the normal vibrant ecosystem she knew and loved. Had she scared its inhabitants away or had someone else? She had to assume the worst.

Sucking in a deep breath, she bolted from her hiding place. This mountain had saved her life once. Would it protect her again?

1

Ten months later, Sanibel Island, Florida

TIGHTENING his grip on the boom, Kevin Slawter adjusted his stance as the wind shifted. He'd arrived at the beach early to get in some windsurfing off the Sanibel Causeway before the waters were filled with boats and jet skis.

It was a cloudless morning. If he was up for more of a challenge, Kevin would have wished for a stiff wind. The strong breeze was enough to keep him gliding along the water but didn't require his total concentration. He'd come out here for some solitary time to clear his head. He didn't want a challenge. He wanted peace. His friends had found it here. Could he? With each visit to the island, Kevin was less inclined to return to active duty. He didn't know if it was this place that pulled him in or his growing distaste for the business of war which caused the turmoil inside.

Being a medic in the Special Forces, he'd seen his fill of death and injury. It was becoming more difficult to bear what he knew would inevitably come with each deploy-ment. The year before last, he'd pressed gauze into the eye socket of his teammate and friend after Troy had attempted to stop a suicide bomber. If Kevin hadn't been in the same marketplace, Troy would most likely have died. He told himself that was reason enough to continue to serve.

Turning his attention back to the surf, Kevin tacked into the wind. The change of direction gave him a view of the narrow causeway beach. When the area started to fill with people he planned to head in, but currently a single woman sifted through the shell line, or trash line as it was locally known, for shells. Unlike most of the shell hunters he'd seen, she was much younger. Even from this distance, her posture and movement spelled youth.

As he periodically checked the beach, watching for the influx of people, he found himself looking for the woman. He'd just spotted her again when a man tore up the beach in her direction. Her back was to him. The soft sand beneath his feet would make it impossible for her to hear him approach. Kevin shouted, but his words were swal-lowed by the sound of the surf.

Turning his sail into the wind, he blasted toward the shore. Damn it. The wind was taking him east of the couple's position. As much as he wanted to steer against it, that would only slow his progress.

He kept his eye on the pair as he shot toward the beach. As soon as the man reached her, he yanked at the backpack she was wearing, trying to pull it free. When she didn't immediately release it, he shoved his foot into her back, slamming her into the sand. Her reflexes where quick, though. Rolling onto her pack, she pulled her assailant to the ground, then jammed her elbow into the man's throat.

Kevin swore as he unhooked his harness. The instant the rail of the board touched the sand, anger propelled him off of it. The wind caught the sail and knocked the rig on its side. He ignored it and took off in a dead run.

Her attacker was wrestling with the straps of her backpack while he dodged her fists and feet. "Hey!" Kevin shouted, closing the distance between them. "Get away from her."

The attacker's head snapped up. It didn't take him two seconds to decide retreat was a better option than dealing with the bull of a man barreling toward him. The woman rolled to her side, protecting her face from the sand kicked up as the man took off.

As much as he wanted to go after the bastard, Kevin's first instinct was to check on the victim. He dropped to his knees beside her. She scooted a few feet away.

Kevin stayed put. Keeping his distance to assure her that he wasn't a threat. Blood oozed from a cut on her cheek. Glancing at the ground, he noted the jagged rock and the spot of blood on it.

The woman was aggressively rubbing her eyes.

"Sand?" Kevin asked.

"What?"

"Do you have sand in your eyes?"

She nodded.

"Let me help you," he said, approaching her slowly. "I'm a medic." Kevin took her wrists and gently pulled her hands away from her face. Sand could do a lot of damage to the cornea. "Do you have any water in your pack?"

"Yes," she answered.

"I'm going to need it to flush your eyes. Okay?"

Nodding again, she slipped the small, simple sack from her shoulders.

When she blindly grappled for the zipper, Kevin took

the bag from her hands. He quickly unzipped it and reached for the water. He didn't miss the 9mm Smith & Wesson at the bottom of her pack. Who the hell carried a weapon to go shelling? Was her attacker after the gun or did she need it for protection? And what the hell had he just walked into?

"I'm Kevin," he introduced himself casually, hoping to put her at ease. "What's your name?"

"River." He didn't miss her hesitation before she answered.

"That's an unusual name. Okay, River, I want you to tilt your head back. I'm going to hold your eyes open while I flush them. All right?"

She turned her face toward the sky and waited, apparently deciding he posed no immediate threat.

He spread her eyelids with his thumb and index finger and was instantly mesmerized. Her irises were the palest shade of blue he'd ever seen—like ice on a frozen pond.

"Go ahead," she said. "I'm ready."

Kevin shook his head, breaking the trance. "You're going to want to flinch but try not to until I'm finished." Carefully, he sloshed water several times into both of her eyes. "Better?" he asked as he dropped his hand from her face.

She blinked several times then directed those blue tourmaline gems on him. The punch to his gut was twice as strong when the sparkle was accompanied by a wide smile.

"Yes. Thank you."

"Good," he said, gathering himself. "Let me wash that blood off your cheek so I can get a closer look at the cut."

"I didn't even feel it," she told him.

"I'm not surprised. Your eyes were more irritating," Kevin splashed some water against her cheek. The cut was small.

"Does it hurt?"

"No," she said, reaching up to touch her face. Kevin once again pulled her hand away.

"There's some nasty stuff on those rocks. You're going to need antibiotics," he told her. "Are you hurt anywhere else?"

She turned her neck and rolled her shoulders, then stood and brushed the sand from her legs. "You said you were a medic?"

"Yes. Army," he answered, pulling his phone from the waterproof lanyard that hung around his neck.

"Who are you calling?"

"The police." Rick Wilcowski was a former team member, his friend and, more importantly at the moment, a detective with the Sanibel Police Department. He needed to know about the attack, particularly since the guy had headed toward Sanibel.

"No. Don't!"

"Why the hell not? You were attacked."

She took the water bottle from his free hand—her touch sending a spark of electricity up his arm. "The man is gone. I was too busy to get a good look at him. Did you?"

"I saw him," Kevin answered, but he let the hand holding the phone drop to his side. He was mesmerized by the movement of her throat as she took several gulps of the liquid.

"Good enough to identify him?" she asked. "Did you get his tag number?"

Kevin continued to stare at her throat as a trickle of water settled in the valley at the base of her neck.

"Hello? You in there?" River asked.

Those eyes were locked on him again. If witches existed, he was staring at one now. She'd robbed him of speech. He snatched the water from her hand and took a slug. Rude. He wiped the rim with the hem of his swim trunks before handing it back to her.

"No, I wasn't close enough and I didn't see a car," Kevin finally answered. Had he been so distracted that he'd missed it? As a matter of fact, he didn't see any cars parked on the beach except his truck. Where was her vehicle?

"Then what's the point in calling the cops? I can't identify him," she persisted.

Her head was cocked as those spellbinding eyes stared up at him in curiosity. She was at least a foot shorter than his six feet two inches. She wore a cream-colored tank top that, from his advantageous angle, showed a hint of cleavage. Her brown shorts were—well—short. Her build was perfect for her height. What the hell was wrong with him? He should be concerned with her injuries instead of sizing her up.

"Because the police should be notified, regardless. You may not be his only victim or target," he explained, managing to get back on track.

She lifted her backpack from the sand. "If you want to notify them, knock yourself out. I can't add anything to it, and I've had all the excitement I can handle for one day— and it's still morning."

"You seem pretty calm for someone who just fought off an attacker." Despite her relaxed demeanor, those eyes continually scanned the surrounding area. She was putting on an act. She was scared. The weapon underscored his suspicion. He'd give her credit, though. She was skilled at pretending. No part of the beach went unnoticed under her gaze.

"You don't know me so you can't judge my reaction to

a given situation." She capped the bottle of water and shoved it into her bag.

He'd been pushing for a stronger reaction and he got one. She had a temper—and backbone. She hadn't backed away from him in spite of his size and looming stance. He should have expected as much since she had been fighting like hell when he reached her side. Given her attitude, why the insistence he not call the authorities?

"Why was he so determined to get your pack?"

"Obviously, he thought I had something of value in it," she answered. She slipped her arms through the thin straps of the bag. "Thanks again for your help," she said as she began to walk away.

"Hold up. How'd you get here?" He gazed up and down the beach. A couple of vehicles had joined his, but with the exception of his truck, the beach had been empty when he'd come ashore.

"I walked, if it's any of your business," she said, trotting toward the sidewalk that led over the last span of water before you reached Sanibel.

"I'll give you a ride."

She didn't lose a step as she looked over her shoulder. "If that's your board drifting out to sea, I think you need to direct your attention elsewhere."

Kevin turned to where he'd left the rig he'd borrowed from his friend, Gibson McKay. The tide was coming in and rising waters had caught the sail. It would be pulled into the bay if he didn't secure it.

"Shit." He backpedaled toward the equipment. "Hang on, would you?" he shouted, but River simply waved her hand over her head. Whether she was waving good-bye or waving him off, he wasn't certain.

2

———

As soon as she was out of sight of her savior, River picked up speed and jogged across the causeway, then made a quick left into an alley near the boat ramps on the other side of the bridge, taking a convoluted route back to her condo. It would cost her a few extra minutes, but neither her rescuer nor the attacker could follow her without her knowing it. She didn't have a reason to trust the striking hunk of a man who had come to her aid, but he hadn't frightened her. Considering her skittishness toward strangers, it didn't make sense.

Regardless of her reaction to him, she didn't want to talk to the police and based on his disapproving scowl at her dismissal of his suggestion, he was going to call—with or without her agreement. She'd kept a low profile since moving to Sanibel and she planned to keep it that way for as long as she was here. While she hadn't changed her name, River Chandler had virtually disappeared when she left North Carolina. She'd been on Sanibel for almost a year and had seen no evidence to dispute that assumption.

She rounded a hedge of hibiscus, turning down the crushed-shell alleyway which led to the rear of her condominium complex. Slowing to a fast walk, she caught her breath. The jog had been an easy trek, it was her nerves that were eating up the oxygen. Damn it.

The assault on the beach couldn't have anything to do with what happened in North Carolina. A lone woman made a tempting target. The guy today wanted her backpack—not her. She'd swear to it.

Besides, her assailant had plenty of time to do some real damage even before that guy, Kevin, had come to her rescue. There was nothing of value in her bag, but an opportunist wouldn't have known that. Water, sunscreen, and keys, along with her ID, made up the contents of the sack. Oh, yeah, and her gun—for all the good it did her today. Had Captain America spotted it when he retrieved the bottle of water? Probably. If he was telling the truth, he was a trained soldier, and a soldier would hardly miss the weapon.

Once inside her unit, she double locked the door. Pressing her shoulder against it, she let out a cleansing breath. It took a minute to get her heart rate back to a normal rhythm. The attack had been an anomaly. It had to be. There was no reason to think it was the beginning of another reign of terror. Damn. She'd gotten comfortable and had dropped her defenses. Whether this was a single incident, or related to her troubles back home, she needed to be more careful

She reset the security system before pulling the handgun from her backpack. As a rule, she'd put the weapon on her nightstand when she returned home, but she hung on to it while she inspected the condo. Dan had made sure she knew how to handle a weapon. Still, the gun felt cold and heavy in her hand as she went from room to room.

Knowing it was obsessive, she hadn't been able to stop herself from checking the closets and under the bed. History told her not looking would nag at her. Might as well do it now rather than in the middle of the night. As she made her rounds, she continually wiped the sweat from her palms onto her shorts.

Nothing she found suggested that her home had been breached, but for the second time in a week her skin prickled. After ten months, surely her stalker would have moved on. As much as she had come to love this island, she yearned to return to the mountains where she was close to the spirit of her family. She'd lost them once. She didn't want to lose her remaining connection to them.

Shaking off the melancholy, she pulled a second phone from the pocket of her shorts. She had calls to make and she dreaded both. Dan would be concerned, and Aunt Amy would be frantic.

A quick check of the cell she used for incoming calls confirmed that no one had tried to reach her today. She dropped that phone on the workbench, holding on to the one she used for outgoing calls. She scrolled to Dan's number and pressed the call button.

"What's up, River?" Dan answered. The worry she expected resonated in his voice. Dan had become family even though they were not related by blood.

"Has anybody asked about me since we last spoke? Anything unusual?"

"No. Nothing. Why? What's happened?"

"A tussle with some guy on the beach," she said, circling the room. "I'm certain all he wanted was my backpack. The beach was desolate except for me and some guy windsurfing." She did her best to sound casual. She didn't want him to worry. An officer with the Department of Natural Resources, Dan Nelson had been the first on the grisly scene fourteen years ago. He'd found her frantically moving from one member of her family to another, pressing articles of clothing from the ransacked suitcases against their wounds —wounds that were no longer bleeding because their hearts had stopped pumping. When Dan had pulled her away, she'd clung to him until her aunt came for her. River and Dan had remained close ever since. Dan had taken it upon himself to try and fill the void left by the death of her father.

"Were you hurt?"

"No. A little sand in my eyes, but they're fine now thanks to the windsurfer. He came onshore and chased the bastard off."

"You sure you're all right?"

"Yes. Shaken but fine," she answered, hoping she sounded more confident than she felt. "Has there been any chatter? Anything I should know about?"

"I haven't heard a whisper about you in months."

"Nothing unusual at the cabin?"

"It's been as quiet and peaceful as a church since you left. Like I promised, I check on it regularly."

"I don't believe this had anything to do with my past. This was too bold a move. The asshole up there preferred to stay in the shadows while terrorizing me. I don't believe he would have attacked me if I hadn't come home unexpectedly that day." This morning had shaken her, but it was nothing compared to the acts that had taken place those last few months at her cabin.

"Have you learned anything further regarding the case?" she asked. While Dan had retired from law enforcement, he had friends in various agencies who knew he was close to her. According to Dan they were happy to keep him in the loop.

"There's been nothing new."

River's pacing came to a stop in front of her workbench. She glanced at the mask in front of her. Cutting all ties with her former life, she'd closed her online graphic design business. Now her work consisted of custom designed, high-end masks. She'd learned there were an endless number of collectors, masquerade parties and, of course, Mardi Gras. She didn't hurt for orders.

Last night she'd left her current project on the bench so the crystals could set. Adorned with glass pieces and cultured pearls, the next step was to fill in the empty spaces with the semi-precious stones she'd purchased for the project. She'd planned to finish it today, but last night's storm changed those plans. Her next design called for miniature shells—tiny, natural reproductions of the larger shells Sanibel was known for. They were tedious to find, but almost always plentiful after a storm. So, this morning she'd set off for an early morning foray to the beach.

She'd been so focused on finding the tiny treasures that she didn't sense the man coming up behind her. It had been stupid to let her guard down and now she had nothing to show for her trip. She'd left her small bag of booty at the beach.

A steady hand was required to work which meant she needed to get her nerves under control. The mask was her most ambitious, detailed, and expensive project to date.

The bejeweled mask stared back at her as if it had something to say. Probably *'get on with it.'* It was right. When the final stones were set, she would add feathers for the finishing touch. They softened the edges and concealed the ribbons that would help to hold the mask in place.

The ribbons. Her stomach rolled as she dropped into the

chair. She always laid the ribbons flat on the surface of the bench to avoid creases. Now they were bunched beneath the mask. She wouldn't have done that—consciously or unconsciously. When it came to her work, she was too damn meticulous.

"River? What's wrong?" Dan asked.

How long had she been silent? "Nothing. Sorry. My mind was wandering."

"Do you want me to come down?"

"If it turns out to be anything more than a purse, or in this case, backpack snatcher, I'll call you and we'll go from there." The last thing she wanted was Dan or her aunt near danger if it had followed her here.

"Did you report the attack?"

"I can't identify him, and he didn't take anything," she said, as if that would explain things. Like the guy on the beach, Dan would have insisted on calling the authorities.

"I didn't mean to get you in a tizzy," she said, trying to lighten his unease.

"I'm not in a 'tizzy'," he said.

"Yes, you are, and I love you for it." She relaxed a bit as she pictured his face turning beet red. Dan was a caring, but far from a demonstrative, individual.

"When was the last time you talked to your aunt?" he asked, redirecting the conversation.

"A week ago. Don't mention this to her. Let me tell her," River said, staring out the sliding glass door. The master suite, along with the living room, had balconies which faced Tarpon Bay. River slept in the smaller of the two bedrooms. Here, she could spread her work out and still have the space for an old-fashioned drafting table where she sketched her designs. Besides, she was more comfortable sleeping in the bedroom which was marginally harder to access from the outside.

She promised Dan she'd call her aunt. First, she needed to take another pass through her place to see if she missed anything. Ribbons didn't get up and dance on their own unless they were part of a Disney movie. This was no Disney movie.

3

───────

While Kevin was wrestling the board and sail from the outgoing tide, he placed the overdue call to Rick. He'd rather be chasing after River. If he hadn't had to rescue the board, he would have taken off after her while he made the call., but the equipment wasn't his and River, along with her assailant, were long gone. Still, the incident needed to be reported.

"What's up?" Rick answered.

"I just witnessed an assault," Kevin said. He held the phone to one ear while he slid the board the rest of the way into the bed of the truck.

"Where?"

"On the causeway," Kevin answered, slamming the tailgate.

"That's Lee County Sheriff's territory. I'll place the call. Where on the causeway? Do they need to come with lights and sirens? Paramedics?"

"Don't press any buttons," Kevin warned off his friend. "There's no one left to talk to, tend to, or arrest. The assailant took off the minute my feet hit the sand. The woman didn't want the police involved and is long gone. Both of them headed toward the island," he continued, "so I wanted to give you a heads up."

"Give me their descriptions. How long ago did this happen?"

Kevin glanced at his dive watch. "I'd say fifteen or twenty minutes since I first spotted the two. I never saw his face, but he was a white male in mid-forties. Average height and weight. Short, dark hair." Kevin hopped into the driver's seat and started the engine. The rumble of his truck must have reverberated through the speaker.

"Stay where you are," Rick told him. "I'm coming to you."

"Why? There's nothing to see. Besides, you said this isn't your jurisdiction." But he knew there was no point in arguing with Rick. Kevin moved his vehicle a few yards to the spot where the woman had been attacked. Grabbing his t-shirt from the passenger seat, he got out of the truck.

"Which beach?"

"First one out of Sanibel." The causeway consisted of bridges and small atolls. "You'll see my truck on the right," Kevin answered. There were three atolls the causeway ran through. They were popular places. You could pull right up to the water's edge and, unlike the beaches on Sanibel, there was no charge for parking.

"Can you describe the woman? What were they driving?"

Kevin clasped the back of his neck and rubbed. "I never saw the guy's vehicle. If he was parked anywhere nearby, it was out of my line of sight."

"And the woman? Did she sprout wings and fly?"

"Funny. She walked."

"And you let her?" Rick had him on speaker. Kevin heard the sound of the truck's engine as Rick stepped on the gas.

"I think forcing her to stay against her will would be breaking some law. I offered to give her a ride, but she took off." And for some reason that irritated the hell out of him.

"At least tell me you can describe her. Did you manage to get her name?"

Kevin understood Rick's frustration. Every member of the team was trained to see the details. It's what kept them alive, but Kevin basically knew squat. One thing he could do, though, was describe the attractive woman. He wouldn't forget those eyes or the fear she quickly reined in.

"River," Kevin told him.

"Did you say river?" Rick asked.

"Yes. River. Like in the Mississippi."

"First or last name?"

The question stopped Kevin. He'd given her his first name. He'd assumed she had responded with the same. Shit. He hadn't asked.

"I think it's her first."

"You're not giving me much to work with," Rick said. "What did this River look like?"

Kevin slipped his shirt over his head then leaned against the grill of his Silverado. As he did, he imagined the woman standing in front of him. "Five-foot-two or three. Long, dark brown hair—almost black. It was tied in a ponytail. Blue eyes the color of ice. They'd be hard to forget."

Rick jotted down some notes then waited for Kevin to continue.

"She was wearing a snug fitting tan tank top and brown shorts. There is a three-inch scar on her right arm.

I'd say she was around one hundred and twenty pounds." He mentally scanned the rest of her body. Bad move. He was getting hard just thinking of her which didn't make a damn bit of sense. She was a stranger, and one he'd probably never see again. Besides, since his fiancé had run off and married another man, he been in a self-imposed moratorium where women were concerned, at least while he remained in the Army. Deployments screwed with relationships. Why was his mind suddenly going in that direction?

Feet. Think of her feet. "She wore cheap, white flip-flops. Her toenails were polished red."

He remembered her hands. Short, unpolished nails. No rings. Why couldn't she have been wearing a wedding ring? That would have dampened his interest.

Rick pulled onto the beach next to Kevin's truck.

"You're not giving me much on the attacker, but the woman certainly made an impression on you," Rick commented as he slammed the door to his vehicle.

"She stuck around longer than the asshole did," Kevin said, scowling at his friend.

Rick gave him a questioning glance before directing his attention to the beach. "Is that where the assault took place?" He pointed to an area of disturbance in the otherwise smooth sand.

"I saw them from the water and got to the beach as fast as the wind would carry me. The wind also determined my landing spot which was down near those trees." Kevin indicated the small grouping of Australian pines on the otherwise shadeless beach. "I shouted at him before my feet hit the sand. That's when the guy took off. She was pounding on him pretty good, but she was no match for him. He could have easily knocked her out and grabbed the backpack."

"You sure that's what he wanted?" Rick asked, as they stood over the spot on the beach where the action had taken place. "The pack?"

"That was my impression. Even with her counter attacks he stayed focused on the bag."

"Any idea what was in the backpack?"

Kevin glanced over the water, replaying the conversation with River. She'd given nothing away except for the flash of fear in her hypnotic eyes. "I don't know what he thought was in it, but there was nothing of value in her pack. I opened it to get a bottle of water to rinse the sand out of her eyes. The man had kicked up a lot of it when he took off." Kevin didn't mention the gun. He didn't know if she had a permit. Why should he care one way or the other?

"What was she doing?"

"What most people do on Sanibel. Looking for shells." Sanibel was known for its shelling. The island's geography made it a landing spot for all varieties. Kevin inspected the base of the protruding stone she'd scraped her cheek on during her struggle. As he suspected, a small, plastic Ziploc bag, half-filled with an assortment of miniscule shells was caught up against its rough side. Her finds from this morning. He picked it up even though he had no way of knowing how to return it to her.

Rick glanced over the area again. "Not much I can do. I'll report it to the Lee County Sheriff's office. They might add a patrol to the causeway."

"No other reports of purse snatchers or assaults along the bridge or on the island?" Kevin asked his friend as they moved toward their vehicles.

"Not on Sanibel. I'll ask the Sheriff's office, but they would have reported any incident on the causeway to us."

"Looks like you're done for the day," Rick commented, indicating the board in the back of Kevin's truck.

"I'd planned to leave once the beach started to fill up. This simply moved up my timetable a bit," Kevin told him. "If you hear anything, will you let me know?"

"I will, but don't hold your breath. We got nothing," Rick said, walking back to his vehicle. "Gib might know this mysterious woman. If she's as stunning as you described and she's staying on the island, it's unlikely she's missed his attention."

As he watched Rick pull out onto the causeway, Kevin thumped his fisted hand against the steering wheel. Why hadn't he gotten the woman's full name? How the hell would he find her? He wanted to check on her status. That cut on her cheek was small but needed attention. He suspected she was too stubborn to have taken his warning seriously.

She handled herself well, though. She was tough. Hell, she'd been kicking the shit out of the man before Kevin hit the beach. He glanced at the plastic bag of shells. Damn it. Why *did* he care? She'd brushed the incident off as if it wasn't a big deal, but he'd seen the flash of fear in those eyes when she glanced at the surrounding beach. He needed to find her.

Checking with Gib was a decent idea. Kevin doubted their friend knew every woman on the island, but it wasn't outside the realm of possibilities. Gibson McKay attracted women. Plain and simple. Whether it was his good looks, charm, his genuine interest in everyone he met or his wicked sense of humor, women adored him. He'd stop to see Gib after he reconnoitered the area.

He'd also visit his former lieutenant. Steve Brody had opened up a security and investigations business on the island It was a long shot, but perhaps he or Troy, who now worked with Steve, would have some advice on how to begin a search for the vanishing woman.

With a partial plan in place, Kevin pulled out onto the road.

4

___

*A*fter going through her condo a second time, River returned to the workroom. She studied the unfinished mask—its hollow eyes staring back at her. She'd didn't want to touch it. The mask now spooked her.

Instead, she'd call her aunt and get that conversation out of the way. She immediately felt guilty for her hesitation to place the call, along with her plans to cut it short. She loved her aunt. The woman had rearranged her life to care for River after the murders, but Aunt Amy's constant concern for her had begun to wear on River. It had been hard to tear free of the apron strings her aunt had woven around her.

Placing her gun on the workbench, River reached for the phone next to the weapon before realizing she'd picked up one of her back-up phones. She removed the cell phones from the pockets of her shorts and placed them on the bench. She stared at the three objects. One phone for outgoing calls, one for incoming—and a back-up phone in each room. She was suspect of everyone she met, and it was hard not to meet people on the island unless she remained quarantined in her unit. She hadn't become a recluse. Occasionally, she'd grab a bite to eat at a local restaurant. She did her own grocery shopping, made the necessary trips to the shipping store, and regularly visited the gun range to practice her shooting skills. But contrary to her isolated mountain community, Sanibel was teeming with people. Yet she remained alone after all these months.

The cell phone designated for incoming calls rang.

"River." Relief resonated in her aunt's voice.

"Damn it. Dan called you, didn't he?" River sighed. She may not be the steadiest person on earth, but she wasn't a broken fourteen-year-old any longer. Her aunt and Dan had been there when she fell apart. They'd helped to pick up the pieces of her life and glued them back together. Still, there were pieces that hadn't been found. It wasn't hard to understand, but difficult to describe. She was empty in places.

She accepted the fact that she'd never feel whole again. River often thought it was a blessing that her parents and brother had left this earth together. She believed neither parent could bear to be without each other or their children. Perhaps her supposition was her way of dealing with the loss—of tamping down her anger. She'd never shared that belief with anyone. Individuals aware of what she'd gone through, suspected she was emotionally damaged. Sharing those thoughts would simply support their suspicions, but no one had known her parents like she had. They belonged together. Billy, she didn't doubt, was wrapped tightly in their arms. They were a family still. It was River who had been left behind. There were times she felt cheated.

"Don't be mad at him. He was worried," Aunt Amy said, pulling River from her mental meanderings.

"He didn't need to make you worry, too." She'd have a

talk with Dan. She expected her requests to be respected. She'd needed their care and comfort after the murders of her family, but it was past time they respected her as an adult. It took her until after her graduation from college before she'd garnered the nerve to tell them the hovering would have to end. When the recent campaign of terror started, however, their protective instincts came roaring back.

"I know you don't need us anymore…"

"I'll always need you in my life," River corrected, her voice softening. "You've always been there for me and I know you always will, but I don't want you worrying about me." Her aunt had been considerably younger than River's mother when she'd taken River in. Aunt Amy had occasionally dated, but never married. River often wondered if she was responsible for her aunt's lack of a family.

"It's hard not to worry," her aunt said.

"I know and I'm grateful that you care. I was getting ready to call you. Has anyone been asking about me? Anything I should know?"

"Nothing out of the ordinary."

River's pacing came to a stop. "What's ordinary?" she asked. Had she been the topic of conversations?

"Old friends occasionally ask how you're doing. Nothing unusual."

"What sort of things do they ask?" River was being silly. Of course, neighbors and such would inquire about the child her aunt had taken in.

"How you're doing. Where you're living? That sort of thing."

River's heart skipped a beat. They were normal, casual questions. Why did they make her nervous? "What do you tell someone if they ask?"

"That you took a job in California. I have to tell them something. Saying I didn't know would seem strange."

Letting out a breath, River had to agree. She and her aunt had been too close for River to just drop off the map and cut all ties. With all their planning, that question hadn't been discussed. Stupid. Well, they'd have to come up with another story when she moved back.

"Sorry if I sounded short with you," River said. "I'm a tad bit jumpy after this morning."

"I'm not surprised. Do you plan on staying there or moving somewhere else?"

"I can't keep running. Besides, I don't think this morning had anything to do with what happened at the cabin. Someone saw an opportunity and took it."

"I hope you're right. You call me tonight. Let me know you're okay."

"I will. Love you," River said.

"Love you, too, honey," her aunt said before she disconnected the call.

River picked up her weapon, checked the safety and slipped it in the waistband of her shorts. Good God, she was getting paranoid if she intended to carry a weapon with her while she was at home.

5

———

*A*fter driving up and down the streets closest to the causeway for nearly an hour, Kevin abandoned his search and headed for his friends' place. If he was lucky, Gib wouldn't be out on a shoot and Steve would be in his office. The businesses sat side-by-side on Periwinkle Way, the main road through Sanibel. The team referred to the two buildings as the compound. When there was trouble—and this group found its share—one or both of the locations acted as a headquarters while whatever issue played out.

Kevin turned into the drive which separated the two buildings. As was his habit when visiting his friends, he pulled up behind the studio, leaving the street parking available for clients.

His luck was improving. Gib's massive truck sat next to Colt's Jeep. Kevin's former commander, Colton James, co-owned the photography studio, *Island Images*, along with Gib. The photo business took up the ground floor. Kevin glanced up the stairs at the two condo units above. Unless Gib was entertaining, it was unlikely he'd be home this time of day. Kevin skirted the building to the front of the business. Colt was a stickler for security since his wife, Cat, had been the target of an assassin a couple of years ago. You either had a key and the alarm code or you entered through the front door.

Kevin did a mental fist pump when he spotted Steve's classic Mustang in front of the single story building next door. The former ranch-style house was now home to Cat's garden design center in addition to Steve's security and investigation business. If Gib was busy, Kevin would run over and talk to Steve. He'd be happy scoring one out of two.

A buzzer sounded as he entered the studio, announcing his arrival. Not wanting to disturb any work that might be going on in the back, Kevin waited. It gave him a chance to view the updated display of wildlife photographs. Who'd have imagined their tough-as-nails commander had such a gift for capturing nature?

"Hey," Colt said, as he entered the lobby. "Good day on the water?"

"Cut things short when some asshole attacked a woman on the beach."

"What happened?"

His former captain hadn't lost his edge since leaving the Army. It had been buried for a while but had never left him. There was a time the team had believed they'd lost Colt. After his last mission to Afghanistan, he'd withdrawn to what he referred to as 'his dark place' where none of them had been able to reach him, Gib had thrown him a lifeline when he'd rekindled his love of photography. Then Colt fell head over heels for Cat, a feisty, strong woman, who was now his wife. She'd managed to drag Colt back over the edge.

"Some bastard apparently wanted the backpack the woman was wearing. I chased him off."

"Did you call Rick?" Colt asked, walking further into the lobby.

"Yes, for all the good it did," Kevin huffed. "The guy was gone the minute my feet hit the sand and the woman didn't want to report the incident. She didn't wait around."

Colt's striking blue eyes stared back at Kevin, studying him. "You did what you could, so what's bothering you?"

"I think she's in some kind of trouble. She held up pretty well, but her fear was palpable. She also needed some medical attention for a cut she received. I want to confirm she had it looked at. Since she's a knock-out, it occurred to me that Gib may know her. He's a heat seeking missile when it comes to women."

"If she's been on the island for any length of time you could be right. He's next-door badgering Steve."

"For what?"

"He's trying to convince Steve to take Josie out for an evening so he can take care of Cece."

"You're kidding." Several months ago, Steve and Josie had celebrated the birth of their first child—a daughter, Carolina Catherine, CeCe for short. The little lady had them all enamored, but Gib had taken his duties as one of her godfathers very seriously.

"Nope."

"I bet he never changed a diaper in his life," Kevin laughed.

"He insisted Josie show him how then proved to her he could handle that part."

"Holy shit. He auditioned for the job of babysitter?"

"Cece has him wrapped around her little pinky," Colt laughed. "Why don't you head next door and enjoy the entertainment. I'd go, but I'm working on a deadline. Check with Steve. He might be able to help," he added.

"He was on my list," Kevin said, turning toward the door.

"Let me know if I can do anything."

Kevin gave his former commander a casual, two-finger salute as he left. Colt would always have the team's back. He'd been a first-class commander and a better friend. He'd made a good life for himself on the island. So had his former teammates, Steve and Troy. Could he do the same?

The tiny bell above the door rang as he entered the building next door. It was followed by the sound of castors rolling across the tile floor. Cat sailed out of her office, still in her chair. Her feet barely reached the floor. She reminded him of a fairy, but he knew better than to underestimate her. Kevin had witnessed her temper. You didn't cross Colt's wife and walk away without a scratch.

"Hi," she said. "I thought you might be a client or customer."

"I'm here to see the guys."

"Joining in the battle over Cece?" Cat grinned.

"No," Kevin laughed. "I'll concede that one to Gib."

Cat smiled, grabbed the inside of the door frame and, using her arms, propelled herself back into her office.

As soon as Cat disappeared, Kevin headed to the other end of the converted home where Steve's office was located. The lively conversation between the two men could be heard through the closed door. If he didn't have a more pressing matter to discuss, he'd enjoy watching them needle one another.

The conversation came to a halt when he entered Steve's office.

"What's up?" Steve asked, turning away from Gib.

"Hey! We're not finished here," Gib said. He been

leaning over the desk trying to maintain Steve's attention. His long blond ponytail swung over his shoulder as he turned to chastise Kevin.

"Yes, we are," Steve told him. "Talk to Josie. It's her call."

"She'll tell me to talk to you."

Steve grinned.

Kevin didn't doubt it. Steve was yanking Gib's chain and getting a kick out of it. Gib was the practical joker of the group. Any chance to even the field was taken.

"I need some help or direction," Kevin interrupted before the two of them started in again.

"What sort of help?" Steve asked.

"A woman was assaulted on the beach this morning." Kevin raised his hand halting any comments. "I reported it to Rick, but there's nothing he can do. I wasn't able to get a good look at her attacker and if he had a vehicle, I didn't see it. The woman didn't want the police involved and took off."

"Then why do you need us?" Steve asked.

"I want to find her. She held herself together well, but she was scared. It was more than just an after effect of the assault. I'd swear to it." He could still see the frantic look in her eyes as she'd scanned the beach. "She was also attractive as hell. I was hoping you would know her," he said, turning to Gib.

Kevin gave a detailed description of the woman, but Gib shook his head.

"She sounds stunning, but I can't say I've met anyone who fits that description."

"And you didn't get a name?" Steve asked.

"I did, but I don't know if it's her first or last."

"What is it?"

"River."

"Doesn't ring any bells either," Gib added.

"You're right," Steve said. "That could be a first or last name. What makes you think she lives on the island?"

"Because she was on foot and headed this way. There were no cars between the beach and Sanibel."

"Logical," Steve agreed, "but you don't have squat as far as information that would be useful in finding her."

"Damn. You guys don't have any suggestions?"

"She must have made a hell of an impression on you," Gib commented.

"She did, but my gut also tells me she's in some serious trouble."

6

———————

*R*iver wanted a shower before she left for the bank to pick up the semi-precious stones that were stored in a safe deposit box there. Hopefully, the shower would wash away some of the anxiety of the day along with the sand. She shoved a dining room chair under the knob of the front door before heading to the bathroom.

Despite her precautions, she rushed through her shower unable to stop the loop of Janet Leigh's death scene from *Psycho* running through her head. This was going to have to stop, she swore as she stepped out onto the bath mat. She was getting paranoid and *that* pissed her off. A chair under the door, carrying a weapon while walking through her home, and now she was speeding through a shower which she would normally find relaxing or rejuvenating, depending on the circumstances. One single incident and she was a frightened fourteen-year-old again.

No, you're not, she scolded the woman in the mirror. She'd been through worse shit than what happened this morning. A single day, no matter how bad, was not going to set her back to the beginning. She wouldn't let it. She'd take the rest of today to regroup then get out again tomorrow and continue her hunt for seashells. She'd damn well be more aware of her surroundings in the future.

Her cheek stung as she applied toner to her face. Damn. It might be her current state of paranoia, but the wound appeared a bit inflamed. The medic was probably right about the rock and the bacteria it could hold in its porous surface. Wasn't there some flesh-eating kind of bacteria? River shivered. Now she'd have that thought stuck in her head.

She slipped on a pair of jeans and a t-shirt then Googled the closest walk-in clinic. She debated swinging by the bank first, but the cut on her cheek was now creeping her out.

The wait to see the doctor was interminable and stressful. She didn't do crowds well. She battled the need to escape the packed waiting area. River wasn't surprised her blood pressure was soaring when the nurse brought her back to an exam room. She blew it off as 'white coat syndrome.' Although she had nothing against doctors, the jam-packed waiting areas ratcheted up her nerves. Dr. Grace materialized a short time later. Like the medic, the doctor was concerned about the source of the small cut. A shot of penicillin in her backside and two prescriptions, one for pills and one for ointment, were River's reward for the visit. She spent almost as much time at the busy pharmacy as she had at the clinic. This time she waited outside in her car to avoid the people milling around while her prescriptions were filled. It was 'season.' The population of the island tripled this time of year and with it the traffic and wait times for anything you wanted or needed. It was too late to go by the bank when she was done dealing with the issues surrounding the tiny cut. By the time she pulled into her parking spot at the condo, she was irritated and exhausted.

She scanned the lot and the building facade. The area was clear. Gathering her prescriptions and purse, she made a beeline for the stairs located at the opposite end of the building from her unit. Like all the buildings, the stairs were not enclosed and that was one of the reasons she had selected this complex. No one would be hiding in a darkened hallway. River pulled her gun from her bag when she reached the steps, checked to made sure the safety was on, then tucked it under her shirt at the back of her jeans. No point in scaring the neighbors.

When she reached the first landing, she surveyed the rear of the building, her eyes quickly taking in the area between the condo and the waters of the bay. Not surprisingly, it was empty. While she had never personally visited the spot, there was a dock and gazebo at the north end of the complex where most residents and guests socialized. Rarely had she noticed anyone wandering this more isolated area of the complex. She trotted up the last few steps, pausing as she approached the walkway which led to her condo. With any luck, the convoluted route would give her time to react if someone was waiting for her. Fortunately, her path was clear.

She was being silly, yet nerves tickled the back of her neck as she approached the door to her unit. She'd intentionally left the stairwell next to her condo for last. If someone was waiting for her, that would be the place—unless they'd already gained entry into her unit. She quietly twisted the doorknob. It was locked. If the door had been unlocked, it would have sent her a clear and an immediate warning.

A scrape of a shoe against concrete was the first confirmation her nerves had been sending her the correct signal.

She rested her hand on the weapon at her back as she prepared to greet the visitor.

She never completed her turn. Instead, River hit the ground hard. The impact was broken only slightly by her purse which landed between her and the solid walkway. One arm was trapped beneath her. Her attacker wasted no time grabbing her free arm, twisting it behind her back until it felt like it was going to pop from its socket. Her face was pressed deeper into the rough, woven surface of the doormat. The doorsill was the only thing she could see. Instinctively, she blindly kicked out with her feet. Sweeping her legs from side to side, she tried to make contact, but her flailing limbs found nothing but air. Her effort was rewarded by a knee pressed deep into her back below her weapon.

Her gun. If he found it, he could use her own weapon against her. With a new burst of energy, she wriggled and writhed beneath him. "What do you want?" she grunted. He answered by grabbing a fistful of hair then slamming her head against the door, stunning her.

"Move," he ordered, his voice laced with anger. He removed his knee from her back and pulled her arm straight up in the air, lifting her upper body off the concrete. He reached for her purse. Her right arm, now free, snapped out to meet his. Her fingernails raked down his exposed arm.

He snatched it out of her range at the same time pressing his booted foot against her hip, shoving her against the concrete walk.

"Bitch," he swore, grabbing her hair again. Too late, she started to scream. He viciously smacked her head against her unit's door. Blinking, River tried to clear her vision, but lights danced in front of her eyes then dimmed as she fell into darkness.

7

Kevin was still with Steve when Rick called to tell him they may have found Kevin's vanishing victim. There had been an assault on a woman whose first name was River. A neighbor had called it in. Rick refused to give him the address, stating it was a police scene. He'd call Kevin when it was clear. Fuck that.

Heading south on Periwinkle Way, he kept an eye open for flashing lights of first responders. Kevin was going on the assumption that River lived on the southern end of Sanibel near the causeway due to the fact that she'd left the beach on foot. Because it was getting late, Kevin didn't have any problem spotting the strobing lights of the police vehicles against the darkening sky. He followed them to their source. The parking lot of the condo complex was full, so he was forced to pull into another building's guest parking area.

He headed directly to the EMS vehicle, hoping he wouldn't find River on a gurney inside. His momentum was stopped when a police officer stepped in front of him.

"You need to get back, sir," the young woman said, stretching her neck to look him in the eye.

"Detective Wilcowski called me," Kevin told her. It wasn't a complete lie. Rick had called him.

The officer walked out of ear shot then spoke into her radio. Kevin moved to side-step her, but she took up her position in front of Kevin again. "You're to wait here," she said.

"Why? Is there a victim?"

"Just wait here, sir."

Kevin was mentally debating how hard he wanted to push the issue when a door shut on the second floor. Rick exited the last unit near the landing and headed for the stairs.

"I told you to stay put," Rick grumbled, as he approached. "How the hell did you find this place?"

"How many crime scenes could this island have? She'd headed in this direction when she walked away. The flashing lights were a give-away. How is she? Is she okay?" His eyes flicked to the EMS van.

"She's upstairs. She has some scrapes, contusions, and a possible concussion. The medics are finishing up with her now."

"I want to see her."

Rick's eyebrows rose. "What's with you? You're not related to her. You didn't witness this attack."

"If I'd caught the asshole this morning, he may not have gotten a second shot at her. I'm responsible for this."

"That's a stretch," Rick huffed. "We don't even know if this is the woman who was attacked or if it was the same guy from the beach."

"Seriously, Rick? What are the chances a person with the same name was attacked twice on the same day by two different people?"

"Come with me," Rick gave in, "but if she doesn't want you here, you leave. And if you stay, you keep out of our way. Understood?"

"Understood."

Kevin matched Rick's long stride. He noted the police tape across the landing to the second set of stairs as they approached the door at the end of the walkway.

"Is this where she was attacked?" Kevin asked.

"A neighbor below heard the scuffle. He didn't realize what was going on at first. He came out to check and spotted a man running out of the stairwell and take off toward the back of the building. He found Ms. Chandler— that's her last name—out cold. He ran back to his place to get his phone, then called us. He waited with her until we arrived."

"Thank God, there are decent people in this world," Kevin commented. He saw the spot of blood on the door-sill. "How bad is she hurt?"

"As I said, unless they say her head injury is more serious than it appears, she'll live—but she'll be sore as hell in the morning." Rick rested his hand on the doorknob but didn't open the door. "There's something else going on with her," Rick added.

"Like what?"

"Don't know. I went through her unit. Each room has a disposable cell phone, which leads me to believe she's running. She hasn't shared any details yet. There wasn't much time to question her before the medics arrived."

While he wished it hadn't, Kevin's gut had been right. There was more going on here than the assault this morning.

River was seated at a glass top dining room table when they entered the condo. Two paramedics bracketed her. One of them was carefully manipulating her right arm, checking its mobility. The other paramedic was applying an ointment to her right cheek. Her left cheek was already sporting a bandage. Eyes flicked in their direction then back to the medic who had a light grip on her chin to keep her from moving.

"You weren't kidding about those eyes. They'd be hard to forget," Rick said in a tone only Kevin could hear, a skill necessary on the front lines.

"Was River able to identify the guy? Did the neighbor get a description? Do we know what the asshole wanted?" Kevin asked, glancing at River. She appeared tiny compared to the two men attending her and neither were as big as Rick or Kevin. Tiny didn't mean weak. She sat as if she had a metal rod for a spine. Her jaw was set.

"The contents of her purse were dumped on the ground next to her. We need her to go through the items to see if anything is missing," Rick said. "As for a description, she says she didn't see anything but his shoes. He came at her from behind. The neighbor claims he only saw him for a second. His description was minimal—white male, dark hair, middle aged. Similar to your man on the beach."

"Damn it," Kevin raked his hand through his hair. "You know this has to be the same person. First someone tries to rip her backpack from her shoulders, and now her purse. What the hell do they want so badly?"

"I've hardly begun to question her. The paramedics took precedent."

"Well, I'm not stopping you and it looks like the EMTs are packing it up," Kevin said as the men next to River snapped off their latex gloves. One of them slipped a paper in front of her which she signed then slid it back toward him. She was refusing further treatment. He'd already determined she was stubborn from their short meeting on the beach. Her current actions confirmed his impression.

Rick joined the group, thanking the first responders as they picked up their gear. As much as Kevin wanted to check on River, he lagged behind. This was Rick's territory, and he'd agreed to his terms.

His friend sat on his haunches, so he was eye level with River. He spoke to her softly. Kevin couldn't make out every word they were saying, but when River's eyes darted to him and then back to Rick, it wasn't hard to piece the words together. When she nodded, Kevin took it as an invitation. He circled the table so her back was never to him. She'd been hit from behind twice today.

He turned the dining room chair next to River around and straddled it. The cheek on the right side of her face showed shallow cuts. None of them were bleeding. Those beautiful eyes reflected pain and exhaustion. He noted her right arm laid in her lap, unmoving.

"Remember me?" he asked. "Sorry I didn't get the bastard on the beach this morning."

"I don't know if this was the same man," River said.

"What did the EMTs say?" Kevin asked, ignoring her comment. "They wanted to take you to the hospital, didn't they?"

"ERs are full of sick people. I passed."

She wasn't hurting so bad that she couldn't attempt a joke.

"I know you have questions for her, but I'd like to check her out while you talk," he said to Rick.

"The paramedics just finished with her."

"I know, but a second opinion never hurt. Is that okay with you, River?" For some damn reason he felt the need to check their work—make sure they hadn't missed anything.

"I'm too tired and sore to argue, so knock yourself out," she said. "I take that back. Getting knocked out isn't recommended." She massaged the side of her head.

"You blacked out completely?"

"The first time my head hit the door I saw stars. I didn't know people actually did that. I always thought it was a metaphor. The second time he used me as a battering ram, everything went dark."

"And you won't go to the hospital?" Kevin asked, raising her eyelids and staring into those intense pupils.

"I'd rather not."

"Stubborn."

"Is that your prognosis or an opinion?"

"Fact. Did you get that cut on your cheek looked at?"

"I was coming back from the pharmacy when I was bushwhacked," she said. "The doctor gave me prescriptions for antibiotics plus a shot in my ass." She rubbed the injection area then grimaced, reaching for her shoulder with her other hand.

"Let me see your arm." Kevin's broad hand covered her shoulder blade. He lifted her elbow and carefully manipulated her arm.

"Does that hurt?"

"Yeah, but I can move it. It'll heal. Don't you have some questions?" she turned to Rick.

WHEN KEVIN FINISHED his cursory exam, he made his way to River's small kitchen. She looked away from the broad-shouldered man with the smooth tone and faced the detective, Rick Wilcowski. He'd given her his name, but she was glad it had been embroidered over the police department logo on his polo shirt. She was having trouble connecting her thoughts, let alone remembering names.

"I gave a statement to the uniformed officer," she said to him.

"I bet you didn't tell them you were assaulted this morning."

She hadn't. Things were getting complicated. She wanted to sort them out before getting in any deeper with the locals.

"It would appear your friend already did that," she said.

"Kevin mentioned it to me, but there was no official report filed. No victim and a partial name make it difficult to write up."

The refrigerator door opened. River glanced back toward the kitchen. Kevin was looking for something in her fridge. He was certainly making himself at home.

"Where do you want to start?" she asked the detective. "This morning or afternoon?"

"Let's start with fourteen years ago," Rick said.

All the blood drained from River's face as darkness threatened to engulf her again.

"Whoa," Kevin said, suddenly appearing at her side. He pressed her head between her knees.

"What the hell did you say to her?"

"I was asking about her history. It could have something to do with today's events. I didn't expect that kind of reaction."

River pushed up against the strong hand pressing across her shoulders. "But you expected a reaction," she insisted. "I'm okay. I should have seen that coming."

"Here," Kevin said, shoving a soda into her hand. Pulling his chair closer, he put one arm across her shoulder, then guided the shaking can to her lips. It irritated her.

"I've got it," she said.

"What happened fourteen years ago?" The medic narrowed his eyes at the detective.

Rick placed his phone face down on the glass tabletop and shoved it across the surface. Kevin reached for it, giving his friend a questioning look. River didn't need an explanation. "Which news service?" she asked.

"*Time* magazine," Rick answered.

"You couldn't have given him one of the abridged versions?"

Kevin flipped the phone so he could read the screen. She found herself leaning into him. The subject never got easier. She'd take her support where she could get it.

"Do you remember the Engleharts?" she asked. *"The family that kills together, stays together?"*

The comment clicked. His grip tightened on her shoulder. "Husband, wife and adult son, right? Fifteen dead over a span of several weeks. They were captured in North Carolina. What do they have to do with you?"

"My mother, father and younger brother were their last victims."

8

---

*R*ick's expression didn't reflect the anxious curiosity or pity she'd come to expect. Instead, his blue green eyes reflected sadness. He hadn't brought up the subject because of his eagerness to hear the gory details of her grisly past. He simply wanted information. Her history was full of law enforcement professionals who relished the idea of rehashing the sensational and gory events surrounding the slaughter of her family. After the stalking began last year, she'd once again become an oddity and a source for those interested in the macabre. The issues at the cabin had brought in a new crop of officers pushing her for graphic details. One positive thing that had come from her move to Sanibel was that she wasn't known here.

She cocked her head to look at Kevin. His face held little expression except for the grim, fine line of his lips. His hand continued to stroke her arm. Neither man appeared anxious to hear a retelling of the gruesome story. Perhaps it was their experiences with war. They'd most likely seen worse.

"I find it hard to believe today's events had anything to do with the murder of my family. Those monsters are in prison and won't be getting out." They'd been convicted of her parents' and brother's murders, due mostly to her testimony. They were never extradited to any other jurisdiction because the number of years that had been added to their life sentences were so excessive, they would never be free to kill again.

"How can you be certain? Serial killers have fans," Rick commented.

"I can't, but the authorities did a thorough investigation last year. No link was found—at least none that I was made aware of."

"What happened last year to bring the authorities back into your life?" Rick, already laser focused, eyed her closely.

"You didn't dig very deep into my background, did you?"

"I haven't had the time to dig into any police reports. If it was mentioned in any of the online stories that I pulled up, I missed it. What happened?" Rick repeated.

River pinched the bridge of her nose. Her head hurt.

"I'd prefer to skip over the details of the day the Engleharts showed up unless it's absolutely necessary," she said. She would never be able to remove those memories from her mind. Walking through them was always difficult and painful. Neither man objected.

"Nothing unexpected happened before, during or after the trial. The case was an easy one for the prosecutors since they had a witness—me. They also had enough physical evidence since they were caught in my dad's car along with personal items they'd taken from my parents. It was pretty much a slam dunk. The news hounds, mostly tabloids, were my biggest problems. Eventually my life normalized—or should I say, as much as possible under the circumstances. I graduated from college and moved into the cabin."

"The cabin where your family was killed?" Rick asked.

"Why?" Kevin asked. Incredulity laced the single word.

River gave him the coldest stare she could muster. It wasn't the first time someone had wondered if she was crazy for moving into the place where her family had been butchered. She'd ceased arguing with them. Admittedly, she was a bit off. She suspected anyone who'd gone through what she had, earned the right to be a little crazy. Maybe that's what it took to survive.

"Because I wanted to," she snapped back. "Do you plan on continually interrupting or can I get on with this?"

Doing her best to ignore the striking man looming next to her, she continued. "The cabin is tucked into a quiet, secluded part of the North Carolina mountains. I lived and worked there in peace for seven years without any issues."

"What sort of work?" Kevin asked.

River's shoulder's slumped. Apparently, the man wasn't trainable. "A graphic design business."

"Go on," Rick prompted.

"Over a year ago, I started receiving unexpected gifts."

"What sort of *gifts*?" Rick asked.

"The first one was a beheaded snake left on my back porch."

"You said your cabin was isolated," Kevin pointed out.

River huffed, tired and frustrated. In spite of her request, they'd be asking questions. The sooner she got the tale out, the better.

"It is, but it backs up to a national preserve. Hikers sometimes explore the area near the cabin. I figured some kids were just getting their kicks."

"But that wasn't it," Rick prompted.

"No, it wasn't. I found the head a few days later in my kitchen, staring up at me from the drain, it's mouth propped open with a toothpick." It was an image she'd have with her for a long time to come.

"Someone got into your place?" Kevin's eyes rounded. "How?"

Pushing back her chair, River stood. "Any chance we can finish this later?" she asked, changing her previous decision to push through the questioning. She pressed her thumbs into her temples as she massaged her forehead with the remaining fingers. "I'd like to go lie down."

"You've had two assaults in one day," Rick said, as if that was all the explanation she needed.

"Headache?" the medic asked. "Where do you keep your pain relievers?"

"Bathroom at the end of the hall." River dropped onto the sofa. The dining room chairs were stiff, and her muscles were beginning to object. Besides, she'd be seated next to the Smith & Wesson she'd tucked into the cushions before the cops arrived.

The room was an open space. The dining and living room were combined. A breakfast bar separated the living area from the kitchen. Rick took up the large guest chair across from her.

Kevin appeared with a bottle of non-aspirin pain relievers. He grabbed her unfinished soda off the table.

"Here," he said. "Caffeine will help, too." As soon as she'd taken the pills, Kevin settled in next to her on the couch. She was quickly getting used to the size of the men. She no longer felt overwhelmed by their stature.

"Where were we?" she asked.

"Were the doors to the cabin locked?" Kevin asked.

"At night? Yes, but rarely during the day when I was home."

"Why the hell not?"

"Do you really need to be here?" River asked, turning her sights on Kevin. "Does anyone lock their doors when they're outside washing their car or cutting the grass? I tended my garden and often took walks down to the creek or hiked into the preserve. It's the country, for God's sake. No one locks their doors every time they step outside even in the city."

"Back off, Kevin," his friend advised. "Let her tell the story her way or you'll have to leave."

"Thank you."

"Did you file a police report?" Rick asked.

"Not when I found the beheaded snake. Like I've said, I assumed it was a sick prank. When I found the snake's head, I called Dan."

"Who's Dan?" Kevin snarled.

"Dan Nelson. He used to be with the Department of Natural Resources. He was the first person to arrive after I found my family. I latched on to him like we'd fallen out of an airplane and he had the only parachute. He still watches out for me even though he retired several years ago."

"What was a forest ranger doing there?"

"DNR is a law enforcement agency," Rick explained. He walked over to the refrigerator and grabbed one of the bottles of water. "Do you mind?" Rick asked River.

"No. Help yourself."

"Was the second incident reported?" Rick continued, retaking his seat across from her.

"Dan pressured me to call the police, but I didn't want the curiosity seekers to start showing up. My story was old news by then. I didn't want to make it new again."

"But with your history..." Kevin started.

"You don't have to remind me of my history. It's not

something I'm likely to ever forget. What purpose would reporting the dead snake have served? You think in rural North Carolina they can afford to have a cop sit on my doorstep 24/7? Nothing of value was ever taken. I wasn't harmed then." River took a sip of her soda. "We had the locks changed and I kept them locked. We installed security cameras, but whoever was behind the campaign, managed to get by them both. I bought a weapon and Dan taught me how to use it."

"How long did this go on?"

"A couple of months."

Kevin bounced to his feet. "Why the hell did you stay? Did you *ever* call the authorities?"

"What's your problem? You have a burr up your ass or something? Of course, I called the authorities when it continued," she snapped. "Can you stop with the criticisms?"

"I'm warning you for the last time," Rick said to his friend. "Sit down, shut up and let her finish." Mouth closed, Kevin sat.

"Obviously, they looked for a link to the Engleharts."

"Did they come up with anything?" Rick asked.

"Nothing. With the exception of the locals, the other agencies were gone by the time I left."

"Who has the lead on the investigation now?"

"I assume the county sheriff is still in charge. If something had turned up, Dan or the sheriff would have let me know."

"What was the final straw? What made you decide to move?" Kevin asked. "You stuck it out for months."

River held out her right arm and pushed up her sleeve. The scar he'd noticed earlier stood out against her tanned skin. "He took a knife to something other than a helpless animal."

"Not to sound cold," Rick said, "but what made him stop with a single slash to your arm?"

"Because I hauled ass after I surprised him. I'd cut my morning walk short. I'm guessing he heard me when I stepped onto the back porch. As soon as I opened the door, I caught the glint of a large hunting knife. The split second it took for that to register was long enough for him to take a swipe at me." She rubbed her hand over the scar. "I threw my full weight against the door. There was a thud. I assumed he'd landed on his ass. If he tried to follow me, he didn't find me. I was unarmed. I'd left my gun in the house." She still kicked herself for the miscalculation.

"Did either man today, in any way, resemble the man from the cabin?" Rick asked.

"I was focused on the knife. I don't remember ever looking at the person wielding it. As for today, my instinct tells me the man who tackled me here was the same one from the beach, but I can't swear to it."

"But not the guy from North Carolina?" Kevin asked.

"I honesty have no idea," River admitted. "Are we done now?"

"What about today? Do you know what he was after?" Kevin pressed.

"Other than name calling, I got nothing from him. I assumed this morning's incident was someone seizing an opportunity. You know? A woman alone on the beach, but after the attack this afternoon I'd be a fool to continue with that line of thought. During both instances, the guy had plenty of time to hurt or even kill me if that's what he'd wanted to do, so I have to believe he was after something. I have no idea what it would be, though." She hesitated. "There's something else. It may, or may not, be connected."

A slight groan escaped as River stood. Her muscles

ached. She'd been slammed to the ground twice in one day. She should have been moving instead of sitting next to the contrary man.

"Let me show you something." They eyed her cautiously. She was used to the look. They weren't the first to question her mental state. She'd gotten accustomed to the questioning stares by people who recognized her name. Their wary expressions put her dent her armor. Was she normal? Disturbed? Long ago, she'd convinced herself what others thought about her didn't matter. She couldn't explain why, but today it mattered.

Neither said a word as they followed her down the hall to her studio.

"This is my workroom. That mask," she said, pointing to the jeweled creation, "is one of my current projects."

"You make masks?" Kevin asked, his eyes widening.

"Yes. One-of-a-kind, made-to-order, masquerade masks. I don't hurt for clients." If she sounded defensive, too bad. She considered her work pieces of art. "I used to do graphic designing. When I left North Carolina, I changed my line of business. As much as I loved my work, we felt the change would help conceal my whereabouts. Making masks was a hobby. I've turned it into a lucrative business."

Kevin walked toward the bench and reached for her creation.

"Don't," River blurted out.

Kevin's arm dropped to his side. "What's the mask got to do with the assaults?"

River moved closer to the workbench. "I don't know if it has anything to do with them. Maybe I'm reading too much into things," she said. "Or going crazy," she muttered under her breath. She'd seen a psychologist after the murders. The memories—the loss—would never go away. It was imprinted on her memory, but he'd helped her to find ways of coping. Most of the time she was able to bury her fears and shut down the horrific images, but she still had her triggers.

"Being scared is normal, under the circumstances," Kevin assured her.

"Most people don't think I'm normal," she quipped. "Anyway," she continued before either man could comment, "a couple of nights ago after I got back from the grocery store, I had the feeling—just a feeling—that someone had been in here. I didn't find anything to support my intuition. The doors were locked. Nothing appeared to be out of place. The property manager has a set of keys, although they don't fit these locks," she added.

"Smart," Rick said. "Are you saying you had the same feeling today?"

"Yes, but this time," she pointed to the mask, "I found that."

"What? Kevin asked, leaning in, getting a closer look at the piece. "It looks expensive."

"Depends on what you consider expensive. When it's finished, the customer will send the balance of the three-thousand-dollar price tag."

"Shit," Kevin commented. "You think someone wanted to steal it?"

"Then why not take it?" she said.

"So, what are you trying to say?" Rick asked.

"The ribbons aren't the way I left them."

"The ribbons?" Rick joined Kevin in getting a closer look at the jeweled mask.

"After I add the ribbons, I never fold them, let alone bunch them up. Even when I package them, the silk strands are wrapped and placed in the carton, so they don't crease. I'd have never left them that way. They're a mess." River let out a breath, feeling a bit more confident. Neither man had immediately brushed her fears aside.

Rick took a few pictures of the mask from several angles with his phone. "Do you mind?" he asked, taking a pen out of his pocket and pointing at the mask.

"Go right ahead. I wanted you to see it like I found it."

The detective picked at the ribbons with the pen, coaxing them out from under her creation.

"There are some empty spots," Kevin commented. "Is something missing?"

"No. Not missing," River answered. "It's not finished. A few semi-precious stones will complete it."

"Is this different from your usual work? Is it unique in anyway?" Rick straightened and turned to her.

"Both. It's the first time I've used stones of this value. Initially, I had some issues with the vendor for the semi-precious stones, but they were settled."

"What sort of issues?" Kevin asked.

"He wanted me to exchange the stones. He claimed he'd sent me another customer's order."

"Did you return them?" Rick asked.

"No. They are exactly the ones I ordered. I suspect he had another buyer willing to pay more. He didn't press the issue."

"Who is your customer?"

"A recording artist. She wants the mask for a stage performance and music video—which is the reason for all the sparkle. The lighting will make this thing sing."

"Anything else in here out of place or missing?" Kevin asked.

"I haven't looked," River said. She hadn't checked the drawers. Why the hell hadn't she checked the drawers? Her heart did a giddy-up when she studied the contents of the top drawer. No snake's head left behind, but a signature, no less.

"What is it?" Kevin asked, tugging her away from the bench.

"My tools. Someone's moved them," she said. She shoved her fingers through her hair. "I'm a bit obsessive compulsive. I put things back in the same order every time." She studied the drawer, fighting back tears. It was happening again. Christ. The disarrayed tools confirmed what she'd been silently denying. Did they believe her? She'd overheard some of the cops in North Carolina talk. Many figured she had a 'troubled mind.' A few of them believed there never was a stalker—that it was a ploy to draw attention to herself—a by-product of her childhood trauma.

Kevin led her out of the workroom. She didn't fight him. She wasn't up to it.

"Who else knows that you, River Chandler, lives here?" he asked.

"Dan and Aunt Amy know my exact location. The Sheriff in North Carolina knows, but he's kept the address out of my file, I'm told. Everything else is listed under my LLC."

"Can I get Dan's number?" Rick asked. "I won't bother your aunt."

"Sure." Right now, she didn't care who did what. All she wanted was to curl up in a ball somewhere. This feeling of doom would pass. She'd been there before. She needed some time to gather herself.

She scribbled down Dan's number and handed it to the detective. "Thanks for your help."

"We'll be nearby if you need us. Put my number in your contacts," Rick said, handing her his business card.

"Call if there's anything out of the ordinary. Even if you think it doesn't qualify as an emergency."

"That's it?" Kevin snapped at Rick. "That's all you're going to do?"

"It's all I *can* do. What did you expect?"

The two carried on a lengthy debate regarding the detective's job. River planted her face in her hands. It was like having two siblings squabbling in the room. Her head was ready to explode.

"Go. Both of you. Now," she said.

"I'll stay. You shouldn't be alone," Kevin said.

"No one is staying."

"But…" Kevin started.

"Thank you, gentlemen," she said, reining in her temper and ending the debate. "But I want you to leave now."

River latched the deadbolt behind them, then pressed her back against the door until she heard their footsteps making their way down the stairs. When those footsteps faded, she ran to the sofa and retrieved her pistol from between the cushions. She was grateful she'd had those few seconds to hide the weapon before the police and EMT's arrived. Her neighbor had helped her inside after she regained consciousness. When he'd gone back to the door to await help, she'd taken the opportunity to hide the gun. She hadn't wanted the questions that would come with its discovery.

With the weapon in her hand, she began a thorough inspection of her condo. The fact that it had already been cleared by the police didn't matter. She wouldn't feel secure until she'd done the same. The paranoia that had been slipping away over the years, was back. She'd been living on borrowed time since the day of the murders. How often could a person dodge fate?

9

———

"**S**he should be more careful," Kevin muttered the next morning as he pulled out of the condo's parking lot behind River's car. She either didn't notice, or didn't care, that she was being tailed. He wasn't in the best of moods. He'd spent most of the night outside her unit, in his truck. Troy had stopped by late in the evening with some provisions. Kevin wasn't surprised by Troy's visit. He'd partnered with Steve in the security firm and knew Kevin had taken up watch duty at River's place. Troy was a part of this close-knit group, as was his wife, Shayne, who worked for Cat at the garden center. Troy still wore a patch over his left eye. There was no hope of restoring it, but the scars from the suicide bombing that emanated below the patch were gradually fading. His plastic surgeon was doing a damn good job. Troy offered to take over the watch for a while, but Kevin had declined. She was his responsibility. If he'd been quicker yesterday, she might not be in danger now. Troy didn't argue. Each one of his friends had the same sense of duty.

River drove north on the main road through Sanibel,

Periwinkle Way. Where the hell was she headed this time of the morning? His question was answered when she made a left turn into a mostly vacant parking area of a strip mall. There was no damn way he could avoid being seen and still keep an eye on her. The jig, as they say, was up.

Kevin recognized the small shopping center from previous visits. As a result, he had a good idea where River was headed so early in the morning. The Sanibel Cafe. It was a popular place for breakfast and lunch on the island. He pulled up behind her. She slid out of her vehicle then leaned against it, waiting for him to join her. The woman was stunning and sexy as hell, especially for someone who hadn't got much, if any, sleep last night. He'd seen the light on in her workroom when he'd patrolled the property during the night. Her shadow had been backlit behind the closed blinds. Were the all-nighters normal for her or had the events of yesterday prevented her from sleeping?

"You're out and about early," he greeted her. Those enchanting blue eyes still took his breath away.

"I needed fuel and didn't feel like making it myself."

"Does the fact that you're not skinning me alive or pointing a gun in my face mean we can sit together and have breakfast?"

"I can be civil," she said, making her way up the ramp toward the corner eatery. "Thanks for not mentioning my gun."

"You don't have a Florida permit for it, I assume," he said, stepping ahead of her to get the door.

"I have one for North Carolina. That should fly here. I didn't want to test it, though." She nodded toward the café. "Let's get in there before it gets busy."

"Crowds bother you?"

"Let's just say I like intimate settings."

Kevin wouldn't mind seeing her in a more intimate setting, but he kept that thought to himself as she walked by him.

A man with graying hair and smiling eyes greeted them. "Good morning."

"'Morning, Richard. I had the yearning for Pina Colada French toast."

"Is this gentleman joining you today?"

"For the moment," she answered, grinning back at Kevin. Her gaze was a punch to his chest. He was beginning to believe in black magic.

"Let's get you seated. Maria will be right over with your coffee," he added.

"Thank you."

Since the restaurant was unlocking its doors as they approached, it was empty except for staff. Their host walked by the vacant seats before offering the two of them a booth tucked into the rear corner of the restaurant. He'd left one menu on the table. Kevin slid it over to River.

"I don't need it. I always order the same thing," she smiled, pushing the menu back across the table.

"I got the impression you didn't go out much."

"I don't, but I force myself not to be a total recluse. And this place treats you like family."

"And knowing you, he knew you wanted this seat." Kevin studied the dining room. There was no other seating behind them, only the restrooms and the kitchen which would have a rear exit. She'd beat him to the seat that faced the interior of the restaurant and the plate glass windows which overlooked the parking lot. The perfect perch to keep your eye on things. There was that cautious streak again. Unfortunately, it meant having his back to the entrance which made Kevin feel exposed.

"Move over," he said, getting up from his seat and slipping in next to her. She didn't have any choice, but to move or make a scene. She didn't appear the type.

A cheerful young lady appeared with a coffee pot and filled the cups on the table. Using an electronic tablet, she entered River's order without asking. Kevin glanced at the menu then and ordered a protein laden breakfast.

"Did you get any sleep last night?"

"As much as you did, I suspect."

"Which would be none. Is that normal for you?"

"Not uncommon. I'd been doing better lately," she said, taking a sip of her coffee. Black he'd noted.

"But you fell back into your pattern again last night?"

"Stressful days bring stressful dreams. I prefer being tired to dreaming." She moved her cup aside as her break-fast order was delivered. "I'll catch up on my rest, eventu-ally. I usually do."

"Can't you take something to help you sleep when you need it?" Kevin dug his fork into a pile of scrambled eggs which had been placed in front of him.

"Are you playing doctor, again?" She didn't wait for an answer. "I have something, but it doesn't prevent the dreams. Being flat-out tired does the trick most of the time."

"Now it's my turn for a question," River said, slicing into her coconut encrusted French toast. "Do you plan on playing bodyguard indefinitely?"

"Until we know the bastard isn't going to bother you again."

"We?"

"My friends and I. Steve Brody owns an investigation business here on the island. Troy McKenzie, another retired member of the team, works with him. Colton James, and his partner, Gib, are photographers, but they come in pretty handy. Colt is our former commander. And, of course, there's Rick."

"Jeezus," River snapped, then quickly lowered her voice. "I don't need or want hordes of people here. I can take care of myself."

"Is that what you were doing yesterday?"

River's eyes narrowed as she scrunched further into the corner. There weren't too many people who questioned her decisions, he'd bet.

"We have a good track record at solving mysteries. Give us a chance. Let me invite them over tonight and you can make a judgement on your own. Plus, you'll get dinner out of it."

River rubbed her temples. "If I say yes, can we change the subject?"

Kevin had won the minor skirmish. It was enough for now.

River peppered him with questions regarding his service—how bases and camps were set up, countries he'd been deployed to, but she carefully avoided subjects the horrors he may have experienced or what he did as a medic. Whether it was due to her own experience with violence or she was being polite, he was relieved he didn't have to brush back the questions.

"What are your plans for the rest of the day?" he asked, as they cleaned their plates. He was surprised when River had finished the large order of French toast then started in on the side of sausage links which had come with her meal. Where the hell did she put it all? She probably didn't eat the rest of the day.

"I want to stop by some of the shops on the island that specialize in seashells," she said. "I don't know if I'm going to have time to gather all I need for my next project. They may have what I'm looking for, or they may be able to get their hands on them." Her shoulders sagged at the admission.

"You wanted to find them yourself, didn't you?"

"Shit happens," she answered.

"How many more do you need?"

"A lot. It would take time. I should be able to find what I need if I didn't have to spend half my time looking over my shoulder."

"Which reminds me," Kevin said, putting his hand over his cup when the server stopped by to top it off. "I have the shells you found yesterday. They're in my truck."

"Thanks," she said. "I pissed you off when I left, didn't I?" There was that spark in her eyes again.

"I was already pissed for not getting to you faster. Unfortunately, the wind wasn't blowing in my favor when I tried to get off the water."

"You did more than most would," she said. "I'm unconvinced my attacker here has anything to do with the events in North Carolina. With the exception of the time I surprised him, the bastard at the cabin never got close to me. Why would he suddenly change his style now?"

"Don't know. We need additional information," Kevin said, reaching for his wallet when the server laid the check on the table.

River pulled cash out of her purse. "Dutch treat," she said, grabbing the check and marching toward the register. Message sent and received. She'd accepted his presence, but not necessarily, his company.

10

———

*R*iver struggled, but she managed to work while Kevin rattled off the names and backgrounds to go with each person who would be coming to her place tonight. He was proud of his friends—it resonated in his tone. She, however, was scared shitless at the thought of meeting them. Since college, she'd virtually cloistered herself in the mountains. She didn't run away like a madman when she found herself surrounded by people, but she extricated herself from the situation as quickly as possible. The clinic and pharmacy had pushed her limits yesterday. Tonight, she'd be interacting with a room full of people. Her stomach was churning as she second guessed her agreement.

As the time grew near, she put her work aside and excused herself. Closing the bathroom door with the heel of her foot, she pulled her tank top over her head. Her home in North Carolina might be in the woods, but it didn't mean she was raised by wolves. Cleaning up before guests arrived was the proper thing to do. Sitting so close to Kevin while she worked, had her perspiring. The room had warmed with his presence. Why the hell did she have to find herself attracted to someone now? He was here because he felt responsible and believed she needed protection. There were a couple of times she felt his gaze held something other than simple concern, but it was probably her imagination. She didn't have much experience with that sort of thing.

River reached behind the shower curtain and turned the water on to warm while she finished undressing. She flicked on the exhaust fan as steam slowly began to fill the mirror. The woman staring back at her wasn't unattractive. She could be if she put some effort into it, but why bother? The men she dated in college freaked out in one of two ways when they discovered her history. They either wanted all the gory details or they trot her out like some sideshow freak. She'd lost interest in dating.

As she tossed her clothes into the hamper next to the tub, the semi-opaque shower curtain appeared to move. For a split-second River assumed she'd brushed against it. That assumption quickly disappeared when the head of a snake rose over the rim of the tub—its tongue flicking in her direction.

She must have screamed when she leaped off the floor and onto the toilet seat because Kevin was beating on the bathroom door calling her name. River gulped in a breath, watching the snake slither over the edge of the tub and onto the tile floor.

"River," Kevin shouted again, thumping against the wooden door. "Answer me!"

The distance to the bathroom door seemed miles away instead of a few feet. Her slithering visitor was now winding his way around the base of the toilet. She was stuck in a scene out of a modern-day Harry Potter movie.

"River!"

She focused on the door and crawled onto the vanity. It wasn't graceful, but River reached the door, knocking bottles to the floor as she did. River didn't recognize the variety of snake, so she wasn't going to get within striking distance.

Kevin's fist was raised as she cracked the door open. "What the hell is going on?"

"There's a snake in here. A big one," she said, catching her breath. "I don't want to let it out." She sure as hell didn't want it slithering through the unit and finding a place to hide.

"Well, you're coming out." In one quick motion, his arm shot through the opening, grabbed her around the waist, and pulled her through. Kevin slammed the door shut behind them.

"Can it fit under the door?"

"Unless it can morph into something much smaller, it's not squeezing under there," she said, pointing to the thin strip of light on the floor emanating from the bathroom. Now that she was safe, River was shivering. Kevin had yet to let her go. She wanted to lean into him and absorb some of his heat.

"Did it bite you?"

"I'm fine, just give me a second," she said, abandoning her battle and closing the gap between them. She laid her head against his chest, savoring the warmth. When Kevin removed his arm from her waist, she wanted to yank it back, but instead of letting her go, he pressed her against him and began rubbing his hands up and down her back. Her muscles melted at his touch. Her eyes grew wide when his ridge rose against her abdomen.

Oh. My. God. She was naked. After spotting the snake, her state of dress—or undress—had completely left her mind. She was no longer freezing. Instead, her skin was ablaze.

She pushed back from the rod pressing against her stomach. Kevin's hands dropped to his side, allowing her to step back. "Thank you."

"No problem," he said, his eyes focused on some spot over her head. "I'll find something to corral the creature."

River leaned against the bedroom door. She allowed herself a moment to catch her breath before straightening her shoulders. She refused to be embarrassed. Kevin had certainly seen his share of naked women. Hell, he probably had his pick. Besides, he was a medic. Think of him as a doctor—a doctor with a hard on. Shit. She had more immediate problems than Kevin right now.

Despite the fact she had wanted a shower, the idea of taking one now gave her chills. As she dug through her dresser for clothing, she made a plan to check the place thoroughly tonight. She'd seen her share of snakes in the mountains, but they'd all been outside—with the exception of the one she'd received as a gift, and it was dead.

Could any of this be connected? Her nemesis in North Carolina had never been this bold. Whoever it was had been covert in their harassment. Was this someone new? She almost hoped it was the same person. She didn't know if she had it in her to deal with a second psycho.

After slipping into a pair of jeans and a blouse, she grabbed a flashlight from the drawer of the nightstand and carefully inspected the shadowed floor of her closet for any unwanted visitors. She kicked a tote bag onto its side. A sigh of relief escaped when nothing hissed or slithered from it.

River completed her inspection of the room by shining the flashlight under her bed then pulling back the covers. Regardless of how much she searched, she doubted she'd get much sleep tonight. The image of the snake slithering out of the tub was going to be hard to forget.

KEVIN WAS ABOUT to knock on her door, when River exited the bedroom. He'd been trying to get the picture of her stripped bare and snuggled up against him out of his mind. She needed his protection—maybe a shoulder to lean on—but she didn't need some horny guy taking advantage of her.

"You okay?" he asked. She looked a little flushed.

"I'm fine. Thank you." Those beautiful eyes rose to meet his.

"You're sure you weren't bitten? Did I hurt you when I pulled you out of there?" He seriously considered offering to examine her but stopped short. Probably not the best idea under the circumstances.

"I'm good. Seriously. I managed to dodge the thing." No longer in a panic, she scanned the room. "Where is it?"

"On your balcony. It's secured," he added. "I borrowed the trash bin from under your sink and duck taped a trash bag over it. He's not going anywhere."

River headed toward the kitchen. "I don't want the trash can back. Okay? It can go with the reptile. Do you know what type of snake it is?"

"No," Kevin answered, following her. "Which is why I want to keep it contained. If it's poisonous, I didn't want to set it free. Rick will know what to do with it either way."

"I just want it gone."

"I can understand. It scared you."

"Ya think?" she said, a small smile edging up the corners of her mouth. "He wasn't my idea of a shower companion."

Her immediate blush was endearing. Adrenaline had blinded him for a second when he pulled her from the bathroom, but as soon as the door latched closed, he was fully aware what he'd had in his arms. A beautiful, sexy woman, totally devoid of clothing. His dick had saluted. Damn thing had a mind of its own.

"I apologize for my inappropriate reaction."

Her eyebrows rose as she cocked her head. "I'm not sure how to take that. I don't get out much, but I'd think a naked woman pressed up against you, regardless of her looks, would gain the same reaction from any man."

"You're beautiful." He was annoyed she'd insinuated otherwise. "My actions were inappropriate. You're under my care."

"Wait just a goddamn second," she snapped. "I'm not under your care or anyone else's. You offered to help, and I agreed, but you're not my guardian. Do you understand?"

Those damn blue eyes—stunning and spitting fire—were locked on his. "Got it," Kevin concurred, taking her chin in his hand. "You're not under my care."

Her eyes flashed like diamonds as she moved closer. When she rose to the balls of her feet he didn't hesitate, lowering his lips to meet hers. His hand fisted in her hair, holding her head in place while he consumed what she offered. Wrapping her arms around his neck, she matched his enthusiasm. Christ! He pulled her so close, air couldn't pass between them if they'd been in the middle of a hurricane. This time there would be no apology for his body's reaction. While their tongues tangoed, she pressed into his rock-hard erection. His hand glided down her arm until it reached her breasts. God. Why hadn't he done this when he had her naked in his arms? He wanted to feel the softness of her skin. Her nipples as they tightened into nubs.

Abruptly, River pushed him away. "What the hell is wrong with me? I'm…"

"Don't you dare apologize," Kevin growled, blocking her path to the door. She shoved him, but he didn't move. He needed to make one thing clear. "It was mutual. We enjoyed it…and we're not done."

Those silver blue eyes shot lasers at him. "We never started."

"You're kidding, right?" This time when she pressed, he stepped aside, smiling as she stormed into her studio and slammed the door.

11

Kevin was still grinning when he called Steve. "If anybody has plans tonight, tell them to cancel."

"We wondered which one of us would receive your Bat Signal. We're all open."

"Is it going to be a problem for you and Josie? We may need her contacts since Don's off communing with nature." If he'd been available, they'd have relied on Don Volpe, another teammate, for his unique computer hacking skills, but even a geek needed a break from the keyboard and the battlefield. Don was spending his leave backpacking through the Pacific Northwest. Josie had numerous contacts in the journalistic world who could prove helpful but having a baby to factor in was something new for this group to consider.

"We've already arranged for someone to babysit Cece," Steve said.

"Gib?"

Steve's laughter reverberated through the phone. "No, not Gib. He's going to have to grovel a bit more before he

71

has the honor. Besides, this is an *all-hands-on deck* situation, isn't it?"

"It is." But not an *all-hands-on River* situation and given the chance, Gib would have his hands on her. Everyone liked Gib—especially women. And Gib liked women. Kevin didn't have a problem with Colt's partner. Hell, Gib was one of the best men he knew. Kevin's eyes swept down the hall to the closed door of River's workroom. He was being an adolescent ass. She was in trouble and Kevin's big worry was whether Gib would score?

"We had an unexpected visitor." Kevin brought his thoughts back to his reason for the call.

"Who?"

"Not a 'who'. A snake. It somehow got into River's condo. I don't think they open doors, and this place was locked up tight. I'll do some checking, but I don't see how it got in here on its own. It's a little too similar to the type of harassment she endured in North Carolina for my liking."

"Where is it now?"

"I've got it trapped in a trash can on the balcony," he said, looking at the gray, plastic container on the other side of the slider. "I was hoping one of you would recognize the species and if it is local to the area."

"We'll check it out. We've made a little headway on River's issue, but we've got more questions for her."

"I'll call Mama's," Kevin said. The Italian restaurant was a favorite among the group. It was always a safe bet when ordering in. "Can one of you pick up the food?"

"No problem. Anything else you need?"

"Have Gib bring my stuff, including my medical kit." Her injuries weren't serious, but he'd feel better having his first-aid equipment nearby.

"You got it."

"Thanks."

After he placed the order for dinner, he'd been tempted to check on River. She'd had a hell of a day and it wasn't over yet. The team would do their best to make her feel comfortable, but there would be questions. Lots of questions.

Rick had inspected the condo yesterday, but he hadn't been searching for a reptile or a means by which one could enter. Kevin noted the security system, but it was simple and basic. It needed some beefing up. The sliding glass doors bothered Kevin, but an intruder would have to be a mountain climber willing to take on the thorny bougainvillea which ran up the side of the building in order to reach the small balconies on the second level.

Silently, Kevin passed the door to River's workroom. At the end of the hall was a linen closet. To his left was a guest bathroom where they'd found their visitor. Based on the items he spotted earlier, it was apparently the bathroom she used on a daily basis.

The bath was directly across from her workroom—which had originally been designed as the master bedroom with a private bath. He had used the attached bath while she'd worked on her mask. Other than hand soap and towel, it was sterile. An opaque window was set high above the combination tub and shower. The window was fixed and didn't open. Still, he'd give the rooms a closer inspection later.

He returned to the living area noting the stark difference between the workroom and the rest of the condo. While the other rooms in her unit screamed minimalist—simple furniture, bare walls and no personal items—her workroom was her home.

Pictures of the family she had lost surrounded her as she worked. One gut-wrenching photograph would be locked in his memory. Void of all human presence it hung above her workbench in a rough-hewn frame. In the center of the shot was a birdbath which rose above a bed of colorful flowers. The wood carving was exquisitely done, but the subject of the art tore at his heart. The base of the pedestal consisted of three distinct pairs of arms which appeared to rise from the earth. One pair was masculine and strong, his muscles defined. The second pair was sleek, feminine, and intertwined with the man's arms. Together their palms held a basin aloft where birds and other creatures of the woods could come to sip the gift of life they offered. The third pair of arms stretched to reach the basin but came up short. After all, they were the arms of an eight-year-old boy. Kevin didn't have to walk her property to know where she'd lost her family. She'd managed to turn the ugly sight into something beautiful—a homage to her loved ones.

River's soul was captured within the room's four walls. Her art, her creativity and her heart, came alive there. The jeweled mask she'd worked on today was an intricate design of colored stones—all bright and cheerful until you noticed the small tear shaped pearls beneath each eye. They told a different story—an underlying sadness was hiding beneath the joyful rainbow of crystals.

Kevin knew better than to get caught up in someone else's pain. He'd seen too much on the battlefield. Too much suffering. It hadn't been possible to shield himself entirely from it, but he should be able to maintain an emotional distance from one small woman.

Resisting the urge to check in on River, Kevin settled down at the small dining room table and began to delve into her past.

After almost fifteen years, it still wasn't difficult to find multiple news articles regarding the Engleharts and the carnage they'd left in their wake. Wikipedia had a page dedicated to them, which is where Kevin found more fact than sensationalism.

As River had told them earlier, her family was the Engleharts' last victims. The Chandlers had arrived at their cabin for a summer vacation. River had taken off to explore with her sketch pad, leaving her family to unpack their belongings. She hadn't known serial killers had been holed-up at the cabin after their recent killing spree. She'd returned to find the bloody, lifeless bodies of her mother, father and little brother on the ground. Her screams drew the Engleharts out of the barnlike structure where her father had parked the car. River managed to lose her pursuers in the forest. There was no reference as to how the authorities were alerted to the crime, but the Engleharts were picked up a day later, driving the Chandler's vehicle.

Kevin glanced toward the hallway then dug into some of the other stories on the killings. The Engleharts hadn't simply killed, they'd butchered their victims—gagging them, then using knives freely on each victim before finally slicing their throats. Massaging his temples, he tried to erase the image of a young River kneeling over the gruesome remains of her family. How does a fourteen-year-old deal with that? Hell, how did anyone deal with it?

He'd seen the worst of humankind on the battlefield. While he never got used to it, he'd learned to expect it. It was war. How many soldier's hands had he held as they'd slipped from this world to the next? How many times had he been burdened with the request to carry a message to their loved ones? He was a trained medic—and a trained soldier. He'd taken his share of lives. There were days he had trouble reconciling the two.

He remembered the day Troy had run toward certain

death trying to stop a suicide bomber. Something in Kevin had changed while he'd battled to save Troy's life. Something he had yet to understand—but he was different. Kevin *knew* he was different. He'd lost something that day, but damned if he could figure out what it was.

How had the slaughter of her family changed River? Had she ever been playful? Outgoing? Had her massive loss turned her into an introvert? Is that why she ran an online business, which would allow her to minimize her interaction with others? He was certain his presence bothered her. She was a loner although she was confident—not to mention stubborn. Recalling her practiced facial expression at the beach, he'd known she'd been scared, but she projected the appearance of someone collected. Some people became extremely adept at hiding the effects of stress.

He was curious about her. Too curious. He had no damn business doing anything other than tending to her wounds and keeping her safe...and wasn't that presumptive of him? His life was in flux. He'd joined the service with every intention of retiring after twenty years. He hadn't planned on leaving before his twenty was up, but his visits to see his friends here—all thriving—had him questioning that commitment.

12

With the information she'd been able to obtain from the local businesses that specialized in shells, River had a good idea of where she was going with the mask and the changes that would have to be made to her design. The acquisitions from vendors would cut into her profits, but she'd have the mask done in time. She spent the afternoon meticulously refining her earlier design, completely immersed in the project.

A knock on the door startled her. The door opened a hair, allowing a visitor to poke her head through the opening.

"Excuse me. Can I come in?" The woman with short, brown hair smiled at her. "Hi," she said, slipping in the door without waiting for the requested invitation. "I'm Shayne. Kevin asked me to check on you."

River was skilled at compartmentalizing. She had fallen back into her work, blocking out the plans for the night. Now, they were front and center. Her palms became slick with sweat.

Laying her mechanical pencil on the table, she stood

and studied her visitor. Between the two of them, they almost made a whole person. Shayne was short—about the same size as River, but with a few less curves.

"I got caught up in my work," River apologized.

"Oh my God!" Shayne started toward the desk where the jeweled mask sat. "Kevin said you made masks, but this is art. It's stunning."

"Thank you. I've got a little ways to go yet." River had set aside the singer's mask to concentrate on shelling and the new project. She'd get back to it. She had to in spite of the fact it now gave her the creeps.

Her guest leaned over the worktable. River didn't have to warn her not to touch. Shayne's hands were firmly grasped behind her back.

"I'm sorry. I shouldn't have kept you all waiting."

"Don't be silly. We've invaded your space."

Shayne's soft smile and casual attitude was putting River at ease. It was as if she'd come to talk her off a ledge. Her presence alone was doing the trick.

"You're used to your own company," Shayne continued. "It took me awhile to get used to the crowd. Now, they're all family."

"A crowd?" River inched back toward that edge.

"Friends. Think of them as friends," Shayne added, quickly. "They will be if you give them a chance. After the bombing, I kept to myself, but they slowly drew me out and then I met Troy."

"A bombing?" River's head was starting to spin.

"It's a long story. I'll tell you the tale some other time. Come on," Shayne said, reaching for River's hand. "I'll run interference."

For the first time since she'd moved into the condo, her living room and kitchen were teeming with people—most of them tall, large men. Her stomach flipped. Shayne gave her hand a squeeze. "They're all pussycats. I swear," her companion said.

More like mountain lions, River thought as she entered the room with Shayne. Each of the men matched Kevin in stature, yet each was distinctively different.

"This handsome pirate," Shayne said, reaching out for the man with a patch over one eye, "is my husband, Troy."

He placed a kiss on the crown of his wife's head. McKenzie was stunningly handsome despite the obvious injury.

"I hear you had a bit of trouble," he commented, wrapping his arm around Shayne's waist.

"Some," River admitted.

"You've handled it well," Rick told her.

"I'm not so sure about that." She made an attempt to smile, but the F1 tornado twisting inside her made it difficult. She hadn't been the focus of this many people since the sentencing of the Engleharts.

"I'm Colt." An extremely tall man with shaggy, black hair and bright blue eyes introduced himself. A partially buttoned Hawaiian style shirt showed off his tanned, toned chest. He was their former commander, if River remembered their backgrounds correctly. "That pixie making herself at home in your kitchen is my wife, Cat."

A short, smiling woman with sable hair waived an oven mitt in her direction. The height difference between the two was, frankly, astonishing.

"And I'm Gib." The man with a thick, blond mane, slid in front of Colt, essentially demanding her attention. He took her hand, bent over it, and laid a soft kiss on her knuckles. Holy shit! The man was sex on legs. When he raised his head, his gray eyes sparkled at her as much as the ruby stud in his left ear.

"Knock it off, Gib," Kevin growled.

"Why?"

"Because she's had a tough day and doesn't need to be fighting you off."

River glanced from one man to the other. Gib's impish grin meant something, but she was so out of her element, she didn't know how to respond to the interaction. Did Gib tease every woman he met? Was Kevin always surly around him. He'd said they were friends.

"Chow's on," the lone man in the kitchen shouted, redirecting everyone's attention. He sported dark brown hair with wisps of silver at the temples. A dish towel was slung over his shoulder, reminding River of her aunt's habit of doing the same.

"Steve, this isn't the base chow hall." A tall, raven-haired woman, hands filled with dishes, elbowed him in the ribs. "My apologies," she said, addressing River. "I'm Josie and this loudmouth is my husband, Steve."

Her husband responded by clasping her jaw and planting a long, hard kiss on her lips. She was beaming when Steve stepped back, taking the plates from her hands.

"You have to excuse those two. They don't get much time alone," Gib explained.

"You call this 'alone'?" Steve laughed.

The chattering and bantering continued as the group lined up cafeteria style to fill their plates. River hung back. Their voices combined until they became a singular roar in her ears. The twister in her stomach notched up to an F2. She made a quick retreat to her workroom, pushing the door closed behind her. Then repeated the process as she entered the bath she rarely used. The sour taste of bile rose in her throat as she lost the contents of her stomach.

～

Kevin had been keeping a discreet eye on River. She wasn't comfortable in crowds. She'd been clear on that point but had still agreed to the get-together all the same. He'd regretted pushing as he watched her color slowly pale. Her hand rested on her stomach, as if trying to quell it. Suddenly, her other hand covered her mouth and she rushed toward her studio. Kevin intercepted Shayne who had started down the hall.

"Let me handle it."

"We overwhelmed her."

Kevin didn't doubt Shayne was right as he opened the door to her workroom. She preferred a solitary life and after today's events, shoving a room full of strangers had tipped the scale. These were his friends, but she didn't know them. Despite her agreement for the gathering, he should have known better.

He passed through the empty workroom and tapped lightly on the bathroom door. "River? Are you all right?" He twisted the knob and opened the door a crack. He wanted to be certain it wasn't locked and if it wasn't, that it remained that way.

"Can you please go away?" Her voice was shaky.

"I'm afraid that's not in my DNA. I'm coming in."

Her sigh was so deep, he could easily hear it, but she didn't voice any objection. Her legs were curled on the bathroom floor. One arm was resting on the closed toilet seat with her head cradled in the crook of her arm. Her left arm lay draped in her lap.

She didn't fight him when he took the wrist from her lap and checked her pulse. It was fast, which didn't surprise him. Her skin was clammy, but not feverish. Those stunning ice-blue eyes were a little bloodshot but, otherwise, clear.

Kevin left her to get some mouthwash from the other bathroom.

Shayne popped into the hallway as he passed through. "Do you need one of us to help or would it be better if we all bugged out of here?" she quietly asked.

"Go ahead and eat. I'll let you know if we have to clear out."

"Here," he said, returning to River and handing her a glass. "This will help." She didn't have to tell him that she'd been sick.

River took the glass in silence, rinsed her mouth then wilted onto the closed toilet seat. "Sorry."

"No reason to be. You went through hell these last two days. Dealing with that rowdy bunch added to your stress. I owe you a big apology. Do you want me to send them home?" He ran a washcloth under cold water, wrung it out and handed to her.

"No," she didn't hesitate. "They were kind enough to offer to help. Chasing them away would be rude. I have some issues I need to get past. Might as well start now." She wiped her face and neck with the cool cloth. Once again, he found himself mesmerized by the divot at the base of her throat. Stupid.

"Do you have something to take for your nerves?" he asked.

"When I need it. I don't need it now." She rose to her feet, standing ramrod straight. "I made a hell of an impression on your friends."

"You'd be surprised how much in common you have with the group out there," Kevin said. "They understand more than most."

"Okay, then," she said, running her fingers through her hair. "Let's see if I can keep from embarrassing myself a second time. I'm going to pass on the food, though."

"No one will be offended," he assured her, leading her out of the workroom.

Shayne was waiting in the hallway. "I'm sorry. I didn't do a very good job of running interference."

"It wasn't your job and it's not your fault," River told her.

Kevin's friends must have rushed through their meal or skipped it all together, because the kitchen had been cleared with the exception of a small pot which remained on the stove.

"We put some soup on warm," Cat answered her unspoken question.

The knot in Kevin's shoulder disappeared when River gave her a small smile.

"Thanks. Maybe later."

"Are you up to answering some questions?" Kevin asked.

She nodded. "I was just getting used to not looking over my shoulder. I guess that was a mistake."

"Can I check out your workroom?" Troy headed for the hallway.

"We've been trying to figure out if your reptilian visitor made its way in here on its own," Kevin explained. "So far, no luck. We still need to look at your office."

"Yes, please. Go ahead." River visibly shivered.

Shayne popped up, almost bouncing out of her shoes. "Can I show Josie and Cat your work? We won't touch it, I promise."

"Sure." River sank to the couch as if the air had been let out of her. Kevin grabbed one of the dining room chairs and seated himself at the end of the sectional, next to River.

"Do you think someone intentionally put the snake in here? How?" she asked, turning toward him.

"At this point, we don't know. I've seen them in lanais and garages," Rick said, "but never inside a house. It's even more suspect with this being a second-floor unit."

"Shit," River swore. "I'd rather deal with a decapitated snake than one slithering around my bathroom."

"You said Dan is the only one with a duplicate key?" Rick questioned her.

"Yes, and I trust Dan implicitly."

"People have been known to get their hands on keys and make copies," Steve suggested. "Where do you keep yours?"

"In my purse, and Dan wouldn't be that careless."

"Does your aunt have a key?" Colt asked.

"No. I gave the duplicate key to Dan because he'd be the one I'd call in an emergency."

"You wouldn't call your aunt?" Kevin cocked his head. Why her aunt wouldn't be first on her list of calls? Odd.

"If I was sick or something like that, but I'm talking about the shit that keeps hitting the fan."

Troy returned to the room with the three women in tow. A slight shake of his head told Kevin, and everyone else present, the snake didn't slip into the condo on its own.

"So? What's next?" River straightened in her seat.

Colt crossed his arms over his chest. He hesitated before speaking—a clear sign to Kevin that Colt was aware of the sensitive nature of the subject. "First and foremost, I want to assure you no one here is a ghoul. Not one of us is eager to discuss what happened to your family, but if at any time you think of something that remotely connects them with the more recent incidents, we need to know."

"Since the shit started last year, I've tried to think of a connection, but I always come up blank. The authorities don't seem to think there's any link."

Shayne reached across for River's hand and squeezed.

"Something may come to you at the oddest moment. Don't fight it, if it does. Trust me. I've been there."

Troy pulled Shayne close. While Kevin hadn't been on the island when Shayne was in trouble, he'd heard about the hell she'd gone through and why she was so familiar with the tricks the mind could play on someone.

"I talked to your friend, Dan," Rick said to River.

"Did he add anything to what River's already told us?" Kevin was curious what her friend could tell them.

"Not much. She was pretty thorough. I did get the names of the investigators who are assigned to the case. I'll get hold of them tomorrow and find out if they shared everything with Dan. They should have been talking to River directly, but I understand with your friend's background and his desire to run interference, they agreed to his request."

"Would you mind going over what you told Rick and Kevin regarding the events behind your move from North Carolina?" Steve asked.

"Is that necessary?" Kevin didn't want her reliving the unpleasantness again. She'd had a shitty day.

"You know it is. Sometimes things get lost in the translation."

"I'm fine, but some of it's not very pretty," River said, her eyes dancing over the ladies in the room.

"You'll never meet three stronger women," Kevin assured her.

"All right, then." River sucked in a deep breath. "Just short of a year ago, I started receiving little gifts…"

13

———

River recounted the events that had taken place in North Carolina adding those which had happened in the last two days. When she'd finished, they all had questions, but their inquiries were soft peddled. She was familiar with the process of being grilled. Were these people afraid to push her? After her earlier performance, she didn't blame them for thinking she might fall apart, but, damn it, it still pissed her off. She may be strung together with spit and bailing wire, but she wasn't a fragile flower who would fall apart if asked a few straightforward questions.

"Look," she said after another soft lob from Steve. "I promise. I'm not going to fall into pieces. If you want to know something, ask it. We'll be here all night at this rate."

Shayne elbowed her husband, a smile on her face. "See? I told you she'd be fine once she got used to us."

"Could any of the *gifts* correlate, in any way, to the murder of your family?" Colt asked.

"Other than the use of a knife, I don't see any link. Neither did the authorities."

Despite her assurance, when they got to the subject of the murder of her family, they remained careful with their questions. While River wasn't made of paper lace, that particular subject was much more difficult to discuss. She was grateful the questions had been brief.

Josie closed her notebook. "I've got enough to get me started. We need to get home," Josie turned to her husband.

"We've got a young lady waiting for us," Steve explained, taking his wife's hand. The others got to their feet, as well.

"Do you have my stuff?" Kevin asked Gib.

"Yeah."

"Can a couple of you stick around for a minute?"

"No problem," Colt told him. Troy nodded in agreement.

"The snake!" How had River forgotten about the snake? Her eyes darted toward the balcony, but the lateral blinds were drawn.

"It's already in my truck," Rick told her. "I'll take it by 'Ding' Darling in the morning. The rangers will deal with it."

River had been meaning to visit the national wildlife refuge. She'd always enjoyed exploring the outdoors, but... But what? Why hadn't she taken the time to visit the sanctuary?

Steve, Josie and Rick said good night before following Kevin and Gib out the door. "I think Kevin's making too big a deal over this," River said to those remaining in the room.

"He's being cautious," Colt said. "Let us check into things a bit. If it turns out to be nothing, we'll be out of your hair—assuming that's where you want us."

"Here's my cell." Cat grabbed a scrap of paper and

scribbled on it. "What's yours? I'll text you everyone's number."

River hesitated. "The police already have my cell."

"You have a team behind you now," Cat explained. "We need to be able to reach you and you, definitely, need to be able to reach us."

She'd given this group permission to help her. "You'll need two numbers. I use one for outgoing and one for incoming."

"What about the other phones?" Troy asked. "I counted at least three additional phones in this place."

"Four. They're back-ups. I keep them charged but I've never had to use them."

"Give the rest of the numbers to Kevin. It's best we have all of them," Colt said.

Surprisingly, no one questioned her need for the additional phones. Most people would think she was obsessive. This group took it in stride. Maybe they did understand her.

Kevin returned, a duffel bag in one hand and a backpack slung over his shoulder. A red cross was displayed prominently on the pack. Cat and Shayne said their goodbyes before departing with their husbands. River was left staring at Kevin's back as he shut and locked the door.

"What's the code," he asked, fingers poised over the touchscreen pad next to the doorframe.

The simple question shook her. She'd spent half her time on earth wrenching back control of her life—learning to be strong and independent. In giving him the code, was she taking a large step backward? Depending on others always hurt in the long run. Raking her fingers through her hair, she stared back at him.

"Something wrong?" Kevin abandoned his place by

the door, moving faster than a big man should. A second later, she felt the heat from his body.

"I don't know if this is all a good idea. I'm used to taking care of myself."

"I think you'd give Cat a run for her money when it comes to stubbornness. We went through this earlier today. It's not a good idea for you to deal with this on your own. If it was the single attack on the beach, that would be one thing, but two assaults in one day? Smart people don't take chances."

It was childish, but his insinuation that she would be stupid to refuse help, grated on her. He held his position, eyes narrowing as he waited for her response. He had the warmest brown eyes—like melted caramel. Her blood slowly heated—not from anger but something else—a growing desire. She jerked away from his touch, walking past him to set the alarm. Desire had no place in her life. Avoiding emotional entanglements saved heartache. Now wasn't the time to explore the effect he had on her.

"I'll get you some sheets," she said. "Sorry, but the couch is all I have to offer." Despite their earlier response to one another, she had no intention of sharing her bed with him.

"That won't be necessary," he stated. "We don't sleep when we're on duty."

So, she was a job. That's how she wanted it, wasn't it? Still, there was a twinge of disappointment mixed with a bit of anger.

"Good night, then." She abruptly turned away.

"Hang on a second. I want to take a look at those cuts on your face."

"They're fine." She didn't want his touch. She craved the sanctuary of her workroom.

"I'm the medic here," he said, grabbing the green Army backpack.

River let out a loud huff, giving up on the argument. He was determined and she was too emotionally exhausted to battle with him. She pulled out a bar stool and slid onto it.

"I can't figure out how to approach you," he said, placing the medical kit on the breakfast bar.

"Excuse me?" Approach her? What did that mean?

"You go from scared, to angry, to cordial in zero to sixty."

"Some people think I'm a certified lunatic." She shrugged. "It ain't much fun from this side, either. You're free to walk out the door if you don't care for my company."

"That wasn't an insult. I'm trying to tread a path which doesn't trigger you."

"Nobody is pleasant all the time. It would be boring."

"True," he agreed, turning toward the sink to wash his hands.

"Can we get on with this? It's not brain surgery." She was being snippy and rude. She'd run the gamut of emotions tonight. She could understand his confusion. She wasn't used to them either. Being alone she was able to control her environment and, therefore, her reaction to it.

Kevin glanced over his shoulder as he continued to wash his hands. "It's in the vicinity, I assume," he smiled.

Damn. The man wasn't just hot, he had a sense of humor. Didn't she have enough on her plate right now? She didn't need to be fighting this attraction, too. The timing sucked.

His fingers stroked her temple as he pushed her hair aside to examine the knot from her meeting with the door.

The action wasn't intended to be sensual, but the touch sent shock waves over every inch of her skin.

"That bump will be there a couple of days. How's the headache?"

"Almost gone," she said, wishing he'd touch her again. Not good.

He cleaned the scratches left by the doormat. After he finished with one side of her face, he removed the bandage the doctor had applied to her other cheek. He studied the wound, applied antiseptic ointment then replaced the bandage with new gauze and tape.

"Did you take your antibiotics?"

It was easier to talk with him when he was all business. "Yes. I'm not a child, you know."

"Far from it," he smiled.

"Are we done now?" River slipped off the stool. "I'd like to get some work in tonight."

"You should rest," he scowled.

River shook her head. Being alone was so much easier. You didn't have to explain your actions to anyone.

"I rested earlier. I'm behind on my projects." She should finish the jeweled mask, but she couldn't bring herself to lay her hands on it. She needed to get past that ominous feeling soon, but for tonight she'd work on the design details of the seashell mask.

"River?"

"Huh? Oh, sorry." It wasn't unusual for her mind to wander, but in her defense, she didn't usually have people around who noticed. "You need me for anything else?"

His head cocked as he scrutinized her. It was hard to tell if he was concerned or wondering how far off the charts she was from normal. It didn't matter.

"No," Kevin answered. "I'll be out here if you need anything."

"Thanks." She considered it an accomplishment she didn't tell him she'd been doing fine before he came along. But after today, having some security nearby would allow her to concentrate on her work without jumping at every little noise.

She grabbed a bottle of water from the refrigerator and was stunned to see the amount of food which had been left behind. "Help yourself to anything in here. I'm sure as hell not going to eat all this."

THE WOMAN WAS A PUZZLE. He hadn't been kidding about her mood swings. That she had them wasn't surprising with her history. He hadn't figured out how to approach her without setting her off. It probably wasn't possible to avoid all the traps. Besides, she'd survived the last fourteen years in better shape than most would have managed, but today had sucked. If she slipped a few rungs on the ladder, she'd deserved some slack.

He used the facilities at the end of the hall. The light from her workroom squeezed under the closed door and out onto the tile floor. How often did she work late?

Ignoring his urge to tell her she needed rest, he returned to the living area and opened the sliding glass door, stepping out onto the small deck. She'd hadn't shut the horizontal blinds to the slider in her workroom. He'd have to discuss that with her. Leaving them open at night wasn't wise under the circumstances. From his current position, he could see her clearly, leaning over the drafting table, pencil in hand, sketching away. Her hair cascaded over her shoulder, blocking his view of her face.

Feeling like a voyeur, he directed his attention toward the surf. He spotted the lights from a few boats still out on the water. Hopefully, they were anchored for the night. The water could be a dangerous place after dark, particularly if there were novices behind the wheel. Other than the boaters, Kevin didn't see any other sign of life. The smell of salt air wafted in on a breeze. The island had a way of settling him. His friends admitted it had the same effect on them. Cat often mused there were mystical spirits in the waters surrounding Sanibel. It was the Irish in her, he suspected, which gave her that magical take on the island. Whatever it was, his former teammates had found peace and love on this small spot of land. Did the island have the same effect on River? Is that what drew her here when she was forced to move?

He glanced back at the workroom and the woman who was so thoroughly involved in her creation. She deserved some peace. Kevin hoped Cat's musings were right.

Leaving the sliding glass door open, he settled into the sofa. River didn't own a television. He'd noted that earlier, but now he wondered why. Was it another way to retreat from the world or did she simply prefer the silence? Stretched out on the couch with the cool sea breeze drifting through the opened door, he understood the appeal. Still, it would have been nice to turn on a sports channel and watch a replay of a football or basketball game. It was going to be a long night.

Through the evening, Kevin had scrolled through so many online sports and news pages, his battery weakened. He moved to the breakfast bar with his phone charging, now playing video games. The last time he'd checked on River via the balcony, had been over an hour ago and now it was 2:00 a.m. The healer in him wanted to force her to get some rest, but common sense told him it would get him nowhere.

She had a front row seat in his head tonight. Not

surprising since he was responsible for her safety and security, but security was sharing that seat with his carnal instincts. Shit. He was screwed up and she was more than a little screwed up. Wouldn't they make a lovely couple? Knowing that didn't stop him from picturing her stretched out across rumpled bedsheets, thoroughly exhausted and satisfied.

Taking a gulp of ice-cold water, he considered dumping the liquid in his lap. He needed to get his mind on something else. There wasn't much to work with regarding her stalker. The information he had was minimal. Personally, he had a hard time believing it didn't have something to do with the murder of her family. What were the odds that so many unconnected events happen to one person? She appeared convinced that was the case—or had someone convinced her of it? Kevin was anxious to hear what the team dug up when he talked to them tomorrow—or today, considering the time.

After rinsing his face in cold water from the kitchen sink, Kevin started searching for the coffee. She had a coffee maker, therefore, she had to have coffee. Right? He found the makings then started a pot. He also figured River had worked herself hard enough today. He'd given her room—aware she didn't like to be pushed or crowded. In addition to the hour, she'd been under a lot of stress today. It was time for her to shut it down for a while.

Bracing himself for an argument, he tapped on the door, but received no response. He softly called her name. Still nothing. Half fearful, he cracked the door open. River's head rested on her arm stretched across the desk. A mechanical pencil was still in her hand, trapped between two slender fingers. Her left hand dangled at her side.

He quickly noted her breathing was even and her color was good. She was exhausted and had every right to be.

Brushing the hair from her face, he waited for a reaction. She remained oblivious to his presence. Slipping the pencil from her fingers, he placed it in the holder. When that action didn't elicit a response, he gingerly lifted her into his arms. She surprised him when she rested her head against his shoulder, snuggling into the crook of his neck.

He carried her into her bedroom but was loath to put her down. He wanted to simply hold her for a while… God, he was being stupid. He tenderly laid her on the bed then tossed the other side of the comforter over her. The activity hadn't awakened her which put a fine point on her need for rest. She snuggled her head into the pillow just like she had his shoulder. If things were different, he'd crawl in next to her and pull her into his arms, keeping her safe. He wanted to get to know her—both as an individual and as a lover, but things weren't different.

14

———————

*R*iver groaned as she awoke. The fact that every muscle in her body ached shouldn't have surprised her. She'd been slammed to the ground twice yesterday. Falling asleep at the drafting table hadn't helped, but she wasn't in the workroom now. She tossed back the comforter. Did she need to add sleepwalking to her list of odd behaviors?

The blinds had been shut, but the sun was still streaming through the slats. The clock at her bedside told her it was mid-morning. If she didn't hurt so much, she'd feel refreshed from the solid, dreamless, sleep. It was normal for her to work until exhaustion overtook her. There were times that meant days without sleep, but she'd discovered dreams were rare when she finally succumbed. A sleep pattern that would be normal to most, tended to have her waking up during the night covered in sweat after sprinting through a thick forest in her dreams.

A brief glimpse in the dresser's mirror told her she needed to clean up. Her face and hair were a sight. The bandage on her cheek didn't help. With some fresh clothing in hand, she made her way to the hall bathroom and downed some pain relievers. The place was quiet. The stillness bothered her, which made little sense. She was used to silence, but after last night, the silence was unnerving. Before she'd conked out, she heard Kevin moving about. Now there was nothing. Had he left? Was she alone? Why should that bother her? She brushed her teeth, ran a comb through her hair then she ventured out to check the condo.

The last thing she expected to see when she entered the living room was a shirtless man on her balcony doing push-ups. She recognized Shayne's pirate, Troy. He grabbed his shirt off the railing, wiped the sweat from his face and chest. The guy was ripped. His chest and abdomen resembled plates of armor. Just because he was married didn't mean River couldn't appreciate the sight. She recalled Kevin's broad chest after he'd cleared the sand from her eyes. She suspected the men were all calendar material.

"I hope I didn't disturb you." Troy stepped into the living room, pulling his t-shirt over his head and ending the show.

"No. Actually, it was so quiet, I came out to see if Kevin—I mean if anyone was here." Did he catch her slip of the tongue?

"He left to catch forty winks. He'll be back later."

"Is it necessary to have someone with me all the time? Seems over the top." For the most part, both Kevin and Troy had stayed out of her way. She suspected the others would as well, but she was used to being on her own even under the worst of circumstances.

"For the time being," Troy answered. "Once we get some pieces of the puzzle put together, we'll reassess."

"I need to discuss fees with Steve." She wasn't a pauper. Far from it. Her mom and dad had invested well.

When she turned twenty-one, she'd had access to an obscene amount of money in her opinion. She'd used a small portion of it to get her graphics business up and running, but once off the ground, it had generated more than enough to support her comfortably.

"This is off the books," Troy told her. "A favor."

"A favor? For whom?" she asked, a small tremble in her voice.

"Kevin asked for help. We're a team. We're family."

"I'm neither," she reminded him.

"You will be," Troy smiled.

What? This was a strange group. "I'll talk to Kevin and Steve. In the meantime, thank you."

"It's our pleasure." Troy made his way to the breakfast bar and grabbed a plastic sack off one of the stools in front of it. "I've got a few things here to increase your security a bit. I didn't want to take the chance of disturbing you while I worked, but I'll get started on it now."

"What sort of things?" River asked. She drew a line at cameras inside her unit.

"Trip alarms for the sliding glass doors and windows. A camera at the front door. Nothing invasive."

"And things I should have had all along." They were all smart ideas which she'd overlooked. Troy, kindly, did not remind her of that fact.

"I started a pot of coffee and there are some bagels in the bag on the counter, if you're interested."

"After I freshen up," she said, making her way slowly toward to bathroom.

"Make the water as hot as you can stand," Troy shouted as she closed the door.

River had been too distracted to move her personal care products to the other bathroom after the incident with the snake. Rather than do it now, she used the toilet bowl brush to poke under the sink and move the shower curtain before getting in the tub. She then happily followed Troy's suggestion and turned the bath into a steam room, flexing her sore muscles under the hot, streaming water.

She stayed in the shower until the water began to cool. It wasn't a miracle cure, but she was less stiff by the time she'd finished. After inspecting the cut from the rock on the beach, she opted to leave it be and let Kevin decide if it needed another bandage. Her stomach fluttered when she thought of seeing him again. Damn.

"How's it going?" River asked when she returned to the living room. Troy was at the slider, muttering under his breath.

"It's not," Troy answered. "The drill wasn't fully charged, and I don't have the charger for it. One of us will have to finish this later."

River shrugged. "I won't be any worse off than I was yesterday." She headed for the kitchen. It was after noon and she'd skipped dinner last night and hadn't had break-fast. Now her stomach was objecting to the missed meals.

"I managed to make some improvements before the drill died on me," Troy said, gathering his tools. "The camera is set up for the front door. I'll link it to your computer and phone, then show you how it works. We'll also be upgrading your alarm system. Your system is decent, but it could use more bells and whistles under the circumstances. We'll get that hooked up to your phone, too."

"After we eat something."

Instead of a bagel, she warmed up enough leftovers for the two of them. It was closer to lunch time than breakfast. River asked him how he'd met Shayne while they shared the meal. It was a casual question, but the answer was anything but normal. Shayne had survived an explosion and the people behind it had come after the remaining witness. Troy joked he'd been saddled with keeping the contrary woman safe at the time, but it was obvious he worshipped her. His emerald green eye sparkled when he talked about his wife.

"I have to get to the bank," she told him after they'd cleaned up the luncheon dishes. "The stones I need to finish the jeweled mask are in a safety deposit box. I won't be gone long."

Troy checked at his watch. "Where's the bank?"

"It's a local bank on Periwinkle Way. Why?"

Troy gnawed on his bottom lip. "Okay. Let me see if I can arrange some back-up," he said, pulling his phone from his pocket.

"That isn't necessary."

"Yes, it is. I can't go into the bank carrying a gun and you're not going in there alone."

"If you drive me there, I can run in and out," she suggested as an alternative, but Troy was already on the phone.

Thirty minutes later she was in the bank with Kevin at her side. Troy had followed in his truck and was currently waiting for them in the parking lot. It was all very cloak and dagger. River felt cornered and manipulated, at the same time feeling comfortable with a couple of men watching her back. Crazy. She was simply going crazy.

"I appreciate your coming to help," she conceded to Kevin, as they pulled out onto Periwinkle Way. "Did you get some rest?"

"Enough."

"Would you like to see the stones?" she asked. Traffic was at a standstill. Not unusual on the main thoroughfare through Sanibel during season.

"Sure."

River opened her purse and retrieved a velvet pouch. Inside the pouch were numerous small plastic sleeves, each containing a stone. "They're only semi-precious stones, but I didn't want to leave them at home. These are tourmalines." She held up several plastic bags so he could see them as traffic came to a stop. "They come in all colors, but these will go perfectly with the design. The center piece is the aquamarine." She slid the other stones back in the pouch and held up the larger one.

"That's an aquamarine?" Kevin asked, turning his attention back to the road as traffic began to move.

"Stunning, isn't it? I was so lucky to find it." River put the stone back in the pouch with the others then dropped it into her purse.

"How do you get your materials? Where are they shipped?"

"All my transactions are done online using my LLC. I have a virtual post office box and I don't receive shipments to my door. They go to a shipping store in California who, in turn, forwards the packages to another store in Fort Myers. I pick them up there."

"You're pretty thorough," Kevin said.

"Dan and I worked through a skip tracer to figure out how to best disappear. So far, everything seems to have worked the way it was intended."

"Until yesterday," Kevin reminded her, pulling into a parking space near her unit.

"I still have a hard time believing it's connected to things in North Carolina. It doesn't fit the pattern."

"You said the knife attack is what prompted the move to Florida?"

"As much as I wanted to stay, it seemed prudent to leave, at least for a while. Besides, my aunt and Dan were constantly fretting over me. We developed this plan, hoping the authorities would eventually find the asshole and I could go home."

They waited while Troy parked across the lot, then trotted up to the passenger side door. "You guys ready?" He looked at River, then Kevin.

"Let's do it." Kevin reached for the glove box and pulled out a handgun. He slid out of the driver's seat while Troy held the door open for River.

"Did you bring a charger for the drill?" Troy reminded him.

Kevin reopened the driver's door. "Almost forgot. It's behind my seat."

As soon as River's feet hit the ground, something whizzed past her ear. Almost instantly, she was on the pavement with Troy covering her from head to toe. "Sniper," he yelled.

"It came from that stand of trees," Kevin shouted.

River didn't know what trees he was talking about because she couldn't see a damn thing but the asphalt under her nose.

"You okay, River?" There was no stress in Troy's voice, which calmed her a bit.

"I think so." The air had been knocked from her lungs when she hit the pavement. Now River was pressed to the ground by a large man. Her breathing came in shallow breaths. As if reading her mind, Troy lifted some of his weight off of her.

"I'm going to get up slowly. As soon as you have room to move, scoot or roll under the truck. Get to the middle and stay there until one of us gives you directions."

River had no intention of arguing. Debating the issue would only put them in further danger. Troy rolled to his right as he lifted his weight off of her, doing exactly what River feared, making sure she was shielded. She quickly scooted under the vehicle. As soon as Troy had his feet under him, he sprinted to the other side of the truck.

"Did you see anything?" Troy asked Kevin.

"No. I was assessing the walkway and staircase."

Troy made a quick, succinct call.

"Rick is on his way with back-up. What do you think, Kev? Move her now or wait?"

"Do what is best for you." She raised her voice to be heard from her hiding place. They were at risk because of her. They should leave her here, but she knew they wouldn't. "I won't be responsible for anyone getting hurt. I won't have any more deaths on my conscience."

The decision didn't have to be made. The sound of sirens grew louder as the emergency vehicles closed the distance. River shimmied her way toward the driver's side of the truck. When neither man moved to let her out, she got the message and stayed put. She angled her head to peer through legs as sturdy as tree trunks. The lot was filling with police units, some officers emerged wearing tactical gear—a couple of them carried long guns. River spotted Rick as he broke free of the pack and ran toward the truck. How the hell did they get here so fast? Or had she just imagined the speed at which everything had happened?

"Were you hurt?" Kevin asked, squatting to bring him closer to her level.

"No. Can I get up now?"

The legs barricading her moved aside. Kevin reached under the truck to give her a hand. She didn't miss the close inspection Kevin gave her as she got to her feet.

"I'm okay," she assured him. She had a few scrapes from the drop to the ground and her subsequent maneuvering under the truck, but she'd literally dodged a bullet so she wouldn't complain.

"What can you tell me?" Rick asked the threesome.

"Single shot from the tree line over there," Troy answered, pointing toward a stand of Australian pines at the end of the parking lot. "Silenced," he added, in a particularly dark tone.

Rick turned back toward the officers. He gave them some orders she couldn't quite make out. Troy and Kevin had each clasped a shoulder and pressed her down, so she was sitting on the running board of the truck, then took up a position in front of her. She couldn't see or hear much, but it was obvious Rick had given the responders their tasks. The guys in tactical gear headed towards the woods behind them. The others spread out, checking the buildings and the property beyond, she assumed.

"What were your positions when it was fired?"

"I was on the passenger side with Troy." River poked her head between the male barricade. "What sounded like a mosquito zipped past my ear. Then I was on the ground." Troy had pushed her to the asphalt so fast, the trip was a blur with the exception of a quick glimpse of Kevin. He'd just raised his head after reaching under the driver's seat for the drill's charger. If he'd been standing erect, he would have been in the line of fire. He could have been killed. This wasn't right. She might be living on borrowed time, but she'd be damned if she'd take someone else with her—especially if that someone had become important to her. Her stomach churned. She swallowed. It didn't help.

"Excuse me," she said, standing, forcing Troy and Kevin apart. She pushed past them and quickly moved toward the stairs. Kevin caught up with her and pulled her back.

"I need to go," she stated, the bile rising in her throat. "Now."

15

______

"*L*et me have your keys." Kevin held out his left palm. His weapon still clutched in his right hand.

River had lost all color and was swallowing repeatedly, fighting the urge to vomit. If, as he suspected, she wasn't already suffering from PTSD when she arrived on Sanibel, the events of the last few days had pushed her over the edge.

Tucking his left hand under her arm, he took on most of her weight as he rushed her up the stairs. Unlocking the door, he felt a dual sense of relief. The place had remained secured, and River was away from the melee below.

River made a beeline for the bathroom. He knew how to care for her physical wounds, but emotionally—psychologically—he was at a loss.

A number of his teammates and friends had battled the demon, most recently Shayne and Troy. Maybe he should talk to one of them. Perhaps they could give him some insight as to how to handle his interactions with River. In the meantime, he was going to see she rested before she was forced to answer questions. He reached in his bag and pulled out a vial along with a disposable syringe. He estimated the dose of Midazolam based on her weight, erring on the side of too little. He was practicing medicine without a license. So, sue him.

When River emerged, Kevin was waiting for her at the breakfast bar.

"Sorry," she said, as she grabbed a bottle of water from refrigerator.

"Stress can do that to anyone."

"Until recently, I could manage the stress—at least in a way that worked for me." Her brow creased and her ice-blue eyes were pinched. "I'm not doing a very good job at the moment, it would seem."

"Give yourself a break." Kevin patted the stool, inviting her to sit. "The last two days would have unsettled the strongest of men."

"I doubt that. Regardless, I'd prefer not having an audience when it happens," she admitted. "What are you doing?" she asked as she scooted onto the seat.

"I want to clean those cuts on your face. You were lying on the ground and could have picked up some dirt. I'm also going to give you a shot for nausea."

"My stomach is fine now. I don't need a shot."

He held her chin while he worked on her face. Those questioning eyes locked onto his. He found it hard to look away.

"When the cops are done, they'll want to ask you questions. I assume you don't want a repeat of what just happened." It wasn't a complete lie.

"No one would. It's not a pleasant experience," she responded, as Kevin administered some ointment to the cut.

He washed his hands again then picked up the syringe.

"You'll feel a little pinch." He cleaned her upper arm with an alcohol swab. "Relax your muscle."

She took a deep breath then let it out, relaxing her bicep on the exhale.

"This is going to sound rude," she said, "but I think I would have handled it better on my own. It's what I'm used to doing. I may huddle in a corner for a while afterwards, but usually pull myself together pretty quickly."

Keeping one eye on River, Kevin put his supplies away.

"That bullet was meant for me, but it would have hit you if you hadn't been reaching for that charger. I don't want any more deaths on my hands," she said. Propping her arm on the counter, she rested her head in her hand. "Is the shot supposed to make you woozy?"

"Why don't you lie down for a while," he suggested, coming up behind her.

"Because you're right. The police will want to talk to me. I'll make some coffee. Caffeine should help." She literally slid off the stool. Kevin was waiting to catch her.

He carried her to her bed and brushed the hair from her face. Damn, she was a beauty. A beauty who would be royally pissed when she realized what he'd done. He wasn't sorry. Her stress level had peaked and would certainly get worse with questioning. And speaking of pissed, Rick wouldn't be too happy with him either when he found out River wasn't available to answer any questions for the next few hours.

Closing the bedroom door behind him, he headed to the front window to see if he could get a read on how soon things would be wrapping up. He didn't expect to see additional emergency vehicles. Particularly one from the county's medical examiner's office. He took out his phone and punched Troy's number.

"What the hell is going on down there?" Troy glanced

up at River's unit then disappeared into the corridor leading to the stairs.

"They found a body."

"What?" Kevin immediately fixed on the wooded area. Like ants at a picnic, forensic units covered the ground where the shot had originated.

"Rick wants River down here to see if she can identify the victim."

"Not going to happen."

"Why not?"

"Because I gave her a shot that will knock her out for a while."

"That will make Rick happy." Sarcasm laced Troy's response.

"Tough shit." Kevin paused remembering the unsteady way River had made her way toward him when she exited the bathroom. "The stress was taking its toll on her."

"And you couldn't watch her decline. Right?"

"Could you? She threw her guts up the minute she hit the bathroom." Kevin glanced toward River's bedroom door.

"Getting in a little deep with her, aren't you?"

"I'm doing what I was trained to do. Help. Just drop it, Troy. Tell me what's going on."

"Like I told you, they found a body. His remains were poorly hidden behind some brush."

"Hidden? As in he didn't get there on his own."

"There are drag marks from one of the large pines to where we found him. Here's where it gets weird."

"It's already weird."

"His hands are missing. Whacked off."

"What the fuck?" Kevin reached for the door, then stopped. He couldn't leave River alone.

"I don't know what's going on, but it's getting uglier by the minute," Troy worried.

"Why cut off his hands?" Kevin circled the dining room, unable to stand still.

"Off the top of my head, the killer could be sending a message to someone or they don't want the man's identity discovered too quickly, but there could be any number of reasons."

"Tortured?" Kevin stopped pacing.

"I don't think so. No one has admitted to hearing any screams and based on the small amount of blood found near his body, my guess is he was dead before he lost his hands."

"No identification on him, I assume?"

"No, which is why Rick wants to see if River can identify him."

"Tell him to take a picture." Kevin was back at the window. Rick was headed in Troy's direction.

"You can't protect her indefinitely," Troy warned him. "You're not giving her the credit she deserves. She's been through hell and made it this far."

Troy was right. Still, Kevin was glad River wouldn't be forced to view the dead body. For a civilian, she'd seen more than her share. A picture would have to do. As for protecting her, he wouldn't be here to do that forever. While he was with her, though, he didn't think he'd be able to pull back from that stance.

"Anything else?" Kevin asked. "Did they find anything else?" he asked as he dropped to the sofa.

"Not that I'm aware of. Here's Rick. Ask him, and while you're at it, break the news about River."

"What about River?"

Rick's voice boomed through Troy's speaker.

"She's asleep."

"Then wake her up. How the hell can anyone sleep with all this shit going on?"

"Because I gave her some help," Kevin admitted. "It will be hours before she's awake."

"You gave her a sedative? Now?"

Yep. Rick was pissed. "If I'd known there was going to be a body…" He'd have done the same thing.

"You damn well knew I'd need to talk to her, regardless. Now I need to know if she recognizes the dead man."

"Take a picture. I did what I determined was best for her. I'd do the same for Shayne, Josie or Cat. If it makes you happy, River will be spitting mad at me when she wakes up."

"You didn't tell her that you slipped her something? Oh, man. You're not helping your case much, are you?" Rick asked.

"What's with you and Troy?"

"You're attracted to her. Why do we have all these screwed up relationships on this island?"

"There is no relationship," Kevin snapped. "How was he killed?" he asked, quickly diverting the conversation.

"Garrote. The coroner will have to make the official call, but I saw my share overseas."

"Then the guy sliced off his victim's hands and took them with him?" Kevin had seen a lot of depraved things while serving, but he was having a hard time digesting the same sort of evil on this quiet island.

"Appears so at this point. We haven't found the appendages."

"And no rifle?"

"Wasn't with the body," Rick answered.

"It didn't get up and walk away. Who took the shot? The victim or the guy who killed him?"

"At this point, I have no idea. I'll be back after we clear

the scene," Rick told him. "In the meantime, I'm sending a picture of the victim to your phone. Show it to River when she wakes up. I want to know if she's seen or recognizes him."

"Roger, that," Kevin said as the dial tone sounded in his ear. A couple of minutes later his phone pinged. Kevin studied the picture. The deceased's age and coloring were similar to the man he'd seen on the beach. If this was the same guy who attacked River on the causeway and outside her door, why was he dead and who killed him?

16

———

*R*iver came awake, fighting her way through a dense fog. She stretched, the action triggering aches and pains which brought her fully awake. She was in her bed and the room was dark with the exception of the light creeping under the closed door. It was enough though, that she could make out a small figure sitting in the corner. She shimmied up on the bed, untangling herself from the covers.

"It's me," Shayne announced. "Kevin guessed you'd be waking up soon. I didn't want you to be alone and wonder what was going on."

River threw her legs over the side of the bed. The clock on the nightstand told her it was after 7:00 p.m. She covered her face with her hands. As her senses sharpened, she heard the voices coming from the living area.

"Who's here?" she asked, running her hands through her hair.

"Same group as last night minus Cat and Josie."

"I can't believe I didn't hear anything. I didn't even hear you come in. Last thing I remember is Kevin giving me something for nausea." She reached for the bedside light.

"About that…" Shayne hesitated.

River flicked on the light, blinking a couple of times. Then it hit her. "The shot wasn't for nausea, was it?"

"No, it wasn't."

"Is he out there?" River rose, throwing the covers back over the bed with more strength than was necessary.

"Yes, and he shouldn't have done what he did without your consent, but in his defense, he was genuinely worried about you."

"That still didn't give him the right…"

"No, it didn't, but you feel better, don't you?"

"That's beside the point," River snarled. They were interrupted by a tap on the door.

"Can I come in?" Kevin asked.

"I think I'll join the others," Shayne said as she got out of her chair and rolled it toward the door. It dawned on River that Shayne had been seated in River's office chair, which shouldn't have surprised her. She didn't have a guest chair in the room.

Shayne muttered something to Kevin as he stepped aside to let her pass. Closing the door behind him, he leaned his back against it. Silence permeated the room.

"I suppose you're wanting an apology."

"Why couldn't you have been honest with me and asked if I needed something?"

"Would you have said 'yes'?" he asked, pushing away from the door.

"Do you know why I live in the woods—alone?"

The wheels behind his dark eyes were turning. "So, no one bothers you?"

"It did help keep the straggling paparazzi away, but the main reason behind the move was to show my aunt I wasn't too fragile to live on my own. She thought I would break. I had to prove to her and myself that I wouldn't—that I could face the deaths of my family and survive it," she said, closing the distance between them. "And I did. I don't like others making decisions for me."

The Adam's apple in Kevin's throat bobbed with each swallow. She was mesmerized.

"A body can only take so much. You've had one thing piled on another these last few days."

"I understand that, but you didn't ask me how I was doing—if I was okay." Her gaze moved from his throat to meet his eyes.

"I didn't have to. I saw how you reacted to the shooting." He met her stare.

"Yes, getting shot at scared the hell out of me, but I'm more terrified of someone else being hurt or killed on my account." He was so close now she felt the heat from his body. "I don't want anything to happen to you."

He tucked a stray hair behind her ear then rested his hand at the base of her neck. The gesture was tender and erotic, which didn't make a damned bit of sense.

"You were sick because you were worried about me?"

As she nodded, he framed her face with his hands and lowered his mouth to meet hers. The kiss took her breath away. It was searing and demanding. Surprising herself, she returned it with the same fervor—the same heat. Enough heat, she thought she might melt into a puddle on the floor. He nipped at her lips from one corner to the other before teasing her mouth open. She pressed against him as their tongues met in a frenzy. When he slipped his leg between hers, she straddled it, rubbing her core against his muscular thigh, trying to relieve the growing ache deep inside her. His mouth traveled down her jaw, nibbling at her ear and suckling the lobe. Her hands burrowed under his shirt, tracing the taut muscles of his back.

A knock on the door startled her. Jumping back, River untangled herself from his arms. What the hell was wrong with her?

"I'm assuming you two have settled things since we haven't heard any shouting."

"Go away, Gib." Kevin's voice was gruff.

River covered her face with her hands. God. What had she been thinking?

"I'm sure you'd like nothing more," Gib continued, "but there's a room full of people out here with things to discuss."

Oh, shit. Had they guessed what was going on? Of course, they had. River's cheeks burned.

"We'll be right out," Kevin answered.

Taking a deep breath, River summoned her courage and faced Kevin. "My apologies. That shouldn't have happened."

He smiled.

"It wasn't very smart considering all that's going on." She took another step away from him. What the hell was he grinning about? He clasped her chin, stopping her retreat.

"It has nothing to do with what's going on. We'll pick this up later," he promised.

"Like hell we will. It was a mistake." She pushed his hand aside and turned toward the door.

"Why was it a mistake?" Kevin asked, placing a hand on her shoulder.

"I like my privacy. I like being alone. Sex is complicated and messy."

"Messy?" Kevin's eyebrows rose.

"Messy as in messing up people's lives." She shrugged off his hand.

"Do you understand the difference between sex and a relationship?" His grin had disappeared. Both anger and confusion now laced his tone.

"I've had sex, if that's what you're asking."

"I'm asking if you've ever been in a relationship with someone—someone special?"

"That's none of your business." She grabbed the doorknob and stepped into the hall. "I'm going to freshen up." Which was true. She also wanted to wash the taste of him from her mouth or it would be hell to concentrate on anything else.

The knock on the door had also knocked some sense into her. She had no business getting involved with anyone. Her life was littered with the dead and injured. She had no desire to leave any more bodies in her wake. Besides, she was damaged goods. There was a black hole in her heart where her family used to reside. She didn't believe there was enough left of it to share with another person.

Contrary to what she'd insinuated, she understood relationships. Her mom and dad had one she would never be able to replicate. River had also had sex for the sake of sex. She'd found it unsatisfying. She'd hoped the words thrown at Kevin would be enough to change his mind—to force him away.

Whether he left under his own steam or at her demand, he was going and so were the rest of them. Relationships of any kind were dangerous—for her and for them. She'd been successful at avoiding them until now. This group had snuck under her radar. The women had welcomed her. The men were protective and respectful. None of them had a gleeful desire to dig into her history.

Then there was Kevin. Damn. There was that flutter again.

But being around her put them in danger. Today proved that. She couldn't let it happen again. It was obvious they weren't going to simply leave because she asked them. They were men of honor. So were the women. They cared. It wasn't going to be easy to chase them away. One painful idea came to mind. She was going to have to hurt them to keep them safe. Hopefully, she could pull it off without them seeing through it.

When she joined the others in the living room, they were all chowing down on sandwiches. Beer, wine, water, and soft drinks were spread across the coffee table.

"There's a plate for you on the counter," Gib told her.

"Thank you." River glanced at the sandwich and chips topped with a napkin. His kindness was making the next move even more difficult.

"You'll probably need the energy later on," Gib joked. "Ouch!"

"Excuse him," Shayne said. "He's either charming people or annoying them."

"What do you mean? I'm always charming," Gib said, rubbing his arm where Shayne had smacked him.

"Have a seat." Kevin indicated the space next to him. The sparkle she'd seen in his eyes earlier was gone. She'd managed to do some damage. She was about to take a sledgehammer to what was left of this attraction.

She ignored him as she marched into the kitchen and pulled a bottle of wine from the small rack on the counter. Gib started to rise. The cold, icy stare she gave him did the trick and had him retaking his seat. Her heart hurt. She felt like she'd kicked a puppy. They were kind people who wanted to help, but their assistance could put them in danger.

The room remained quiet while she opened the bottle. She filled her glass then raised it. "I want to thank you all for everything you've done."

"What's going on?" Kevin asked, breaking the silence.

"I won't be taking advantage of your time or your kindness any longer."

"You're not taking advantage of us," Shayne grinned. "We're friends."

"We're acquaintances," River corrected her in a cold, business-like tone. "And while I appreciate your help and the offer of friendship, I prefer my singular lifestyle to this room full of people."

Shayne's sparkling smile morphed into a thin, tight line, the edges turning down. Her eyes dulled, covered by a thin sheen of moisture. River turned away from her.

"What the hell happened between the two of you in there?" Colt's head snapped in Kevin's direction.

Eyes narrowing, Kevin didn't respond. Instead, he glared at River. "My friends are trying to help you. Is this how you repay them?"

"That was your idea. Not mine. I should have said no when you first suggested it. If you'll let me know how much I owe you for your security and the food, I'll get the funds to you."

"You don't owe us a damn thing," Steve said. He set his beer on the table with a loud thud. River thought the glass top might have cracked. It was the least of her problems.

Troy pulled his wife to her feet and headed for the door.

"Hold up, Troy," Rick said, standing to face the two. "I still have questions regarding the shooting I need to ask River. I need you and Kevin to stay behind so we can go over the events of today."

His one, sharp, emerald-green eye bore into her. "Gib, would you take Shayne home?"

"No problem. You can pick her up at Colt's," Gib told him. "Josie and Cece are visiting Cat. We'll keep her company until you get there."

But Gib didn't head to the door. River took a step back from the counter as he stormed toward her. The charmer wasn't so charming anymore. He leaned over the breakfast bar—his lively grey eyes had transformed into steel. "I don't know what brought this on, but whatever it was, you had absolutely no reason to hurt Shayne."

RIVER'S back was so damn straight you could have hammered her into the ground like a steel rod. Her jaw was clenched so tight it had to hurt. Her eyes though— Kevin swore there was sadness in her crystal blue eyes, or it could be a reflection of his own mood. He was caught somewhere between anger and sorrow.

"What the hell is wrong with you? If this is about…"

"Let's get on with this so I can get out of here," Troy snapped. "I don't give a damn why she's got a burr up her ass. I need to get to Shayne."

Kevin dropped the subject for now. He'd find out what was going on with River after everyone had left.

River opted to stay in the kitchen. She was working on her second glass of wine—her other hand clutched the bottle, posed for another pour. He hadn't seen her drink, but then again, he didn't know crap about her, except that ugly portion of her childhood, and how she felt in his arms. After the way she'd treated his friends, all interest in her should have died. It hadn't, but now wasn't the time to puzzle it out.

"Do you recognize this man?" Rick held up his phone. There was no way River would be able to make out the face from where she stood. Kevin assumed the action was a tactic to bring her closer for the discussion or, it could be Rick was still pissed enough that he was making her come to him.

River slid from behind the granite breakfast bar, after topping off her glass of wine. Her eyes narrowed as she approached Rick's extended hand. As soon as she saw the photo clearly, Kevin bet she'd stop in her tracks. Six feet out, she did.

"No. Is he the one who shot at us?"

"We don't think so. This guy was found dead in the stand of trees," Rick told her.

"Dead? How? Who is he?"

Kevin noted the hands tremble, but she was doing a decent job of holding it together. Trouble was, it wasn't going to get easier for her.

"We were hoping you'd recognize him. There was no identification on the body."

"Let me see the picture again."

Rick handed her his phone as she set down her glass. Some color faded from her cheeks, but Kevin didn't note any other reaction to the photo.

"How did he die?" she asked again, retrieving her glass and taking a hefty sip.

"The coroner hasn't given an official cause of death, but I'm pretty certain he was strangled," Rick told her.

"So, there were two people out there? And you don't believe this one fired the shot at us?"

"At you," Troy pointed out.

River nodded. "I am sorry my presence put you in danger. It won't happen again."

Kevin noted the slackening of Troy's jaw. Still, his friend didn't acknowledge her apology.

"This man didn't do any shooting. At least, not today," Rick told her.

"How can you be certain?"

Troy snatched the phone from River's hand. Kevin understood his intentions a minute too late. Troy had already scrolled to the next photo and shoved the phone at River. She went from pale to white. Rushing toward her, Kevin stopped in his tracks when those ice-blue eyes flashed up at him. Tossing the phone to the couch as if it had burned her fingers, she stumbled back toward the kitchen. Leaning against the counter, her hands trembled as she took another fortifying sip of the wine.

"Was that necessary?" Kevin couldn't blame Troy for his hostility toward River. He adored his wife, but the action had been unlike him.

"Why?" River asked. "Why did he cut off the hands? Is someone sending me a message?"

"It's possible, or someone is trying to make his identification difficult," Rick said.

River set the glass aside, letting her head drop into her hands. Kevin could only imagine the memories running through her head. Her family had been slaughtered—stabbed and sliced with knives. The dismemberment of the victim hit all too close to her history. Her agony was so visible, it hurt to watch. Instinct almost brought him to his feet again, but common sense stopped him. She didn't want his help. She chose to carry this weight alone. Why?

Kevin side-eyed his friends. They, too, were uncomfortable. Troy's head hung low, studying his hands, avoiding the painful scene. Rick fiddled with his phone, giving River time to gather herself.

A deep breath, followed by a loud sigh, signaled River

was ready to continue. She raised her head and focused on Rick.

"How can I help?"

The question and tone caught Kevin off guard. Gone was the anger and pain. The softness and concern he'd witnessed the last two days had returned. Interesting.

"You don't recognize him?" Rick asked again.

"No. Not at all. If I ran into him somewhere, I don't remember." River hesitated. "And you don't think the killer was sending me some kind of message? A warning of some sort?"

"You'd have to be alive to receive a message," Rick asserted. "From what the guys have told me, the gunman was going for a head shot."

Kevin didn't know what to make of River's expression. Resignation? Disappointment?

"Can you think of a reason why someone would want you dead?"

"No," she answered Rick. "Well, maybe the Engleharts. I'm sure they would like a crack at me, but they're locked up for the rest of their lives. Everything that's happened in the past year or so has been meant to frighten me. If someone wanted me dead, I've been an easy target. This is something new."

"Give me your version of what happened today." In addition to recording the interview, Rick took out the small pad he kept in his pocket along with a pen. Kevin knew old habits die hard.

The events were related in a steady, disconnected voice, but she was anything but calm. Her fingers traced the sides of the wine tumbler. Her eyes no longer sparkled like ice on a sunny day. When she got to the part where Troy had slammed her to the ground, she stopped to thank him again. She finished relating the events up until she fell victim to the injection Kevin had given her.

"Does that dovetail with your end of things?" He looked to Kevin.

Kevin nodded, keeping his attention fixed on River. She'd remembered every detail. Is that how she remembered the scene that she came upon at fourteen years of age? Were the memories crisp and clear or had they begun to fade around the edges? If they had, today probably brought them back into focus.

"Troy?" Rick glanced at his friend.

"That covers it," Troy answered the unspoken question.

"Can you think of anything else?" Rick asked River. "Anything? Anyone we should follow up with?

River's brows knitted together as she gave the question more thought, then quietly shook her head. Kevin fought the urge to go to her. Why the hell would someone prefer to suffer alone when there were people willing to offer support?

"If we're done," Troy said, "I want to pick up Shayne."

"We're done," Rick told him. "I'll follow you over to Colt's."

"Give me a minute here," Kevin said. "Then I'll see you all over there."

"Josie and Steve are ready to leave. They'll need to get Cece to bed," Rick reminded him from the door.

"I won't be long."

"She doesn't want our help," Troy reminded him. "She's made herself clear."

"I'll be along in a minute," Kevin reiterated, refusing to get pulled into an argument.

The door clicked shut. Silence claimed the room. River held her ground, wine glass still clutched in her hand.

"I don't have anything to say to you," River said, breaking the silence.

"I think you do. I brought my friends into this mess with your agreement. Granted, I pushed, but you accepted their help then threw dirt in their faces. I think you owe us an explanation."

"It was a mistake."

Kevin was done talking to her from across the room. He'd planned to corner her in the kitchen but stopped short of doing so. He did, however, block her exit from the small space. "Why?"

It had taken River a while to come down off her peak of temper after Kevin had left. He'd pushed. He'd wanted answers. He wanted the reason behind her sudden change in demeanor, and why she'd hurt his friends. She'd refused to be baited. She was a loner. It was safer for her and everyone else if she stayed that way. If she'd told him she feared for his safety and those in his close-knit group, they were the type to tell her to stop being a hero and would form a tighter circle around her. Insulting them seemed like the best way to be rid of all of them. They'd be fools to want to see her again after her performance. Her face burned at the way she'd treated Shayne. One day she'd apologize, assuming she got the chance.

He'd called her a coward.

Fuck him. River yanked the chair away from her workbench. Dropping into the seat, she picked up the small brush she used to add adhesive to the stones before setting them in place. Her hand shook, damn it. Why did his accusation get under her skin? He had no idea how hard it was to put one foot in front of the other each day—to push past the guilt of leaving her family to die.

Hadn't she stared sheer evil in the face when she'd testified against those bastards? She'd tackled her nightmares by moving into the cabin where her family had been slaughtered. Who was he to accuse her of hiding? She kept to herself to avoid assholes like him who assumed they had the right to sit in judgement of her actions or reactions.

River's ears burned and her skin flushed, anger replacing her earlier embarrassment. Swearing at her shaking hands, she threw the brush onto the bench. She wouldn't work on the mask with an unsteady hand. The client was expecting perfection. They were paying for it.

Her eyes were drawn to the large photograph mounted on the wall above her workspace. She'd sketched the pictures the artist had used to carve the base of the birdbath. It had been easy to remember her father's strong arms as they lifted Billy in the air or hugged her mom tight. River hadn't needed photos to recreate the lithe limbs of her mother or the pudgy fingers of her little brother. The sketch had been done from memory. To this day, she didn't question the way she chose to honor them. Her family had loved the land and the creatures that shared it. In River's mind, the fountain offered life in place of death.

She missed her home and the family who had been gone half her life. How would she be different if they'd survived? Would her career choice have been different? Would she be married and have a gaggle of kids? Would she still be the target of a stalker? Which led her back to the question of whether the death of her family had anything to do with her current problems. She ran her fingers up the bridge of her nose and massaged her forehead. There were so many thoughts banging around, it hurt.

Opening the drawer by the computer, she pulled out her sketch pad. No work would be accomplished tonight, and experience told her sleep would be elusive. So, she did what had become a habit when she was anxious. She began to freestyle—drawing whatever came to mind.

Her pencil flew across the thick, white paper. The outline of the headless snake quickly—almost automatically—appeared. She filled in the details—the scales, the narrowing of the tail. She cut a sharp slash across the page where the head had been cut off. She ripped the page free of the pad. The head of the snake emerged on the next sheet. It rose from the drain of the kitchen sink—its mouth gaping wide, propped open with a broken toothpick. She filled the next page with the frightening, and sad, image of the dead rabbit tucked into her bed—as a child would do with a precious stuffed toy. An eviscerated raccoon followed, propped on the outdoor rocker. A bird, neck broken, strung up on the rafter of her front porch. The images tumbled out like individual frames from a movie until her pencil grew heavy and her hand cramped. Her final sketch showed the blade of the knife as she opened the door to the cabin.

River exhaled, dropping the pad and pencil onto the drafting table. She'd spent months fighting those memories, pushing them into the cracks and crevices of her mind, but tonight they'd refused to stay hidden. The stress of the evening and the process of bringing the images to light drained her. She rested her head on her arms then let the exhaustion consume her.

~

KEVIN CURSED as he made his way up the stairs to Colt's home above the photography studio. River was the most stubborn, pig-headed woman he'd ever met. He didn't understand why the hell he cared. She'd hurt his friends and, with the exception of Rick, was refusing all assistance. Rick would have been out the door with the rest of them had there been a second detective on Sanibel's small police force. What the hell was it about her that drew him?

He tapped on the door twice before entering the home. He'd have been surprised if anyone could have heard his knock over Cece's wailing. Apparently, the young lady was not happy and was making her displeasure known. Gib was doing his best to charm the baby—cooing, tickling and rocking her. The crying didn't seem to bother him. He was thrilled he'd been given temporary childcare privileges.

The men hovered by the couch where the three women huddled together. Shayne was squeezed between Cat and Josie.

"I'm sorry, Shayne," he said, approaching them.

"It's not your fault. She blindsided me for a second," she said, giving him a smile.

"I pushed her. I guess I pushed too hard."

"What happened between you two?" Steve asked.

"Nothing that I didn't think was mutual," Kevin admitted.

"Apparently, it wasn't," Troy growled.

"Give it a rest," Shayne told her husband, reaching for his hand. "We've all had our breaking points." She glanced at the women at her side.

"We have," Cat agreed. "And each of us handled it differently."

"Lashing out may be her way of dealing with stress. She admitted she's not used to crowds. We witnessed her reaction to us during our first get-together," Shayne reminded him. "We all should have known better than to gang up on her. Regardless, I wish she'd accept our support."

"Get her to change her mind," Josie ordered Kevin as she took the crying baby from Gib's arms.

"How? She's closed up tighter than a drum," Kevin responded.

"I bet I could get her to talk." Gib volunteered, grinning.

"Leave her be for the time being. I'll see her tomorrow. See if I can't talk some sense into her." Kevin scrubbed his face with his hand. "I can't make sense of this. Do you guys see a pattern? Anything? You're the investigators."

"Don't sell yourself short in that category," Colt corrected him. "You investigate every time you work on a patient. You determine the cause of the injury and what they need, then you work to solve it. Medicine is a hell of a lot more meticulous than crime solving."

"If it hadn't been for your quick thinking and know-how, I wouldn't be here. I would never have had this chance with Shayne." Troy pulled his petite wife closer before laying a kiss on her hair.

Kevin hadn't thought of it in those terms. His instincts kicked in when someone needed medical attention.

"I haven't figured her out yet, let alone the shit that's been happening to her," he admitted.

"Because we don't have much to work with right now," Rick said. "The case didn't go away because she got her back up. I can't drop it because she'd be unhappy with us."

"She was hoping for another detective, but I explained you're it. She'll cooperate."

"I still have people in North Carolina to talk to," Rick continued, "and I'm hoping we can identify our victim shortly. He may be the clue we need. There has to be a reason someone took the time to lop off his hands and remove all his identification—assuming he had some on him."

"I'm still digging, too," Josie added. Her voice was softer now that Cece had fallen asleep in her arms. "I'll touch base with my sources again tomorrow. The police don't always get the juicy tidbits reporters dig up and most of those don't make the news."

"I've got to get these ladies home." Steve grabbed the diaper bag—and wasn't it a sight to see his former Special Ops lieutenant hauling diapers instead of weapons of war?

"Sounds good," Rick said.

"If I find out anything," Josie added, "I'll pass the info to Steve."

As the family made their way toward the rear door, Kevin followed as far as the kitchen. He snagged a beer from the fridge, returning to the living room to join those who remained. Straddling one of the dining room chairs, the beer dangling between two of his fingers, he faced his friends.

"Okay," he said. "Be honest. Give me your impressions."

"Of what?" Colt asked. "River or the shitshow surrounding her?"

"Both. I feel like I'm in the middle of a dust storm and can't see anything clearly. One minute she's cautious but accepting. The next she's tossing us out on our ear. She lives quietly on the island for almost a year and suddenly is attacked three times. Is she hiding something? Can we trust her? Should we even try?"

"You can't see the forest because you're too focused on the tree. Or in this case, River. You're attracted to her," Cat told him. "Everything else is in your periphery."

"What do you mean?" Kevin raised his eyebrows at her blunt assessment.

"Kev, it's how you're built," Troy explained. "You've always had the ability to block out the chaff while you dealt with the problem at hand. It's what makes you a good medic."

"She doesn't need a medic. She needs someone to watch her back."

"You can't save everyone," Colt reminded him, solemnly.

The room grew silent. Colt rarely spoke of his last mission to Afghanistan. He'd been their commander when the team was ambushed at a friendly village. Many of those in the village had died that day. Colt had taken on the responsibility of their deaths. The team couldn't convince him otherwise. He'd left the Army and moved to Sanibel. Gib and Cat had worked some sort of magic. Between the two of them, their old commander was back.

"You couldn't prevent the attacker from reaching her at the beach. You see that as a failure. You feel responsible," Colt said. "You need to give yourself a break and her some room. It's pretty obvious she'll rebel if you don't. She needs time to get used to having people around her who care."

"Where's her aunt?" Gib asked. "Where's this friend of hers, Dan, while all this shit is going down?"

"She probably told them to stay away." Kevin would bet she hadn't told them much, if anything.

"Would you stay away?" Gib didn't let up.

"Hell, no." Kevin scanned the room. "And don't tell me any of you would either."

"You know better, but she's not ready for an army to back her up," Colt told him. "We'll remain in the background, but we'll be right behind you—assuming you can make any inroads after tonight."

Kevin nodded. "Can you guys see something surrounding this mystery that I'm not?"

"We're missing a lot of info." Rick ran his thumb and index finger along his chin and jaw line. "Instinct tells me the mayhem at the cabin is connected to the murders of her family. The authorities initially tried to tie them together but dropped that line of investigation. I haven't been able connect the two yet, but the way the animals were eviscerated was too close to the way her family was butchered."

"If it's so clear to you, why did they give up on it?" Kevin asked.

"The detective in charge didn't disagree with me, but he said they'd exhausted all leads in that direction."

"What about the Englehart family?" Troy questioned Rick. "Steve and I didn't turn up any mention of relatives in our search. Did you find anything different?"

"A couple of distant relatives," Rick answered. "Third or fourth cousins, I think. They've lived on the West Coast all their lives. Sheriff Chamblee never found any connection between the extended family other than bloodline. The cousins didn't even know they were related to the Engleharts until the FBI tracked them down, and they want nothing to do with them."

"Where are they, specifically?" Colt asked.

"Washington State. The investigators visited them again when the harassment started last year," Rick explained. "They're clean."

"We're basically stuck then," Kevin lamented.

"It's still too early to be stuck," Troy commented. "If you want to continue to play guardian after tonight, I can make a trip up to North Carolina. Nose around a bit."

"To do some digging?" Kevin stared at his friend. He was surprised by the offer considering the events of that evening, but Shayne was beaming at her husband.

"I don't think River will go for it." He was concerned how River would react to the continuing investigation.

"We won't tell her unless we have to. I won't approach her aunt or Dan. I'll check out the area. Poke my head around. Talk to a few neighbors. I can come up with a cover story that won't put anybody on alert." Troy paused. "You want her safe, don't you?"

Kevin scratched the back of his neck. He trusted Troy, and River's problems weren't suddenly going to disappear.

"Thanks. I'll pay for your plane ticket."

"Put away your wallet for now," Gib interrupted. "I'll see if my friend's jet is available. It will get us there fast and give us the flexibility we need."

"Us?" Troy asked, raising his eyebrow.

"Why not? We can tag team."

Troy rolled his remaining eye. "Ah, maybe I'll fly commercial."

18

―――――――

*E*arly the next morning, Kevin pulled his truck up in front of River's condo. At Cat's strong suggestion, his first stop had been Bailey's Market for flowers then he swung by the restaurant to pick up her favorite breakfast. He grabbed the *to-go* box from the Sanibel Café and the bundle of flowers from the passenger seat.

A police cruiser was parked in the lot. As he made his way over to talk with the officer, the woman was grinning. "Is that your insurance?" she asked, indicating his full hands.

"Can't hurt," he answered, stepping back as the officer opened her vehicle's door. "I'm Kevin Slawter." He tucked the bouquet under one arm and offered her his hand.

"Sarah Stanton," she said, accepting his outstretched hand.

"I assume it's been quiet?" Rick would have been on the phone with him if anything had been reported.

"Nothing unusual. I checked the stairwell and the bayside of her unit a number of times. Scared a couple of lizards, but other than that, nothing's moved. The light was on all night in one of the rooms. Second balcony to my right," the officer told him.

Kevin wasn't surprised. Had she fallen asleep or worked through the night? She'd dozed off at her drafting table once that he knew of. Either way, he'd best be prepared for an irritable female.

"How long are you going to be here?" Kevin asked.

"Long enough to see if you get your ass kicked to the curb. Rick wants you to call him if you can't cover her."

Kevin would like to cover River from head-to-toe. Right now, he needed to start from scratch with her. Win her trust again.

"Let's see if flowers and/or French toast gets me in the door," he said heading for the stairwell.

Tucking the bouquet under his arm again, he tapped on the door. When the soft rap didn't get a response, he knocked harder. Nothing. Was she ignoring him? With the equipment they'd installed, she would know he was at the door. He juggled the items in his hands and pulled his phone from his pocket. If she didn't answer his call, he'd have the officer come up. River might answer the door for her. If that didn't work, they'd be finding another way to get in there. Kevin's tension was ramping up. Chill. She's pissed at you, he reminded himself.

Quickly finding her number, his finger was hovering over the call button when the door opened. River stood in front of him, blocking his entry. She looked tired, irritated —and enticing.

"What do you want?" she asked, unbundling her messy hair from an elastic band. She ran her fingers through it before pulling it back into a ponytail. The action appeared automatic but had a certain sensuality to it. Her pouty lips begged to be kissed. Don't go there.

"I brought you breakfast," he said, holding out the food

container. "And an apology," he added, pulling the flowers from beneath his arm.

Those ice-blue eyes narrowed, tightening at the corners. Her aquiline nose twitched as her attention slipped to the container. "What's in there?"

"Pina Colada French toast."

She took a step back. He gave himself a mental fist bump.

Shutting the door after him, she grabbed the flowers along with the container of food. Placing both gifts on the breakfast bar, she opened the to-go box and removed the small, plastic container which held the sweet, pineapple topping. She eyed him skeptically. He'd remained in the living room, figuring it best to wait for a further invitation.

"I'm going to clean up," she said. "Warm this in the oven and find something to put the flowers in. I don't have a vase, so use whatever will work."

"No problem," he said, but she'd already disappeared down the hallway.

He found one of those single-use aluminum baking pans and put the bread into the oven, setting it on warm. He couldn't come up with anything but a stunted pitcher for the flowers. She'd said "whatever", so he filled it with water, cutting off some of the stems so the blooms didn't fall out of the vessel. He sat them on the breakfast bar along with a paper napkin and utensils from the drawer. She didn't keep much in the place. It underscored the fact she had no plans to stay. Why did that bother him? She had roots elsewhere. It was natural to want to go home— unless going home could get you killed. Not that she was all that safe here.

Kevin checked the coffeemaker, confirmed it was prepped for several cups, then hit the brew button.

Because the place was small, he heard the water from the shower shut off. Reaching in the oven for the French toast, he stopped when he heard the whir of her hair dryer.

He switched off the oven but left the breakfast in it to keep it warm. Leaving the kitchen, he ducked into her studio. With her thick head of hair, he should have sufficient time to check out her office. It wasn't snooping. Yeah, it was, but he was curious what had kept her up most of the night.

The pages that littered the drafting table stood out in stark contrast to the obsessive neatness of the rest of the room. The inconsistency drew him closer. He picked up the papers, a knot forming in his stomach as he viewed the first image—a bird hung from some rafters—her cabin's porch, he'd bet. When he got to the drawing of the rabbit in her bed and what he assumed was blood soaking through the covers, his jaw tightened. God, the visions that must be trapped in her mind. If these sketches were anything close to the actual events, they were horrific. She'd been living in the middle of a nightmare yet had stuck it out until the knife attack. The woman had guts or was stubborn—or both.

When the hairdryer shut off, Kevin slipped back into the kitchen. He grabbed a plate from the cabinet, trying to dismiss the images he'd just seen, which would be a damn hard task. He placed the coconut encrusted toast along with a cup of coffee on the breakfast bar before retrieving his own coffee from the countertop.

When she came around the corner, she looked refreshed and less stressed. A sparkle had returned to those stunning eyes. Her hair was loose and draped over her shoulders. She'd slipped into jeans and a tank top covered by an opened, long sleeve shirt with rolled up cuffs. She took his breath away. Shit.

"Did you eat?" River asked, hopping onto the stool.

"Before I left Gib's. Did you get any sleep last night?"

"You bribed your way in here with breakfast." Her eyes narrowed. "It doesn't mean we're suddenly friends."

Taking a sip of coffee, he watched her through the rising steam. The statement was a small kick in the gut. He'd known it wasn't going to be easy to get back into her good graces. At least his ass hadn't been kicked to the curb—yet.

"Look," she said, aimlessly rearranging the food on her plate, "I've got work to catch up on. Don't you have something to do?"

"Not really. I thought I'd hang out on your living room balcony for a while. Enjoy the view. I won't get in your way."

"You won't get in my way because you won't be here. I'm behind on my work. I don't need distractions." She glanced back at him as she rinsed her dishes before putting them in the dishwasher.

Kevin liked the idea of being a distraction. He considered it a back-handed compliment.

"Why are you still here?" she asked, looking over her shoulder at him.

"Why are you so damned stubborn?" He quickly regretted the snappish question. The same tone had gotten them kicked out of her place last night. He was trying to make inroads, not further the divide. "Sorry. I was hoping to give the police officer outside a break by sticking around for a while today."

River's back straightened. "There's a policeman outside?"

In addition to her tussled look when she answered the door, the fact she hadn't noticed the police presence, added to his assumption that she had, indeed, fallen asleep while working.

"Policewoman," Kevin corrected. "She's been there all night. She could use a break."

River looked toward the front windows.

"Did you think Rick would leave you on your own?"

Her shoulders slumped in resignation. She wasn't stupid. She simply hadn't given it any thought. After seeing her sketches, it was obvious her mind had been elsewhere.

Her head fell, causing her silky hair to cascade forward, shielding her face. "Fine," she sighed. "Stay. Inside or out. I'm going to get some work done."

"River?" Kevin said as she reached into the refrigerator. "I owe you an apology for last night. I shouldn't have pressed the way I did."

Without a word, she grabbed a bottle of water and headed toward her work room. He didn't know how to interpret her silent exit.

RIVER TOOK a minute to gather herself once she was behind closed doors. She'd hoped she wouldn't see Kevin again—that her rude remarks had chased them all away. In all honesty, her stomach fluttered when she'd seen him on the security monitor. She'd debated answering the door, but logic quickly told her if she didn't answer, she would be inviting more trouble. He'd been getting ready to place a call and, if it was to the police, she didn't want them coming back. She hadn't been aware they had never left.

He'd brought her breakfast and flowers. She'd never

received flowers from anyone other than Aunt Amy or Dan on her birthday. And he'd remembered her breakfast order. The thoughtful bribe had worked and melted some of the ice she'd been shielding herself with since last evening. It pissed her off she had to battle to keep those feelings and yearnings at bay. Why did this man have her defenses falling?

She gathered up the sketches she'd drawn last night. She should tear them up. Better yet, burn them. The act of producing them had been painful, but perhaps keeping them would save her from experiencing that pain again. She stuffed them in a portfolio she seldom used and set it on the top shelf of the closet. Hopefully, she'd cleansed those memories from her mind.

Digging back into the project, the world faded into the background. She spent the morning setting the final stones in place then adding the last touches to the mask. Then she took time to study and admire the finished product. She never sold anything she wasn't proud of, but this project had been particularly challenging. The circumstances in her personal life only served to heighten that challenge, but the mask had transformed into the work of art she had originally imagined. She hoped the client would be as pleased with the outcome.

The mask would require additional support. The usual ribbons wouldn't be enough to hold it in place. The stones made the mask heavier than most and her client made it clear she planned to be active during the performance when she wore it. They'd discussed the possibility and the options to address it, eventually coming up with a solution they both believed would work. It would be the last step before shipping the mask out.

She was tired. She hadn't slept, but a few hours in the last two days. Stress sat on her shoulders like ten-pound weights. A nap would be nice, but she was running danger-ously close to missing the completion date for the project so she started in on the additional strapping which would be hidden by the wig her client planned to wear.

An hour and a half later, the mask was officially complete. As River pulled a box and packing material from her supply closet, her stomach growled. A tap on the door made her jump.

"River?" Kevin, of course. Who else would it be?

Yanking the door open, her vision was filled with a broad, muscled chest struggling against a snug polo shirt. Her mouth went dry.

"You okay?"

Those caramel-colored eyes bore into hers. She licked her lips. "Uh, yeah. Fine," she answered, shaking her head. "Just hungry."

"That's what I figured. I'm a little hungry myself."

For the same thing? Christ. Get yourself under control.

"I can warm up some of those leftovers, if you want," he said, dropping his forearm which had been showing off some mighty fine pecs as he'd braced it against the doorframe.

"You're not here to wait on me," she said. "Besides, I owe you lunch." She shut her mouth so quickly, her teeth rattled. What the hell was wrong with her? She was ready to invite him out to lunch.

"You're not suggesting we leave here?"

His stunned expression tripped the switch in the oppo-site direction.

"And I know you're not suggesting I'm going to be a prisoner. Are you?" Her hands fisted.

"You were shot at!"

"I sort of remember that." She'd never forget. Her presence had almost gotten him killed.

"Look." He let out a huff. "I worry. I worry about you. I worry about people in general."

She took in the short, clipped sentences. His statement was part confession and part annoyance with himself. He cared for people—not for her in particular, but he cared for people—and that made her an ass for her snarky tone and insults.

"It's why you do what you do," she said, letting the comment out on a soft breath. He was a healer and hero. A protector. The least she could do was respect him even if she resented the constraints he wanted to put on her.

"I'll make a deal with you," she said, relaxing her stance. His eyes narrowed in suspicion. "While I don't frequently roam the island, I'm not going to be trapped in here."

"I get the feeling I'm not going to like where this is going."

"When I do venture out, I'll let you guys know." It killed her to even suggest they ride shotgun and put them in danger, but she hoped it would keep them from round the clock surveillance of her—which she had no doubt was the plan.

"That guy had a rifle," Kevin pointed out. His effort to keep his voice level was almost visible.

"I totally get that, but I'm not going to let anyone determine my movements." He'd probably just filed her under the "too stupid to live" category and she wouldn't deny it, if accused. One day her number would be up. There wasn't a day she didn't wake, wondering if that day would be the day she'd be free of her anxiety—whether it was by breaking the shackles of fear, or by joining her family. After all, she should have died fourteen years ago.

She set the completed mask inside the box on her work desk. She'd finish the packing later.

"I'm heading to Grandma Dot's. I have a craving for a grouper sandwich. Then I'm going to do a bit of shelling." What she had was a craving for a little independence and perhaps a bit of fresh air. He was going to blow a gasket when he saw her destination.

The woman had a death wish, Kevin swore as he followed River out of the complex. She hadn't waited for him. She'd simply grabbed her purse, breezed by him and headed out the door. He'd quickly set the alarm and raced to the ground floor, but River was already in her car and on the move. Either she liked to get under his skin, or she was sending a message that he wasn't needed—or both.

When she made a left turn off of Periwinkle Way, his jaw literally dropped as River pulled up to the front of a small restaurant. It sat on a dock next to a marina which was packed with boats of all sizes. The location wasn't the issue, the structure was—or lack of it. Most of the seating was outdoors under a covered patio. There appeared to be some seating inside the building, but he held little hope River would reach for the door. She didn't.

He pulled out the chair across from her. There was no position he could take that would allow him to have a visual of the entire area. Fortunately, it was a bit late in the day for lunch, so the small restaurant was sparsely populated. That didn't mean the area was safe. Boats, which would make excellent hiding places, surrounded them. Since she hadn't preplanned her foray and they hadn't been followed, the chances were low of her being targeted.

"What is it with you?" he asked. "You're a sitting duck out here."

"I've lived in fear. I still live in fear, but I have to occasionally remind myself it doesn't own me."

"Can I convince you to go inside?" he asked, scanning the area. He was surprised to see her hand was stretched across the table, palm up. He stared at it for a second, then mirrored her action, clasping his fingers with hers.

"Will you leave, if I do? I don't want you hurt." Her glacier blue eyes shimmered with unshed tears.

"Do you hear yourself? You're admitting you're a target." He didn't realize he was holding her hand so tightly until she grimaced. He relaxed his fingers.

"If it's going to happen, it's going to happen," she said. "It won't matter where I sit or where I go, if someone wants to get to me, they'll manage to do it."

"Do you have a death wish?" he asked, scanning the area again.

"I have an acceptance," she started, then stopped as a young woman appeared with menus.

Kevin was annoyed by the interruption. She was opening up. He quickly ordered the first item under sandwiches on the menu then held his tongue while River studied it. She seemed to relish taking her time, eventually requesting her earlier stated wish for a grouper sandwich.

As soon as the server left, Kevin jumped on her last remark. "What the hell do you mean by you have 'an acceptance'?"

"Let's drop the subject. I'd like a few minutes to forget everything and enjoy this beautiful weather."

The weather was perfect. So was the woman sitting across from him. He should have pressed but he didn't. A break from constant stress was what she needed.

"When do you head back to your base?" she asked, removing the paper straw from its wrapper.

"I've got a couple of weeks. Then a few months at Fort Bragg before we're deployed."

"You mean I only have to put up with you for a few weeks, at most?" Her smile was broad, and her eyes sparkled.

"Does that mean you're accepting our assistance?" Again, he glanced at the area surrounding them—the boats, the nearby condos and water. He didn't like it here, but she appeared content and he was hard pressed to argue with her when she was obviously relaxed.

How often did she allow herself to unwind? He had his share of stress during deployments, but relaxation was a key to mental and physical health. One of the reasons he came to Sanibel was to hang out and kick back with his friends. He'd do the same if he was home with his family in Arizona. He had a network of friends and family who could draw him out of soldier mode. River had none from what he could see. A maiden aunt and a retired law officer were the only people she held close.

Kevin took a large bite of the fish sandwich. "Something's changed with you," he commented, talking around a mouthful of damn good fish. "What happened to the woman who was spitting fire yesterday?"

"And throwing insults?" she asked, pulling her attention away from the water. Her eyes were no longer sparkling. Instead, there was a seriousness—and a sadness in her eyes.

"Unless I pulled out my gun, insults were all I had to chase you all away. It didn't work very well, apparently, so

I'm trying a new tactic Honesty." She paused. "I don't want to see your friends again."

"Why? They want to help. My friends," he said, "are the best people I know."

"And that's why." Her lips trembled. "They are good people and helping me could get them killed. I'd like you to leave, too. I can't watch someone I care about die again. What can I say to make you go away?"

At that minute, Kevin felt his heart tumble. He didn't have time to dwell on the unexpected emotion. His phone was ringing. Annoyed, he pulled it from his back pocket.

"Hey, Rick. What's up?" Kevin paused, then smiled at River. "We're at a place called Grandma Dot's having lunch. Why?" He listened as his friend relayed the gut-wrenching information, hoping his expression didn't give away the context of the one-sided conversation. A public restaurant wasn't the place to break this kind of news. River had put down her sandwich. Her eyes were pinched as she watched him intently. "Anything else?" Kevin asked.

Kevin didn't catch Rick's answer because River's phone began chirping frantically. The alarm system they'd set up at her condo had gone off. His phone vibrated simultaneously. She didn't know he'd had Troy connect the alarm to his cell. She'd be pissed, but that was a battle for another day. He reached for River's arm as she rushed by him, but she dodged it, sprinting for her car.

"Someone's at River's condo. We're headed back." Kevin disconnected the call and threw some money on the table.

"Ride with me," he shouted as she climbed into her vehicle. "We'll come back for your car." She ignored him, slamming the car door. She pulled out onto the busy road, barely missing another vehicle as she stepped on the gas. The woman was dead set on getting herself killed. Did she really not care one way or the other if she lived? How would she react when he broke the news that her friend, Dan, had been murdered?

Common sense told her to wait for Kevin. Going up against an intruder alone—who was no doubt armed—wasn't the smartest move. The whole point of this break-in may be to draw her out. So be it. She was tired of being on the defensive end of things.

As soon as she turned onto her street, she pulled her gun from her purse. Today she was running toward the battle instead of away from it. It was about damn time.

She tuned out the squeal of tires in the lot below as she raced up the stairs. If the son-of-a-bitch was still here, she damn well was going to make sure he didn't get away. As she rounded the corner from the stairwell, she spotted the door to her unit ajar. Ignoring the flicker of nerves, she slipped to the other side of the doorway, her gun drawn. She prayed she had the guts to use it. With her free hand, she flung the door open the rest of the way. Before it could hit the wall, Kevin appeared, stopping its momentum and any noise that would make.

The man must have moved like a bolt of lightning to catch up with her. River wasn't surprised when he motioned for her to get behind him, but this was her place —her problem. No one else was going to die because of her.

Quickly scanning the room, she started to enter when Kevin ducked in front of her. Half tempted to push her foot into the back of his knee, she thought better of it. The sound of a man his size hitting the floor would alert the intruder. She quickly followed him into the workroom.

The slider was open. The drafting table, which would normally block access to the sliding glass door, had been tossed on its side. There was no beating Kevin to the deck. He was bigger, faster, and blocked her way with his muscular arm. She wasn't strong enough or dumb enough to challenge him, but if he saw the bastard and didn't shoot, she would and damn the consequences.

The decision didn't have to be made. The deck was empty, the ground and landscape beyond were desolate. The trellis reflected the escape route. Several vines from the bougainvillea had torn away and lay on the ground below. Their visitor would have cuts and scratches from the thorny vine. If the structure had been your typical wooden trellis, it would have never supported a grown man, but the designers had made the support of metal and had anchored it well.

"What the hell were you thinking?" She was still leaning over the railing looking for anyone or anything to tear into when Kevin verbally started lashing out.

"I was thinking the bastard wasn't getting away this time. I'm tired of this shit. I want it ended." He was already towering over her, so it wasn't much of a stretch to get in his face.

"It might have ended with your life," he growled.

"Either way, it would have ended." She started around him.

"Were you on a damn suicide mission?" His voice snapped out like a whip.

She stopped. His words piercing deeper than any of her previous thoughts or words—or misplaced wishes.

"I don't know," she whispered. She glanced at the balcony then back at Kevin. "I don't know."

Kevin gathered her into his arms, holding her tightly against his chest. Anxious, she fought the stillness.

"Just give yourself a minute. Give *me* a minute," he said.

"He's getting away," she mumbled into his shirt, but she stopped struggling to break free.

"He's already gone," he assured her. His tone left no room for doubt.

"I wanted to stop him. I wanted this to stop." A tear tickled her nose. She brushed it away. "Why won't it stop?"

As his lips touched her hair, they both stilled. Not surprisingly, Kevin heard the footsteps approaching through the living area. He positioned River closer to the open slider. "Get ready to follow his escape route," he ordered. "Just in case."

Yeah, right. She wasn't leaving him, and if it was one of her tormentors, she wanted a piece of the bastard. Taking a step back and to the side, she raised her weapon. Kevin muttered something, but she ignored him. She was totally focused on the doorway. They'd left the front door wide open as they'd rushed in. Anyone could have walked in—friend or foe. They were both erring on the side of foe.

"Stay here," he said softly as he moved toward the entrance—his gun pointing low and gripped with both hands.

Kevin barely stepped into the hallway before he turned back toward her. "It's Rick."

The detective, dressed in khakis and a police department issued polo shirt, entered the room. "Are you both okay?"

"No one's hurt," Kevin told him.

"Have you cleared the place?" he asked Kevin.

"Haven't had time."

"Let's do it."

River waited in her office. They didn't need her, and she'd just be in the way. Instead, she studied her surrounding space. The discarded drafting table appeared to be intact, despite its lopsided angle.

Her stomach lurched the second she spotted the box on the floor which held the jeweled mask. Carefully, she sat it on her workbench. Air slowly escaped her lungs as she lifted the object from the container. Thank God. It was undamaged.

The room was a mess, but a quick glance told her nothing of value was missing. What the hell did he want?

"Did either of you see him?" Rick asked, returning to the room with Kevin.

"I didn't," River answered, placing the mask back in the box.

"The man must move like a cheetah," Kevin added. "He was on the ground and out of sight before either of us got to the balcony. He's long gone by now. Still, shouldn't we be searching for him?"

Rick inspected the trellis then pivoted to River. "Pull up the security video while I call the station. Steve will be here any second," he told them.

River pulled her chair over to her computer. Kevin and Rick hovered closely over her shoulder while she brought up the security video from the two cameras they'd installed out front. She took a deep breath and clicked on the videos.

The larger of the two images was clear, but she couldn't see where it would be of much help to the authorities. Whoever broke into her place had either spotted or knew the whereabouts of the cameras. He wore a windbreaker with a hood that covered almost his entire face. What wasn't covered, he diverted from the camera as he worked the lock.

"This guy knows what he's doing," Rick commented.

"It didn't take him any time to get past the new locks Troy installed."

"The alarm is silent. What caused him to bolt?"

"We made some noise coming in," Kevin admitted.

River remembered the sound of Kevin's tires squealing as he tore into the parking lot. She'd probably been making just as much noise. The screaming tires hadn't registered at the time because she'd been focused on her goal.

"I'm headed back," a warning was shouted from the living room.

River recognized Steve's voice. She'd reluctantly agreed to allow them to hook the security system into Steve's business, but she'd refused any other links, including the police. She had enough trouble dealing with these few men. If she needed the police, she'd call them. She'd wound up with Rick, anyway.

"What's the status?" Steve asked as he entered the room.

"He was in and out like a shot. Other than the open slider and the drafting table he knocked to the floor nothing appears to be disturbed."

"Did you check the other rooms?"

"Yep. They're clear. Besides, there wouldn't have been time to go through this place and still disappear before we got here."

"Any idea what he wanted?" Steve addressed the two men.

"Excuse me, but I'm right here," River said. It annoyed the hell out of her when people talked around her as if she wasn't there.

"Are you okay?" Steve paused. "I'm sorry about your friend."

"My friend?" An icy cold suddenly enveloped her.

Steve quickly turned his attention to Kevin. "She doesn't know?"

"I was still talking to Rick when the security alarm sounded. I haven't had the chance to tell her."

"Tell me what?"

Kevin ran his hand over his face. The room became so quiet, or her senses so heightened, she swore she heard the rasp of his beard against his palm. This couldn't be good.

"What is it?" Her pulse began to gallop. "What the hell is it?"

20

───────

God. He didn't want to be the one to tell her. This was going to rip her apart but drawing it out wasn't going to help—it would only add to her stress.

Squatting in front of her, he took her fisted hand from her chest. He clasped it along with her other hand.

"I'm sorry, River. Dan was found dead this morning."

"No! No. It can't be. Not Dan." He felt her fingers clench. "He's fine. It's got to be some sort of mistake. I'll call him now. I'll prove it."

Kevin rose to his feet, bringing her with him. He pulled her close, stroking her hair as he spoke. "It's no mistake, honey. I'm so, so sorry."

The sobs racked her body. Sobs too big for such a small person. He felt the pain rip through her with each gasp for breath. He gathered her closer, wanting to absorb the hurt, knowing it was impossible. She pressed her face into his chest, mumbling words of heartache and loss. Her grief was palpable. Kevin closed his eyes at the sound of her anguish. Laying his cheek against her crown, he whispered soothing words—words she couldn't hear above her own cries.

Steve tapped him on the shoulder and passed him a wad of tissues. Prying her fingers away from his shirt, Kevin stuffed them into her hand. She sniffled loudly as he led her out of the room so Rick could process it for anything left by the intruder.

When they reached the living room sofa, River collapsed onto it. Her brow furrowed as silent tears continued to escape and trickle down her cheeks. She didn't bother to wipe them away. He took the tissue from her and padded her cheeks. The pain in her glacier-blue eyes killed him.

"How?" she asked. "He's never been sick."

Kevin pinched the bridge of his nose. "I'm sorry," he found himself repeating. "Dan didn't die of natural causes. He was murdered."

She stilled. Like one of those street artists who pose as a statute, she sat frozen. Her eyes were fixed and unblinking. If not for the rapid rise and fall of her chest, she could have passed as one.

"Steve. Get me a cold cloth and a cola, if you can find one," Kevin directed his friend who had followed him out of the workroom. "If not, start some coffee." Once she recovered her senses, River would want answers. Right now, she needed something for the shock. He pressed the cool dish towel to her cheek and forehead. She jerked back, her eyes blinking.

"Here," he said, taking the cola from Steve. "Sip this."

She clutched the can with both hands and took the instructed sip. He recognized the internal battle she was fighting to hold it together.

"How?" she asked, locking eyes with Kevin. Her backbone incrementally reassembled itself until she was ramrod straight. "When did it happen?"

"It was a blow to the back of the head. The time of death hasn't been pinpointed."

"I spoke with him the day I met you. It was the last time we talked." Her voice hitched.

"Does he have family close by? Somebody who would have missed him for a couple of days?" Steve took a seat across from her.

"He has a son, Jacob, but he lives out of state. I know they were close, but I don't know if they were in touch daily." River knuckled a tear from her cheek. "Why would anyone want to kill him?"

"I don't know," Kevin answered, but it was too much of a coincidence not to be connected with the shit that had been going on.

"I need to be there. I need to pack." She sprang to her feet, almost knocking him back.

"It's not safe for you to be there and you're in no condition to drive."

Anger leapfrogged her grief. She twisted away from him, heading toward her bedroom.

"River, please. You can't go home." Kevin took a few steps toward her but kept his distance. He didn't want her to feel crowded or bullied.

"Why the hell not?" She swung on him. "It's my home."

"At the moment, it's a crime scene," Steve announced.

For the second time in a few short minutes, Kevin watched her color pale. "Damn it, Steve."

"Sorry. I wasn't thinking. Josie and I didn't get much sleep last night, but that's no excuse. I'm sorry, River."

"Dan was killed in my cabin?" Her eyes flew from one man to the other. "He's dead because of me?"

"No. Not because of you," Kevin argued, stepping to her side. "You have nothing to do with his death."

"The hell I don't. I'm the one who's been stalked. I'm the one who called him about the assault on the beach. Knowing Dan, he would have gone out to the cabin to check on it after my call."

"Kevin's right," Rick said emerging from the hall, carrying the shipping box containing the mask. "It appears the attempts to terrorize you at your cabin don't have anything to do with the break-ins or attacks here. Let's have a seat," he added.

"What are you doing with that?" she asked, indicating the box he was holding.

"I'll get to it in a minute." Rick herded them back into the living room.

Kevin put his arm around River and walked with her to the sofa. He couldn't seem to keep his hands off of her and she didn't fight him. Was it surrender or trust? The later, he hoped. She was strong, independent, caring…and she was becoming all too important to him.

"I still need to get back to North Carolina. He was my friend. I need to be there," River insisted, her voice trembling. Her posture shifted a split second later. "And I damn well want to know who the hell killed him."

"We'll get you back there when it's time. And you have my word if the locals don't figure it out, we will," Kevin said, as he looked to his two friends for confirmation. He wasn't surprised when they both nodded in agreement. Brotherhood. It would always be there.

"I don't want anyone else involved." River's voice was firm. "There are too many dead and injured in my wake." Her tone held both sadness and determination.

"You're not a fool." Kevin held up his hands to ward off the volley she was preparing to shoot his way. He welcomed the burst of anger. He preferred it to her sadness.

"We know how to handle ourselves and you need us, but we need to work together to get to the bottom of this. Hear us out," Kevin implored.

This wasn't the best time to confront her with their discoveries or anything else, for that matter. She'd just lost someone close to her but based on what Rick had told him on the phone, things were changing—and changing fast.

She crossed her arms and began to rub them as if to warm herself. She was still borderline shocky. He grabbed the throw from the back of the couch and draped it over her shoulders. The sideway glance she threw at him told him she was getting her feet back under her—metaphorically speaking.

"What is it you want to tell me?"

"Eric Kane. Do you recognize the name?"

"He's the man who sold me the semi-precious stones I used in the mask. Why?"

"He's also the man who was killed here yesterday," Rick said. "You didn't recognize him."

"We never met, and I know you checked his website. If there's a picture of him on it, I didn't see it. We always communicated via email."

"How did you I.D. him?" Kevin asked Rick.

"We sent his photo to the Tampa PD. They ran it through their face recognition software."

"I assume they identified him?"

"It got us started," Rick confirmed. "We were able to dig up the rest."

"What's this got to do with Dan?" River scooted toward the edge of the couch.

"Nothing," Rick answered, "which is my point. It looks

like what's been happening here has something to do with those gems you bought from Kane."

"I don't get it." The fingers of her hands were knitted together. The thumb of her right hand pressed circles into the palm of her left.

"Eric Kane had a legitimate business—the one you contacted to purchase the stones, but he was involved with a nasty organization known for stealing and fencing stolen gems." Rick carefully removed the mask from the box.

"The stones I purchased from him were valuable?"

"You said he wanted the aquamarine back. He didn't ask for any other stone?"

"No, he didn't," she confirmed. River stared at the mask as if she'd never seen it before. "He told me he'd sent the wrong stone—that the one I received was promised to another buyer. Aquamarines aren't precious stones. Why would anyone murder someone over it?"

"The FBI hooked me up with a member of Jeweler's Security Alliance. He's guessing your stone isn't an aquamarine," Rick told her. "Based on what I described, he believes it could be a blue diamond."

RIVER DIGESTED the information while she rubbed her burning eyes. The tears she'd shed hadn't helped. Her head hurt almost as much as her heart.

"The shit going on here has nothing to do with Dan's death? The bastard wanted the stone?"

"That's our assumption at the moment. If the fence, Kane, had a buyer for the stone and mistakenly sent it to you, he would have been desperate to get it back. His name has popped up in connection with several investigations of SATG enterprises. They're ruthless and extremely dangerous. People don't live to make a second mistake."

"SATGs?" Kevin asked.

"South American Theft Groups," Rick explained. "You don't want to screw up if you're doing business with them. The outcome is never good."

"Which explains the loss of hands," Kevin stated. He'd remained at her side, which gave her some comfort and strength. She didn't understand it, nor would she admit it, but she was glad he was there.

"I suspect it was a warning to others. Yes. The loss of his hands and, therefore, fingerprints, didn't cost us much time. We had the results back in hours. SATG members would know that. They are cold-blooded, but sophisticated and organized."

"How the hell did he get away with running a gem business?" River jumped at the sound of Steve's voice. She'd forgotten he was there. He had moved from his earlier perch on the couch and was now settled in the corner of her small kitchen.

"He'd been picked up for questioning a couple of times, but never charged with any crime. Technically, he was clean. The legitimate business was a good front for his fencing work."

"Which explains why he wanted the stone back, but what about the guy who killed him? Why take a shot at us?" Kevin asked.

"Unless we find him, we may never know. He might have been trying to frighten us away and force River to be on her own. On her own, she, along with the diamond, would be easy targets."

River couldn't sit still anymore. Invisible spiders crawled over her skin. "You know what's stupid?" She rose to her feet and began pacing the room. "All the guy had to do is tell me he'd sent me a valuable stone instead of an aquamarine. I'd have sent it back in a heartbeat. He doesn't appear to have been very smart."

"He was probably afraid if he told you about the diamond, it would have sent up red flags for you. They're rare and not part of his catalog. His initial attempt to get the stone back by exchanging it failed," Rick explained. "By coming after you and the stone, he was showing his intent to right the mistake. Besides, being on the move was better than being a sitting duck. When he failed to get the diamond, the SATG group brought someone in to finish the job."

"Why did Kane go after me on the beach? I didn't have the stones on me."

"You said you'd suspected someone had been in your condo. It could be he'd already searched your place and didn't find the stone. He was probably getting desperate and took a chance you kept them with you," Kevin suggested.

"I'm surprised he lasted as long as he did," Steve commented.

"I'll need the stone, River." Rick handed her the mask he'd placed on the dining room table.

Damn. She'd just finished it. Now she'd have to find a replacement for the stone. It was the least of her worries right now, though.

"I'll take care of it as soon as we're done here. Who's going to tell me what happened to Dan." She did her damndest to let her anger show over her grief. She'd finish grieving Dan in private.

"We found him this morning." Steve pushed away from the countertop.

"We?" The air left her lungs in a rush. "Who's 'we'?" she asked him.

"Troy and Colt. They went up there to look into your stalker."

"After I asked you to stay out of it?" She was having no trouble keeping the fire within her lit.

"Hear him out." Kevin walked over to stand in front of her. "You can tear into me later. I take responsibility for giving the nod to continue the investigation."

She glared at him knowing it wouldn't do any good to argue the point. Taking a seat at the dining room table, she braced herself. His friends had found Dan. They were there now. She could use their help to find his killer.

"Go ahead," she said to Steve, taking a deep breath. Still, she wasn't able to stop her lips from trembling when she asked, "He was dead when they found him?"

"Yes," Steve confirmed. "Troy and Colt flew up there early this morning. They went to check your cabin out. The rear door was open. Dan was on the floor. No sign of a struggle. There was nothing they could do for him. I'm sorry."

How long had he laid there? Did he ever regain consciousness? Did he know he was alone when he died? River swallowed hard. "What else? How was he killed?"

Steve looked at Kevin.

"You don't need his permission to talk to me. I'm the one asking the questions."

"He was struck on the head from behind. Troy said there was a piece of firewood next to the body," Steve continued. "He suspects it was the murder weapon. This was either a crime of opportunity or someone wanted it to look that way."

Her firewood. She'd supplied the murder weapon. She flinched when she imagined the crack of the wood against her friend's skull. Her hands knotted, twisting the hem of her shirt until her fingers hurt. More death at a place she loved. Maybe her aunt was right. Maybe the place was jinxed.

River didn't pull away when Kevin reached for one of her hands and began to massage her aching fingers. "It's not your fault. Don't do this to yourself."

"Don't even think about it," she snapped, remembering his high-handed way of dealing with her last upset. "I don't want another shot."

"I wasn't suggesting it. I won't give you anything you don't ask for. Okay?"

River nodded, straightening her back. "Anything else?" she asked them.

"At this point, not much," Rick joined the conversation. He'd taken the seat across from her when she was at the dining room table. He'd remained there. "Troy and Colt have been dealing with the local authorities since they arrived. Answering questions, for the most part. Do we have your permission for them to stay at the cabin after it's cleared and to do some snooping?"

"If it will help find Dan's killer, then yes. They can have anything they need." She wanted that more than anything on the planet. "Does anyone know if my aunt has been notified?"

"The local authorities didn't say," Rick told her.

"I'd best go call her before they do." River stood, sliding her hand from Kevin's. She immediately missed his warmth. "Do you need me for anything else?"

"When the guys report back in, we may have some questions you can help with, but we're okay for now. Kevin and Steve will be here, if you think of anything to add."

"Oh! The stone," she said, returning for the mask. "Give me a minute." She'd need to add getting a replacement gem to her list of things to do. The task was small in comparison to the rest of the thoughts spinning around her.

River retreated to her workroom where she didn't waste any time removing the blue gem from the mask. She was glad to be rid of it. With any luck her recent problems would follow the stone.

"I'm going to assume you're right and this isn't an aquamarine," she said, returning to the living room and dropping the stone into Rick's palm.

"How did they find her?" Kevin asked. "You agreed she took the right precautions. She wasn't easy to find." He'd taken up space next to River again. This push/pull of wishing he'd keep his distance and wanting him close was making her head spin.

"She did everything right when she left North Carolina," Rick agreed. He pulled out a small plastic bag from his back pocket, depositing the stone into it. "But it couldn't hold up against a professional organization. The SATGs are sophisticated and deadly. She's lucky you were nearby when they showed up," he said to Kevin.

The comment wasn't caustic. She didn't take it as a rebuke of her attempts to push Kevin and his friends away, but a sincere regard for River's safety. She wasn't used to this kind of support—this level of concern.

21

---

evin locked the door behind Rick and set the alarm. Rick had arranged for a local gemologist to examine the stone prior to handing it over to the FBI. He was anxious to be rid of the case. STAGs were considered organized crime and the case would fall under the Federal RICO statute. The small Sanibel Police Department wasn't equipped to deal with an organization of that size.

"What are you going to do about her?" Steve asked.

"That's an open-ended question. You want to be more specific?" Kevin headed toward the refrigerator and grabbed a bottle of water from it, wishing she stocked something stronger.

"She's hurting."

"You think I don't know that? You think I don't want to go in there?" he asked, gesturing toward the hall. "You saw what happened when I pushed her too hard. I don't want us kicked out again." He slammed the bottle down against the counter.

"You got in here this morning."

"I'm flat out of Pina Colada French toast."

"What?"

"Never mind," he muttered. "I'll give her some privacy while she talks to her aunt then I'll check on her."

"I'm surprised her Aunt didn't call her first."

"Could be the authorities had trouble connecting with the next of kin." Kevin took a slug of water. "Amy's not Dan's family. She wouldn't be first on their list." River, on the other hand, owned the property where Dan had been killed. Her name would be at the top of the list of calls.

"How come they reached out to Rick instead of River directly?" Kevin wasn't involved in too many investigations, but the act seemed odd.

"My guess?" Steve's eyes narrowed—a bit of anger seeping through. "Rick had already been in touch with them, and they didn't want to be the ones to break the news to her, so they passed that nasty job onto Rick— which you wound up doing. I suspect she won't have to wait long before she hears from them."

Kevin wished she didn't have to make the call to her aunt. River was already strung so tight she could snap at any minute. The conversation was going to be tortuous for both of them.

"Why haven't the police contacted River?" Kevin wondered. "I would think it would be one of their first calls. He was killed at her place."

"They'll be talking to her. Like you said, he was killed at her cabin, but Rick managed to put them off until we could break the news. They were happy to leave that job to one of us."

How many hours over the years had River spent with the police going over events that affected her life? He couldn't imagine it got any easier.

"Are you going to be okay with her?" Steve asked,

pocketing his phone. "I can ask if Josie, Shayne or Cat can come over if she'd prefer their company to yours."

Kevin's attention had been lingering on River, listening for any sign of distress. He returned his focus to Steve.

"You know," Steve said, "she's not much different from the women in our group. Each one of them has an independent streak a mile wide and they'd all been loners until they met up with us. They also share some form of trauma. They'll be here for her if she wants the support."

"I know they would," Kevin said. "But for now, let me try to reach her. If I can't handle it, I'll call for back-up," he said, clasping Steve on the shoulder. "Do you know anything other than what you shared with River?"

"Troy and Colt did a quick search of the place before the cops arrived. They'll give it a thorough going over when the scene is released. If the sheriff missed anything, they'll find it."

"Wasn't Gib supposed to go with Troy?"

"Gib was being Gib—doing his best to get under Troy's skin. Colt's better suited for the task. Gib's covering their business while charming the ladies."

"I bet he is," Kevin muttered. He'd best not be charming this one.

"Did they find anything of interest at the cabin when they arrived?"

"Nothing."

Kevin lowered his voice. "No sign someone was planning on leaving another calling card?"

"None. That wouldn't make much sense since River isn't there."

"Unless Dan's death was a brutal message. It's got to be tearing her apart. She's blaming herself. You heard her. What if that was the point? That's more than harassment. It's emotional torture." Kevin fisted his hands. They were supposed to be used for healing, but he could easily kill the bastard who was tormenting River.

"How would this mysterious person know Dan was going to be there?" Steve argued. "Give Colt and Troy some time. While the cops are processing the scene, the guys are out asking questions. Talking to neighbors—if you can call people who live miles away neighbors. They also have a meeting with the lead detective on River's case this afternoon. Hopefully, we'll have additional information by this evening."

"Call me when you know something," Kevin said, following Steve to the door.

"I'll stop by later to restock you guys. I think Rick will be with me. If that's a problem for her, one of us can bow out."

"She's stronger than she looks," Kevin said. He pictured her on the beach when she fought off her attacker. He was convinced her reticence had more to do with their safety than a real dislike of people. "I'll talk to her and warn you off if she objects."

Kevin stood outside her room. It was quiet. Either her aunt was doing all the talking or their conversation was over. He tapped on the door.

"Come in," she said. Her voice sounded a bit husky and shaky. She'd been crying. Upon opening the door, her eyes confirmed it. Those sparkling blue eyes were red and brimming with tears. She wiped them away as he entered then she pulled back her shoulders, transforming into the self-reliant, independent woman. All the contradicting features fit. Vulnerable yet strong. He was so fucked..

"How are you doing?"

"Not bad," she answered, swinging around in her desk chair. "I managed to find a vendor who has an aquamarine that will fit the mask."

"That was quick. I can ask Rick to run him through the system."

"I already did. He's checking them out and will get back with me."

"Smart." Kevin was feeling tongue tied. The urge to wrap her in his arms was so overpowering he had to fold them over his chest to avoid a slip.

"I need to get the mask out of here before I head north."

"You still have a couple of days. Can I help with anything?"

River shook her head as another transformation took place. Her shoulders sagged and the light went out of her eyes. It was as if a shadow had passed over her. Her emotions appeared to be constantly in flux. "I hate that his death has a connection to me. God. What if it's my fault?"

Kevin gave up the fight. He found himself in front of River, cupping her elbows and coaxing her out of her chair. "Would you mind if I held you?" he asked. "I really need to hold you."

She surprised him when she didn't argue and went quietly into his arms, laying her head against his chest. He rested his cheek against the crown of her head for a second time that day. He wished—actually wished—empaths existed, and he was one of their ranks. He wanted to draw the fear, pain and hurt from her. Hadn't she suffered enough?

Still, she'd managed to remain strong. Was she naturally tough or did that strength rise out of the ashes of her family's slaughter? He ran his hand over her hair then laid a kiss against it.

He continued to hold her even when her shoulders relaxed, her tension easing. Comfort was the only form of care he had to give. There was no bandage, no surgery, no medicine that could heal her wounds.

HER HANDS DROPPED to his waist, creating some breathing room between them.

"Did you talk to your aunt?" he asked.

She felt his warm breath as it bathed her face. "My phone rang before I could place the call. She'd just heard the news."

"Let's sit down." He steered her toward the living room. She was too tired—too whipped to argue. The sofa sunk when he took up the seat next to her.

"How'd she take it?"

"Pretty much how I expected. Stunned and sad. We cried." River paused. "He was a kind and decent man."

"I'm sorry," Kevin said again, taking her hand in his. It was warm against her frigid skin.

"Aunt Amy believes the cabin is bad luck. Maybe it is."

"Places and people aren't bad luck." Kevin said, releasing her hand. A chill settled over her as he left her side.

"Dan didn't have enemies. I don't understand why anyone would kill him."

"How close were your aunt and Dan?"

"I don't know how to describe their relationship." River's gaze drifted out through the sliding glass doors. "They liked one another. They were friends, but they didn't socialize. I was the common denominator. They both stepped in to help raise me, but each in their own way. Aunt Amy has always been a bit of a loner. I may have inherited that gene from her side of the family. Dan was outgoing." She paused, willing her voice to steady. After a deep breath, she continued.

"While Aunt Amy took over *mom* duties—helping with my studies, shopping for prom dresses, that sort of thing—Dan became my cheerleader. He attended almost every school event. He didn't have to do that. He had a family of his own. For some reason, I gravitated to him when I needed to talk about relationships. God help the boy who hurt my feelings." River was surprised she could still smile. "He took me to my high school's Father/Daughter dance so I wouldn't miss out." Her breath hitched at the memory. "He never tried to take my dad's place. He'd simply lessen the loss when he could." She would always be grateful that he was first on the scene. She couldn't imagine those early years without Dan in her life. As she grew older, he became her best friend.

"He asked Aunt Amy if it would be okay," she continued. "I later learned he'd contacted the school to find out the date. Then cleared it with his supervisor so there would be no conflict with his work schedule. Only after everything was in place did he ask to escort me. He didn't want to disappoint me if I'd said yes and his deck wasn't clear."

Kevin now stood in front of her—a glass of wine in one hand and a bottle of water in the other. She took the wine.

"I've never known a better man than him, other than my father. I want the bastard who killed him," she said, angrily slashing away the tears. "I want him in prison with the scum who killed my family. Dan was family."

"We'll do everything we can to see to it. Troy and Colt are already on the ground." His mouth was drawn in a straight line. His brown eyes, pinched. He shared her anger.

"You were all still willing to help me after I insulted you

and chased you out." Still a bit shaky, she used both hands to lift the glass of wine to her lips.

"It's not in our make-up to stand down when someone needs help." Kevin shrugged. "Troy and Colt plan to be discreet."

"Let them loose," she said. "I don't care who they disturb, as long as someone finds out who did this."

22

Kevin touched base with Troy and Colt while River sequestered herself in her room to talk to Dan's family. Regardless of what he'd told her, it was evident she took responsibility for her friend's death. Guilt was a heavy burden to bear. It was no stranger to him or his friends. He wanted to be with River to help her past it. He wanted to be with her—period.

The timing sucked. It always sucked. She didn't need some moonstruck medic hovering over her. She was under personal siege and had lost a close friend. She'd had enough sense to back away from their earlier sensual encounters. He needed to show the same common sense. Didn't she have enough to deal with without getting involved with someone else who'd be leaving her? How would his deployment affect her if they got involved? Who was he kidding? They were already involved.

A knock on the front door interrupted his musings. Rick slipped in first when Kevin opened the door, followed by Steve and Gib. Each of them carried two six packs of beer. They loaded the refrigerator with the brews, each helping themselves to one as they did. Rick grabbed an extra.

"You look like you could use one," he said, holding the bottle out for Kevin.

"She's had a rough day," Kevin explained, twisting the top off the beer. "She's talking to Dan's son now. The authorities called earlier and interviewed her."

"Shitty day, I'd say," Gib agreed, taking a pull from his cold one. "Does she have an issue with us being here?"

"None. She wants Dan's killer caught. She's more than happy to have us step in if that's what it takes."

"Interesting lady," Rick commented. "First she kicks us out because she worries we'll get hurt. Now it sounds like she's on a crusade to avenge his killer."

"I don't know about avenge," Kevin answered. "But she wants the person caught and sharing a cell with her parents' killers."

It wasn't long before the door to her room opened, followed by the closing of the bathroom door. When she finally rounded the corner into the living area, it was obvious she'd been crying again, but her eyes were now dry. She stood as tall as her short height would allow.

"I appreciate that you're willing to help after I was such an ass." She glanced at each of them. "I owe you all an apology."

Gib rose before Kevin could intercept him. "We're all good," he said, placing a light kiss on her cheek. "I'd be on edge if I had to spend time around this guy," he added, nodding in Kevin's direction. "Say the word and I'll kick him out so we can be alone."

The wink Gib gave her apparently made a crack in her wall of grief. She hesitantly returned his coquettish smile. Despite the source, Kevin was relieved to see it. Timid as it was, it still brightened her face.

"Is the stone precious?" she asked Rick. Kevin took some satisfaction when she seated herself on the cushion next to him.

"Extremely. It's a blue diamond. The FBI should be able to trace its origins. It's their case now," he told her.

"And the murder?"

"We still have the lead on that, but I suspect it will wind up in their court eventually. We're working with them for the time being."

"Don't make us pull it out of you," Kevin warned to Rick, picking up his beer. "Is River safe?"

"The FBI isn't happy," Rick huffed, "but I think so."

"You're driving *me* nuts," Gib kneaded his friend. "Spill."

"The FBI was brainstorming the idea of keeping the information regarding the stone under wraps. They wouldn't be able to keep the murder out of the news but staying silent on the whereabouts of the diamond could draw out the interested parties."

"Hoping the SATG would make another move to recover it? They want to use it as bait?" Kevin's question came out a slow growl. Such a plan would put River in the crosshairs again.

"There was a suggestion to that effect, but that was nixed once word leaked out that the stone was in the possession of the FBI."

"Thanks, Rick," Kevin said, knowing where the leak had originated. "What else have you got?"

"You first," Steve said to Rick. "I'll piggyback on to your findings."

Rick pulled out his ever-present notebook. "I've talked to the cops who were assigned the case. It's early. They don't have much at this point. They've confirmed the blow to the head was the cause of death."

River scooted closer to Kevin, leaning into him.

"What else?" Kevin asked, taking her hand—anchoring her.

"No one saw anyone coming or going from the cabin."

"That's not surprising," River confirmed. "Its isolation appealed to me. At least it did when I moved in."

"They won't be getting fingerprints off the piece of wood. The surface is too uneven—too rough. There is always the possibility of some DNA if the perpetrator wasn't wearing gloves, but it will take time."

"So, they haven't found much," River said.

"Troy and Colt will go over the place with a fine-tooth comb when they get back in there. The authorities are being helpful, but they don't have much to share."

"What about the FBI?" Gib asked.

"Why would the FBI get involved?" River cocked her head toward Gib.

"They were part of the investigation into the death of your parents. This could possibly lead back to their murder." Gib glanced at the others in the room. "Couldn't it?"

"Any connection?" Kevin asked Rick.

"Nothing is impossible, but I don't see one—at least not yet. Steve?"

"You're the expert on bringing in the Feds, Rick, but something did pop up on Josie's radar."

The air stilled. As a successful freelance journalist, Josie had an extensive list of contacts in the field. What she couldn't find out herself, she often called on her colleagues in the press for help.

"Well?" Rick prodded.

"It may be nothing, but as we know, the Engleharts do not have close family. Strangely, over the past year each of them has been visited by the same person. A minister."

"What's so unusual about that?" Kevin prodded. "It's not uncommon to have the clergy visit in prison, is it?"

"No. Some prisons have a minister on staff. Most, however, rely on visiting ministers," Rick explained. "What put this particular clergyman on Josie's radar?"

"According to her contact," Steve continued, pulling his phone from his back pocket, "the Engleharts had refused all outreach from any ministry prior this particular preacher showing up."

"What made this guy so special to the Engleharts? How does he play into River's problems?" Kevin gave River a quick glance. She was totally focused on Steve, listening intently. Her sadness temporarily pushed aside by the mystery.

Steve laid his phone on the coffee table and tapped a call button.

"Hi," Josie answered.

"Hey, Babe. I have River, Kevin, Rick and Gib here. Can you explain what you found out about the Engleharts' visitor?"

"Hi, everyone," she started out. The 'hellos' flew around the table.

"This may not mean a damn thing," Josie warned them. "Hasan is a reporter for the Charlotte Observer. He covers most of their crime beat. He wasn't there fourteen years ago, but since he landed in North Carolina, he's kept an ear to the ground with regard to the Engleharts. River, I don't mean to sound like I'm sensationalizing what happened to your family, but their murders were big news and fourteen years isn't all that long ago."

"Go ahead and tell us what you found out. I know you mean no harm. North Carolina is one big, small town. It's one of the reasons I have a home in the country—as far away from local gossip as possible."

Kevin held River's hand snuggly. He was rewarded with a warm smile and a quick squeeze back.

"Okay." Josie took a deep breath. "Hasan developed an interest in the Engleharts when he took the job at the paper. Other than hurricanes, it was the biggest story the paper had ever covered. He made some connections with Central Prison outside Raleigh, as any good reporter would. The Engleharts aren't the only interesting inmates housed there. Having a contact on the inside is just good investigative reporting."

Josie hesitated. "I feel like one of those paparazzi you were trying so hard to avoid."

"Go on," River prompted. "I can tell the difference and I appreciate you're helping me out."

"A while back, his contact called and told him there was something unusual about a visitor who'd been coming to see the Engleharts. A pastor would visit each family member individually. He wasn't allowed to see them as a group. It's against prison policy."

"Steve said they'd refused all pastoral offers in the past."

"That's what caught his contact's attention. Once Hasan had the name of the pastor, he checked further. Joseph Roxbury has a small congregation in Webster, North Carolina..."

"Webster?" River's eyebrows almost reached her hairline. "That's clear across the state. It's got to be a couple a hundred miles from Raleigh."

"Closer to three hundred," Josie corrected. "And by small congregation, I mean small—twenty people or so and they meet in his barn."

"How did he get through to the Engleharts and why did they invite him in?" Rick asked. "I suppose he could be an honest, God-fearing preacher, but then why the small flock?"

"Six hundred miles round-trip is a lot of driving," Kevin noted. "How often does he show up? When did this start?"

"Let her finish." Steve raised a hand, calling a halt to the questions.

Everyone stared at the phone on the table as if Josie were perched on it.

"Hasan interviewed Roxbury, but he didn't get anything noteworthy out of him. The pastor claimed his visits were private ministry, which didn't surprise him. Hasan did a bit of background on the Reverend. He's not a licensed minister. He can't even marry anyone."

"You'd know all about that, wouldn't you Steve?" Gib laughed, slapping his friend on the back.

"Not now, Gib." There was a snap in Steve's tone.

"Roxbury," Josie continued, "appears to have taken up the cloth shortly before he started visiting the Engleharts. He's not married. No children. Hasan said he's about forty years old. Roxbury's name is on the property deed. No mortgage. His mother owned it free and clear. Now he does."

"Where is his mother now?" Rick asked.

"She passed away. Nothing suspicious there," Josie noted. "Hasan had planned to return for one of Roxbury's services, but he hasn't made it back. The paper has cut staff and the story was going nowhere, so he's had to put it on the back burner."

"It will be on our front burner tomorrow," Steve announced. "Colt is making the trip to Webster."

"I thought he and Troy would be sticking close to River's place—trying to dig up leads there." Kevin eyed Steve.

"You go where the leads take you," Rick explained. "It may not be much, but it's the first one we've gotten."

"Besides, Webster isn't far from River's cabin. It shouldn't take him long to get a read on Roxbury," Steve added.

Kevin was extremely aware of Colt's interrogation skills and his ability to read the tell signs people inadvertently gave off. "Assuming he's there."

"If he can be found, Colt will find him. And Troy's working on getting in to visit one of the Engleharts," Steve added.

"I want to go with him," River told them. "I need to head back sometime soon anyway."

"No, you won't." Kevin quickly regretted the words and tone.

"Don't start," she snapped. "I haven't seen them in fourteen years. If they are behind the harassment or had anything to do with Dan's murder, I want to see their eyes when I accuse them. I want to be there to see them react."

"It might not be a bad idea," Rick suggested. "Facing the sole survivor of their rampage may set them off. One of them could let something slip."

"And what about the agony River will go through seeing them again?"

He faced River. "It's not my call and I shouldn't have said that but think of the pain they've already caused you. Do you want to give them even more of your soul?"

"You have that wrong." River shot him a pointed look. "They never took any of it. I would give my life to have my family back on this earth, but I would never let them take that part of me. I made sure they got word that I'd moved into the cabin. I wanted them to know they wouldn't win. I want them to know they still can't."

"You've been in touch with the Engleharts?" Steve asked.

"No. Dan got word through to them."

"Weren't you taking a chance letting them know where you were?" This time it was Gib asking the question.

"They were in prison. I didn't see it as an issue. I may have made an error in judgement there."

Kevin was a bit stunned when she shrugged. Why did she have such little regard for her safety?

"Good work, Josie," Rick said. "One of these days, I'm going to steal you away from Steve and put you to work on the force."

"Like hell," Steve laughed.

"Steve, are you on your way home?"

"I'll leave in a few minutes. Is Cece asleep?"

"She's being contrary so you may catch her awake if you hurry."

Steve disconnected the call and got to his feet. "That's it for me tonight. Rick, can you find someone to pull strings at Central Prison?"

"Never hurts to make a call." He joined Steve as he moved toward the door. "I'll also touch base with the local authorities again tomorrow."

"Let me know when you want to leave for North Carolina. I'll make the arrangements," Gib volunteered.

"What are you? Our local travel agent?" Kevin half laughed. Gib could arrange just about anything and avoided all inquiries into how he made it happen.

"One of my many skills," he quipped. "Besides, I'm sure you've got better things to do than waste the night fretting," he added, wiggling his eyebrows at River.

River's thoughts bounced from one side of her head to the other as she watched Kevin set the alarm system. Did they really have a lead on the person who had been terrorizing her? It was a slim chance but knowing the investigation into her tormentor was no longer at a standstill was rejuvenating, in a way.

Thinking of the Engleharts, she felt both anger and trepidation. She wanted to spit in their eye. Prove to them they hadn't beaten her—that they would never get the best of her. Would her unexpected appearance trigger something in them? Maybe goad them into bragging about what they'd been able to do from prison. How would they react to the news of Dan's death, or did they already know?

"Are you all right?" Kevin's gaze covered every inch of her. His brow creased in worry.

"I'm fine."

"You've been through hell today."

"I won't deny it, but it's not your job to make things right—to make me feel better." She surprised herself when she reached out for his hand then tugged him down next to her.

"I'm going to hurt and grieve for Dan for some time to come. There's nothing you can do except what you're doing now—be here for me."

"You loved Dan," Kevin said, cupping her face with his palm.

"He was my rock when I lost my parents."

"And your aunt? Wasn't she there for you?"

"She was. She watched over me like a mother hawk. Caring for me and soothing me. Dan was a straight talker. I took comfort from my aunt and drew my strength from Dan. Whoever did this to him, can't take that away from me. I won't let them, and I won't let them get away with taking a good man from this earth."

She didn't realize she was still holding Kevin's hand until he laid his other hand on top of hers. There was strength there, too. Not just physical, but emotional.

"I'm glad he was there when you needed him."

"I'm glad you're here when I need you."

His head came up as his eyes pinned her. His brow rose. "Need?"

River freed one of her hands and used it to caress his chin. Like him, his jaw was strong, yet there was a tenderness beneath the surface. She couldn't take her eyes from him. Physically, he took her breath away. He was caring, dedicated, and protective. She was falling for him. Damn it. It would only complicate things, but at the moment, she didn't care.

"It seems I need you on many levels. I shouldn't be thinking of physical needs at a time of loss, but as much as I want your compassion and support—I want you."

She let her hand slide from his face as he pulled back.

"Are you looking for a distraction?"

A deep sigh escaped. "Maybe. I don't know. I won't deny I want to feel something other than sorrow and fear." Mortification replaced nervousness. She'd never invited a man to her bed.

"I am attracted to you," she admitted, her skin warming with embarrassment, "but I can't honestly say which of those reasons prompted my suggestion. It was wrong of me to ask. I'm sorry," she said softly, getting to her feet. This had been a huge mistake. All she wanted to do was retreat.

Kevin's hand slid down her arm as she turned to leave. His fingers knitted with hers when they met. "Are you saying you changed your mind?"

"I insulted you."

With a quick tug of her arm, he pulled her with him as he dropped back onto the couch. He settled her onto his lap. "Affirming life in the face of death is a natural response. I don't find it insulting."

He lowered his head, touching his lips to hers. They were surprisingly soft and gentle. After their previous encounters, she expected a hot, urgent meeting of their bodies. The kiss was tender and seductive. Had she ever been seduced? When his tongue began to brush her lips like an artist caressing a canvas, she ceased questioning. Instead, she welcomed him in.

The gentleness vanished as their tongues began a furious, heated tango. One hand raked through his hair, pulling him closer. Her other hand traced the sculpted planes of his chest over his tight-fitting polo.

In one smooth movement, he rose with her in his arms. Then she was flying—literally and figuratively. The sensation didn't stop her exploration. Any part of his anatomy she could reach, she touched. Lifting her head, she nipped his jawline. It was rough with a day's growth of beard. She flicked her tongue out and licked it. She barely noticed his stumble.

When he gently deposited her on the bed, she continued to cling to his neck, urging him closer. She felt him smile as she dotted his jaw with kisses. His hand slid down her ribs until they reached her waist. Her nerves hummed to a rhythm she wasn't familiar with as his hand slipped under her shirt and caressed her back. A quick snap of his fingers and her bra was undone. He cupped her breasts, brushing her tender flesh with the pad of his thumbs. She was melting under his touch until those nimble fingers found her nipples then her back arched like a bow strung too tight. Blood raced through her veins like a high-speed train before settling in her most sensitive spot. She was tingling in areas that rarely called out for attention. Now they demanded it.

Their connection was abruptly broken as Kevin released her. "Why did you stop?" She grasped the hem of his shirt, trying to reel him back in. She wanted him closer —plastered to her skin. She searched his face, trying to find some indication of what he was thinking. His caramel-colored eyes met hers. The desire reflected in them put her fears aside.

"I think we need to lose some of this clothing," he explained, pulling his shirt over his head.

Shimmying out of her jeans, she paused—the demin mid-way over her hips. He'd been shirtless on the beach, but she'd been distracted then. Now she took the time to admire the chiseled physique. Lordy, he was a sight to behold.

"Do you need some help?" he asked with a sly grin.

She'd been caught ogling him. She discovered she didn't care. She waited, her eyes not leaving the specimen in front of her.

Kevin grinned as he obliged her silent request. He stepped out of his chinos, tossing them over the foot of the bed. Oh, Lord, his chest was nothing compared to the full-frontal view. You'd have thought she'd never seen a naked man in her life. In truth, she'd never seen one as stunning as Kevin.

Bending over, he kissed the skin just below her navel. Electrical currents rippled through her body. As he caressed the exposed flesh her head fell back. She struggled with the need to writhe as his tongue lapped the area between the zipper's threads. Damn. She should be naked. She needed to be naked.

As if answering her silent plea, her lower half was suddenly stripped bare. The tongue that had so deftly traced her tender flesh, now sampled the dampness between her legs. Cupping her buttocks, he lifted her slightly, adjusting her position. Instinct had her widening her thighs as his tongue began to do magical things. He spread the soft flesh surrounding her core, then slid his tongue inside. She almost flew off the bed, but he held her close. As he tasted and laved, her muscles corded. The sensation was so intense she wanted it to stop yet wanted whatever was coming next. When his attention moved to her clit and he began to suckle, her breath came in fits. Fireworks slowly began to build until they culminated in a full Fourth of July finale. She screamed, crying out his name. Kevin rode the waves with her, holding her in place, savoring her even as the sensation diminished. Finally, as she caught her breath, she collapsed onto the mattress. Kevin had yet to move. He was still poised between her legs, wearing a salacious grin.

What did you say when someone took you to a place you had never been—a place you didn't even believe existed outside of romance stories?

"Wow." Well, that was certainly profound, but it must have been satisfactory because his smile grew wider as he slid up the length of her. He coaxed her shirt over her head tossing it, along with her bra, to the corner of the room.

She lay motionless, selfishly waiting for what would come next. She didn't have to wait long. He took one breast into his mouth, suckled, nipped and feasted upon it. The heels of her feet pressed hard against the mattress as he turned his attention to the other breast. Enough with the tormenting.

She urged him up where once again their lips met in a frenzy. This time the kiss was fast, furious and carnal. River hung on for dear life. She was spiraling into a realm unfamiliar to her. Her heart pounded against her breastbone so hard it hurt. She didn't care.

His hands found their way to her hips. When he lifted them off the bed, her eyes flew open to find him staring into hers. Sparks. Later she would swear there had been actual sparks in his dark brown eyes.

He paused, silently seeking permission. She answered by shifting her position to meet his jutting erection. He needed no further invitation.

It was his turn to arch back as he filled her, then stilled. Whether for his pleasure or to give her time to adjust to the invasion, she didn't care. She needed him to move—now. Tightening her sensitive muscles around him, she pulled away slightly. When his eyes met hers, the corners of his mouth ticked up. He retreated further before slowly filling her again. He repeated the move again and again. It was torture. Sweet, unbearable torture.

"Damn it," she swore, squirming to bring him deeper inside. "Stop teasing!"

His eyes darkened as his tempo increased. This time his movements weren't gentle, but fast, hard and breathtaking.

Her body rocked to match his movements. Her back stiffened and her thighs tightened as she reached for the precipice. Then she broke. Spasms racked her body. She screamed at the sheer ecstasy of it. Kevin shouted somewhere in the distant fog.

When the indescribable sensation ebbed, Kevin dropped to her side. His skin was damp with perspiration. The fragrance of musk filled the room. He pulled her close and kissed her temple before rising up on his elbow.

"You okay?" he asked, brushing the hair from her face.

"I had no idea," she whispered, as her breathing slowed. She rested her head against his chest and let the night claim her.

24

————

oading up on caffeine to make up for his sleepless night, Kevin sat at the breakfast bar, sipping a cup of coffee. He could have dozed last evening. He was a light sleeper. But sleeping would have robbed him of the serenity he found holding River close. Kevin had lain in the dark, stroking River's hair as she breathed softly against his chest. If he'd been used, it was the best use of his body he could remember.

He already missed the feel of her skin against his. He wanted to see her smile more often. She'd teased him that first day on the beach, but these last few days had robbed her of any reason to smile. Last night, though, her ice-blue eyes had beamed. He wanted to hear her laugh… Damn, he was getting in deep—too deep under their current circumstances. River would be going home to North Carolina. He'd be returning to base and then deploying. There was no time to develop a relationship, assuming she wanted one with him. She didn't know him. Yet she'd spent the night sleeping peacefully in his arms.

Kevin couldn't imagine how Steve managed to leave

Josie so soon after they'd met and married. The deployment that followed had been hell on Steve and almost cost him his wife. There would have never been a Cece if fate—and hate—hadn't intervened and brought the two of them back together. The distance had distracted Steve. Worse, it had made Josie question their whirlwind romance.

Shouldn't that be enough incentive to stop his wistful thinking? It was nonsensical to be wishing for something deeper with River. The distance would eventually tear them apart.

For God's sake, he wasn't a teenager. They'd slept together. They'd had sex. Damn good sex, but it didn't have to mean anything more. It may have been all she wanted.

The focus of his thoughts entered the room, wearing a pair of shorts and a tank top the showed off her curves. Curves he'd become very familiar with last night. Her eyes sparkled like shattered glass and a small grin brightened her face. The knot he'd been tying himself into loosened.

"Good morning," she said, her smile widening.

If he hadn't been sitting, her grin would have knocked him on his ass.

She walked into the kitchen and grabbed a mug from the cupboard. Coffee pot in hand, she eyed him as she poured herself a cup. Her brow crinkled and her eyes narrowed. "What's with the silent treatment? Are you upset about last night?"

"Uh, no." He stumbled over his words. "I thought your eyes were your most stunning feature, but your smile..." His voice trailed off. "You're beautiful," he simply stated.

He rose from his seat just as she dipped her head, averting those eyes. He lifted her chin then dusted her lips with a kiss. "Good morning," he said, returning her greeting.

She smiled softly. "Thank you for last night."

He should step away, instead he leaned in for another tender kiss. "It was all my pleasure."

Picking up her cup, she put a little distance between them before taking a sip. "I'm going to head to the beach today—see if I can find some shells for my next project. Are you sticking around or am I no longer considered a target and can go on my own?"

He was hit with a taste of bitterness, laced with a twinge of sadness. Had his first assessment of their evening been right?

"Second question, first." His tone was sharper than he'd intended based on her wide-eyed expression. Last night she hadn't asked for more than his body. He'd given it to her freely and enjoyed hers in return. Why was he pissed off now?

"Chances are low you're in any danger on Sanibel. Odds are that issue left with the diamond. However, the North Carolina problem may take a while to resolve."

"If at all," she added. "Why do you think you'll get lucky when the police haven't found a thing?"

'Get lucky.' Her phrasing hit another nerve. He ignored it. "We already have a possible lead they didn't have. Give them a chance."

"I didn't mean any insult."

"To me or to them?" Kevin asked. Apparently, the nerve didn't plan on being ignored.

"Excuse me?" Her head came up. "Did I say something wrong?"

Gears churning behind those crystal blue eyes. When had he become so sensitive and insensitive? This wasn't about him.

"No. I didn't get much sleep last night. It left me a bit short-tempered this morning, I guess."

"Why don't you catch some rest. I'll be gone a couple of hours, at most."

She wasn't pushing him out. She'd asked a simple question and he'd twisted it into something personal. He needed to get his head screwed on straight.

"I've managed on less sleep," he told her. "Let me change into something other than these jeans. Did you want to grab some breakfast?"

"I'll pop a bagel in the toaster," she said, reaching into the freezer. "Would you like one?"

"Sounds good," he said, turning his back to dig through his duffel. He pushed his personal feelings aside. He was here for a reason. The chances of another attack while she was on the island were slim, but the feeling he'd missed something nagged at him.

RIVER SORTED through the trash line on the causeway, one of the best places to find miniature shells. Kevin had attempted to help, but they quickly discovered his fingers were too big to pick up the tiny crustaceans. Still, he continued to sift through the debris, pointing out ones he guessed might suit her needs.

They'd been at it a couple of hours, mostly in silence, when her back and legs began to object. *The Sanibel Stoop*, as the shell hunting position was called, could not be sustained all day. She groaned a little as she stretched to her full height.

"Are you done?" he asked, rising from his squatting position.

The question was asked in a perfunctory tone. The

tenderness of last night was gone. Why had she expected something different? He'd been accommodating, which was a cruel way to think of their night together. She'd needed affection. He'd given her that and more. Now there was a coldness she hadn't seen or noticed. It was pretty obvious she was responsible for it, but she didn't know why.

It was for the best. He'd be leaving. Getting close to people was a mistake. Kevin—and especially Dan—were proof enough.

"For today," she answered. "If you don't mind, I'd like to stop by some of those shell shops and see if they've had any success. If that's a problem, I can do it later."

Kevin simply nodded. As soon as she clicked her seatbelt, he was pulling onto the causeway, heading into Sanibel. His silence was beginning to unnerve her. "Did I do or say something to earn the silent treatment?"

"I've got a lot of things on my mind."

Things that had little to do with her, apparently. She, on the other hand, built the short interlude into something romantic. She'd put hearts and flowers around their evening together. Was she that desperate for affection that she created it where it didn't exist?

"Do you know when you're heading back to North Carolina?" he asked as he made a right onto Periwinkle Way. "We'll need to let Gib know."

The question snapped her back to her reality. It was selfish to be lingering on her personal wants. Dan was gone. Kevin kept his eyes on the road. He hadn't even glanced her way when he'd asked the question. Apparently, she'd lost not one, but two people in the last twenty-four hours. Her friend and surrogate father in the most horrendous way. It was the deepest hurt. But it would appear she'd also lost Kevin's respect. She pinched the bridge of her nose, hoping to hold back the tears that came too easily these days. She was still processing Dan's death. It was a normal response, but she'd be damned if she'd let Kevin see her cry.

"Jacob will call me as soon as he's made arrangements. He's still waiting for the coroner's office."

Another nod was his only reaction to her response. She forced the issue and hurt aside to concentrate on what she needed to accomplish before her departure.

The stops were quick and successful. One shop had gone through their inventory and had a bag of shells ready for River. With what was promised by the other vendors, she should have sufficient materials to finish the mask, and most would be ready in time to take with her when she left for Dan's funeral.

She had no idea if she'd return to Sanibel for the long term. She'd have to come back to pack her things, but other than the condo she had no ties to the island. The pastel painted houses passed in a blur as Kevin headed south on Periwinkle Way. She refused to look at him. Embarrassment, anger and sadness all battled inside her, each one seeking dominance. She was stronger than this. Smarter than this.

Last night was a mistake. That much was obvious in the bright light of the Florida sunshine. It had been wrong to seek solace in Kevin's arms, but it had felt so right. Was it simply her seeking an affirmation of life as he'd asked? If it was, it was a resounding affirmation.

As they pulled up to the condo, she spotted Gib waiting by his truck. The man's features would make any woman think of rumpled sheets and hot, sweaty bodies, but the attraction wasn't there for her. Her gaze went from Kevin to Gib and back again. No, last night hadn't been sex for the sake of sex. It had been something much deeper—for her anyway.

"Were you expecting Gib?"

"No, but it can't be urgent, or someone would have called." He pulled into the parking space next to Gib.

"What's up?" Kevin asked his friend.

"Nothing yet. I understand Colt is on his way to meet the Reverend and Troy is attempting to arrange a meeting with one of the Engleharts. Nothing new on either front."

"I want to be there for any meeting with the Engleharts," River reminded him.

"Troy knows you do. We've allotted plenty of time to get you there."

River didn't know whether to be relieved or anxious.

"Then why the trip out here?" Kevin asked.

"Just a neighborly visit," he said smiling. "See if there's anything you guys need."

"Can you take over here while I catch a few winks at your place?" Kevin asked.

"Ah, yeah. Sure," Gib answered, but his raised eyebrows told River he hadn't expected the request any more than she had.

"There's nothing pressing at the studio, so no problem. Steve wants to meet back here tonight to update everyone." He glanced at River, then Kevin. "What's going on?" he asked.

"I just need to get some rest," Kevin answered quickly. It was just as well Kevin spoke up first because River didn't have an answer to Gib's question.

Kevin grabbed his duffel from the living room and headed out. "Text me when we're ready to meet," he called over his shoulder.

"What's going on?" Gib repeated the question, this time to River.

"What are you talking about?" River made her way to the kitchen and opened the refrigerator door. Anything to avoid eye contact. She could guess what had gotten under Kevin's skin and the last thing she wanted to do was discuss it with Mr. Hottie. Kevin and Gib were friends. Eyeing a bottle of wine, she glanced at the clock and opted for the alcohol instead of water.

"I'm talking about you and Kevin. What happened between you two?"

"I have no idea. I suspect he's grown tired of babysitting me."

"That doesn't sound like Kevin. Something else is going on."

"You'll have to take his personality change up with him. I've got enough on my plate." She snagged a glass from the cabinet, filled it to the top with Pinot Grigio, then took a large sip. Gib's intense stare was unnerving. His friends would eventually find out what happened and that she was to blame for hurting him. She was getting to be an expert at alienating people.

She grabbed a disposable aluminum pan, snatched the bag of shells off the counter then placed them in it. Running cold water over the shells loosened the sand and debris that washed ashore with the tiny treasures. She repeated the process several times before laying them out on a paper towel on the counter to dry. River didn't have to look to know Gib's eyes remained cemented on her as she proceeded with her task. She could feel them.

"If you plan to stick around, why don't you make yourself comfortable? I'm going to wash this sand from my feet then get to work." The single bag of shells she received from the vendor today would allow her to get started and, with any luck, allow her to keep her mind off Kevin and Dan for a while.

"Why don't you take a break first?" Gib asked. "It's a

pretty afternoon. Join me on the deck. I'll grab a beer and we can relax and talk."

River eyed him suspiciously. No one had to tell her he was the charmer of the group. A ladies' man, if the term was still in use. She didn't need another man clouding up her life.

"Come on," he cajoled. "I'd enjoy the company and you look like you could use a rest."

The sliders were open. A breeze drifted in off the bay. River glanced at the man with the gray, sparkling eyes. She wanted to be alone. At the same time, she didn't.

"For a few minutes," she relented. "As long as we don't bring up the crap that's been going on here."

After Gib helped himself to one of the remaining beers, they settled into the cheap plastic chairs she'd purchased for the deck. Since she'd never planned on a long-term stay, the inexpensive chairs had served her needs.

Gib kept his agreement and avoided any talk of the death of her friend, the attacks or her problems in North Carolina. Instead, the man chatted about his friends, individually and as couples. River developed a deeper understanding of each of them, particularly the women's ability to empathize with her. Gib was a natural storyteller. He rattled on—telling tales that had her laughing. Laughing. She wouldn't have believed laughter was possible before they'd sat down. Maybe it was the result of the second glass of wine or Gib's ability to put her at ease. Between his GQ looks and personality, she had no doubt half the ladies on the island were enamored of him.

After a couple of hours of distracting conversation, she decided to put some time in on the shell mask before the company arrived. Gib had received a text telling him his friends would be over after Rick got off his shift. River assumed Kevin would be in the group.

What had he been doing all day? Had he needed rest, or had it been an excuse to get away from her? It didn't matter. It would seem they were both on the same page regarding their lack of judgment last evening. They were adults. If she read him right, he was too much a gentleman to make an issue of it in front of his friends. He was a compassionate man—one she'd taken advantage of in her grief and fear.

25

—————

"Y ou with us, Kevin?"

Kevin's head came up in response to Steve's question. River was in a better mood than when he'd left earlier in the day. He'd let his mind wander. Gib had spent the afternoon with her and the two seemed to be getting along well.

"Just thinking," Kevin said. "Go ahead. Place the call."

The purpose of the gathering was to get and give updates on what they'd been able to discover in the last twenty-four hours. They'd been waiting for Rick before they placed the call to Colt and Troy. Rick had been delayed, which annoyed Kevin as it had allowed him to dwell on the fact that he'd acted like an ass this morning. He owed River an apology but now that Rick had arrived their mission came first.

Colt picked up on the first ring. "I was getting ready to call you," he said.

"Rick was running behind," Steve explained.

"What did you find out from the preacher?" Kevin asked. "Anything useful?"

"The Good Reverend Roxbury," Colt stated. "He was an interesting study."

Kevin leaned in closer to the phone. Colt wouldn't have missed a thing. He was intuitive in addition to being a trained interrogator.

"How so?" River asked.

"Hey, River," Colt said, acknowledging her presence. "How are you doing?"

"Hanging in there. What's with Roxbury?"

"There's something definitely off. He was nervous. Defensive. Twitchy—although in that neck of the woods I wouldn't be surprised to find he had access to a meth lab. Anyway, he gave me a tour of his property while he lauded his ministry—which apparently centers on revenge and justice. He's a quack, that's for sure. I know more about the Bible than he does."

"That's saying a lot," Gib laughed.

"How did you get him to talk? If he was defensive, I'm surprised you got anything out of him," Steve questioned his former commander.

"Fed him a load of bullshit. Told him a friend of a friend who was a member of his flock suggested I reach out to him. I threw enough at him that his head should still be spinning."

"Can you tie him to River in any way?" Kevin was anxious for answers. So, apparently, was River. Her knee was pumping up and down like a piston. He wanted to reach over and lay his hand on it—give her some reassurance, but he couldn't assure her of anything. Besides, she'd probably push him away.

"I brought up the Engleharts. The questions startled him for a second, but he recovered quickly. He said they reached out to him and he'd visited at Mrs. Engleharts' request. He wouldn't comment further on them, claiming their conversations were privileged."

"He's not a priest," Steve noted.

"No, but I couldn't beat the information out of him."

"Why not?" Gib asked with a curve to his lips. Rick batted his arm. The two were a side show even when things were on fire.

"Besides," Colt continued, "I don't want him clamming up on me. He might have been defensive, but he was talking. I may need to see him again. Rick?"

"Here." Rick edged forward in his seat, leaning closer to the phone.

"We need more info on Roxbury than Josie has been able to dig up. Have you made any inquiries into his background?"

"Not yet. I'll work on him tomorrow."

"We need to know how he hooked up with the Engleharts. What's their connection?"

"I'll see what I can find from this end," Rick offered. "Troy, you're meeting with Zeke Englehart is the day after tomorrow. I'll text you the details."

"Good. I'll see what I can get out of him."

"I want to be there," River almost grabbed the phone off the table. "I told you I wanted to be there," she repeated.

"They're expecting two of you," Rick assured her. "The prison doesn't know you'll be the second visitor."

Kevin was watching River intently. He saw her shoulders relax a bit at Rick's answer, but her fingers were knotted. Her thumb was drawing circles in her palm. He'd seen her do that a dozen times—a signal, he'd learned, that her tension level had ratcheted up. Instinct urged him to go to her. Common sense held him back. She'd managed just fine before he came along. He hadn't met many women with the dog-headedness and backbone of River Chandler. Cat, Josie and Shayne were the only ones who came to mind who had the fortitude and tenacity she possessed.

"I need to get packed." River rose to her feet. "Where do you guys want to meet? My place?"

"What time is he scheduled to be at the prison," Gib asked Rick.

"One o'clock in the afternoon."

The team worked out some general logistics. Gib's friend would fly River into Raleigh which was the closest airport to the prison. Troy and Colt would meet her there. She'd ride back to her cabin with them when the meeting at the correctional facility was over.

"I'm going, too," Kevin added.

Her eyes widened. "I've imposed on you enough.".

Kevin wasn't surprised by her reaction. He'd acted like an ass this morning. She was quite capable of handling herself and the guys would have her back, but this had all started that day at the beach when he'd chased off her attacker. He wanted to see this through. To see where things led—not this dangerous puzzle—but between them.

He'd gotten very little rest today, instead he spent a great deal of time contemplating the comments he and River had exchanged this morning. He concluded he'd overreacted. When this was behind them, if she wanted nothing more from him, he hoped they'd part friends.

"You've never imposed, and I'd still like to help." It was the best apology he could come up with in front of others. Anything more, might embarrass her.

"Thank you," she smiled this time. It lit up the room. "It's going to get a bit crowded up there," River added.

"We've reserved a room at the resort on the other side of the preserve. We'll stay at the resort if you prefer the cabin," Troy offered.

"The birdbath," River blurted out, her thoughts changing direction. "Is it okay? Has anyone damaged it?"

"It's untouched except for the birds who visit it. It's a beautiful piece, River," Colt complimented her. "A heartfelt tribute to your family. If you have no objection, I'd like to take a few photos of it."

"Please. It would be my honor."

"What's the plan for tomorrow?" Rick asked.

"We'll keep poking around. We missed a few neighbors on our first sweep and didn't get a chance to go into the little town nearest you."

"Small towns are a good source of gossip," Steve agreed. "Call if you find out anything of interest. Rick and I will do the same."

"Roger," Colt said, slipping back into his military jargon. "We'll talk tomorrow night."

The phone went silent. Rick stood as he slipped it into his pocket. "Kevin?"

"What?"

"You're on duty tonight again, if no one objects." He glanced at River.

"Whatever works for ya'll," she answered.

Kevin walked with his friends to the door.

"Don't screw up again," Gib warned him with a grin.

Ignoring the barb, Kevin shut the door behind them and set the alarm. River had yet to move from her spot on the couch. Those glacial blue eyes watched him warily as he crossed the room. How did he make things right between them?

26

———

*R*iver conceded the staring match and focused on her hands. She had convinced herself she'd made a mistake in taking him to her bed. Kevin had every reason to feel she'd used him as an escape. It was true. The pleasure he'd offered had temporarily overridden the grief of losing Dan, but she'd felt something deeper. Their love-making had not only given her an escape from the pain but had also touched her heart—her soul. How was that a mistake?

No one fell in love this quickly, did they? She had no idea how it felt to be in love. It was times like these she missed her mother the most. Her Aunt Amy was a rock—a strong, no-nonsense woman. She'd given up a lot to care for her niece, and River couldn't love her more, but River never opened up to her about boys or the other things teenage girls fretted over. The two of them had never shared that kind of bond for some reason.

It was years after the murders before she was old enough to understand the love between her mother and dad had been rare—a rare and special gift. Her parents had loved deeply, but they had also been partners and friends. They hadn't had enough time on this earth to pass on their working formula. The snippets River did remember of the two together were her only road maps. She held on to them tightly. Still, she suspected she would never experience that depth of feeling with anyone.

As Kevin's shadow settled over her, she managed to swallow in spite of her dry mouth. She should apologize for last night. Or should she thank him? God! She was so fucked up. Why would she add a man to her confusion?

Squatting in front of her, Kevin waited patiently until she raised her gaze to meet his. When she did, he reached for her hand and nestled it in his palms. Electricity danced across her fingertips, making its way through every inch of her being. Surprisingly, there was warmth in his eyes—a mixture of compassion and heat.

"Do I owe you an apology?" she asked.

Removing one of his hands from hers, he lifted her chin then touched his lips to hers. She didn't pull away, but didn't fall into it, as much as she wanted to.

"Why would you owe me an apology?" He brushed his thumb over her chin.

"For last night." She hesitated, briefly closing her eyes. "You were angry this morning, weren't you?"

"I was," he admitted. "I believed I'd been dismissed— that our time together meant nothing to you. It was an unfair assumption on my part."

"I did take solace in your arms." His grip loosened, but she held on tight. "But I received so much more. I can't explain it. I felt something I've never knew existed." She paused, reaching deep for courage. "I'd like to share my bed with you again tonight." Instead of confident, she sounded wanting and pitiful.

She closed her eyes, embarrassed by her unexpected

confession and fear she'd see rejection on his face. As much as she wished it, he didn't move. He stayed firmly planted in front of her—her hand still clasped in his.

He nudged her head up again with the tip of his finger. She sucked it up, meeting his gaze head-on. There was no disdain in his expression. Warmth, bordering on heat, flared in his dark eyes.

"It would seem we're both new to this."

The statement caught her off guard. "New to what?"

"These feelings. The insecurity of not knowing what the other is thinking. Maybe we could talk about it?"

How many men would admit that? How many would offer discussion instead of something carnal? Feelings rushed through her mind and her heart. He was a good man. She didn't deserve his understanding or compassion. One of their hearts would break. She'd been training for fourteen years to defend her heart. Instinctively, she would continue to protect it, but this man had managed to break through her outer barriers and touch it. How much more could she expose and survive? Right or wrong, though, she wanted him. His pull was too strong.

"Maybe." She hooked her arms around his neck. "But could we talk later?"

No explaining was necessary. His lips met hers as his fingers slid to the buttons of her blouse. When her breasts were free and he cupped them in his hands, she demanded more. Tugging at the hem of his shirt, she struggled to pull it free. He took her hands in his, ending her battle to strip him.

"I think we can find a better place to continue this." Holding her hand, he led her to the bedroom. She began to shrug out of her blouse, when he stopped her with a light touch to her shoulder.

"Give me a second then let me have the honor," he said.

He pulled several packets from his pocket and tossed them onto the nightstand. She grinned at the number of condoms before turning back to watch him shuck out of his jeans and his shirt. The simple act of removing his clothing was enough to get her juices flowing—literally.

Poised on the edge of the bed, she stared at his erection, which was now pointed directly at her like a divining rod. She reached out and wrapped her fingers around the soft, firm flesh. His head lolled back as she tentatively began to stroke it. Her tongue flicked out to taste him.

"Not yet," he warned her, stepping back. She hardly recognized the gruff, strained voice. "As much as I'd enjoy that, this will be over before we get started if you keep it up."

"That was my plan…To keep it up," she grinned.

He was chuckling as he slipped her blouse from her shoulders. Her jeans disappeared just as swiftly. She heard the material crumple as her clothing landed in the corner.

"Now, let's get serious," he told her, laying her back against the mattress.

The air surrounding them heated like a sizzling summer afternoon, forecasting an intense electrical storm. Instead of the flash and bang of the night before, Kevin surprised her with a touch that was measured and gentle. He feathered his fingertips over her skin. From her forehead to her toes, not an inch was left unattended. She was a canvas, lovingly being stroked by an artist. When his fingers brushed a particularly sensitive spot, he lingered there for a while.

When he found his way back to her breasts, she was squirming beneath him. Her breasts weren't the only areas that were demanding attention. She urged him upward, tugging at his shoulders. She wanted his mouth on hers. She wanted him inside her.

With one last pass over her tender nipple, he rested on his elbows, hovering above her. Peering down, he smiled—a smile of contentment and anticipation. River reeled him in for a kiss—one that was hot, hungry and urgent. She wrapped her legs around his thighs, inching them up, lifting her hips as she did.

"Let's slow the pace a bit," he said, edging back. "We've got all night."

"What if I don't want to wait all night?"

"You won't have to, but for this minute, let's take this slow and easy. Enjoy."

She could do that. As much as she wished for the fireworks and ecstasy she'd experienced the prior evening, this tenderness was almost as exhilarating. The dusting of his fingertips. The teasing with his tongue. Every movement, every touch, raked shivers through her body.

Then he stretched out beside her. She was on fire and he was…what? Taking a break?

The glint in his eye should have told her otherwise. His hands began to stroke, pet and tease. How many damn hands did he have? Her hips rose and her thigh muscles tightened to the point of snapping as he returned his attention to the ache between her legs. The sensation was too much. She let those surgical fingers take her over the edge.

Collapsing against the mattress, her breathing came in fits and starts. Kevin was once again propped on one elbow gazing at her as if she were a unique piece of art. A satisfactory grin graced his face as he brushed the damp hair away from her forehead.

"What about you?"

Kevin smiled. "I said, we have all night."

RIVER SLIPPED from the bed before the sun was up. Kevin heard the bathroom door close, the toilet flush, followed by the sound of running water. He was tempted to join her in the shower. Just the thought had him rising for the occasion. But the water shut off quickly, so he waited. When she didn't return to the warmth of their bed he tossed back the covers. Pulling on his jeans, he stepped into the hall. While the bathroom door was open, the door to her studio was closed. He should have joined her in the shower.

The aroma of coffee caught his attention. He poured a cup, noting the shells she'd cleaned and left to dry were no longer on the counter. It confirmed his assumption she was already at work.

He tapped on the workroom door then let himself in. River glanced over her shoulder and smiled. "'Morning," she said.

"'Morning. You're up and at it early." Tiny shells were spread out over a black cloth on top of her workspace. The mask in front of her had a penciled designed etched on it.

"I wanted to get a start on the mask before we left," she explained. "If I get these set early enough, then it should be okay to take with me. I may have to finish it up there."

"You're not planning on coming back?" Kevin put his coffee aside and laid his hands on her shoulders. She'd been relaxed and fluid in his arms. Now her neck was corded tight.

Dropping her pencil, she picked up her cup of coffee. "I don't know. To be honest with you, it's one of the reasons I came in here instead of returning to bed. I needed to think."

"Why don't we find something to go with this coffee and talk."

He was rewarded with a smile for the suggestion.

"We did use up a lot of energy last night."

River gathered eggs, bread, and some sausage she'd rediscovered in the back of the freezer. She scrambled cheese into the eggs as he popped the pre-cooked sausage in the microwave.

Settling in at the dining room table, they each scarfed up a few forkfuls before Kevin stop eating.

"Do you want to come back here?" he asked, holding her gaze.

"My plan was to rent this place to vacationers after I lived here for one year. HOA by-laws," she added. "I should know better by now than to think things turn out the way you plan them."

"So, you were going to move back to North Carolina, all along?" The idea of her alone in the cabin saddened him. His home, when he was stateside, was also North Carolina, but he had friends at Fort Bragg in addition to his friends here. Based on their conversations, she didn't have many, if any, friends at home.

"That was the original plan. After a year, if they hadn't caught the person behind the harassment, I figured he—or she— had probably moved on."

"But no one has been arrested, and now with Dan being killed at the same location…"

It was River's turn to drop her fork. "I know. The cabin is my home. It's not just a place to hang my hat—it's a part of me. But how do I live there, constantly looking over my shoulder? And why was Dan killed there? Did it have something to do with me or my family? I don't know if I can stay there with that on my conscience."

"From what you told me I don't think Dan would want you to feel that way." Kevin reached across the table and placed his hand over her small fist.

"He wouldn't," she said, a small smile gracing her face. "Unlike my aunt, Dan understood my determination to stay put. He wasn't easily intimidated. A little of his stubbornness rubbed off on me."

"I can tell," Kevin grinned. "Your aunt wanted you to leave?"

"She never wanted me to live there—that goes way back." River's head dropped back against her shoulders. "Oh, the battles we fought. She considers the cabin a place of evil. She's never stepped foot on the property since the murders. Dan kept it up until I moved in."

"That must have made for a tense situation," Kevin said, bringing her eyes back down to his.

"I was fourteen when I moved in with her. A teenager, grieving, but with all the answers and a chip bigger than Mount Everest on my shoulder. I know I wouldn't have had the patience she'd possessed during those first couple of years."

"She must care a great deal about you," Kevin stated.

"I know she does, but I'm not moving back in with her, which she may suggest. We're both grown women with ideas and beliefs that clash. For the first time, though, I don't know if I should live at the cabin. There's been so many deaths."

"What made you decide to move there after college?" Kevin asked as he collected their dishes and set them in the sink. He returned to the table with the carafe of coffee.

"It was always a special place with wonderful memories when my family was alive. I didn't want anyone to steal those from me. Walking away would have given the Engleharts the power to do that. Besides, the cabin gave me solitude." She smiled as he topped off her cup. "If you haven't noticed, my social skills aren't the best."

"You'd do fine if you gave yourself half a chance," he countered. "I think it's more of a preference than a trait."

"You could be right, but I haven't had the need to develop that skill."

She sipped her coffee and stared out the window behind him.

"Back to your return to North Carolina," he said. "What are you thinking?"

"I'm definitely going back to the cabin. I don't want to kick your friends out, but I need to see if I can do it. It's been my home. It shouldn't scare me."

Kevin stopped fighting the urge to hold her. He abandoned the cup he'd just filled and in a few short minutes, they were on the couch with her in his lap. He held her tight. She was scared—and grieving. Losing her family and her friend were bad enough, but now she was contemplating losing her remaining physical connection to them.

"And the terrorizing? What if it returns once you're there?" It scared the hell out of him.

"You know? Until the knife attack, I was mildly upset by the events—but not terrified. I figured somebody would either catch the bastard or he'd get bored and leave if he didn't get a rise out of me. I retreated to Sanibel not because of the attacks, but because Aunt Amy and Don were frightened for me. Staying there, was adding to their burden. I've caused them so much trouble."

She scooted off his lap but didn't go far. She leaned into him, resting her head on his broad shoulder. "I'd considered selling the cabin, but just thinking about it is like selling a piece of my soul. It's a place of horrific memories, but beautiful memories, too. I walk the same trails I walked with my family. I cook in the same kitchen where my mom fried trout that dad and Billy caught. Well, it was mostly my dad who caught the fish, but everyone praised my brother on his fishing skills. I want the fucking bastard that's trying to steal that from me."

"So, returning to the cabin will serve two purposes? Test how much the death of your friend affects your being there and to see if the guilty party starts another round of harassment?"

"I can deal with the second more easily than the first, but I won't know if I can deal with either until I try. It may take me some time to figure those things out.

"What about Sanibel? Do you like it here?"

"I haven't regretted the move, except for the incidents with the jewel. This place is so different from my mountain, but it is beautiful in a different way and…" she paused. "Medicinal, I guess would be a fitting word. I can't think of another way to describe it. I feel at peace when I'm alone on the beach listening to the waves roll in to kiss the shore while delivering the beautiful little treasures they offer me."

"I'm glad you chose Sanibel," Kevin said, hugging her closer. "Have you considered staying?"

"Why do you want to know? You're leaving shortly, aren't you?"

Kevin grinned. At the forefront of her mind was how he might figure into the picture if she stayed or moved.

"I have, at the very least, one more deployment," he told her. "I'm at a crossroads myself. I love the military. I'm good at what I do, but I've watched my friends grow and make new lives for themselves. It's tempting. I came here to try it on, so to speak."

"Have you made up your mind?"

"No," he said, kissing her lightly. "A few other issues came up that redirected my attention."

"I'm sorry," she apologized.

"I'm not. I'll figure it out, just as you will. Do what's in your heart, River. If I, or anyone of us can help, reach out. You've got friends here, if you'll accept them."

"Friends with benefits?" she smiled, touching his face.

He kissed her, hard and deep. "Only if those benefits apply to me."

---

27

*A*fter cleaning up the breakfast dishes, Kevin convinced her he was an expert on packing since he'd done it so many times, so he volunteered to tackle her clothing. Initially, she was hesitant to let him pack her things, but he'd seen more than her underwear last night. She did draw the line when it came to her personal hygiene products.

Kevin had the easier job in River's opinion. She had no idea whether she was returning. All her tools, supplies and designs would have to go. She was fortunate Gib had a friend willing to fly them to North Carolina, otherwise she'd have had to ship everything. For some reason the task of packing was getting her down. Had this place become home? Deja vu all over again. It was the same feeling that had enveloped her when she'd loaded her possessions into her Subaru the day she'd left her cabin. This was supposed to be a temporary stop on a road she'd expected to travel alone. Lonely, but safe from heartache.

The drawers of her dresser opened and closed as Kevin moved about her room, gathering her things. It seemed natural to have him nearby. What was going on with her?

Shaking off the odd sensation, she gathered her tools, glues, sketch pads and materials, then packed them carefully in boxes. She'd saved the boxes and packing materials, knowing this day would eventually come. But going home wasn't the celebration she'd expected.

This place had grown on her—or was it because of the company of late? Then there was the ominous meeting awaiting her. She'd be facing at least one of the family members who had killed her loved ones. She expected she'd be attending Dan's memorial—seeing him off on his final journey home to be with his wife. Linda Thompson had died years before River had met Dan. He spoke of her often and it was obvious how much he'd missed her. That loss may be why she and Dan had related with each other so easily. They'd each had a hole that needed filling.

The melancholy continued to settle over her as she took in the space surrounding her. This room had become a virtual cage since she'd moved in. She tried to fit in a morning run and an occasional meal out—she'd refused to be a hermit. Work kept her busy, thank God, but her work kept her within the four walls of this room. So much for winning the battle against darkness.

With her emotions sagging, she'd made it a point to avoid the photographs of her family scattered around the room. Normally, they would fill her with warmth. Today, she was afraid they would make her weep.

"Damn it," she muttered, tossing tubes of epoxy into a box. She was stronger than that. She'd let the recent crap she'd been going through get to her. Her parents would be disappointed, and it would make Billy anxious. She could picture his rounded face scrunched up in concern. Pulling back her shoulders, she raised her head, and focused on the picture which was the centerpiece of the room.

While it wasn't a photograph of her family, it embodied their essence—love, kindness, teamwork, and strength. God, she missed them.

River didn't think any artist could capture what she'd been trying to relate in her sketch, yet the wood sculptor had done an amazing job of doing just that. The femininity and strength of her mother. The enthusiasm and eagerness of her little brother as he reached up to help. The tender, yet strong, hands of her father as he supported, not just the basin, but his family.

She could still feel Kevin's hands as he'd gently tended to her wounds and, later, intimately traced the lines of her body. She'd seen the strength, when he rescued her from the snake, then protected her from the gunman.

How would her dad feel about Kevin? She smiled, knowing he'd trust her judgment. *"Your mom and I have tried to give you the tools to make the right decisions,"* he'd told her on her fourteenth birthday. *"I expect you to use them."* He never had the chance to see if she made use of those tools. She'd tried to make him proud. She'd started by standing up in court and facing the family that had taken hers.

She had never expected to—never wanted to—see the Engleharts again, but she needed to know if they were behind this systematic terrorism. They had reveled in the killings. It had been written on their faces during the trial. Occasionally, one of them would glance her way, a depraved grin on their face. An attorney would quickly elbow them, forcing them to turn around.

Would those same faces give something away this time? She was scared, but she'd be damned if she'd give them a pass. If they were behind any of this shit, they wouldn't get away with it this time either.

~

KEVIN STOOD in the doorway to River's studio. She didn't acknowledge his presence. He suspected she didn't even know he was there. Her focus was solely on the photograph above her workspace.

"Hi," he said softly, not wanting to startle her. If he did, she didn't show. How often had he seen her fight to conceal her emotions? Last night, at least, she'd set some of them free.

"Hi." A tender smile lit up her face. "Your timing is perfect."

"How so?"

"I was working myself up into a fit of anger over the Engleharts. I sometimes forget they don't deserve my energy."

"You're right. They don't," he agreed. "You were thinking of your family, though, so it's understandable. The sculpture is moving," he said, indicating the picture with a nod of his head. "You designed it, didn't you?"

"I drew the sketch, but the woodworking artist deserves credit for capturing what I was trying to say."

"You both told a story," Kevin confirmed, gazing at the photo.

"If the Engleharts are somehow behind the shit that's been happening to me, I want to know. If not, I want to find out who is," she said. "Will you help me end this?"

It was an invitation he hadn't expected, but one he would do everything to see through. "I'll do all I can." Surprising him again, she pulled him down to kiss him.

"Thank you."

"You're welcome. We'll continue this later." He raised his eyebrows and smiled. "We have company coming."

"I expected as much. Do they have more news?"

"Nothing urgent or Steve would have shared it with me. Cat and Josie would like to join the guys, if you have no objection. Cece, too."

"None, but I'm surprised they want to come. I've either been snapping at them or running from them."

"Trust me, they understand."

"I guess we'd better feed them," she said, checking the clock.

They settled on a delivery from a local pizza place. The team would gladly bring the food, but River insisted on making the arrangements and the purchase.

The meal arrived, followed shortly by Steve, Josie and Cece. Kevin watched as Cece reached for River. She appeared stunned and hesitant, but after a nod from Josie, took the child into her arms. The sight was another gut punch for Kevin. River was constantly knocking the air from his lungs. Smiling, Cece reached up and pinched River's cheek before falling into a fit of giggles. River immediately recognized the game and softly pinched Cece's chubby cheek, bringing on more laughter from the little girl.

Both laughing, River headed back to the kitchen with Cece on her hip. Setting out the food and dishes one-handed while keeping up a conversation with the tittering child. Kevin was enthralled. He couldn't take his eyes off the two of them.

"I'd better get in there and help. She's a natural," Josie whispered, as she passed Kevin, sending him a wink as she did.

Kevin couldn't dwell on Josie's comment, or admire the way River so easily dealt with the child. That time was stolen with the arrival of Shayne, Cat, Rick and Gib. The pizza was passed around the room and everyone ate their fill—with the exception of Cece who played with any food within her reach. Kevin stole glances of River as she reached to wipe the child's face or chuckle at one of Gib's obvious passes. He regretted the social part of this evening would end too soon. River was relaxed and laughing, something he hadn't seen her do much, but they'd be leaving in the morning and there were still questions to be asked and plans to be made.

"Colt said to call when we're ready," Cat said, reading his mind.

"Get them on the phone," Rick added. "I've got a bit to add to last night's discussion."

It was Troy who answered, however. "Hey, guys."

"Where's Colt?" Cat immediately asked.

"Not to worry, Cat. He ran downstairs to grab a couple of brews. We checked into the resort this afternoon. We've done all we can at the cabin. We've also talked to your closest neighbors, although I wouldn't call them close. Your place is really out in the sticks, River."

"Part of its appeal," she said.

"Is Shayne there?" Troy asked.

"I'm here."

"Sorry I didn't have time to call today."

"I wouldn't have had time to talk. Snowbirds were flocking into the garden center like mosquitos on a summer night."

"Call me when you get home, baby."

"You two can have phone sex tonight," Gib interrupted.

Kevin noted the sparkle in Gib's gray eyes and the slight blush on Shayne's cheeks. Troy had shared the fact it had been Gib who'd been instrumental in pushing the two of them together. Initially, the couple barely tolerated one another.

"And speaking of calls," Gib added. "I spoke with

TAC Air at Raleigh-Durham International Airport. I'll shoot you their exact location. They're expecting you and Colt in the morning. River and Kevin should be arriving around 11:00 a.m. You'll have plenty of time to get to the prison."

"Is everyone there?" Colt's deep voice resonated through the telephone, joining the conversation.

"Here, and ready to get started," Rick announced.

"Did you find anything of interest on Roxbury?" Troy asked, his voice becoming clearer as he approached the phone at the other end.

"Nothing major, but he has a record," Rick told them. "One assault charge, and a string of misdemeanors. The assault charge was dropped. The misdemeanors were for harassment, disturbing the peace, that kind of shit. He did community service."

"Any recent run-ins with the law?" Troy probed further.

"Not in the last couple of years. He either cleaned up his act when he found God, or people aren't reporting it."

"I haven't found anyone to say differently, but I plan to go back tomorrow. Troy will meet you at the airport, Kevin. I want to keep working the Roxbury angle. There are too many questions about him that beg for answers," Colt explained.

"We're still meeting with the son tomorrow?" River asked.

"Unless we hear something different from the prison or Rick, we're still scheduled to question Zeke," Troy confirmed. "You positive you want to do this?"

"In all honesty, no, but I think my being there will get a reaction that might be helpful. Besides, I want them to know they didn't break me."

Kevin squeezed River close then placed a kiss on her

temple. His friends thought nothing of the gesture. Relationships had a way of blossoming on this island.

"The cabin has been cleaned up, but if you want, we can get another room at the resort for you," Colt offered.

"Thank you, but I'm staying at the cabin." River stated. "I have to make up my mind whether I'm going to keep it. It's seen so much loss..." Her voice trailed off. "I need to spend some time there in order to make that decision."

"Anything else on the Engleharts?" Steve asked Rick, his tone low. Cece was already asleep in the crook of Steve's arm. Kevin suspected it was way past her bedtime.

"I don't think the warden held anything back. The family hasn't caused any trouble. For the most part, they're kept away from the general population. Even convicted felons don't like child killers. Their single visitor in all this time has been the Reverend. He scheduled another visit for the end of the month—a couple of weeks from now." Rick took a pull from his beer.

"He didn't mention that to me," Colt told the group. "But he wouldn't open up about them, so it's not surprising. I think Troy and River are our best bet to get information out of the Engleharts, if there's any to get."

"Are we sure we're not missing something?" Kevin asked. "I feel like we're putting all our efforts in one direction. Could there be another avenue we need to explore?"

"River," Cat said, making her way to the kitchen, "I suggest you spend some time giving thought to anything odd or out of the ordinary that's happened to you, other than the obvious." River and Shayne joined Cat as she began to clean up. "Any former friends, vendors or clients —anyone who might have an axe to grind."

"They can pop up and surprise you. Trust me," Josie added. She took Cece from Steve's arms and tucked her in her carrier. "I'm still reaching out to my contacts, but nothing new has turned up. There wasn't a lot of media interest in events surrounding your gaslighting."

"You're certain the break-ins here weren't connected to the stalking in North Carolina?" Kevin asked Rick.

"Pretty damn sure. There's been no threat to River since it was made clear the diamond was removed from her possession. The SATG group would get the hell out of the area. There's no way they'd stick around with the FBI involved. Not when they don't have a chance of recovering the stone. They've written that one off as a loss."

"And they wouldn't hold River responsible?" Gib questioned Rick.

"It wouldn't serve them any purpose and would cause them more trouble than they needed. They sent the message they wanted to send when they killed the dealer who screwed up. We made it clear River wasn't aware she had the diamond. No. I'd bet my next paycheck they've packed up and gone home."

"Speaking of home," Josie said, her voice softening, "it's time to get this young lady to bed."

"I guess we've covered all we can cover for now. We'll see you two tomorrow," Kevin confirmed before disconnecting the call.

After River said her goodnights, Kevin walked his friends to the door, then set the alarm. Once they were secure, he faced River and opened his arms. They'd done all they could do tonight. He had something else in mind for the remainder of the evening.

28

River was grateful they hadn't discussed what was to come in the following days. Instead, they exuberantly enjoyed one another's bodies. She suspected she was more than infatuated with Kevin, but having never been in love, how would she know? Regardless, common sense told her to keep it to herself. She'd be leaving Sanibel permanently, sooner or later. Kevin would be returning to duty and shipping out. Thoughts of anything deeper developing between them were wasted and would lead to heartbreak. She'd be grateful for her time with him and live with those memories when he was gone.

Shayne delivered them to the airport early the next morning. She told River to give her husband a kiss for her. It was easy to see how much she missed Troy. River suffered a bit of guilt for stealing him for a while.

Troy and Shayne were quickly forgotten when she stepped inside the small jet. "Holy, crap," she exclaimed. "Who owns this thing?" The inside wasn't huge, but it was luxurious. Plush leather seats, crisp, clean lines, tasteful yet minimal decor.

"A friend of Gib's."

"Some friend," she said, as she settled into a cushy seat next to the window.

"He's pretty mysterious about the whole thing. Knowing Gib, he gets his kicks by keeping us in suspense."

"I get the impression everyone loves Gib," River remarked, buckling her seat belt as the plane taxied onto the runway.

"I've never met anyone like him, but don't let his good looks and charm fool you. He's tough as nails and he'd lay down his life for any one of us. He took a bullet for Cat. He doesn't have our military training, but we'd all trust him with our lives."

River glanced out the small window as the runway rushed by. The plane left the ground, forcing River deep into her seat. She gripped the armrest. Flying didn't terrify her, but it wasn't high on her list of fun things to do.

"Look at me instead of the ground." Kevin gently pried her hand from the seat's arm. "It makes take-offs a bit easier in my opinion."

"You're not afraid of flying." She couldn't imagine him afraid of much.

"No. I've been on so many planes you get used to them."

"Take-offs always screw with my equilibrium." Her grip loosened as the plane began to level off. "Thanks."

"Any excuse to hold your hand."

He'd done more than that last night. That hand had wandered, caressed and aroused. She had met him, stroke for stroke. She imagined he had a few nail marks across his back as she'd dug in and held on for the ride. The image made her smile.

"Let's talk boyfriends," Kevin said, leaning back in his seat.

"Excuse me?" A bit stunned by the question, she stared at him. After last night's lovemaking, he wanted to ask about her old boyfriends?

"Cat was right when she suggested we run through your background outside of the death of your family. Is it possible there's another reason for targeting you?"

River relaxed into her seat. "My love life, if you can even call it that, has been sparse. I dated infrequently in college and a few times since graduating. All partings were mutual. There were never any sparks—good or bad," she added. Kevin grinned. Did he know he set off sparks within her? Did he feel the same?

"Okay. Any vendors, college professors, clients you've had issues with? Anyone you dealt with who struck you as odd?"

River took a few minutes to ruminate her professional history. She'd had some picky clients and a few college professors she'd like to forget, but nothing significant came to mind.

She blew out a long breath. "With the exception of the gem dealer, all the drama in my life has taken place due to the death of my family. Besides dealing with the trial, there were death threats."

"What? Why?"

"I never understood the why of it. Dan told me most of it was bluster. A few crazies firmly believed my testimony was believed over the Engleharts' denials because I came from a wealthy family and they were poor. It was all a bunch of crap and died down soon enough. The evidence against the Engleharts was overwhelming."

"It was your quick thinking and testimony that nailed them."

"True. The police didn't have any real leads. They knew there were multiple killers, but they hadn't developed any substantial leads until my family was killed. Whether they would have caught up with them because they stole my dad's car, is questionable. The Engleharts would have dumped it and stolen another. That was their pattern. They'd hiked to our cabin after ditching their last ride."

"Were any of the threats you received serious enough to warrant another look now?"

River glanced out the window as clouds, instead of a runway, floated by. Dan would know, she almost said. "Rick might want to ask the authorities when he talks to them. I don't remember the details. I was still trying to process the loss of my family and deal with the trial. I can ask my aunt when I see her."

"When will that be?"

"I'll call her in the morning. By the time we get back from the prison tonight, it'll be late."

"You didn't tell her you were coming?" Kevin's eyebrows rose.

"No. She'd ask all sorts of questions." Aunt Amy would vehemently object to her visit to the prison and River didn't see any reason to cause her upset. She'd put her aunt through enough during her lifetime.

"I'd assumed you were close."

"We are." River didn't care for his assumption. "I didn't want to worry her. She'd want to talk me out of going to the prison."

"What have you told her about this past week?" His eyes bore into hers.

"As little as possible."

"You could write a novel about the shit that's happened to you in the last seven days. Won't she be a bit upset she's been excluded?"

"I know my aunt. You don't." The idea of dissecting each day was exhausting. Being barraged by questions would make it much harder to relate the events—and her aunt would take each day apart piece by piece.

"You're right," Kevin said, returning to his seat. He'd grabbed two bottles of water from the small refrigerator at the front of the cabin. He handed her one. "I don't know her. Why don't you tell me what she's like? What does she do?"

"She owns a catering business. It's small but has an excellent reputation."

"You sound proud of her."

"I am. Besides taking me in, she built the business from the ground up. Clawed her way to being successful. She found a niche that makes her stand out from the other caterers in the area. Not only is she a great cook—who is embarrassed by my lack of culinary skills—but she can market."

"What's her special 'niche'?"

"In addition to the traditional menu items, she creates delicacies made exclusively with local produce and meats. No one else goes to the trouble of providing the unique variety she does. She's worked hard to build her business."

"Like you did. You started your graphics design business from scratch," Kevin commented.

"With the help of a hefty inheritance which was waiting for me when I turned twenty-one. I had a foot up when I started the business. She didn't."

"You're an heiress?" he joked, taking a slug of water.

"I'm not near that category. My family left me well off, but I'd rather have them than the money."

Kevin took her hand. "I know you would."

They spent the remainder of the flight trading stories about their histories and families. They'd been together for days, but they'd barely touched on their personal lives, unless that history had something to do with her recent problems. As they flew north, he'd occasionally dig a bit deeper than casual conversation. She suspected it was his attempt to jog her memory toward something significant as Cat had suggested. It didn't.

What it did accomplish, however, was pass the time—to the extent that she was surprised when they started to descend. Her pulse kicked-up a notch as the wheels hit the runway and the pilot throttled back. Her heart pounded remembering the last time she'd seen the Engleharts. She was a frightened, yet determined, fourteen-year-old. She wasn't fourteen anymore, but she was still determined. She'd be damned if she let them frighten her. They were the ones behind bars. Still, facing evil a second time had not been on her bingo card.

Kevin deboarded the plane first, turning back to offer his steady hand to River as she made her way down the steps. Troy was waiting for them. She'd almost forgotten how striking the man was even with his facial injuries. The man was dressed warmer for the cool North Carolina spring, but the heavier clothes didn't hide the strong build beneath.

"Did you have a good flight? I know it can be hard spending time with this guy," Troy laughed.

"I could get used to flying in one of these," she said, indicating the small jet. And, boy, wasn't that the truth. She'd be spoiled getting on a commercial airline from this point forward. She raised up on her toes and placed a kiss on Troy's cheek. "That's from Shayne. She dropped us off this morning."

"We talked after she did."

"I feel bad keeping you up here."

"It's what we do. Hopefully, we can be of some help."

"I'm going to find a way of making this up to you all," she asserted as the three made their way to the cargo area at the rear of the plane. Kevin and Troy unloaded her boxes and their luggage.

"We're doing this as a favor."

Troy was smiling as he chastised her, so she didn't take offense to the statement, but she was determined to find a way to repay them for their assistance. They'd gone above and beyond on her behalf. Right now, though, she needed to focus her attention elsewhere.

River had opted for the back seat of the large SUV Troy had rented. The closer they got to the prison, the more frequently Kevin glanced over his shoulder at her. His lips were drawn tight. His eyes questioning. Concern was written clearly across his brow. She wanted to tell him not to worry. This was her load to bear, but he wouldn't have listened. While guilt gnawed at her conscience for the burden he'd taken up, she was glad he was with her today.

They'd been forced to take a longer route to the prison due to an accident which had shut down part of I-40. Still, the ride was relatively short. Troy explained the prison protocol to River. Kevin reminded her to stay by Troy's side—as if that warning was necessary.

"Have you considered what you're going to say to him?"

River was surprised it had taken this long for him to ask. "No. I'm going to let Troy do the talking. I'm more interested in his reaction to me. Zeke doesn't know I'm the second visitor, does he?" she asked, turning to Troy.

"No. He knows I'm an investigator, but not the details of our visit. I assume he agreed because they don't get many visitors."

"Why are you meeting with the son? Who made that decision?" Kevin asked. "I assume the Engleharts didn't flip a coin."

"The warden made the decision. We were lucky to get permission to see any of them."

"He'd be in his thirties now," River mused.

"I think it would be better for you if you were meeting with the mother," Kevin argued.

"Stop worrying." River reached through opening between the seats and took his hand.

"We didn't get a choice," Troy repeated. "Besides, Zeke will be behind plexiglass and a guard will be nearby. Meeting the son could play to our advantage. It wouldn't be the first time a man bragged about his exploits to an attractive woman."

Kevin scowled at Troy over the last remark. Troy didn't notice or didn't care. She settled back into her seat and studied the massive complex as they approached the prison. The huge institutional tan and brown buildings were surrounded by fencing topped with barb and razor wire. It was ominous and depressing. The vision wasn't one that would leave her anytime soon.

"I'll follow your lead," she said to Troy, turning away from the window. "If there's anything you want me to steer clear of, say so now."

"Let me give him a shot before you speak up. If you don't want to talk to him at all, that's okay, too."

They pulled up to the guard's station used by visitors. Troy opened his window and pulled out his identification. While the guard checked the visitor's log, he looked over his shoulder at River. "If Zeke recognizes you, we may have to change tactics and use that to our advantage. Think you can handle that?"

"I'll sure as hell try. We came here for answers. I don't want to leave without getting them."

Parking in a space near the visitor center, both Troy

and Kevin checked their watches. "How long?" Kevin asked.

"We have him for forty-five minutes, but it will be his call if he wants to use all the time allotted. Assuming he does, add in the time it will take to get through security. I'd say at least an hour. Maybe a bit more."

Troy jumped out and helped River down from her seat. "Don't worry," he said to Kevin. "I've got her."

"I've got myself," River corrected him. She looked over her shoulder to assure Kevin, but his seat was empty. Suddenly, Troy bobbed to the side and Kevin was standing in front of her. His lips touched hers. Not hungry—but hurting. Rising to the balls of her feet, she returned the kiss. She stroked his cheek, hoping to brush away his fear for her safety. "I'll be fine," she whispered, cupping his jaw. "I promise. Nothing is going to happen to me in there."

29

Troy tossed the keys to Kevin then rushed her toward the building. River shivered as they made their way across the parking lot. She could see her breath. They cast no shadows as the sky was gloomy and dark. She felt the chilled air through her clothes. It wasn't cold enough to snow but damned it if didn't feel like it. How quickly she'd forgotten what early spring was like in the mountains. Occasionally, there would be warm, sunny days, but mostly it was damp and cold this time of year.

Once they were inside, they were forced to go through several layers of security checkpoints. At each stop, she had to swallow the rising anxiety. She wasn't going to let Zeke Englehart see her sweat.

Finally, they were led into a visitation area. The tan walls and closely cropped brown carpeting matched the dreary colors on the exterior of the buildings. River counted a dozen cubicles for visitors to meet with prisoners. Partitions extended from the wall giving each cubicle some semblance of privacy. A small counter stretched beneath the plexiglass that divided the visitors from the prisoners. A telephone handset hung on each partition wall. The set-up was duplicated on the prisoners' side. The place was cold and unwelcoming.

With the exception of the guard who stood near the door, Troy and River were alone. The two of them had been told that they'd have the room to themselves. Englehart was not a popular prisoner and, therefore, the prison did their best to keep him isolated as to not cause trouble. Other inmates scheduled to meet with family were being directed to different visitation areas. Troy pulled a chair from the next cubicle over and indicated for River to take a seat. Then they waited.

River almost didn't recognize Zeke when he was led into the room. He'd grown up, and bulked up, from the scrawny young man she'd seen at the trial. While his physical appearance had changed, the madness and evil reflected in his eyes remained.

Taking the seat across from them, he barely spared Troy a glance before zeroing in on River. There was no recognition in his appraisal of her. It was more sexual than anything else.

Troy tapped on the glass, returning Zeke's attention to him. He indicated the phone and they both picked up the communication device. Troy held the handset loosely to his right ear so River could lean in and pick up the other end of the conversation.

"Who do I owe for this visit? I haven't seen such a mighty fine piece of meat since I arrived here."

Troy's grip on the phone tightened, if his white knuckles were any indication. She patted his thigh, knowing Englehart wouldn't see the signal she was giving him. She could handle the insults.

Troy introduced himself as a private investigator but avoided introducing River. He'd given her a small note pad and pen when they'd entered the building. She pulled it out of her back pocket, giving Englehart the impression she was the note-taker.

"We need some information," Troy started. "What can you tell us about Reverend Roxbury?"

"This is about Roxbury? What I say to my minister is confidential." Zeke turned his head slightly to look at Troy. He narrowed his gaze, clearly annoyed that his attention had been taken away from River.

"While I've no doubt your conversations would be interesting to hear about, I'm not looking to invade your spiritual privacy. I'm asking how you met him."

"Why should I tell you? Why do you want to know?"

"He's come up in one of our investigations. It seems strange that a relatively new and unknown minister would be serving your religious needs. I understand you've had several offers from other preachers to do the same."

River scribbled on her pad, only occasionally glancing up.

"Ma heard about him. She liked what he had to say. He's come to see us a few times. What's it to you?"

"Has he helped?"

"In what way? He ain't gonna get us out of here."

Had they expected him to? How odd, but River had to remember they were all a bit crazy. Correction, they were mad as hatters, in her opinion.

"Spiritually," Troy clarified. River had no idea where this was going.

"What the hell is this? Some sort of a reference check on the reverend?"

"In a sense. He may have been involved in some trouble with a friend of ours. You're an interesting member of his rather small following. It's possible you could give us some knowledge or insight."

Englehart quieted. He obviously recognized a fishing expedition. They might all be crazy, but crazy didn't mean stupid.

"Who's your delicious friend?" Zeke asked, his cold eyes drifting over River. "We weren't properly introduced." The man was all but drooling. From the salacious looks she was getting; he could care less about her name. It was only a means to change the subject and focus his attention on her.

"River Chandler."

River blinked. Had the sudden announcement surprised Englehart as much as it had her? She was certain they'd eventually get around to her identity, but Troy dropped the bomb without warning. Shooting a glance in Troy's direction, she noted he was studying Englehart intently. River didn't have any trouble gauging the monster's reaction. An unholy excitement rose from within him. She saw it in his eyes. The look sent shivers through her.

"Hot damn." The wicked excitement had Zeke surging to his feet, leaning closer to the plexiglass. She couldn't miss the ridge that formed in the loose-fitting prison pants. The guard shoved him back down into his chair. Troy had noticed the reaction, as well. Quickly acting as a shield, he'd shifted his weight so his torso temporarily blocked her view of Zeke.

Once he was reseated, he continued his litany. "You sure turned out mighty fine," Zeke said, licking his lips. "Wait until Ma and Pa learn you're all grown up and pretty as a shiny penny."

"All grown up and thriving unlike you."

"What are you doing here? What happened to bring you here after all this time?" The words snapped out like a curse. Then just as quickly, his persona changed. "Did you miss me?" He puckered his lips and threw air kisses in her direction. She reminded herself that the man was certifiable. His actions made her skin crawl, but she managed to keep her expression blank. This Zeke wanted a rise out of her. He wasn't going to get it.

"We're wasting our time with him, you know?" She looked at Troy. "He's still a moron."

"Fuck you."

"You wish." This time she gave Englehart a wry grin.

She saw the light the moment it blinked on behind the madness in his eyes. "Somebody's after the one that got away. That's why you're here." His gaze drifted over her, mentally stripping her of her clothing. "You wouldn't get away from me now. Imagine the fun we'd have before I sliced and diced you." One of his hands disappeared beneath the counter. His arm continued to move as he stroked himself. She glanced at the guard. Either he didn't see Zeke's attempt at self-gratification or didn't care.

"Enough!" Troy cut him off, slamming his fist against the counter. "What do you know about the threats to Ms. Chandler?"

"I'm done talking to you, asshole," he said to Troy. "I will talk to this luscious lady or I'll tell the guard to take me back to my cell."

Troy pressed the receiver against his bulky thigh and leaned over to whisper to River.

"Can you do this? Can you keep the bastard talking—see if he slips up?" he asked.

She took a deep breath. "I'll do my best."

"What the hell are you two whispering to each other? You getting a piece of her ass?" Englehart yelled into his end of the phone.

River yanked the phone from Troy's hand. "What's it to you? Aren't you getting enough in here? Oh, wait. It's your ass they're getting a piece of, isn't it?" She slung his words back at him.

"Bitch."

"Is that what they call you? A mama's boy must be easy pickings." They hadn't gotten anywhere with civil conversation except to confirm he was still an evil, crazy, son-of-a-bitch. Perhaps pissing him off would do the trick. Apparently, she'd hit a target. If looks really could kill, she'd be dead on the floor.

"You don't want to know what I'd do to you if I get my hands on you." His eyes were steely black. His left hand fisted while his right held the phone so tight, she thought the receiver might snap.

"But that's not going to happen, is it? You're in here for the rest of your rotten, scum-sucking life. It doesn't mean you didn't find someone to complete the job you were incapable of finishing. A fourteen-year-old girl brought you down. I'll do it again, if necessary."

"You can't touch me in here." He was defiant.

"Your life can be made worse," Troy warned him.

"Go to hell," Englehart sneered.

"Why won't you talk about the Reverend? Is he involved?" River asked.

"What I discuss with my minister is off limits."

"Here we go again," River gave him an exaggerated eye roll and shook her head. Both actions intended to piss Zeke off. "He's not a priest. He's not sworn to any oath of confidentiality. Maybe we'll just see what he has to say about you."

"You think he'll talk? Ha! He's a rabbit."

River leaned closer to the divider. "Who's he afraid of? It can't be you."

Englehart's mouth snapped shut. Interesting. She caught Troy's nod of the head and kept going.

"Do you have any privileges in here? You'd best enjoy them while you can." River was shooting blind on the last remark. She knew nothing of prisons or privileges inmates receive—just what she saw in the movies. Still, it felt like a good parting shot.

"Are we done?" she asked Troy.

He nodded, taking the phone from her to hang it up. Just before the click, Englehart yelled into his end of the line. "You won't get anything out of that limp dick."

THE MINUTE the pair exited the building, Kevin was out of the vehicle and halfway across the parking lot. He took off his windbreaker and threw it over River's shoulders. It was getting late and the temperature was dropping.

"How are you doing?"

"Fine." She tucked the jacket around her.

"How'd it go?" The short, snappy response told him different.

Troy grinned. "Metaphorically speaking, she packs a hell of a punch."

"We didn't get anything out of him," River grumbled. "A slow strip tease would have worked better."

"What?" Kevin asked over Troy's laughter. "And what's so damn funny?"

Kevin helped River into the rear seat, then jumped in after her. "Does someone want to explain what happened?" he asked as soon as Troy slipped into the driver's seat. Even with all his deployments, Kevin swore the last hour had been the longest of his life.

"He wouldn't tell us anything," River said.

Kevin pulled her close. She was shaking. "We need some heat back here," he snapped at Troy as soon as the engine was engaged. He suspected it wasn't just the cold that was affecting River. "You two spent a long time with someone who wouldn't talk."

"He didn't confess to anything, but River pushed him into saying plenty," Troy responded.

"Why don't you start at the beginning," Kevin suggested, as they pulled out on to the highway.

By the time they were done relating the visit, Kevin swore if the bastard ever got out of prison, he'd wring his neck for the things he'd said to River.

"Your lady has balls of steel," Troy grinned at them in the rearview mirror. "Zeke didn't hide his interest in her, so she played him like a fiddle. He confirmed what we already suspected. In spite of being housed separately, the family seems to communicate freely. Then there's Roxbury. Engle-hart could have given us something useless about the guy—something innocuous. Instead, he kept repeating the same mantra—which just happens to be the exact same thing the reverend told Colt. It's like they're reading from a script they weren't allowed to deviate from. I've got to wonder, who gave them that script?"

"Where does that leave us?" Kevin asked.

"Reverend Limp Dick," Troy chuckled. "See if you can raise Colt."

30

———

They met up with Colt at the resort. The four of them took a corner booth in the lounge. This wasn't River's first visit to The Carolina Inn. She occasionally met her aunt here for dinner, but they hadn't spent any time in the bar area. It was off-season so the place was virtually empty. Most of the guests were in the dining room this time of night. The soft clinking of silverware told her the number of diners were also slim.

The guys ordered burgers along with local brews. River opted for the French Onion soup and an Old Fashioned, with a double shot of bourbon.

When the drinks arrived, she took a large gulp. She raised her glass again when she noted the three men were watching her.

"What?"

"Are you all right?" Kevin asked.

"I will be in a minute," she said, this time taking a smaller sip. She pressed her back into the cushioned booth and waited for the buzz to kick in.

Troy picked up her drink and took a whiff. "Whoa.

We'd best get this show on the road before she slides onto the floor."

"Ha, ha. I've had stronger and I think I earned it after facing Zeke Englehart today." She visibly shivered at the statement.

"Can't argue that," Troy said. "The guy was enough to make *my* skin crawl. If there hadn't been a barrier between us, I would have pounded the shit out of him for the way the lecher ogled you."

"You agreed my presence might prompt a response. We got one."

"One you turned to our advantage."

"I still don't see how I helped. He didn't tell us anything useful."

"You made him nervous. He didn't have any reason to be jittery unless you'd touched a nerve," Troy said.

"You think he knows what's been going on and his family is involved?" Colt asked.

"He knows something."

"Did you dig up anything on Roxbury?" Kevin asked Colt. "Rick says he's reached a dead end."

"There's something definitely off with the Reverend. I found a couple of locals who said they were invited to attend his church, but never went back after the first service."

"Why?" River asked.

"They didn't go for his dark take on Christianity. He appears to be a "fire-and-brimstone" theologian rather than a "love-your-neighbor" kind. Both of them used the word 'uncomfortable' when they discussed his sermonizing."

"Those are individual opinions," Kevin pointed out. "There are plenty of wacko preachers out there who see more evil than good. It doesn't tie him to River."

"No. It doesn't. He did have a rifle propped against the wall of his barn."

"Which means nothing," River said, fighting with a string of cheese from the top of her soup. "I'd bet at least ninety percent of North Carolinians own guns. There's not a person who lives in the country who doesn't own at least one. A rifle comes in handy for hunting and chasing away unwelcome visitors."

"If he is involved with the harassment, how did he hook up with the Engleharts?" Kevin asked. "According to the prison authorities the Engleharts reached out to Roxbury—not the other way around."

"How would they know to reach out to him? There's got to be a connection," Colt said. "My gut tells me Roxbury is involved. Troy? You up to some stake-outs?"

The question cut through the pleasant haze the alcohol and warm food had provided. "Stake-outs?" River cocked her head toward Colt, but her movement was restricted. Kevin's arm rested on her shoulder, holding her in place. When had that happened?

"Are you serious? I'm no investigator, but it doesn't sound like you have much more than a hunch about the guy. Is that reason enough to sit out in the cold?"

"You're back in town. If Roxbury is connected, he's going to know. If he's connected, he's going to react to the news. Is that your thinking?" Kevin asked his friends.

"Exactly." Troy took a sip of his beer. "If he found out about the visit to the Engleharts, he may be getting nervous. We need to find out if any of the Engleharts made calls after your visit."

"That's a lot of ifs," River commented. "You're not positive if Roxbury or the Engleharts are involved in this shit."

"If not them, then who?" Colt asked.

River's head dropped back against Kevin's arm. "I don't know." She left her head resting against Kevin's muscular forearm and closed her eyes. Her head hurt. Whether it was from the potent drink or the long, stressful day, she didn't know or care. She wanted to go home.

"How the hell did Roxbury connect with the Engleharts?" Kevin asked. "No way we can get his phone records, I assume?" he asked, glancing from Troy to Colt.

"Not going to legally happen with what little we have," Colt confirmed. "And we don't have anyone who can do a bit of surreptitious snooping this time."

River raised her head and let out a long breath. "Why don't I go see Roxbury?"

"The hell you will," Kevin blurted out.

She straightened her back at the comment and shuffled in her seat, putting a little distance between them. Sadly, it was only a few inches, but she was making a point. "Don't start telling me what I can and can't do," she said. Silence. Apparently, Kevin was smart enough to hold his tongue.

"You believe I got a reaction out of Englehart which was helpful," she said to Troy. "Why can't we use the same tactic on Roxbury?"

"The situation is a bit different," Colt began. "As badly as he put it, Kevin's insinuation is correct. This time there wouldn't be any plexiglass protecting you."

"One of you would be there," she said. She sure as hell didn't plan on meeting the guy on her own.

"Of course," Colt told her, "but assuming he knows you're here, he'll be expecting you. His reaction could be practiced. A visit might tell us something, but it's nothing worth putting you in danger."

"But what if he doesn't know I'm here? His reaction would be genuine."

"If he doesn't know you're here, then my bet is he isn't involved."

River rubbed her forehead between her thumb and forefinger. "And, therefore, he wouldn't have any reaction to seeing me. Wouldn't that, in itself, tell you something?"

"It's possible," Troy answered her question.

"She's been put through enough without adding another face-to-face meeting with her possible stalker," Kevin argued.

"I agree," Colt said. "Give us some time, River. Rick is trying to persuade the warden to review the Engleharts' mail and call logs to see if there are any red flags. I think Rick has him convinced that you might be in danger due to the Engleharts' association with Roxbury. If he agrees, we may learn a lot more about the connection between the reverend and the Engleharts."

"Plus, Josie's still digging, and something may turn up while Colt and I are on recon," Troy added. "We'll give your idea consideration if we don't get anywhere. I don't think we need to shove you out there just yet."

"I don't like sitting around."

"Go figure," Kevin muttered.

She caught the comment as he moved closer to her once again. She reached for what was left of her drink, but Kevin nudged it away. She glared at him. "I also don't like being told what I can and can't do."

"Another news flash," Kevin said. This time not hiding his sarcasm. "Are you always a mean drunk?"

She was ready to tear into him when Colt and Troy slid out of the booth.

"We'll catch up with you guys tomorrow," Troy said, making a quick retreat.

River was torn between being polite and pissed. She opted to remain silent until the two men had left.

"What the hell is your problem?" she asked Kevin.

"I don't have one. C'mon. Let's get you to bed. You've had enough for one day."

She stumbled as she got out of the booth. The action had her grabbing at Kevin for support, but when he caught her, her immediate instinct was to push him away. He was getting way too bossy, but his arm steadied her on the uneven surface, so she swore at him silently instead as they made their way toward the door.

As soon as they stepped outside, she forgot she was mad at him. Instead, she was glad for his warmth. She was shivering when Kevin lifted her into a massive pick-up truck and buckled her in.

KEVIN FOLLOWED the GPS route to River's cabin. Fortunately, it was in memory since the guys had, apparently, done the same. While her cabin was a straight shot through the woods, the road bypassing the national preserve took them away from her home before turning back toward it. River wasn't available to give directions. She'd fallen asleep—or passed out—the minute the heat in the cab cranked in. He suspected it was a bit of both. The double shot of bourbon would hit a small-framed woman hard. Add in the stress of seeing Zeke Englehart, and her body had reached its limits for today. Her breathing was steady, and her color was good, so he wasn't particularly worried. She'd simply hit the metaphorical wall.

From what Troy had told him, she'd put Englehart in his place. Better yet, she'd instilled some fear in the bastard —but not near as much as he deserved. Kevin couldn't imagine how tortuous the meeting had been for her, but she'd not only handled herself well today, but given back better than she got. His chest puffed out a bit in pride.

He shouldn't be getting this close, but while he'd waited for River and Troy to emerge from the prison, he admitted it was already too late. Whatever happened between them happened. They'd have to deal with it. He wasn't turning away from his emotions any longer.

The sun had already set when he pulled up to the cabin. Kevin glanced at River. She was out cold. Her head rested in the space between the seat rest and window. Her hands lay limply in her lap. He opted to leave her rest while he made a quick check of their surroundings and the house.

Retrieving his weapon from the center console, he left the engine running and the heat on. After hitting the lock button on the key fob, he trotted around the side of the home. There was no reason to suspect they had a visitor—and no reason to be assured they didn't have one.

He circled the cabin, checking the doors and windows. All remained closed and latched. The flashlight on his phone wasn't that strong and limited his distance vision, but he saw nothing to set off his radar as he skirted the perimeter.

Making his way back to the front of the cabin, he unlocked the door. He entered the code he'd been given for the security system. River hated the electronic warning system. She'd told him it stole something from the serenity of the place.

The cabin had a limited number of rooms, but they were spacious enough for the family of four who spent their summers here. He did wonder how they managed with two kids and one bathroom. It must have made for some interesting mornings. An open kitchen and dining area were to his right. He didn't want to leave River alone much longer. He made a quick search of the bedrooms, one of which obviously served as her workroom while she was here. There was no place to hide in the bath.

Kevin trotted back to the vehicle. River was still asleep, her head lolling slightly to the side. She was going to have a crick in her neck in the morning. She didn't stir when he opened the passenger side door. Unclipping her seat belt, he lifted her into his arms. She squirmed a little, but those ice blue eyes never opened. Instead, she snuggled closer. His heart warmed.

Shoving the cabin door closed with his foot, he carried River into the bedroom. He'd lock up after he got her settled.

Tossing back the covers, he laid River on the queen size bed. He should get her out of her clothing. She'd be more comfortable in her night clothes, or better yet, nothing at all—which was a selfish thought. His mind was already wandering, imagining tracing the series of goosebumps on her normally smooth and silky skin. He turned away and began quietly searching her chest of drawers. He found a pair of cotton pajama bottoms and a well-worn, large t-shirt.

He took his time, savoring the act of undressing her. He promised to repeat the action when she was an active participant. He managed to get her into the loose-fitting clothing. He stopped at one point, concerned that nothing seemed to disturb her, but her vitals were good. As he suspected earlier, either the liquor or exhaustion, or a combination of both, had taken their toll on her today. Pulling the covers over her, he left the room. He'd wanted to climb in bed with her, but he had a few things to take care of before he settled in for the night.

He found a large flashlight under the kitchen sink. Locking the door behind him, he made a thorough recon of the area. Colt and Troy would have checked the grounds this morning, but that was no guarantee the property hadn't been visited in the meantime. Other than a few critters scurrying about, he saw nothing that got his guard up.

Even at night, it was easy to understand the appeal this place had for River. There was solitude in addition to the sounds and fragrances of nature. The earthy smell of decaying leaves mixed with the rich soil that created nutrients for the plants. He caught the slight whiff of some early blooming flowers. While many would claim this place devoid of any noise, Kevin could hear night creatures scurrying through the woods along with the rustling of coniferous branches as the cold breezed brushed them against one another. There was the trickle of water nearby. Similar to being at the beach as the waves rolled gently onshore, it gave him a sense of peace.

When he returned to the cabin, he set the alarm and nudged up the thermostat a notch before returning to the bedroom. Stripping down to his boxers, he draped his clothes over the footboard, then crawled into the bed beside her. Pulling her close, he fell into a light sleep.

31

aking a sip of the hot coffee Kevin had brewed, River rested her forearms against the log railing which surrounded the front porch of her cabin. Anger, sadness, and fear wrestled within her. She battled each one into submission. She wouldn't allow her stalker the satisfaction of rattling her. Her heart had ached when she'd left this place. It would shatter if she sold it.

This had been her home in spite of the fact that she should have died here—would have, if she'd hadn't been a disobeying, obstinate adolescent all those years ago. She pushed the deathly images aside once again.

River scanned the woodlands surrounding the cabin, listening to the mountain breeze as it tickled the leaves of the towering evergreens. Water, no longer frozen solid, bubbled over river stones in a nearby stream, hidden by mountainous terrain. Birdsong would soon be filling the air.

It wouldn't be much longer before the flowers at the base of the birdbath would push their way through the damp earth, reaching for the light. Their fragrance and colors would attract butterflies and other nectar seeking insects throughout the summer. The garden and birdbath were located where the detached garage once stood. Years earlier, in anger and pain, she'd torn the building down—slat-by-wooden-slat. Her hands were bloodied, but the act had been cleansing. Later, when she'd dug up the soil and planted the flowering perennials, she'd cried buckets, but the ground that had once been saturated with death, now welcomed life. Despite all that had happened, she couldn't picture anyone else living here—or God forbid, level the place.

In spite of her isolation, she was aware many of the locals saw the memorial as a sad reminder of what had happened. To River, it was a homage to her family. Their deaths did not erase them from this earth. They were still here, pushing her forward.

She tugged her sweater tighter against the chill. Spring came grudgingly to these mountains. It would have been hard to imagine a year ago, but the warm Florida sunshine had its draw, especially this time of year.

She expected Kevin to come storming out any minute. She gotten dressed, grabbed a cup of coffee and stepped outside while he was in the shower. She didn't expect he'd be in the bathroom long. His protective instinct wouldn't allow it, which was both annoying and endearing. Taking care of herself was something she'd been damn proud of until recent events. Now someone cared about her—someone she shouldn't care about in return. He'd be leaving soon. God knew, she didn't need the heartache any more than he did.

"You shouldn't be out here by yourself," Kevin scolded her a few seconds later when he stepped out onto the porch. Surprisingly, steam wasn't streaming from his ears, but those dark, worried eyes bore into hers. Lordy, he was magnificent.

"I needed a little time alone out here," she found herself responding. Her heart stopped fluttering and the ache returned. She and Dan had exchanged the exact same words the day she'd left for Sanibel.

"You okay?" Kevin asked, those eyes narrowing.

Sucking in a breath, she exhaled slowly. Dan would lecture her if he were here. He'd constantly reminded her to honor the dead—not dwell on their deaths, but had she honored them, or had she come up short in that area? How would she honor Dan? What would he want her to do?

"I'm going to take a shower," she said, stepping around him. He laid his hand on her shoulder.

"What's wrong? Did something happen?"

River raised her hands to cover her face. When had she become so insensitive of others? Her silence and disregard for his obvious concern was selfish.

"I'm fine," she said, letting her hands fall. "I was piling one thought on top of another. I'll sort it out."

"Sometimes voicing your concerns or worries helps. I'm a good listener." Kevin opened the door, guiding her inside.

She raised herself to her toes, kissing him on the cheek before laying her head on his chest. He pulled her closer.

"Are you going to tell me what's going on?" he asked again. "I appreciate the show of affection, but you have me a bit concerned."

"Which is why I love you." The words were out of her mouth before her brain had engaged. Oh, shit. Maybe he didn't hear her. Maybe she imagined she'd said it. Her emotions were twisted up in knots this morning. He didn't release her but continued to hold her firmly against his chest. In the silence she heard the beat of his heart as it ratcheted up. Crap. She hadn't imagined it and he'd definitely heard her.

"I'm sorry," she said. "I don't know where that came from."

"Did you mean it?"

How did she answer? It wasn't fair to lay that at his feet. She was bitchy, neurotic and a target.

"River?"

"Truth?"

"Nothing but."

This time when she stepped back, his arms fell to his sides. She gazed up into his eyes and, not for the first time in her life, she wanted to run. The reason may be different, but the urge was there. She stood her ground and kept his gaze.

"I don't know. I know I feel different with you. I want to be near you. Knowing you will be leaving hurts, like a splinter in my heart. If that's the definition of love, then I guess I'm there."

"You don't seem very happy about it," Kevin's eyes were narrowed as if he were straining to see through to her soul. His lips formed a line as straight as a carpenter's level.

"I can give you a hundred reasons why," she answered, "but I think we'd best save this conversation for later. I need to stop by the police station before I see my aunt. I should also check to see if there is any additional information on Dan's memorial service. She'll want to know." River paused. "Can we talk tonight when I'm not as rushed, and my mind is clear? Hopefully clear, I should say."

His answer was a kiss. It was deep, demanding, and giving. She responded with the same vigor and enthusiasm. Her center warmed. The bedroom was only a few feet away. A few more steps and they would be there—then Kevin broke away.

"Go take your shower," he said, turning her by her shoulders so that she faced the bathroom. "I'll fix us something to eat."

River slipped from the bath to the bedroom wrapped in a large towel. Kevin had to rein in the primal instinct to follow her. Instead, he broke several eggs into a bowl and began to scramble them, doing his best to distract himself from the knowledge there was nothing beneath the towel but the body he was beginning to know simply by touch. She'd asked for some time. He'd give it to her, but his carnal and emotional needs battled inside him. He wanted her love because he'd come to the realization he was in love with her. Bad timing on both their parts.

As soon as he'd exited the bath this morning, he'd caught sight of her through the living room window as she stood on the porch. The urge to yank her back inside and away from any possible harm had him rushing toward the door, but he'd stopped. The wistful way she'd stared at the sculpture touched his heart. It wasn't possible to be her protector forever—nor would the tough woman want him to be. In addition, what sort of relationship would they have if he didn't trust her to make her own decisions?

So, he'd watched her, and the area beyond, as he gave her some time alone with her family. She had a deep connection to this place—one that would be hard, if not impossible, to break. There was the obvious beauty of the mountains along with the memories of her mother, father and little brother. It wasn't possible for him to imagine the pain of losing her entire family the way she had or of being the one who'd been left behind. How often did River feel alone in this world—even deserted? Based on their conversations, Dan and her aunt had tried to fill the void, how could anyone ever take the place of a loving parent, let alone two?

When his heart and his nerves told him she'd been outside alone too long, he hustled her inside. The confession of love had surprised them both. He wanted to delve into the revelation, but she'd been right. Her plate was full this morning. Tonight would be soon enough.

Speaking of plates, he found her small stash of dishes. Nothing fancy, but they served their purpose. The microwave pinged as River exited the bedroom.

"Something smells good," she said.

"Eggs and sausage. Troy and Colt left some provisions, but not a large variety."

"Sounds great. I'm hungry. Last night's soup didn't fill much of a hole."

"How's the head?" he asked. "I expected a bit of a hangover this morning."

"I wasn't lying when I said I can hold my liquor. No aftereffects. I think I was just tired and worn out. The bourbon added a punch."

"Your body needed it," Kevin commented as he dumped the eggs in the hot skillet. "You were in there a while," he said, indicating the bedroom. "Did you call your aunt?"

"No, not yet. I did call Dan's son, Jacob. The memorial is the day after tomorrow. Would you go with me?"

"I'd be honored to pay my respects." Kevin had already planned to go. It was going to be rough on her. She'd need support. Besides, you never knew who might show up. It would be a good idea for Colt or Troy to also be there. They'd be extra eyes watching for anything unusual.

"So, you still have to call you aunt?" Kevin asked, cutting into a sausage link.

"Yes." River rubbed the bridge of her nose.

"Are you nervous about calling her?"

"A little. She's going to be surprised I'm here. I didn't tell her when I was coming."

"I'd think she'd be happy you're back."

She puffed out her cheeks. "She would be—if I wasn't staying here. I told you, she's always been against my moving into the cabin. Knowing Dan was killed here, she'll think I'm nuts. I expect that to be a point of contention."

"You're an adult. You're free to make your own decisions." He reached across the table and took her hand. "Are you concerned she'll be upset I'm here?"

"She'll be fixated on my staying at the cabin. You'll only be a blip on her radar."

"I can understand her aversion. She lost her sister here. As I said, you're an adult. You have the right to be here and, if you're happy here, then she should be happy for you."

River pushed back from the table. "She is happy for me, but she can't get past her hatred of this place. She claims the property is jinxed or evil."

"Could she have a point?" He joined her at the sink.

"Huh?" The skin across her forehead rippled. Her eyes were wide.

"What I'm asking is there something here that draws evil, for lack of a better word, to this place? Is it possible there's something of value on this land? Something that would make it worth the campaign of harassment to get you off of it?"

Shaking her head, she ran water in the sink and added

dish soap. "I lived here for years before the gaslighting started."

"Maybe they were in jail or out of the country."

"You must read too many thrillers," she said. "Even if it were the case, they would have gotten what they wanted when I left for Florida."

"I'll ask Troy and Colt if either of them checked the property." He dried the dish she'd handed him. He smiled at her exaggerated eye roll.

"Knock yourselves out," she told him.

River gave him the details of Dan's memorial then went to her office to call her aunt. Kevin noted the changes in River's demeanor when she spoke about her aunt. There was the obvious affection for the woman who helped raise her, but there was also an underlying anxiety. Was it guilt? She'd mentioned a number of times that she felt she'd interfered with Amy's personal life when she'd been saddled with a teen to raise. Kevin was looking forward to meeting Amy and getting his take on her. She'd made major changes to her life to take on an orphaned niece. She deserved kudos for that alone. The alternative would have been the social services system for River. For a young teenage girl, the results could have been disastrous.

Kevin took the time to text Colt and Troy then waited for one of them to call him back. He didn't have to wait long.

"How are things there?" Colt asked, skipping the niceties.

"Quiet. River is talking to her aunt now. If Amy isn't tied up, we'll head over there when they're finished." Kevin glanced at the closed door. "I assume Troy has watch duty since you're the one who's calling?"

"He took over this morning. No movements last night," he reported.

"I'll send a text with the information for Dan's service. I'll go with River, but if one of you is free, I'd like another set of eyes."

"Whoever has the cleanest shirt will be there."

"Did you search the property for anything unusual or out of place while you were here?" Kevin asked.

"We walked it. Didn't notice anything. Why? Something off?"

"No. I had this hairbrained idea that River might have been chased off so someone would be free to search the property at will." It did sound crazy when he said it out loud.

"You're not thinking buried treasure?"

"Nothing that exotic. Why would anyone go to the trouble they did to chase her away? Was there something here they needed time to find?"

"I think you're reaching. We'll go over the grounds again, but remember she's been gone for months. If your theory has merit, they've had plenty of time to find whatever it was they wanted. By now, nature would have covered their tracks."

Kevin huffed. "I'm grasping at straws, I guess. You still think Roxbury is our best lead?"

"Right now, it's all we have to go on. It's a good lead with a connection to the Engleharts."

"Did Rick get anything from the prison yet?" The door to River's workroom opened. She leaned into the doorjamb waiting for him to finish. He didn't think he'd ever get tired of the sight of her.

"I talked to Rick last night. He hasn't spoken with the warden again. He's pushed as hard as he thinks he can without severing that tie altogether. The guy's radar is up. Rick thinks he's a straight shooter and won't let the matter drop. We're going to have to wait for him to get back to us."

"Thanks, Colt. Call if anything turns up. And get some rest."

"Are we ready to hit the road?" Kevin asked River as he pocketed his phone. She gave him a small smile. He was becoming familiar with her body language and facial expressions. In this case, they told him the conversation wasn't as stressful as she'd expected.

"Looks like," she said. "Aunt Amy is home. She's prepping for an event tonight. Don't be surprised if we wind up being taste-testers."

"I think I can handle that."

"You just had breakfast."

"So?" He grinned at her raised brows. Those blue eyes glinted from the sunlight streaming through the windows. He was surprised how easily they still robbed him of his breath.

32

Kevin had insisted on driving even though she could have made the drive with her eyes closed. Now she wished she'd argued the point. If she'd been behind the wheel, her mind would be occupied with something other than the admission she'd blurted out earlier.

River gave him points for not pushing the subject. His singular response to her declaration of love had been the searing kiss that almost had her stripping him bare where they stood. What had possessed her to give voice to her feelings? It didn't matter. She'd said it and she'd promised to discuss it tonight. At the moment, she had no idea what would come out of her mouth, but she'd be honest with him. He deserved no less.

They made the final turn onto Mill Creek Road. She'd warned her aunt she was bringing a friend. During the call, Aunt Amy had peppered her with questions. River had put her off. What had surprised River was her aunt hadn't said a single word about her staying in the cabin. Perhaps she was distracted learning River hadn't returned alone.

Like most of the properties in the area, Aunt Amy's home sat on a couple of acres of land. People liked their open spaces out here. She lived close enough to Asheville to service her customers, but far enough away to avoid most of the tourists who flocked to the area.

Kevin pulled into the driveway and parked near the front walk. "She's not going to be surprised by my presence, is she?" he asked.

The drive had been made in silence. Both of them internalizing their thoughts. Now that they had arrived at their destination, it would seem their minds were focusing on the current issue.

"She knows I'm bringing someone with me, and she knows about most of the shit that went down in Florida. I left out a few details—like getting shot at. Do not tell her. She'll freak out."

"Anything else I should veer away from?" he asked, opening the driver's side door. "Does she know you were accosted twice?"

"Yes. I think I told her everything, but the events surrounding the shooting since it wasn't connected to this end of things. I didn't see any point in worrying her," she said slipping off the seat.

"And us? Does she know you and I have a relationship?" Kevin took her by the elbow as they made their way up the walk.

"She'll figure it out quick enough."

The door swung open as they stepped onto the porch. Aunt Amy stood in the front door of the old farmhouse with a dish towel thrown over her shoulder. River smiled. Some things never changed. There was always a dish towel.

River stepped into her aunt's open arms. As soon as they locked around her, she began to cry. "Dan's gone," she said. "Why? Why did they have to kill him?" As her aunt squeezed her tight, River opened the flood gates and bawled. Dan had been a huge part of her life. Like Aunt Amy, he'd been there when she needed him.

With one last squeeze, River took a step back and met the eyes of the tall woman she hadn't seen in eight months. She smelled of spices, something lemony and home. She'd altered the direction of her life to step up and take in a frightened fourteen-year-old girl. River was old enough to realize she'd been a handful—a teenager filled with guilt, anger and grief—but Aunt Amy had done exactly that.

She hadn't changed much while River had been gone. She'd kept her pixie hairstyle, a style that suited her both in features and career—no hair to get in her way while preparing her catering jobs. River noted the gray streaks in her dark brown hair. Had it been there when she'd left, or had the last year been particularly hard on her aunt? She was forty-eight years old but looked older. A sliver of shame engulfed River. Had she been so wrapped up in herself that she hadn't bothered to pay closer attention to her aunt?

"This is Kevin Slawter," she said, grabbing his hand and pulling him to her side. "He's the man who came to my rescue on the beach when I was attacked."

"Nice to meet you, Ms. Scott," Kevin said, extending his hand.

"Did you follow her here to protect her or for another reason?"

"Aunt Amy. It's none of your business." River hadn't dated much when she'd lived with her aunt and there was never anyone special in college. She'd never brought someone to meet her aunt.

"I'm here for moral support," Kevin told her.

"Sorry. Didn't mean to be short. This is all very upsetting besides being so rushed at the moment. Why don't we get in from out of the dampness?" Her aunt stepped into the entry hall. "Do you mind if I work while we talk?"

River relaxed a bit. She remembered her aunt was on a deadline. It wasn't unusual for her to be tense when she was pushed.

"I warned Kevin we'd probably wind up taste testers," she smiled. "I've missed your cooking."

"Sadly, you didn't inherit that gene."

"No, I lean more to the artistic side," River teased.

"Hey, I'm artistic, too. I just do it with food."

"Good thing. I don't think there would be a lot of demand for your stick figure seating plans."

Her aunt laughed as she entered her kitchen. This was her comfort zone. She was always happiest in the midst of cooking.

"I think I have an hors d'oeuvre or two to spare."

The room hadn't changed since River had last visited. The kitchen had been enlarged years before to accommodate restaurant-size double ovens, cooktop and sink. A humongous worktable filled the center of the room.

"What's the venue?" River asked, pulling out one of the stools from under the countertop.

"A nice-sized book club in South Asheville," Aunt Amy answered.

"Biltmore Forest?" River asked, grinning. Only a book club in Biltmore Forest would have their gathering catered. It was the wealthiest neighborhood in Asheville, sitting next to the famous Biltmore Estates. "That's fantastic."

"It's not a big deal," her aunt commented as she piped filling into small phyllo shells.

"You should be excited. There's a lot of old money in that neighborhood. This might turn into something bigger."

"You know I don't do big events. I'd need a bigger kitchen, have to hire help—I'd need more of everything. I've put what I can into this business. It's a Catch 22. I would have to cater bigger events to grow, but I can't grow unless I get bigger events. The other option is to gamble— to take out a loan, move to a commercial location, and hire staff." Her aunt shrugged. "This is fine. I'm happy with this set-up. I do a good business. You know that."

"I do. I didn't mean to touch a nerve." River couldn't blame her aunt for not wanting to go through the hassle of a loan and the debt that would hang over her head. Aunt Amy had always said she was happy with the way things were. River hadn't pushed. Perhaps it was time they talked about it. River was flush, thanks to the trust and portfolio left to her by her parents. She'd make time to sit down with her aunt and discuss her business after the current crisis passed.

"No nerve touched, sweetie."

Two small plates appeared on the countertop in front of River and Kevin. A half-dozen hors d'oeuvres adorned each piece of china.

"These look delicious," Kevin said, complimenting her aunt.

"What are these creations?" River asked.

"You should remember most of them, but these two are new," she said, pointing out two items on the plate. "The puffed pastry is stuffed with quail and a Boursin cheese and the bacon wrapped item is rabbit rumaki. I was lucky to get my hands-on fresh game this late in the season. Now, you didn't come here for recipes," her aunt said. "When is the memorial?"

Aunt Amy slid the tray she'd been working on into one of the massive ovens, set the timer, then turned to meet River's stare. The sadness in her aunt's eyes reflected the break in River's heart. Kevin reached for her hand, giving it a squeeze. Her aunt handed her a napkin.

"Tomorrow evening," she said, gathering herself. River gave her the details while Aunt Amy flew through the large kitchen. She continued to hold Kevin's hand under the table. It grounded her and kept her from breaking down as little memories of her time with Dan kept popping into her head. Kevin peppered her aunt with questions about River teenage years, doing his best to keep things light. She was grateful for the mini mental diversions.

They conversed until all the food was prepared and ready for transport. River and Kevin helped load the catering van.

"Do you want us to pick you up tomorrow night?" River asked.

"No. I have a meeting with a prospective client in the afternoon, so I'll leave from there. I may even be a little late."

"Okay," River said, hesitating. "Look for us when you get there."

She stood silently until her aunt's vehicle disappeared over a hill. When she turned back toward their car, Kevin was staring at her.

"What?" she asked.

"I don't think your aunt likes me."

~

"You don't know that," River answered. "She was rushed, and the subject of Dan's death isn't exactly a positive topic of conversation. Do you care one way or the other?"

"She's important to you, so yes, I guess I do," Kevin said. He shut the passenger door as River buckled up. He may not have the skills to read people like some of his friends, but the vibes coming from her aunt were not warm or welcoming.

"How long has she had the business?"

"For as long as I can remember. Fortunately, I was old enough she didn't have to devote all her time to me. I was able to give her a hand with minor tasks while I was there."

"She said you couldn't cook."

River swatted him as he slid into the driver's seat. "I can cook, but I'm definitely not a gourmet chef."

"Your job was the cleanup, wasn't it?"

"We all have our talents."

Kevin laughed. River's eyes sparkled like rare diamonds as she giggled. She didn't laugh enough, but there hadn't been much to laugh about lately. He wanted to change that.

As he shifted the rental into reverse, his phone rang. He shoved the car back into park. "What's up, Rick?"

"A couple of things, although neither may add up to much. Kane's wife has disappeared."

"Who?"

"The gem dealer. The authorities can't locate his wife. They don't know if she's missing or running."

Kevin relaxed, letting out a deep breath. "Either way, it has nothing to do with River."

"I tend to agree, but it may be a piece of the puzzle we're missing."

"How?" He reached for River's hand and gave it a squeeze. Her shoulders had squared, and her attention was fixed on him.

"At this point, I have no idea."

"Great. You'll let us know, I assume, if you figure it out?" Kevin didn't see how the disappearance of the dead man's wife affected River. If it did, Rick would get to the bottom of it.

"You know it. Keep your guard up. I don't like loose ends."

"None of us do. Have you shared this with Colt or Troy?"

"They know."

"Put the phone on speaker," River broke in. Those sparkling eyes had narrowed. He wouldn't say she was angry, but annoyed fit the bill.

"Any reason I can't put you on speaker?" Kevin asked.

"You mean you haven't done that yet? Is she pissed?" Rick asked.

"Ah, maybe," he said, noting the tight line of her lips.

Rick was laughing when Kevin hit the speaker button. "Okay. Get on with it."

"Hey, River," Rick said.

"Hi. What's going on?"

"As I told Kevin, it may have nothing to do with us, but Eric Kane's wife has disappeared. She may have gone to ground—hiding from the SATG. If she was aware of her husband's side business, that would be enough to make her nervous and take off. Another obvious possibility is they've already found her."

"Neither sounds good for her. How does that affect me?" she asked. Her back was propped up against the door as she spoke into the phone Kevin had laid on the console between them.

"It probably doesn't, but I don't like surprises. There's always the outside chance she holds you responsible for her husband's murder."

"That's nuts," River responded, her brow crinkled.

"The world is full of nuts and it only takes one to create a disaster."

"We'll keep our eyes open," Kevin said. "Do you have a photo you can send?"

"I should have one shortly. I'll forward it to you and the guys."

"What's the other thing you wanted to relay. You said there were a couple of items."

"I got a call from Warden Brandley. He's been busy. He went through the correspondence and call transcripts of the Engleharts. He didn't come across River's name, or anyone named Chandler, but there were several references to a "her" during their conversations with the pastor. He's going back through the documents again to see if he can put them in context."

"Did he say what caught his attention? That's a pretty vague reference." Kevin commented. He glanced at River. If she was alarmed, she wasn't showing it.

"He didn't want to get into specifics until he had the chance to review the documents again, but he thought it was unusual the person's name was never referenced. He believed it was as if they went out of their way to avoid it."

"That doesn't help us. Can we get our hands on the phone transcripts?" Kevin shifted in his seat.

"Not without a warrant and we have absolutely no grounds or standing for one. As far as those conversations go, we have to rely on Brandley. He's an officer of the law. I'm banking on him wanting to get to the truth, if he can."

"You're thinking the '*her*' they're referring to in the calls is River?"

"I don't know that. I'm letting you know we have information that may, or may not, be pertinent to River."

"We're finding new threads instead of tying up the ones we already have," River said, letting out a frustrated breath.

"It's all part of an investigation," Rick told her. "Sometimes we need those threads to tie all the pieces together."

Her lips were drawn tight. Her shoulders rounded. She seemed to be fixated at something on the floorboard. Kevin reached for her hand. The steel in her spine had softened. Temporarily, he hoped.

"How long? How long can this go on?" Her face was drawn. Sadness laced her question.

"I wish we had the answer, but these things aren't always resolved quickly." Kevin refused to lie to her.

"We're making progress," Rick chimed in.

"I know you are, but I'm so tired. I've been dealing with this for so long."

And today had been another stressful day on top of how many stressful days? Kevin leaned over the console and kissed her cheek, taking a teardrop with him. "You're not alone in this," he assured her.

"Don't give up on us," Rick said firmly. "We're not going to drop this."

Running her fingers through her hair, she attempted a smile. It wasn't very convincing.

"Anything else?" Kevin asked his friend.

"Not at this end. We've got all we're going to get on Roxbury from the local authorities. It's going to be up to Colt and Troy to find anything else."

Kevin put the SUV in reverse and backed out onto the street. "Thanks, Rick. Keep us posted."

"You know it."

River didn't speak as they drove. He could feel the tension emanating from her. The road was desolate. Kevin quickly checked behind him, then shoved the car into park. "What's wrong?" he asked.

"What isn't?" she huffed.

"Can you be more specific?" He checked the rearview

mirror again. "Was it your visit with your aunt or the phone call that got to you?"

Her forefinger traced the depression between her nose and upper lip. The road in front of them held her interest more than he did.

"I believed this was over when the Engleharts went to prison. Then those poor mutilated creatures were left for me. Now, Dan is dead. What's next? Will they go after Aunt Amy? Will they go after you?" She began massaging her temples. "My head hurts. I can't think."

Selfless and independent. She worried about others but didn't want them to be concerned about her. He wanted to take her in his arms—to tell her everything would be okay —but he would be lying. He didn't have the answers. Sometimes they never come. The fear was eating at her and he didn't know how to alleviate it.

33

When they pulled up to the cabin, River couldn't move. She didn't have the energy to get out of the car. Empty—she felt empty. The passenger door opened, startling her.

"It's okay," Kevin said. "Let's get you inside." As soon as she unlatched her seatbelt, he lifted her into his arms, surprising her for a second time.

"I can walk." Admittedly, she didn't put much effort in the objection. Instead, she let herself sink into his warmth.

"I'm not sick or injured," she told him as they entered the cabin. "You can put me down." Her energy may be zapped, but her wits were returning.

"No, but you are hurting," he said, laying her on the bed.

She did hurt. There was an ache in her heart and soul. Why had today been so rough on her? She'd certainly had worse.

"You had a lot thrown at you today and a lot to go through tomorrow. Why don't we just sit here," he said, lowering himself to the mattress, "and talk about something else?"

"I can work," she threw her legs over the side of the bed. "It always takes my mind off of things."

Standing, Kevin planted himself in front of her and reached for the buttons of her shirt. "I can think of something else you could focus on."

"Ah, yes," she said, some of the tension escaping with the sigh. "That might work."

"Might?" he asked, slipping her shirt over her head with excruciating slowness. "I think we can do better than that."

When he flicked open the front clasp of her bra, her mind was definitely not on work.

The world ebbed away as they made love—slowly and tenderly, then climbing the peaks to urgency before cresting them. He tasted, teased, and caressed every inch of her body until she was consumed by nothing else. The energy she hadn't possessed to get out of the car, thankfully, came roaring back. She met his moves, stroke by stroke until she was sent careening over the cliff.

Totally spent, she fell back against the warm sheets. She didn't move when Kevin slipped out of the bed, leaned over and kissed her forehead.

"I'll be right back, love," he said, stepping into his jeans. "I'm going to button up the place."

A few minutes later, the front door shut. 'Button up' evidently meant securing the property. She rolled out of bed and padded to the bathroom. It was now dark. She didn't check the time. She didn't want to. She was going to make time stop, if only for tonight.

As River climbed back into bed, the front door clicked. She listened to Kevin's footsteps as he went through the cabin, checking doors, windows—every nook and cranny, she assumed. It should have made her nervous, sad or angry. Instead, it made her feel safe and loved. He'd called her 'love'. She hadn't missed the endearment. She also remembered they had a conversation to finish. She'd promised to tell the truth, and as she had witnessed throughout her life, the truth wasn't always pleasant. Right now, though, she wanted to spend time in his arms.

The refrigerator door shut. A few minutes later, Kevin's large form was backlit in the doorway. She was propped against the pillows, the covers tucked under her arms, waiting for him.

He handed her a bottle of water. She hadn't realized she was so thirsty. After she consumed more than half the bottle, she handed it back to him.

"Don't you want any?" she asked as he capped it.

"I downed one in the kitchen. Are you hungry?"

"Oh, yeah," she said, patting the mattress next to her. "I'm definitely hungry, but not for food."

He shrugged out of his clothing, until all that was left was a smile. "Let's see if I can help satiate your appetite."

River didn't know where she got the energy or stamina, but the entangling of bodies was even more fervent than their earlier lovemaking. When her muscles eventually turned to jelly, she draped herself across the hard planes of his damp chest, inhaling his musky scent as he stroked her hair. She wanted to stay here forever. Secure, happy, and loved.

Love. She owed him a conversation. She'd promised. She started to rise when Kevin pressed a finger to her lips before coaxing her head back against his shoulder.

"We were supposed to talk," she mumbled. God, she was tired.

"Sleep," he answered. "We've got all the time in the world."

If only, she thought as she drifted off.

RIVER WAS in her workroom when Kevin returned from his expansive exploration of the area surrounding her cabin. He'd gotten a few hours sleep before quietly slipping out of bed. River had been exhausted prior to reaching the cabin —physically and emotionally. He'd been surprised, then driven, by her enthusiastic response to him in bed. The sex had been mind-blowing and at the same time more intimate than anything he'd ever experienced.

She'd fallen asleep in his arms. She'd wanted to talk. He wasn't surprised, but her words drifted off as her eyes closed. They needed to talk but, admittedly, there was some trepidation at the outcome of the conversation, so he'd let her sleep.

The door to the workroom was shut. He didn't take offense. He'd seen her at work. She was in a zone—a different one than the one they'd shared hours before. Her current focus would keep her mind off the coming evening for a while. No doubt tonight would be the hardest thing she would have to face since the death of her family.

He grabbed a cup of coffee and took it out to the porch. It was easy to understand her love of the place. He gaged he'd walked several miles this morning without seeing or finding a single trace of another human being. If he hadn't been searching for signs of unwanted company, the hike would have been pleasant on this cool, crisp spring morning. Would she move back here if they didn't find the person responsible for terrorizing her? It tore at him to imagine being deployed and wondering if she was safe. They had a lot to discuss. Decisions to make.

He leaned his chair back against the cabin wall and

propped his feet up on the railing. Leaning his head back, he spotted a spider web in the upper corner of the porch. Dew still covered it. The sun sparkled off the tiny specks of water. It was reminiscent of the light in River's eyes when she smiled. She didn't smile enough. Hard to do when you were constantly looking over your shoulder. He was familiar with the feeling, but he only had to live with it when he was deployed. She lived with it every day. Damned if he didn't want to be the one to wrench that fear from her life.

He walked the perimeter several more times. Nothing changed. He checked in with Rick, Steve and Colt for updates, but nothing new was reported. Troy was still watching Roxbury, the warden hadn't gotten back to Rick, and Steve and Josie hadn't dug up anything else. Damn it.

By mid-afternoon, Kevin felt it was time River took a break other than her short trips to the bathroom. He tapped on the door. When she didn't respond to his knock, he let himself in.

Not for the first time, he found her with her head on the desk, asleep. It seemed to be a habit. Her head was pillowed on her left arm which was stretched across the flat surface. The right arm rested in her lap. He held his ground as he watched her for a few minutes. She was beautiful, but he found her strength the greatest pull for him. She should be a basket case. Yet she kept putting one foot in front of the other. She was loyal to the memory of her family. She proved she was caring when she'd tried to drive him and his friends away for fear she'd put them in danger. An independent loner which he suspected was a result of losing her family and fear of getting close to anyone else.

He was afraid of what she'd planned to tell him when they finally made their way back to the discussion of love. He loved her. Admitting it freely now, but first things first.

They'd get through today and deal with matters of the heart tomorrow.

Brushing his hand softly over her hair with the intent to wake her gently, he gazed at the mask she'd worked on most of the day. She'd made amazing progress and what she'd completed was stunning.

He pressed a kiss to her crown then whispered in her ear. "River? Wake up."

She blinked her eyes and rolled her shoulders as she pulled herself up straight. "I fell asleep," she said, swiping the hair from her face.

"I noticed. We have a few hours before we need to be at the service. I'm guessing you'll want some time to clean up. Then we can get something to eat."

The confused expression of being awakened from a sound sleep transformed into one of sadness. He hadn't expected different. It was one of the reasons he'd delayed interrupting her.

"You must be starving," she said, rising from her chair.

"I grabbed something from the kitchen, but you haven't eaten since last night."

"I don't need much fuel to run on," she said. "I lost track of time, then fell asleep. Damn. Let me take a shower and get changed."

"How's the project coming?" he asked.

"Not bad," she said, turning back to the workbench. "I hope the client likes it. Thank God this wasn't a rush job. I still need those shells from the other vendors to finish up."

"I can't imagine the client wouldn't be pleased," Kevin said, leaning in toward the mask. He kept his hands clasped behind his back to resist the urge to touch it.

"Feathers won't be suitable for this mask. I'm thinking of some sort of coral or pen shell. Something in a fan shape to set into the sides. They would give it a winged appearance."

"What's a pen shell?"

"It's a large, single layer shell which resembles the quill of a pen. Their interior side is iridescent. They are also extremely fragile. It's hard to find ones that are unbroken. I'll see what the vendors have. If they come up empty, I'll head to the beach when I get back to Sanibel."

"You're going back? To stay?" Why was where she went so important to him? The island had become his second home, but he didn't live there.

"I haven't made up my mind what I'm doing, but if I return here permanently, I still need to go back to clear out the unit in order to rent it out." She gave him a timid smile.

Her fragrance lingered after she'd exited the room. He closed his eyes and inhaled her scent, imprinting it on his memory. Kevin had no business making decisions for her. He didn't like her being alone—and she was alone and isolated in more ways than he'd first realized. Her Aunt Amy didn't strike Kevin as the warm and fuzzy type and appeared to leave River to her own life. With Dan gone, who did she have here? On Sanibel, she'd have his friends. Friends that would eventually draw her out of her self-imposed isolation. She'd also have them to call on, should she need help.

It wasn't his decision, but it wasn't going to stop him from making the argument.

34

———

They stopped to grab some bar-b-que at a local eatery, then finished the ninety-minute drive to the Blue Ridge Lodge. Located on the edge of the Pisgah National Forest, Dan's son, Jacob, had arranged to have the service held there. According to River, the lodge had a room large enough to accommodate Dan's friend's, former co-workers and family, but also housed his favorite bar. It would be packed after the service—everyone raising toasts to the man.

They were early, still the parking lot was full when they arrived. Kevin pulled the SUV into an overflow area. The lobby was full of people who weren't ready to take their seats. A man standing near the door to the assembly room, waved at River. Kevin immediately saw the resemblance to the picture of Dan that River kept in her office.

Kevin followed as River weaved her way through the crowd, keeping his eye out for anyone who might be particularly focused on her. When she reached Jacob Thompson, the two hugged tightly. He wasn't surprised when River repeated 'I'm sorry' over and over again. It was all the confirmation Kevin needed to know she still blamed herself for her friend's death. To Jacob's credit, he continually assured her it wasn't her fault.

River's voice was a bit shaky as she introduced the two men. Jacob was tall with an average build. His handshake was firm. Kevin guessed him to be a few years older than River.

"I've reserved a seat for the two of you up front," he said after the introductions.

"I'd like to say a few words about your dad."

"I expected you would," Jacob said. "He loved you, River. If he never said it, you need to know it."

"He wasn't big on touchy-feely words, but I knew it. Thank you for sharing him with me. Some kids would have been jealous of his attention."

"And dad would have been madder than hell if we had been. No, he stepped in where he was needed. We all understood."

"Why did he have to go to the cabin?" she muttered.

"He once told me that every time he was out there, he felt like he'd missed something. It was the investigator in him, I guess. Maybe something finally clicked because he'd just been out there the day before."

"Did he give you any idea what drew him back there?" Kevin asked.

"Are you looking into his murder?"

"Unofficially," Kevin answered. "Some of my friends are investigators. We might see something looking at it from a different angle."

"He didn't tell me he was going back. I didn't know he had until I got the call, they'd found him," Jacob said. "Damn it, I wish I could help more."

"I can't help thinking if he hadn't been out there…" River started.

"Stop it. You didn't kill him. Dad wouldn't want you to take on that mantle of guilt," Jacob said, glancing over his shoulder at the room filling with more people. "Look, I've got to see to the other guests. You'll always be part of our family, River. Don't be a stranger."

The two men exchanged phone numbers. "I'm glad River has someone to watch out for her."

"She can handle herself, but I'm happy to be here as backup. Call me if you think of anything, and again, my condolences on your loss."

"Thank you." Jacob offered his hand to Kevin, gripping it tightly. I hope you'll stay afterwards and join us in a toast to my dad." Jacob waded his way through a group of people gathered in the lobby.

"He seems like a decent man," Kevin commented.

"We spent some time together when we were young, but I hadn't seen much of him in recent years. He's turned out much like his dad," she said.

Her lips trembled. God, he hated to see her hurting, but all he could do for this pain was to be here for her. "Do you want to take a seat or are there people here you'd like to see?"

"Honestly, I don't know many of Dan's friends. They probably know about me and what he did for me, but I didn't meet many of them." She paused. "Except for that one."

"Who?"

She pointed to a heavyset man, who had just entered the door. "He was Dan's boss when my family was killed," she said, heading toward the newcomer. Kevin followed in her wake. He wasn't letting her out of her sight in this crowd.

River introduced Kevin to Ralph Pugliesi after the two had finished a long, tight hug.

"My you've grown into a beautiful young lady. Dan and I kept in touch. He was proud of the woman you've become."

Kevin handed her another tissue. He'd stuffed his pockets, anticipating the need.

"Did I ever tell you how much I admired your strength?" Pugliesi started. "I don't think we would have gotten the bastards without your help and testimony. Nothing shook you off your goal. You were amazing then. I'm sure you're just as amazing now. Dan told me about the harassment you've been through recently. I understand they haven't resolved the case. I've been wondering if Dan's death is connected. It's not out of the realm of possibilities."

Kevin's jaw tightened. He didn't think Pugliesi meant any harm by the comment, but it had to cut at River. She'd been blaming herself just minutes before. She didn't need someone else reinforcing her belief. Kevin acknowledged the man with a nod then steered River away from him.

The door to the lodge continually opened and closed. Each time, Kevin glanced in its direction. A man almost a head taller than the others in the room entered. Colt had arrived. They had no plans to connect. Colt was here to get a feel of the room. He was the best at reading tell signs. If anyone sent off signals that were out of the norm for the situation, his former commander would pick up on them.

Kevin took a seat next to River in the front row. Two sprays of flowers flanked the large photo of Dan Thompson in his uniform. A podium had been set up on the left. River had told Kevin that Dan's wishes had been to be cremated and his ashes spread throughout the parks he once worked. It was against all policies, but she was convinced his friends would see that it happened. He'd do the same for his friends, so he understood.

The service was traditional. A minister had a few words to say while a slideshow displayed pictures of Dan throughout his life. There was one with River when she graduated high school. Jacob took the podium after the preacher and eulogized his dad, relating heartfelt moments and telling stories which brought laughter to the gathering. Kevin's phone vibrated while Jacob was still speaking. Hoping he didn't attract too much attention, he pulled the cell from his pocket. He had a text from Colt. *Meet me in the back.*

"I'll be right back," he whispered in River's ear.

No one paid attention as he made his way toward the exit to meet Colt. Kevin spotted River's Aunt Amy on the other side of the room, sitting in the back row. She'd probably arrived late and didn't want to disturb anyone.

Colt was waiting for him at the door.

"Roxbury has left his farm and is headed toward River's cabin," Colt said as Kevin closed the gap between them.

"That doesn't mean it's his destination." But the hairs on the back of Kevin's neck rose.

"No, it doesn't, but my instinct tells me it is. Troy's on his tail. I need to leave now if I want to get to the cabin when they do."

"Do you need me?" Kevin glanced at the front of the room. He didn't want to leave River alone right now. As strong as she was, this was going to be tough on her.

"No. Until the cabin is secure, you stay with River. Do you have your weapon?"

Colt had a sense for things and if he was asking about Kevin's sidearm, it meant all his Spidey senses were flaring. "It's in the vehicle."

"Hang out here with River as long as you can. One of

us will text you with an update," Colt said then silently slipped from the room.

River was getting to her feet when Kevin returned to his chair. She gave him a timid smile when she reached the podium. She had a couple of false starts, then gathered herself and began to speak. His heart hurt for her as she recalled how Dan had stepped in when she lost her parents. The picture she painted was of a man who already had a family and still found room in his heart for a sad and angry teen. She stood straight, undeterred and didn't shed a tear. He was proud as hell of her.

As the mourners filed out of the room, some headed toward the exit while others made their way to the lounge to continue to celebrate Dan's life.

"I want to go back to the cabin," River told Kevin. "I'm not in the mood to mingle."

"We should go in for a while. I'd like to raise a glass to Dan."

"I'm tired," she said. "Please?"

She didn't have to tell him she was wasted. It was written all over her face. She'd managed to honor Dan without breaking down, but the effort had taken its toll. She was easy to gage. Her ice blue eyes reflected pain, sorrow and weariness.

"We can't, River. We can't leave yet."

35

———————

"Ⓦhat's going on?" River asked. She was tired, but it didn't make her stupid. Something had happened when Kevin had excused himself.

He guided her to a relatively quiet corner. The lobby was still full of family and friends either getting ready to leave or move on to the bar. "What's going on?" she asked, again. Kevin hesitated, which scared the hell out of her.

"Colt just left. He's headed to your place and wants us to wait here until he can check it out."

"What was he doing here? Why is he going to my place?"

"I'll tell you in a minute," Kevin said as he glanced over her shoulder. "Your aunt is headed this way."

River nodded. A few steps, and she and her aunt were hugging the stuffing out of each other. River needed to absorb some of her strength. She'd always been there when River needed her. Now wasn't any different.

"You doing okay, honey? You did great up there. It was a beautiful tribute to a wonderful man."

"Thank you," River answered softly. "Eulogizing him isn't enough. I feel like I need to do something more."

"You already have," her aunt said. "You made him proud."

"I want his killer." River was surprised at the anger and vehemence of her statement. Apparently, her aunt was taken aback by her stark tone. The dark-haired woman's eyebrows rose to meet her widow's peak and her eyes rounded.

"I'm sorry, but I'm sick and tired of the creatures who belong under rocks taking away the people I love. What if you're next? I want the asshole."

"Honey, don't get yourself all riled up. The police will get to the bottom of this."

"If they don't, I'm hiring someone who can," River threatened.

Aunt Amy gazed at Kevin. "Is he helping with that?"

"I'm just a friend here to support River," Kevin said, placing his hand on her shoulder and giving it a squeeze.

The gesture appeared supportive, but the strength of his grip told River not to go down that road. Resting a hand on his, she signaled she understood the message. She didn't know why he was hesitant to discuss what he and his friends were up to, but there had to be a reason.

"Be happy he's here," River smiled at her aunt. "Otherwise, I'd be hanging around you and crying my eyes out while you tried to work." Kevin's grip relaxed but stayed anchored on her shoulder.

"Do you want to stop by tonight?" Aunt Amy asked.

River was glad for the change of subject as she sensed a lowering of tensions in both her aunt and Kevin. She was also anxious for the chatter to end. She wanted to get back to the conversation that had been interrupted by her aunt's appearance.

"We'd love to," River answered, "but I'm tired. Can we get together one night for dinner? Call me and let me know what night works best for you. I'm working on a project, but I can always use a break."

"How long are you staying?"

"I haven't made up my mind."

Her aunt hesitated. "I'll call you," she said, giving River a hug and a kiss on the cheek.

"You're not staying for a drink?" Kevin asked.

"No. I can use the time to plan menus for events I've got coming up. You two try to enjoy yourselves."

"Okay," she started in on Kevin as soon as her aunt had exited the building. "What's this about not going back to the cabin?" His announcement had acted as a shot of adrenaline. Her exhaustion had faded. She imagined it would come slamming back at some point, but right now she was wide awake.

"Colt told me Roxbury was on the move."

"Is that where you disappeared to? He didn't stay long. Why was he here?"

"He came to pay his respects…"

"And didn't ride with us because?"

"This will go a lot faster if you let me finish."

River crossed her arms over her chest. "Go ahead."

"Colt received a text from Troy who has been keeping an eye on Roxbury. They also tagged Roxbury's truck with a GPS device. He took off in the direction of your cabin, although they can't swear at this point he's headed there. Colt wanted to get to your place, in case his gut is right. I've not known it to ever be wrong. One of them will notify me if it's safe to go back."

"I still don't understand why we can't head out. Certainly, they'll both beat us there. We could be halfway home when they give us the *all clear*." And if they didn't, she wanted to be there to kick the shit out of the bastard.

"I don't know what Colt and Troy have in mind. Their actions will depend on Roxbury's. We don't want to stumble into anything."

River sighed. She wanted to go. Not because she was tired, but because she wanted to do something. Surprisingly, she wanted to hurt somebody. Why now? Why had Dan's death tripped that switch?

"You okay?"

She unclenched her jaw. "If he's the one who killed Dan," she said, "I want to hurt him. I want to get my hands on him." She gulped for air. "What's wrong with me? I didn't wish for the deaths of the people who killed my dad, mom and Billy. Why am I so damn vengeful now?"

"If you're asking me, I'd say it's past time."

River stared at him. "What the hell is that supposed to mean?"

"I'm a medic, not a psychologist, River," he said, steering her toward the bar, "but you've been through hell —from the time you were fourteen until now. You've been stoic, strong, and obeying all the rules. My guess is you're sick and tired of following them."

She chewed on that while he ordered drinks for the both of them. Besides being a basket case and trying to hold it together after the murder of her family, she wasn't physically capable of lashing out at the guilty parties. Besides, her aunt was one step away from putting her in a psychiatric center for counseling. To avoid it, she'd seen a counselor, remained calm throughout the trial, and learned to withhold her anger and tamper her grief. He was right. She didn't want to hold back any longer.

Kevin handed her an Old Fashioned, then clinked his beer against her glass. "To Dan," he said.

"To Dan. He'd have liked you, you know?" she told him before taking a sip.

"Does that mean I've passed some sort of test?" Kevin's grin was a balm to the soul when she needed it.

"I didn't need Dan's approval to date anyone, but he often put on his *dad* hat when I was dating in high school. Looking back, it was fun to watch the boys squirm, although embarrassing at the time."

She quickly finished her drink, but Kevin was still nursing his. River wasn't in the mood to wait. "Can we go? Certainly, we'll hear from one of your friends on the way back." She rocked on her feet from heel to toe, her urgency to move was eating at her.

Kevin studied her silently.

"If you are worried I plan on doing physical harm to the bastard, I'm not, even though it would give me a great deal of satisfaction."

"Okay. Let's go," he said, setting his bottle on the bar. "If we haven't heard from Troy or Colt by the time we reach the cabin, we wait. I'll contact them, if I can, but we're not going in blind. Do I have your agreement?"

River nodded. "Agreed."

SIMILAR TO THE trip to the lodge, the return journey was also silent. River stared out the window into the darkness. Kevin wasn't concerned. The woman had her shit together. She was grounded despite all she'd been through. Her fit of temper tonight actually relieved some of his concerns. She had a safety valve and blowing off steam was normal, and in his opinion, a bit past due.

The silence was broken when Kevin's phone rang. He pulled over to the side of the road then quickly swiped the display to answer. He knew better than to connect his smartphone to a rental vehicle. The information could wind up anywhere.

"What's happening?" Kevin asked Colt.

"Our collective guts were on target. Roxbury showed up. He had a dead opossum with him when Troy tackled him."

"What's going on?" River unlatched her seatbelt and faced Kevin straight on.

"I'm putting you on speaker."

"The cops are on the way," Colt continued.

"Roxbury's at my place?" River asked.

"He had another gift for you," Colt answered. "This time we gave him a little welcoming party."

"Son of a bitch," River swore. "Has he said anything? Did he admit he killed Dan?"

"He's been rather quiet for a preacher. We haven't been able to persuade him to talk. The cops will take him in for questioning. There are too many open questions. Too many similarities to what happened last year."

Kevin didn't comment on Colt's assessment. Questioning someone did not mean an arrest was imminent and if he was arrested, the most they had on him at the moment was a misdemeanor. He'd walk—for the time being anyway. River's darkened eyes and down-turned mouth told him she'd come to the same assumption.

"Don't suppose either of you laid a hand on him?" Kevin asked.

"Us? We're law-abiding citizens," Troy responded. "I can't help it if he's a clumsy bastard."

Kevin smiled. "I owe you guys."

"We look out for one another," Colt said. "The cops just pulled up. We'll see you when you get here."

"It's not enough," River said, as the call disconnected.

"What's not enough?" Kevin asked, pulling onto the empty road. After her comments at the memorial, he suspected she'd wished his friends had done more than rough up the reverend.

"They were never able to find any connection between my 'gifts', as Colt called them, and anyone in particular. Roxbury showing up with a dead opossum isn't enough to cement a connection. Suspicious as hell, yes, but not proof he was behind the shit that happened. And what about Dan? Will they question him about his murder?"

"They will. Based on Rick's conversations with the cops up here, they took what happened to Dan personally. They considered him one of their own. Roxbury is going to be the subject of a thorough investigation. Do you trust the local sheriff?"

"I don't have any reason not to but that still doesn't mean Roxbury won't walk out of the sheriff's office. Unless they find a link between him and Dan's murder, he'll be out shortly. Leaving dead animals on my doorstep isn't going to get him thrown in jail without bail."

And that was exactly what Kevin was afraid of. "Give them a chance. Give us a chance. If there's something to find, we'll find it."

River dropped farther back into her seat. "I don't have a choice, do I?"

"There's a vote of confidence," Kevin muttered. Her remark cut at him.

"Sorry. I'm grateful for what you and your friends are doing, I really am. Lately, all of this shit feels endless. When my family was killed, the conviction was finite. The Engleharts where sent to prison. Sure, there were appeals, but the case was ironclad. This feels different—like a race-track with no finish line."

He'd seen her down, but never out. "From what you've told me about your family and Dan, I don't think they'd give up. I don't think you will either."

"I didn't say I was giving up."

"Then don't act like it."

36

"Wait here until I see where things stand," Kevin said, opening the car door. "I want to scope out whether it's best for you to hang back or be front and center."

"I want to be face-to-face with the son-of-a-bitch." She was pissed now. Kevin had prodded her temper and she was glad for it. He was right. She'd slipped into self-pity mode too often lately. She didn't like it and it did her no good.

They were parked in a stand of trees near her cabin. The two sheriff's vehicles were easily visible parked in front of her home. There were no flashing lights. The glow emanating from her cabin and the head lights of the vehicles, illuminated the scene. It was enough. She could identify the target of her fury. A thin, reed of a man with dark hair faced one of the officers. She noted his hands weren't restrained. Why should that surprise her? Who locks up a man for having a dead opossum in these parts? The most they'd have on him was trespassing—unless he was stupid and talkative. Why had the guys even bothered to call the authorities? It was a waste—or had they intended it as a warning?

The other officer, rounder and older than the one with Roxbury, stood with Troy and Colt. Kevin joined his friends. The three men towered over the deputy. River suspected the man had been in law enforcement for quite some time because their size and number didn't appear to intimidate him.

As much as she wanted to kick the man's ass, under the circumstances she wouldn't get within three feet of him if she tried. And since the pastor wasn't restrained, Kevin wouldn't be inviting her over to join the party. Annoyed, she sat, studied, and contemplated. She'd never seen him before—she was sure of it. His appearance wasn't the least bit scary to her. With his hunched shoulders and downcast eyes, he appeared more subservient than menacing. How the hell did the man attract a congregation regardless of its size? From her design and art classes, she'd learned to read body language and this guy was a follower in her opinion, not a leader. He certainly didn't look like a murderer. She supposed a murderer could look like anyone. They said Ted Bundy was attractive and charming. She'd seen three killers up close, but she didn't think they weren't typical, if there was such a thing. They were mad as hatters— Hannibal Lector clones—just not as smart.

She turned her attention away from the suspect and back to the group of men. Kevin's body language told her he wasn't happy. His arms flew as he talked then settled, fisted on his hips. She caught the glance in her direction, but his look didn't linger. Colt clasped his friend's shoulder and said something to him. Whatever it was, it appeared to settle Kevin, though his stance remained erect and foreboding.

The older officer shook hands with each man, then

left to join his partner. Together, the two cops put Roxbury into the back of one of the units. River was done waiting. She slid out of the SUV and was halfway to the cabin when she met up with Kevin. He guided her through the brush with the flashlight he'd retrieved from the glove box when he'd first exited the vehicle. She knew these woods and didn't need the assistance, but she didn't object.

"What happened?" she asked. "Is he under arrest?"

"Not yet," Kevin said, his voice seething with displeasure. "They're taking him in for questioning."

"They don't have cause to charge him, do they?" she asked as they approached Colt and Troy.

"Misdemeanor trespassing and hunting out of season," Troy said.

"In one breath he claimed he didn't know he was on your property. In the next breath he called you the devil's handmaiden."

"I don't even know the man."

"Which brings us back to the Engleharts. What are they feeding him?" Kevin asked.

"I agree," Colt said. "The question is why? And why now?"

"He sounds delusional," River mused.

"I wouldn't be surprised." Kevin pulled her close. His large, warm hands caressed her arms, settling her.

"But there's nothing to prove, or disprove, what he's claiming at the moment," Colt explained. "As for being on your property, you said yourself people have wandered onto it because its location next to the nature preserve. He was carrying a rifle, but that's not unusual for the area, nor is it illegal."

Shit, shit and double shit. "All your time, the stakeout, it's blown. He can recognize you now and knows you're keeping an eye on me. He'll be all the more cautious, assuming he's the right guy."

"He's the guy who's been terrorizing you," Kevin swore. "But we have to prove it."

"Now what?"

"We're going to make a run out to his place while he's occupied. Check the place out," Kevin told her. "It will be hours, if not tomorrow, before Roxbury is released."

"I hope you're right. Doesn't sound as if they have much reason to hold him." Frustrated, she retreated toward the cabin. "I'm going inside. It's chilly out here." She wasn't surprised when the men followed. "Are you seriously going out there tonight?"

"He lives alone. We won't get a better opportunity and time to search the place," Kevin said.

"I hope it helps. I'm getting tired of running into brick walls," she said. "I'll change clothes and be right with you." She was still dressed for the memorial.

"You need to stay here," Kevin said.

"Excuse me? Why the hell would I do that?"

"You're safe here. Roxbury won't bother you tonight. He has a big place, and we need to move fast," Kevin explained. "We know how to get through a search quickly and silently. If you're with us, that won't be possible— you'll be a distraction, one that could be dangerous for us."

"Besides, we may need you on the outside to bail us out," Troy smiled.

"I know you want to be there," Kevin said, ignoring his friend's attempt to lighten the situation. "But I need you to stay here. Roxbury will be tied up with the police for hours. Those cops didn't like what happened to you. They know the bastard was up to something. Even if they can't hold him, they're going to drag him over the coals for as long as they can."

"What am I supposed to do while you're gone?"

"Get some rest. You said you were tired."

"Yeah. Right," she said, rolling her eyes. "Like I'm going to take a nap while you're out breaking and entering."

"You mentioned it's not uncommon for people to leave their doors open in these parts," he said, laying a kiss on her forehead. "There may be no 'breaking' involved, if we're lucky."

She crossed her arms under her breasts. "I still don't like it."

"I know. One of us can stay if it will make you feel better."

"I'm not talking about me. I can take care of myself. I have a gun and I know how to use it. I'm worried about you—and them." She nodded her head in Colt's and Troy's direction.

He cupped her face in his hands and reeled her in for a kiss. Her skin tingled. Her toes curled. The thrill of it didn't seem to end, nor did she want it to. A cough from the other side of the room was a cold splash of water.

"Go," she said, torn between hauling him back for another kiss—and being pissed at being left behind.

"Maybe we shouldn't have left her," Kevin second-guessed their decision. Colt was behind the wheel while Kevin rode shotgun. "She could have waited in the truck."

"And just like you said, she'd be a distraction," Troy reminded him.

Kevin agreed, yet something niggled at the back of his mind. "How did Roxbury know River would be gone tonight? Hell, how did he even know River was back in North Carolina?"

"It's a small community," Troy interjected from the rear seat. "Word travels fast."

"If he was aware of Dan's memorial, he could have easily connected the dots. Dan was an integral part of the initial investigation. First on the scene. His unusual connection with River. People here would remember him and know she wouldn't miss it," Colt added.

Kevin stared out the passenger side window into the darkness. "We need to talk to the Engleharts again if we can't get anything out of Roxbury. There's got to be a link. It's too big of a coincidence."

"They've been in prison almost fifteen years. Why go after River now?" Troy asked.

"That's the $750 question, isn't it?" Kevin let the conversation ruminate in his head for a minute then asked his friends. "What do you think of the timing of Roxbury's appearance tonight? Was he late? If we'd come straight back from the service, we'd have been there when he arrived. Did he plan to do something more than leave a dead critter on her porch?"

"It didn't come up while I was tackling him," Troy said.

"You want to head back?" Colt asked. "If your gut is telling you something, we need to listen to it."

"This may be our only chance to get into his place. There are a lot of unanswered questions surrounding his visit tonight. We may get some of those answers at his place."

"I barely had time to glance at the room before Troy called. Did you pick up anything at the memorial?" Colt asked.

"Dan's son, Jacob, said the night his dad was killed was his second visit to the cabin in two days."

"Did he say why?" Troy asked.

"He didn't know. It would be a good idea to have a look at Dan's phone. Maybe he spoke to someone who could give us a lead."

"Possibly," Colt agreed. "Let's see if we can get our hands on his cell first thing tomorrow. Do you think his son will be on board?"

"He wants his dad's killers. I don't see a problem."

"It might not hurt to check out Dan's place. There may be notes. He wasn't just a wildlife officer but a cop before he retired. Old habits die hard," Colt added.

"The sheriff probably has them, if there were any," Kevin noted.

"Not if they didn't understand their significance. We'll take a look to be sure," Colt said.

"If Dan saw something peculiar on the property, you two didn't see it, did you?" Kevin was getting damn frustrated. They were spinning their wheels and getting nowhere.

"Nope," Troy confirmed. "Nothing was out of the ordinary. With the exception of a lack of food, which was to be expected, the place was neat and clean. I suspect Dan kept it up while she was gone."

"We may be focused too much on Dan's trips, or trip, to the cabin," Kevin mused. "He may have simply been at the wrong place, at the wrong time."

"It's always a possibility," Colt agreed, as he tapped the brakes. They approached a mailbox on the side of the road. Next to it were a pair of tire ruts in the bare winter ground. The tracks led to a group of buildings set back into a stand of trees.

"Is this his place?"

"Yeah," Colt answered, slowing to a crawl. "Looks quiet."

They parked in a thicket of trees less than a half a mile from the property. Colt switched off the interior light before they exited the vehicle. They all checked their weapons. No light was needed. They'd done it a thousand times.

"I'll take the barn," Kevin volunteered. "You said it appeared to be his base, Colt?"

"Yeah. Troy, check the outbuildings and the grounds. I'll be in the house. Phones on vibrate. Text if anything develops."

"We'll meet at the car," Kevin suggested.

The three marched out of the woods, separating when they reached Roxbury's home. The place was dark. That struck Kevin as unusual as Roxbury should have known it would be dark when he'd returned from his mission. His senses notched up another level.

Once they reached the buildings, they silently parted ways. Kevin pulled the massive barn door open and slipped inside. The building had been here awhile. He stilled after closing the door behind him, listening for any sounds. Sounds that would alert him to human or other possible creatures. Once he was satisfied he was alone, he flicked on his flashlight. The place was uncannily neat—the last thing he expected for a barn.

The room was divided into two distinct areas. A cross hung from a loft to his right. Bales of hay lined up like church pews in front of a roughly hewn pulpit. The picture it made was eerie.

Kevin directed his attention to the opposite end of the building. The rifle Colt had mentioned was no longer in the corner. It was probably the one Roxbury had on him tonight. Two work surfaces were flush against the inside of the barn. Knives, shears and various other tools necessary for hunting hung on the wall above a stainless-steel table. None of those finds were surprising.

A tall, red Craftsman toolbox stood next to the bench. It had a lock, but the genius had left the key in it. Kevin opened the top drawer. Swiftly, he sorted through it and the other drawers. He found nothing out of the norm for any garage or, in this case, barn.

He checked the benches, even searching the underside of each. Nothing. Turning his attention to the other end of the building—the man's church. Kevin hadn't asked the name Roxbury had given the group or his ministry. It didn't matter. It was obvious it was austere. The square bales of hay couldn't be all that comfortable to sit on for very long. Perhaps it was some sort of penance he required of his flock. There were no hymnals or prayer books. The pulpit was a simple wood frame with no hiding places. Assuming he wrote them down, where did he keep his sermons? He'd like to get his hands on them. However unlikely, their contents could possibly hold a key to this mystery. At the very least, they'd give him an insight into the man.

To the left of the pulpit, a ladder leaned against the loft. Kevin checked its sturdiness before making his way up its rungs. Scanning the loft with his flashlight, he noted a makeshift desk at the far end and made his way to it.

The writing surface was supported by two bales of hay on each side. A weather-worn sheet of wood lay across them. A three-legged, old fashioned milking stool apparently made do as his chair. There were a few items strewn across the improvised desk. A pad from a local dairy market and a couple of pencils. A battery powered lantern served as his lamp.

There was nothing on the page of the notepad. Did he

use this space for preparing his homilies? It didn't feel right. Where was his Bible? There were no religious articles of any kind. It didn't strike Kevin as a place of contemplation or prayer. It was dark, depressing and cold, which shouldn't be surprising considering Colt's take on the preacher.

Regardless of how odd the place struck Kevin, there was nothing useful here. The barn was a bust. He took a few steps toward the ladder and stopped, then retraced his steps. Slipping his hand between the bales of hay that supported the right side of the wooden plank, he felt around. Nothing. Abandoning that search he slid his long fingers between the two bales on the left side and—bingo.

Kevin inspected the cell phone. It wasn't one of the newer versions. It's simplicity and style told him it was a burner. He flipped it open and quickly scanned the call log. Two numbers appeared on the call list. Just two. An anomaly for any cell phone. He took out his phone and snapped a picture of the screen, recording the numbers.

His phone vibrated as he exited the barn. It was a group text from Troy. Two words. *Car. Now.*

37

"What are you doing here?" River asked her aunt as she stepped through the doorway and gave her a hug. "You said you had work to do."

"I do, but I was worried. The service had to be rough on you." Her aunt scanned the cabin. "Where's your friend?"

"Kevin had some things to do."

"I'm not sure I like you being alone here," her aunt said.

"Why do I have to keep reminding people I can take care of myself? Besides, they caught the guy who was leaving the dead animals."

"They did? Why didn't you call me? Who is it? Do you know him?"

"I'm sorry. I should have called you," River apologized. "My mind has been going in a million different directions." She reached in the refrigerator, pulling out a bottle of wine one of the guys had stocked for her. "Have a seat and I'll tell you what I can."

Instead of sitting, her aunt reached into the cupboard and pulled out a couple of wine glasses. Aunt Amy was much taller than River, who took after her mother. River had the same dark hair, small build and her distinctive blue eyes. It was hard to look in the mirror and not see her mom looking back at her.

"I still don't like you being here alone. When is your sexy soldier coming back?"

River stopped in the process of uncorking the wine. "He is sexy, but I keep telling you he's not mine." She recognized the sadness in her tone. "He'll be going back to his base then be deployed to God knows where. We live two separate lives." She poured wine into the glasses. "Besides, my life is crazy enough without adding a long-distance relationship to it."

"Did you two have a fight?"

"Pardon?" River asked taking the chair opposite her aunt.

"He's not here. You sound down. It made me wonder if you had an argument."

"No." River was growing a bit annoyed at the pointed questions regarding her relationship with Kevin. "Like I said, he had some things to do. I just got back from Dan's memorial, of course, I'm down."

She took a sip of her wine. Her aunt took a gulp. River's brow crinkled. "Is something bothering you?"

"Yes. No. Maybe. I shouldn't worry about you. I know that. You have your head on straight," she said taking another slug of wine. "Subject dropped, okay? Let's get back to tonight."

River nodded, grateful for the change in subject.

"What happened? I'm surprised the place isn't still crawling with cops."

"It was never 'crawling' with cops," River corrected

her. "The sheriff already had our trespasser in custody when Kevin and I got back from the memorial."

"How'd the sheriff know he was here? Have they been watching your place?"

"Unfortunately, not. A couple of Kevin's friends came up to help. They caught Reverend Roxbury as he approached the place and called the sheriff."

"Roxbury?"

"Yeah. He's a preacher the next county over."

"Roxbury." Her aunt's nose scrunched up. "Hold sermons in his barn. Right? He's some kind of a nutcase, from what I hear. Why would he want to harass you?"

The questions flew at her. "I have no idea. I understand he denied everything. He's being questioned at the sheriff's office now. Kevin and his friends are pretty certain he's the guilty party, though. They're out at Roxbury's place now checking it out while he's tied up."

Her aunt's eyes rounded in alarm. Shit. She shouldn't have mentioned the night maneuvers which bordered on illegal, if not outright illegal. "Don't tell anyone. One of them is a private investigator. If they find anything, they'll notify the authorities."

"Kevin must care a great deal about you if he's willing to break the law," her aunt said, pouring herself another drink.

"They're all honorable men. The last thing I want to do is get them in trouble, so please, don't mention this to anyone."

"Of course not."

River needed to get her aunt out of here before the guys returned. She'd already let one thing slip. She didn't want to put them in an awkward position of having to explain where they'd been. How did she chase her away without hurting her feelings? She never stopped by for a visit. Actually, this was the first time River had seen her aunt in the cabin since the deaths of her family. Guilt crept in as she sought a way to push her out.

"Do they think he had anything to do with Dan's murder?" her aunt asked, reaching for the bottle of wine. It was empty. River didn't offer to retrieve another.

"You mean the sheriff? I don't know what they think," she answered. "They'd be stupid not to question him about it and they've never appeared to me as stupid."

"I hope they have the bastard."

"That makes two of us." River was startled when her phone pinged in the back pocket of her jeans. She'd forgotten she'd slipped it in there when she'd exited the car.

"What was that?" her aunt asked. The woman had always possessed the hearing of an owl. River couldn't get away with anything when she was a kid.

"My phone," she said, pulling it out and unlocking the screen. Her heart sank as she read the text. "Shit."

"What is it?"

"It's a text from Kevin. They let Roxbury go."

"You said they'd keep him."

"Apparently, they didn't think the same way we did. They must have had a reason." She let the air escape her lungs. "Kevin's on his way back."

"I'll stay until he gets here." Her aunt stood next to her massaging her shoulder.

"No!" River stepped away. If Roxbury was innocent, he should be on his way home, relieved his trouble was over. If he was involved in the shitshow surrounding her, he could be headed back to the cabin. For all Roxbury knew, she had three very big men to protect her. She couldn't imagine anyone being that stupid, but to be safe, it would be better if Aunt Amy was somewhere far away.

"I'll be fine. If there was reason to worry, Kevin would have said something." And if she didn't text him back, he'd be frantic. She responded with a quick *Okay* then laid the phone on the table.

"I don't mind staying. I'd feel better if you weren't alone."

"It'll be fine. Go home. Work on your menus. I'll call you tomorrow." River steered her aunt toward the door. The sooner she was gone, the better River would feel for her aunt's safety.

"Okay. Okay." Aunt Amy raised her hands in defeat. "I almost forgot. I brought some homemade breads and a pie for you and your friend."

"Thank you," River said, giving her aunt a squeeze.

The rear hatch popped open as they approached the SUV. "It's all in that box," her aunt pointed to a cardboard carton on the rubber mat. "Sorry I forgot to bring it in with me earlier."

"No problem," River said, reaching for the baked goods. "These will be consumed in no…"

She tensed as she caught a movement out of the corner of her eye. She never completed the turn to identify the distraction. Her head snapped to the side as she was forcefully whacked on the temple. The sudden pain was followed by the same damn twinkling of lights she'd seen after the hit on the head at the condo. She collapsed over the carton she'd been about to pick up.

38

"What did she say?" Troy asked, as they barreled down the narrow road. Colt was silent as he maneuvered the vehicle through the dark countryside. The tight turns took all his concentration at the speed they were going.

"She texted 'okay'," Kevin answered.

"Just 'okay'? What did you text her? Hell, why didn't you call her?"

"I didn't want her to panic."

"Historically, that sort of response hasn't gone well."

Troy was right. Kevin grabbed his phone to place the call at the same moment Colt made a quick maneuver into a hairpin turn. His phone went flying across the floor of the backseat. Minutes ticked by until he found it under the driver's seat.

"Something's wrong," Kevin said. "She's not answering."

"Maybe she fell asleep," Troy suggested.

"Nice try, but that's BS and you know it. She hasn't been out of arms reach of her phone since the first attack at her condo. Can't this thing go any faster?" Kevin asked Colt.

"Not without going over one of these embankments. Try her again."

"Why the hell didn't they keep him longer?" Kevin's earlier instinct came back to haunt him. His gut had told him not to leave River alone. Shit. His next attempt to reach her got the same results. He left a voice mail urging her to call. Then he texted her—again. His heart crawled up his throat. Why the hell didn't she answer?

"We didn't make the sheriff aware of our plans for a little B&E," Colt said, flooring the gas as they hit a straight-away. "They didn't know we needed time."

"Do we want the cops in on this now?" Troy asked, pulling out his phone.

"They're the ones who let Roxbury walk," Kevin barked.

"All they have on him right now are misdemeanors. We expected them to hold him. I got the impression the cops believed the same thing. Regardless, someone made the call to let him go. They weren't getting anything out of him, anyway. They said he made one call then clammed up."

"He lawyered up? For a misdemeanor?"

"Yeah. It doesn't make any sense," Troy agreed.

"He called somebody else," Kevin swore. "Nobody, not even a dumb fuck, calls a lawyer for a misdemeanor. We have a second party we've overlooked."

Kevin tried River's number again. Why the hell wouldn't she pick up? He could think of all sorts of logical reasons she didn't answer but, once again, his gut was telling him something had gone wrong. He was terrified for her. Damn. He'd worked under fire, for God's sake—but this was different. This was River.

His hands were so slick with sweat, he almost dropped the phone again but caught it before it hit the floorboard. His fumbling fingers caused the display to switch from contacts to his photos. The last picture he took was front and center. Roxbury's call log.

"Do these numbers mean anything to you?" he asked, shoving his phone at Troy.

"This is Roxbury's call log? That's it? Only two numbers?"

"I scrolled through the list. There were just those two."

"I recognize the second number. I've called it enough recently. It belongs to Central Prison." Troy picked up his phone off the console, double checking his call list. "I don't have any idea who the other number belongs to. I'd say that's your second party."

"When was the last call to the prison?" Colt asked.

Kevin enlarged the screen. "Yesterday afternoon."

"Troy, get a hold of Rick. See if he can get a transcript of yesterday's call."

"Already on it."

Troy's request to Rick was brief. The team didn't have to make long explanations to one another. Mentally, they worked in sync. They always had, which is what had made them such a great team. The new members of the team were good. Damn good. You didn't get a green beret if you weren't, but the mental telepathy the original James Gang shared, had yet to develop.

Kevin tried River again, and again had no results. They were nearing her cabin. He had the urge to get out of the car and run, as if that would get him there faster.

"Did you find out anything?" Troy answered his phone a few minutes later. "Interesting. What? Okay, thanks. One of us will keep you up to date."

"What happening?" Kevin asked, leaning through the opening between the front seats.

"Brandley is a man of his word. He took the call transcripts and copies of correspondence home with him."

"And?" Kevin prodded.

"The initial suggestion for the Engleharts to agree to meet with Roxbury came from a third party in a letter just about a year ago. It suggested Roxbury could help them and, I'm quoting here, 'find solace and resolution for unfinished deeds'."

River. She was an *unfinished deed* as far as the Engleharts were concerned. The one that got away. The one who survived their killing spree. "They didn't think that was strange?" He wasn't near as calm on the inside as he sounded.

"At the time?"

"No. It's not unusual for prisoners to get weird mail. I doubt the warden would have given it any thought if we hadn't been poking around."

"Who sent the letter?" Colt asked, turning down the long gravel road leading to River's cabin.

"Somebody calling herself Grace. And before you ask, the return address was a post office box. Similar to the one River uses—one that can't be easily traced back to anybody. It didn't stand out because they had no reason to be suspicious." He paused. "There were several letters from the mysterious Grace. All of them a bit cryptic, but not enough to raise flags of the average low-wage prison worker who reviews them. The warden requested and received scanned copies. He picked up on the odd wording and a strange addition to the letters."

"What sort of addition?" Kevin was ready to strangle the life out of Troy for drawing this out.

"Below Grace's name on each letter were four stick

figures. Three of the figures, two adults and a child he'd guessed, appear to be on the ground. The third figure was in the distance.

"God damn, son-of-a-bitch," Kevin swore, pounding his fist into the back of Troy's seat.

"Do you know who it is?" Colt floored the SUV, kicking up gravel behind it.

"I have an idea, but it doesn't make any sense."

SOMETHING WAS POUNDING inside River's skull, trying like hell to escape. The jostling her body was taking wasn't helping the pain. Shaking her head to clear the fog, the darkness almost swallowed her again. She fought it.

Her battle was aided by the pain shooting up her arm. Something sharp was digging into her forearm which was pressed against the floor. Instinctively, she rolled away from it, but not before tearing her shirt and the skin beneath it. Her ankles had been bound together. Her hands taped behind her back. She swallowed a moment of panic. She needed to think.

Taking a deep breath, she let it out slowly, assessing the area around her. The texture of the surface she rocked against finally registered. She was laying on the rubber mat of a cargo hold—an SUV cargo hold. It was dark. Too dark to make out much of anything. She was moving, that much she was sure of. They had to be in the country. It was the only place they could traverse without any ambient light streaming in through the windows. The only thing she could distinguish was the outline of the seat in front of her.

While her vision was limited, her sense of smell was something different. The aroma of baked goods and the waning fragrance of cooked meat and spices hung in the air. This had to be her aunt's car. Oh, God. If her aunt was dead because of her…

River's body wilted into the rubber mat. She was so tired of losing people she loved. Was there anyone left to miss her? Kevin. She'd tried to keep her emotional distance because she couldn't bear losing anyone else. Now, it was possible—even probable—he would be the one losing her.

The vehicle continued to bounce over rough terrain. Who was behind the wheel? Roxbury? Most likely. And where was Aunt Amy? She'd been right behind her when someone had bashed River over the head. Could she be out cold in the rear seat or had he left her back at the cabin? That would make the most sense. One kidnap victim would be easier to deal with than two. She prayed Kevin would find her aunt alive and well.

What did Roxbury want with River? To carry out some sick ritual for the Engleharts? She could still see her family laying in pools of their own blood. Their bodies slashed and stabbed. Had Roxbury been taxed with finishing the job the Engleharts had started?

As the pounding in her head lessened, the road noise grew louder. They weren't on a paved road. Gravel crunched beneath the wheels. If they'd been traveling on side roads since she was abducted then chances were, they weren't all that far from her cabin. Speed wasn't your friend on the mountain's backroads. The countryside had a way of letting you know who was in charge. It wasn't unusual to slide off an embankment or into a tree it you didn't take your time.

The continued silence, excluding the movement of the vehicle, convinced River she was alone with her kidnapper. Would it be possible to reason with him? She caught her laugh before it escaped. If the Engleharts were able to influence him, he wasn't capable of listening to reason. He was probably just as crazy as his mentors—maybe more so.

Eventually, he'd have to stop. The question was, what would she do when he did? *Fight.* She silently heard the collective voices of her family shout at her. But how and with what? She'd have to be ready the minute the hatch opened—which would be impossible if she couldn't free herself.

Twisting her wrists, she tested the bindings. They were tight but didn't cut off circulation to her hands. Still, no matter how she twisted or pulled, she couldn't wrestle herself free of the sticky tape. Panic rose in her throat. She was familiar with panic—and it didn't help.

She stopped struggling long enough to draw in another deep breath and take a moment to think. Her arm began to throb. Her sleeve was damp where blood seeped from the cut. *Cut.* If the object could cut through her blouse and skin, then it should cut through the tape that bound her.

Squirming back toward her original position, she stretched her arms out behind her, blindly searching for the sharp protrusion. A slice of her finger announced her discovery. She'd yet to figure out what the object was, but it didn't matter. It was a possible means to freeing her. The tape caught on her first try. While the space between her wrists would have been ideal, unable to see, she was happy to hit any part of the tape.

The first layer of the sticky binding tore as she pulled it across the sharp edge. Unfortunately, it wasn't enough. Slamming her bound wrists against the sharp object, she continued to drag her wrists across it until the last pass tore into her skin. Pulling her arms apart, one hand broke free of its bondage.

Her victory was followed by a flash of fear. She'd been concentrating on freeing herself, not listening for sounds from her captor. Now she listened intently. Other than the continuing crunch of the tires against a rough gravel or dirt road, it remained quiet. Eerily quiet.

Slipping her left arm under her body, she debated how best to remove the tape which bound her legs. Sitting up was out of the question. Roxbury would notice the movement over the seatback. Remaining on her side, she pulled her legs up toward her chest and found the ragged end of the bindings. Instinctively, she wanted to rip it off. Time was of the essence, but she held back, remembering the ripping sound of the all-purpose tape as it was torn off a roll. She opted for quiet in lieu of speed.

Her hands were covered with blood and sweat, and her outstretched arms ached, but she managed to coax the tape from around her ankles. Exhausted from the task, she took a second to rest and listen. The silence was starting to get to her. It wasn't uncommon for River to talk to herself. Didn't everyone cuss at other drivers, or in this case, mumble or complain about the road conditions? And the road had gotten very rough. River was sure they had left a county-maintained gravel road and were now headed up an old logging or forestry road. The grade was steep. Where the hell was he taking her?

Wherever it was, there was nothing she could do about the destination, but she could prepare for their eventual arrival. River rolled onto her stomach and reached blindly for anything she could use as a weapon. Since the area was small, it didn't take long to determine the cargo hold had been cleared of everything. The box she'd been reaching for when she was walloped was gone. It may have contained a knife or other kitchen utensils, but that wistful thought was quickly dashed. She didn't dare take the chance of moving the mat beneath her even with the possibility of finding some sort of weapon. The action would require too much movement and noise that could alert her captor.

The front of the vehicle unexpectedly lurched upward, bringing the car to an abrupt stop. River was thrown to the back of the cargo hold and pressed up against the liftgate. The engine quieted and the dome light flashed on when the driver's door opened.

River's stomach tightened. She had nothing to defend herself with except her wits. She didn't know Roxbury, but he'd been clever enough to terrorize her for months without getting caught. He had a plan. She didn't—but she did have the element of surprise on her side. She was unbound and the reverend didn't know it.

It happened in an instant. A click sounded, the hatch instantly opening. She fell from the vehicle, hitting the ground hard. The landing didn't stop her, though. The steep incline had her rolling downhill, away from the vehicle. Covering her face with her hands to protect her eyes, she let gravity aid her escape. Rocks and twigs dug into her as she went. Her elbows and hips were being battered. The initial excitement of freedom was replaced by fear. She could be hurdling toward a ravine.

The journey came to an end as quickly as it had begun. The air was forced from her lungs as she crashed into the sturdy trunk of a large pine. Scrambling to her knees, she sucked in a deep breath, replacing the air she'd lost. It hurt like hell, but she could breathe. She'd be black and blue if she survived, but she didn't think her ribs were broken. Using the tree to steady her, she got to her feet, then took off into a stand of trees.

"River! It's Aunt Amy. Where are you?"

Aunt Amy? River froze. She was tucked behind an evergreen shrub, still sucking in air—her brain working as fast as her lungs. She stood, ready to call out when her aunt shouted.

"Roxbury hit his head when we crashed. We need to make a run for it while we can. Can you hear me?"

Loud and clear. A bell rang in River's head. Too clear and too loud—and too confident. Could Roxbury be using Aunt Amy to draw River out? Then why was her voice unwavering? Something was off. Her instinct was to keep running, but Roxbury was incapacitated, so she couldn't desert her aunt out here.

River made her way back toward the vehicle, keeping out of sight. She watched the beam of a flashlight as it swept the area next to the car. Still, she couldn't make out the person holding it. Dropping to her knees, River searched the ground until she found a rock—large enough to make noise when it landed, but small enough that River wouldn't have a problem chucking it a good distance from where she stood.

With all the strength she could muster, she hurled the stone in the direction beyond the rear of the vehicle. The forest gods were with her once again, because the stone had clear sailing until it hit a tree several yards in the distance. The light swung in the direction of the falling stone.

"River?" Her aunt came around the back of the vehicle, backlit by the interior light of the SUV. She held the flashlight in one hand—and a gun in the other. Where the hell had Aunt Amy gotten a weapon? She must have taken Roxbury's gun. *But he carries a rifle…*

River was being paranoid, but instinct urged her to be sure. Roxbury may have opted for a handgun tonight, but he hadn't had one on him when he'd been taken into custody and he hadn't made it back to his home or the guys would have let her know. Still, that didn't mean he didn't have one stashed away somewhere else.

Creeping back to the SUV, she scouted the area as she went. There was no sign of anyone else. No one lurked near the vehicle. No one lay unconscious or incapacitated in or near it. Her aunt's purse sat on the passenger seat.

River's heart banged against her breastbone before shattering into a million pieces. Her aunt hadn't come with anyone. She hadn't been a captive. Aunt Amy was alone and hunting for River.

39

———

The area in front of River's home was illuminated by light streaming from the open door. The sight sent them bounding from the car. No words were spoken as they drew their weapons. Colt and Troy circled the building while Kevin headed to the cabin. When he spotted River's phone on the dining room table, his neck corded. He wanted to howl in anger and fear. She wouldn't voluntarily leave it behind. No way. After a quick search of the place, he returned to the main room. In addition to River's phone, two glasses of wine occupied the table. Rose colored lipstick clung to the rim of one of them.

Picking up her phone, he scrolled through her texts and call logs. They didn't reveal anything unusual. A call to Dan's son and a couple to and from her aunt. The recent text messages were between Kevin and River.

He tucked the phone into the back pocket of his jeans as Colt and Troy entered the cabin.

"Nothing in here?" Colt asked.

"Her phone and two glasses of wine. I can only think of one person River would let in."

"Her aunt?" Troy asked. "What brought you to that conclusion?"

"Stick figures and wine."

"Explain," Colt said curtly.

"The first time I met her aunt, River joked about Amy's lack of artistic skills—commenting they were limited to stick figures. Then there's the wine. River was entertaining. She wasn't afraid. And there's lipstick on one of the glasses. River wasn't wearing any tonight." Kevin noticed everything about her. She never wore anything on those soft lips, but gloss.

"This isn't going to be enough to drag in the sheriff. If they couldn't hold Roxbury," Colt said, "they're damn well not coming out to search for a woman who might be taking a late-night stroll through the woods."

"And leaving the door open and her phone on the table?" Kevin snapped.

"It's not enough and arguing is wasting time," Troy told him.

Kevin eyed his friends closely. "Do you guys have something in mind?"

"Troy," Colt said, "you can track Amy's cell, I assume?"

Within a few minutes, Troy had her location. "She's in the nature preserve."

"Are they close by?" Kevin asked since River's cabin backed up to the preserve. But that wouldn't make sense. Why would Amy take the car where she could go on foot?

"Doesn't look like it," Troy confirmed his suspicion. "She's off a maintenance road."

"Can we get to her from here?"

"We can," Troy said. "It's hard to tell which route would be faster—on foot or in the car. We'd have to drive to the other side of the preserve to access the road, but once there it would take us deeper into the woods."

"Then we split up," Kevin said.

Troy opted to go with Kevin. Despite the loss of one eye, Troy could see in the dark like an owl. Colt took the truck. They would meet where Troy had last picked up Amy's signal.

It was a cold evening, but Kevin was sweating bullets. It wasn't the exertion of racing through rough terrain, but the fear of what was happening to River. Her aunt had to be the one who'd lured her out of the cabin tonight. Leaving her phone on the table and the door wide open, told him she'd not suspected a thing. Why should she? She loved her aunt. She believed the feeling was reciprocal. What did Amy want? Kevin was now convinced she was behind the gaslighting of River last year.

The questions ran through his head as he dodged a low-hanging branch. "Why?" he muttered aloud.

"Why what?" Troy responded, keeping his voice low. Whispers carried.

"Why would her aunt want to harm River? What was the trigger?"

"That's something we'll have to ask her when we find them," Troy responded, not slowing down.

The two of them made their way quickly through the maze of trees. He could smell the decaying leaves, some type of early blooming flower, and the distinct aroma of pine trees. The ground was damp in places, shaded on sunny days by the evergreens which dotted this part of the forest. Kevin moved swiftly, keeping pace with Troy, but his footing could have been better if he had on his Rockports instead of the shoes he'd worn to the memorial. He hadn't taken the time to change. Wishes didn't get you anywhere and were distracting. He needed to focus.

They'd traveled several miles through the woods when they came to an abrupt stop. Kevin spotted it at the same time Troy had—a beam light in the distance. Whoever it was, it wasn't River. She was too smart to draw attention to herself. The frantic movement of the light told Kevin the person was anxious and desperately searching for something or someone. He figured it was the latter.

Using simple hand signals, Kevin indicated to Troy to head to the right which would put him behind the light source. He headed toward the left to cut them off.

Picking up speed now that they had a target in sight, he steadied his breathing further, refusing to allow any audible escape of air to pinpoint his location. He might be able to control his intake of oxygen, but it didn't mean he was any less scared.

During his tours, there were times they had no more cover than the crumbling wall of a bombed out-building while RPG rockets sailed over their heads. He'd held the hands of men and women who wouldn't make it to see another sunrise. He could put his emotions aside while sealing off an artery or transfusing blood under fire. None of that compared to the fear of knowing River's life was in their hands.

He slid over a large, fallen tree, cocking his head as he hit the soft dirt. A sound. Man, or beast? He stilled, waiting to hear it again. He immediately ruled Troy out. You wouldn't know he was near until his knife was at your throat.

He listened, focusing on the direction of the initial noise. Discarded leaves rustled again, closer this time. Experience and instincts told him it wasn't an animal. To his right off in the distance, the light still swept the area. Definitely someone searching.

Kevin made his way toward the sound of rushed

breathing. If it was River, he didn't dare call out and make her stalker aware of their presence. He darted behind a shrub, making his way up the hill to intercept his target. Once he was certain he was above it, he ducked behind a wide tree trunk and waited.

RIVER'S INITIAL RESPONSE—AFTER the gut punch of realizing her aunt was behind her kidnapping—was to get in the abandoned car and take off, but she wasn't going anywhere on wheels. There was no key and, damn it, no phone left behind. By the time she finished her search of the car, the light had turned back in River's direction. She scrambled away from the vehicle and up the hill.

Diving into the night, she ran as fast as she dared. Tripping over a tree root or scaring one of the inhabitants could give away her location. Taking a chance, she took a quick glance over her shoulder. She was relieved to see she'd put some, if not much, distance between her and the sweeping beam of her aunt's flashlight. But the move cost her.

Her next step was into thin air. In an instant of panic, she thought she'd stepped off the edge of an overhang, but she quickly landed, face down in moist soil. What the hell would cause a chasm this large? Right now, the reason didn't matter. Spitting out dirt, she crawled to the end of the hole. Tracing her hands up the side of the pit, she figured it was about four feet deep. At just over five feet, hefting herself out of it wasn't going to be easy.

In her search for a foothold, the shape and depth of the hole became clear. Her stomach rolled and her skin prickled. She was standing in a grave. One that had yet to be filled—and she had a pretty good idea who was the intended inhabitant. The knowledge gave her all the incentive she needed. She found a nearby root and anchored herself to it as she swung her legs up over the edge. Taking a deep breath, she ran for the shelter of the trees.

She didn't know what part of the preserve she was in, which was a problem. She suspected it was also deliberate. River's two previous escapes had partially been a result of her familiarity with the area. How well did her aunt know this particular stretch of woods? Her Aunt Amy enjoyed hunting for small game. While the preserve was off limits to hunters, any violation would be small compared to what she had in mind for River. Poaching a rabbit or two would be small change. Was this one of her hunting grounds? If it hadn't been previously, it was now.

Proceeding with more caution, River avoided other obstacles as she clawed her way up the slope. The black clothing she'd worn to the memorial helped her blend in with the darkness. If she was able to reach the top of the hill, she should be able to get her bearings.

She slipped on a patch of wet leaves which sent her sprawling onto the forest floor. Her teeth dug into her bottom lip when she hit the ground. She tasted blood. It was a small sacrifice for not announcing her location. Crawling away from the slick spot, she returned to her feet. The landscape blended in with the night sky. She had no idea how far she had to go, but she was on an incline. Eventually, she'd reach the peak. She batted away branches she could see and took the slap of those she couldn't.

Once again, she zigged when she should have zagged. Her toe caught the root of a large tree and she went sailing. She reached out to break her fall. An arm shot out from behind the tree, catching her by the waist and pulling her to safety.

"Shhhh, River. It's me." A warm breath kissed her ear.

He didn't have to tell her. She'd known it was Kevin the instant he touched her. "It's Aunt Amy," she said, choking out the words while he held her tight.

"I'm sorry, honey." He cradled her head snuggly against his chest.

"She has a gun," River mumbled the warning.

Stepping back, he pressed a finger to her lips, hushing her. He held up his weapon for her to see. The site, along with the man, were reassuring. He knew what he was doing. He trained for it. She suspected his friends were nearby. She wanted to ask him but heeded his warning and remained quiet.

Kevin gave her shoulder a quick squeeze then left her behind the wide trunk of the tree while he moved to watch the approach of her aunt—made obvious by the beam of light which continued to search the forest. God. Aunt Amy. Now that she wasn't running for her life, River could think. The betrayal hit her hard. Her lips quivered. Her aunt had dug a grave for her. She kept coming back to the question. Why? Why did her aunt want her dead?

Keeping his eyes on his target, Kevin reached over and placed his hand on her back, rubbing it gently. Had he sensed her tension, or had he known instinctually what she was thinking? Either way, his intimate gesture had her pulse gearing down a notch. She wasn't alone. She hadn't broken when she was fourteen. She hadn't broken last year. She wouldn't break now.

Pulling her shoulders back, she straightened to her full height. Kevin's hand moved from her back to her shoulder, gripping it tightly. River understood the command. She didn't move further and remained silent, but it didn't stop her from watching the beam of light as it appeared to their left. Her breath hitched.

What was Kevin waiting for? Was the plan to hide until

her aunt passed? Aunt Amy wasn't going to give up. River knew too much now. Besides, she was done running. She wanted answers. The urge to tackle the woman she'd known and loved for years was almost overwhelming, but River knew she wouldn't be able to take two steps toward her with Kevin at her side.

Suddenly, the beam of light jerked upward as a shot rang out. Unseen wildlife could be heard scurrying deeper into the forest. A few seconds later Troy shouted, "Clear."

"You stay here," Kevin told her as he headed toward the sound of Troy's voice.

"The hell I will. I have more right to know what's going on than anyone." She sidestepped the fallen tree trunk Kevin had easily vaulted over.

"Then stay back until I make sure the situation is secure," he told her.

She wasn't one for taking orders, but under the circumstances, she'd default to the man with battle experience.

The distant voices became a clear litany of hate filled profanity as they approached.

"Goddamn bitch," Aunt Amy squealed.

River's agreement to Kevin's request didn't last long. With a mixture of anger and pain, she turned toward her aunt who continued to sling insults. Troy had her in an armlock. Her weapon was in his waistband. Her flashlight lay on the ground casting long shadows of the rough landscape.

"Why?" She verbalized the question that had been running through her head. Fury leapfrogged over the pain. "Why, damn it? Anger filled the hole where her heart had been. She wanted to slap the shit out of the woman who'd help raise her. "Answer the damn question. Why do you want me dead?"

Kevin pulled River against his chest, holding her a safe

distance from her aunt. River wasn't sure who he was protecting. River or Aunt Amy.

"Because you're not." She spat out the words. "This is all your fault. If you hadn't run away that day, you'd have died with the rest of your family."

River didn't think she could be anymore shocked. Her head snapped back as if she'd been hit. The words were a blow to her heart. "I thought you loved me."

"That just proves how naïve you are. I loved the money you brought with you. How the hell do you think I built my kitchen? Catering ladies' lunches and tea parties?"

"You stole from my trust fund?"

Her aunt quieted. Had it just dawned on her that she was speaking too freely?

"Then River took over the accounts and you lost your money tree. Right?" Kevin prodded when her aunt didn't answer. "So, you thought you'd inherit from her."

River didn't recognize the woman struggling to get away from Troy. It was as if she had dual personalities. She was stunned. Hurt, livid, and stunned.

"You killed Dan." Kevin made the statement in a cold harsh tone.

"Why would she kill Dan?"

"To get you back here," Troy answered for her.

There was no response, other than the steely, tight-lipped expression filled with hate. She'd already said enough to incriminate herself in kidnapping and attempted murder. Had she killed Dan for the sole purpose of luring River back? River stumbled over to a fallen tree and vomited. She continued to wretch even as Kevin pulled back her hair.

She wiped her mouth on her sleeve. She didn't seem to have much control over her tears or stomach these days. As she straightened, Kevin stepped up and brushed the hair from her face.

"Colt's waiting for us near the car," Troy said, raising his voice as he jerked the arm of his squirming captive. "He's called the sheriff. They should be there by the time we meet up with them."

"Roger," Kevin responded. "Let's get this over with."

Over with. Was it? There were so many questions to be answered.

"You're safe," Kevin said. "We'll get this sorted out."

How did he know what she was thinking before she verbalized it? When was the last time someone understood her? The answer shrouded her in sadness. Her mom and dad had always been able to read her, but no one else had possessed the ability to see inside her soul. Not her aunt. Not Dan. Not even her therapist. But she had a bond with Kevin—a bond that would soon be broken.

40

As the sun rose, Kevin sat on the couch with River tucked up next to him, her head resting on his shoulder. Neither of them had slept since returning to the cabin. River was too pent up over the events that had unfolded last evening. Once home, she'd been on a mission to erase all evidence that a forensic team had ever been in the cabin. Kevin scrubbed tables, floors, doorknobs and whatever else River pointed to, all the while keeping one eye on her to be sure she suffered no ill effects due to the knock on the head. Troy and Colt were currently outside on the phone with Rick.

He thought back to last night's trek down the mountain to the abandoned SUV. The hike had been filled with tension. So much tension, Kevin had half expected a tree branch to snap as they passed by. River had trudged down the hill like a cast member of *The Walking Dead*.

When they reached the vehicle, they'd been met by Colt, the sheriff and a contingent of deputies. A forensic team had already started on the abandoned car. Amy Scott was immediately taken into custody. There were enough witnesses and evidence to warrant the arrest. Statements were taken, adding to the physical evidence that had been collected. Contact information was exchanged before they were dismissed and told to remain available for additional questioning.

Despite River's objections, Kevin had insisted she be checked out at the hospital after they'd left the scene. He was concerned there were wounds hidden under the layers of dirt that cover her. He hadn't known until they'd reached the hospital that she'd been unconscious again. He waited with Troy and Colt as the ER staff cleaned her up and checked her injuries which were, thankfully, mostly scrapes and bruises.

In spite of consuming copious amounts of hot coffee, River was still cold. Shock. It wasn't surprising considering the night she'd had. He pulled the throw from over the back of the couch and wrapped it around her shoulders. It tore him up to see her in so much pain. With all the tools in his medical pack, there were none he could pull out to fix this. She was grieving at the loss of another family member—her last family member—not from death, but from betrayal.

And it wasn't going to get any easier any time soon. Sheriff Chamblee had called at the crack of dawn. He wanted them all in for questioning sooner rather than later. They'd been lucky to have some time to decompress. If Rick hadn't interceded last evening, giving his word as a fellow officer that his friends would show up when requested, the four of them would have, in all probability, spent the night at the county jail answering questions.

Troy and Colt had arrived early, bearing bagels and breakfast sandwiches. Kevin had managed to get River to nibble on some food. She needed something in her stomach to absorb the caffeine. It was going to be a long day and there was no way of telling when they'd get the chance to eat again.

Tucking a leg beneath her, River repositioned herself.

"You okay?" Kevin asked. The question was automatic. How could she be?

"Do you think Aunt Amy had anything to do with the murder of my mom, dad and Billy?"

"I can't see that angle."

"I know it's a long stretch…" River paused as the front door opened.

"What's a long stretch?" Colt asked.

"River's afraid her aunt may have had something to do with her family's murder," Kevin explained.

"You can rule that fear out," Colt said, dropping into one of the empty chairs. Troy headed for the coffee maker.

"How?"

"Rick has been in touch with both the Sheriff and Warden Brandley. I think we can fill in a few blanks now. The rest will come in dribbles and drabs."

"What did Rick have to say?" Kevin asked, taking River's hand.

"There is a tie in between your aunt and the Engleharts," Colt said, steepling his fingers, "but it's not what you were thinking. The way we figure it, she was using them to set Roxbury up to take the fall. When something happened to you, she would be able walk away scot-free, no pun intended."

"I don't understand. She knew the Engleharts and Roxbury?" Nails dug into Kevin's palm.

"It was a convoluted plan. Your aunt must have invested a great deal of time in it. Years." Colt shook his head. "Not to sound cold, but the amount of patience it took to attempt to pull this off is amazing."

"Did they get along?" Troy asked. He leaned against the kitchen counter, sipping a cup of coffee.

"Excuse me?"

"Were your aunt and mom close to each other?" Troy clarified.

"They got along well, at least in my presence," she said, cocking her head to look at Troy. "We spent holidays and birthdays together, but other than those special occasions, they both had their own lives. Mom trusted her enough to make her my guardian in her will."

"Other than custody of you and the administrative costs of caring for you, she didn't get a dime, did she?" Kevin asked, understanding the direction the conversation was taking.

"What are you trying to say?" River asked, her brow furrowed.

"It looks like your aunt expected a financial windfall from the death of her sister. When she didn't get it, she directed her anger at you."

"I didn't pick up on that."

"You were her meal ticket. She'd be careful not to alienate the fatted calf. You'd best have a forensic accountant go over your books. I'd bet she did some skimming from your trust funds. I assume you had her removed from everything when you turned twenty-one?" Kevin asked.

"Yes," River huffed, "which would explain her objection to the change. She said she didn't want me carrying too large of a load while I was in college. I figured she was trying to be helpful, but I wanted to stand on my own."

"You need an expert to look into that aspect," Kevin suggested.

River sighed. "I'll contact my attorney and have her recommend someone. If Aunt Amy did siphon off money, my current accountant didn't catch it, assuming he wasn't involved."

"An easy way would be to pad the expenses she submitted. In seven years, that could add up to quite a bit," Troy suggested.

River glanced from one man to another. "My brain is swimming in questions. How were the Engleharts and Roxbury involved in all this crap?"

"I think they'll confirm your aunt, not Roxbury, was the one doing the harassment last year—leaving the mutilated animals," Kevin said. "You mentioned she used local products in her catering business. Did that include local game?"

"Yes. In addition to getting meats from local ranches and hunters, she did some of the hunting herself. She enjoyed it."

"So, not only is she familiar with this place, she's also skilled at hunting and dressing her prey." Kevin paused. "Do you remember the drawings you made in Sanibel? The drawings of the animals and the knife as it slashed you?"

"I was upset that night."

"That was obvious from the sketches. The drawing of the knife has been nagging me. I couldn't figure out what it was until now. The hand you drew holding the knife belonged to a woman."

"I must have subconsciously known that. You think it was Aunt Amy?"

"It's just an educated guess, but a good bet," Troy confirmed. "She might have been there to leave you another present, but you interrupted her. The incident pushed you over a line she hadn't intended for you to cross. In setting up Roxbury, she scared you away."

"I moved because I was concerned about them—not

me. She and Dan were worried sick about my staying there."

"I'm sure Dan's unease was real," Kevin said, "but your aunt had no choice but to put on an act and pretend to be upset. If she didn't it would look odd. She overplayed her hand and you left."

"Which screwed up her plans. She had to get you back here," Troy continued. "She'd spent months setting up Roxbury to take the fall. Your death on Sanibel would have raised too many alarms. Especially with Dan. He would have become suspicious since only the two of them knew your location."

"We'll have to look into it more closely, but I also think your aunt was in Sanibel for a while," Colt said, pushing to his feet and stretching his muscles. It had been a long night for all of them.

"What? Why? When?"

"You said there were times you felt someone had been in your condo, but you couldn't prove it. Then there was the snake. Somebody put that thing in your unit."

Kevin felt River shiver. He remembered her terror as he pulled her from the bathroom. He'd also never forget her naked form wrapped around him.

"We're big on going with our guts here," Colt added, pacing as he spoke. "But if she could chase you away, maybe she could chase you back home. That idea would have fallen apart when the SATG showed up on the scene looking for that stone. Amy had to think of another way to force you back here."

"Josie uncovered a developer who plans to build a resort nearby," Colt said. "Did you know about that?"

"I'd heard some talk before I received a letter asking if I was willing to sell to them. But what's that got to do with this?"

"It's all pieces of the puzzle," Kevin explained. "You told them no. Right?"

"Of course. This is my home. My family died here. I don't want anyone digging up this place and putting a swimming pool where their bodies were found."

"Rick plans to check into the developer to see if they contacted your aunt and she perhaps had some sort of understanding with them. It would have been another incentive for her to get you back here as soon as possible. Here, she had control over your demise."

"There's any number of things that could have gotten me to come home. She didn't have to kill Dan," River argued. She left Kevin's side and went to stand by the window. Her gaze locked on the world outside her cabin.

"Jacob said his dad went back to the cabin the night he was killed." Kevin glanced at his friends. They were skilled in the art of solving mysteries, but they remained silent, letting him take the lead.

"Dan may have spotted something the day before which made him curious," he said, joining her at the window. "He might have called your aunt to tell her or question her about it. The other, less likely, option is she asked him to meet her here. I'm guessing he'd have questioned that. You said she never came out here. Dan might have thought that request strange."

"What could he have seen?" River asked, turning back to the room.

"Any number of things. Stakes left by a surveyor. Something as simple as a window blind being open which he'd left closed on his last visit. We'll eventually find out why he returned that night and why she was here. He may have been getting too curious or she needed an excuse to bring you home. Whatever the reason, she took that opportunity to kill him."

"That's evil. I can't believe she's that evil."

"Too many people are twisted inside. We don't always see it." Colt snatched his mug off the coffee table. "You loved Dan. The lure made perfect sense to her."

"And Roxbury and the Engleharts? How do they play into this?" River asked.

"I think we can connect most of the dots on that one, too," Kevin answered. "The warden said the Engleharts were encouraged to contact Roxbury by someone who called herself Grace. Based on information the warden shared, I think we can safely assume that your aunt is Grace."

"For what reason?"

"When she started gaslighting you, she needed someone to take the fall for the harassment and your eventual death. She reached out to this odd-ball, fire-and-brimstone preacher and hooked him up with the Engleharts, keeping in the shadows as she did."

"How did she manage that?"

"Rick will request copies of the letters," Colt said, "but Amy's been writing the Engleharts and even called them. By connecting the Engleharts with Roxbury she accomplished one of her goals. The authorities would immediately latch onto the relationship between the preacher and the Engleharts when something happened to you, which suited your aunt's purpose. The Engleharts looked at the relationship as a way to exact some revenge on you from behind bars. You didn't just mar their perfect record but were instrumental in putting them away for life."

"What, exactly, did Roxbury do?" River looked at each of the men.

"Roxbury was a pawn of both your aunt and the Engleharts. He was picked up this morning for questioning again. When faced with the possibility of being implicated in Dan's death and your attempted murder, he spilled everything he knew," Colt said.

"None of it would have been believed if it hadn't been for last night and your aunt panicking," Troy added.

"Roxbury never met your aunt. She was just a voice at the other end of the line. It looks like the Engleharts had him convinced to take her word and orders as gospel."

"When we searched Roxbury's property last night, we found a burner phone. There were two numbers in the contact list," Kevin said. "One belonged to the prison. It's the number someone would call to set up a visitation with one of the prisoners. I'm betting the second number will be traced back to your aunt."

"I'm still confused." River massaged her brow. "What are you seeing that I'm not?"

"Try not to view it as a complete picture," Kevin said, kneading her shoulders. "We don't have one yet. Think of it as a puzzle with some pieces still missing. You know what the outcome should be, but it will take time to get there."

River returned to the couch. She crossed her legs, yoga style. Her back, once again, was straight as if a steel rod had replaced her spine. Her curiosity was overriding her sadness.

"Correct me if I'm headed in the wrong direction," Kevin said. He stood behind River, his hands once again on her shoulders. "Here's my theory. Amy purchased two burner phones and sent one to Roxbury after he started seeing the Engleharts. His instructions were to check on you while you were here and report back to the Engleharts and to her via the number she gave him. Her sole purpose was to have a fall guy—to set him up as your stalker and, if she'd succeeded, your murderer."

"I agree," Troy said. "Initially, he was just watching you. Amy was the one behind the mutilated animals which explains him having a dead, but intact, opossum, when we caught him."

"I'm on the same page with them," Colt agreed. "As I said before, she's been building this web for a long time. It's going to take a while to unravel it."

"Roxbury and the Engleharts weren't directly involved in the harassment?"

"They are far from innocent. The Engleharts reveled in the terror you were going through. That's sick, but it's no crime. Last night, however, was another step to set up Roxbury." Kevin gave her a reassuring squeeze. "Your aunt gave him his marching orders not knowing Colt and Troy were keeping tabs on the preacher. Other than our team, no one knew they were here. Amy was at the service, so she'd have an alibi if her name ever came up. He wasn't supposed to get caught but if he did leave any evidence behind, it would tie him to the past harassment. She was probably counting on it. Amy kept him involved so there would be a fall guy when the time came for one. If he mentioned the Engleharts, they'd be more than happy to point a finger back his way. There's not much more the system can do to them. My best guess is they enjoyed toying with him. It probably gave them a perverse sense of satisfaction."

"I don't doubt that," River agreed.

"He made one phone call when he was picked up and it wasn't to a lawyer," Troy said. He dumped the remains of the coffee pot into the sink. "We tried the number. It went straight to an automated voice mail. No name attached to it. The cops will check it out, but odds are it was to the second number on his burner phone—your aunt's phone."

"Amy had to act quickly once Roxbury notified her that he'd been picked up," Colt explained. He drained his coffee cup and headed toward the kitchen. "There was a second call to the same number after he was released. Roxbury had to be free in order to become a suspect in your disappearance. He was told to call her as soon as he was released. That was her cue to move."

"Why go to the trouble of killing me and burying me in the forest? Wouldn't it have been easier and faster for her if I was just found dead? Wasn't she taking a chance my remains wouldn't be found?"

"I suspect an anonymous tip would have led them to you. She most likely had a plan to connect Roxbury to the grave and, even in her panic, stuck with her plan," Kevin said. He came around the front of the couch and offered her his hand. When she took it, he pulled her to her feet and encircled her in his arms.

"What if you'd been here?" River asked.

"Until she talks, all we can do is guess. She might have waited for an opportunity to grab you. She might have tried to kill us both. We'll have to wait for those answers, if we get them at all," he said, hugging her tightly.

"And nothing of this had to do with the shit that happened on Sanibel? Did they ever find out what happened to Kane's wife?" She pulled away from Kevin, her gaze passing from man to man.

"Other than your aunt's surreptitious visits, nothing else looks like it's connected to your aunt. Mrs. Kane's body—or what was left of it—was found floating off the coast near Miami," Colt told her. "Another lesson from the SATG."

"Do you have any idea what spooked your aunt last night?" Colt asked, rinsing his cup. "She had to be freaked out to take off with you without setting the scene. She'd been doing a damned good job of that all along."

"I think I might have triggered that. I let it slip that you were all at Roxbury's."

"That would have done it," Troy leaned against the door jamb. "She panicked. Panicked people make mistakes."

"I'm sorry, River," Kevin said. They'd been discussing her planned murder like it was an episode of *48 Hours*.

"You've got nothing to be sorry for," she said, laying a kiss on his cheek. "You saved my life. If you all hadn't helped, I'd still be clueless or dead."

"I think we need to get our asses down to the Sheriff's office," Troy interjected. "They've been patient and we need their help to fill in some holes."

———

41

A concern River hadn't voiced to any of them, was the fear of running into her aunt. She wasn't ready to face her. Anger battled with heartache. She needed time to digest and dissect her aunt's role in all this. Fortunately, that particular worry was a waste of energy. Her aunt was in the county jail. The sheriff's office was located in another building.

"Ms. Chandler?"

River had been studying her hands. The sheriff had ushered her into his office when they arrived at the station. The guys were elsewhere—presumably being questioned. It was odd to be on her own. She'd spent so much time with Kevin recently, she now felt strangely abandoned. Shit. He'd be going back to his base, then he'd be deployed. There were times when she thought they could do this thing. Be apart and still be together. There was no guarantee he'd come back to her. She'd already lost too many people. Selfish. She recognized the selfishness of it, but it was better to cut the ties than spend months wondering if he'd come home. He deserved someone stronger and unafraid.

"Ms. Chandler? Are you all right?" the sheriff asked.

"Sorry," she said, bringing her gaze up to meet his.

"No problem, Ms. Chandler. You've got a lot on your mind."

"Call me River, Sheriff. We've known each other a long time."

"Sadly enough, that's a fact. Since we're on a first name basis, call me Lance."

Lance Chamblee had been a deputy when River's family was murdered. She'd occasionally see him when she was in town. She voted for him for sheriff. He'd personally taken the lead on her case when she was receiving the *gifts* which had been left for her. He'd done his best. People trusted their neighbors here. If it hadn't been for Kevin and his friends, she seriously doubted anyone close enough to know her family would ever suspect her aunt was behind this craziness.

They spent a great deal of time breaking down interactions with her aunt before and after the death of her parents and brother. Either Aunt Amy was skilled at covering up any negative feelings or River was extremely bad at reading them. She opted for her aunt's skill at hiding her sick mind or her mother would have never named her the guardian of her children.

"Did your aunt ever ask you for money? Ever tell you her business was in trouble?"

"Never. It wasn't until recently that I gave it any thought. I could have helped her out if she needed something. It was selfish of me not to have asked. I'd planned to rectify that when we got this shit behind us."

"And it looks like she was responsible for this *shit*," Chamblee said, rubbing his jaw. He was a handsome man.

River guessed he was in his late thirties. Young for a sheriff but this was a small town, and he was more than qualified from what she knew.

"They'll be looking at her books—and yours too."

"I'll make them available. I plan on hiring a forensic accountant to review them, as well. I'm assuming that won't be a problem?"

"They can work together." Chamblee paused. "Would Ms. Scott have received the bulk of your estate if something happened to you?"

"Not everything. A big chunk would go to charity, but the majority, including the cabin, would have gone to her." River had become a dollar sign as far as her aunt was concerned. It made her sick inside.

"I never looked into your aunt when your harassment began. I can't apologize enough for that." Chamblee threw his pen on his desk and ran a hand through his hair. His jaw tightened.

"You had no reason to. Hell, she played the part perfectly. Has she talked at all?" River had gotten past the crying stage. She was still stunned and hurt. She suspected the pain would remain with her for a long time.

"She refuses to answer questions and has contacted an attorney. What we know is what she told you and your friends."

"She killed Dan," River stated flatly. She didn't doubt Kevin's assumption now—not after seeing the hate behind those wild eyes.

"I suspect so, but we still have to prove it. Did your aunt say anything you can think of that would help?" Chamblee picked up the pen he'd thrown down. He was recording the conversation, but he still took notes on a yellow pad. Highlights, she supposed.

"When she came by the cabin, she said she'd come to

check on me. I should have been on alert then since she hadn't stepped foot in the place since my family was murdered. She asked me a lot of questions about Kevin. Pressed me to the point I got annoyed." It was easy to understand her interest now. Kevin and his friends were possible wrenches in her plan.

"She was very curious about Roxbury. I couldn't tell her much. I didn't know much at that time." She looked at her hands as she literally twiddled her thumbs around each other.

"The fact that your friends were at his place must have scared her."

River's head snapped up.

"They're not in any trouble, although they did get a stern warning," he said, answering her unspoken question.

"They were just trying to help."

"And if they hadn't been helping, you might not be sitting in that uncomfortable chair right now, so I'm grateful they had your back. I wouldn't mind having one or two of them on the force."

"I think they're all happy doing what they do," she responded. Was Kevin happy? He said he was thinking about leaving the service. If he decided to leave, he'd head to South Florida and join his friends there. She understood that. Now wasn't the time to think about it.

"Getting back to Ms. Scott, how did she respond when you mentioned your friends were making a visit to Roxbury's place?"

"She didn't react at all, not that I could tell. I guess she's a pretty good actress."

"She had everyone fooled, it would seem."

"There was one question I'll never forget." River remembered her aunt chugging her glass of wine before asking the question. "She wanted to know if Roxbury had killed Dan. How could she ask me that when she knew?"

"River, you have my word, we'll see Dan gets justice," he assured her. "Is there anything else you can tell me?"

"I walked out to the car with her to get some baked goods she had for us. That's when I was hit on the head." She should have pocketed her phone. While she hadn't suspected her aunt of anything at the time, they still could have been targets. Going anywhere without her phone under the circumstances was taking chances. It was a lesson learned too late.

"Have you seen a doctor?"

"Yes. Last night. I apparently have a hard head." River took a deep breath. "When I regained consciousness, I didn't hear anyone speak. I assumed she was a victim, too. It wasn't until I was free that I discovered she was the one behind my abduction."

The sheriff nodded, his jaw clenched. He was angry on her behalf. That knowledge loosened the knot in her stomach—just a hair. He got to his feet.

"You'll be hearing from the District Attorney, but I think we've covered all we can for now. If you think of anything else, contact me," he said, extending his hand.

"Thank you," she said as he escorted her to the door.

"I wish I could have done more when this all started. If I had, things may have never gotten this far."

"I know you did your best."

"Your friends figured it out."

On cue, the men he was referring to, rounded the corner and headed down the hall toward her. Kevin reached her first, pulling her into his arms. The knot which had begun to loosen in the sheriff's office, unraveled at his touch.

"Let's go home," he said.

Home. She had no family. Did that mean she had no home?

~

THEY STOPPED FOR A FAST-FOOD DINNER. River picked at her sandwich and nibbled on a few fries, but Kevin was unsuccessful at getting her to eat. The mystery was solved and she was safe, but the resolution came at the loss of her remaining family member.

Over cold hamburgers and soft drinks they picked apart the questions they'd been asked by the authorities. Using those questions, they filled in the holes in their theories. A clearer picture began to develop.

With River's permission, the authorities had quickly opened the spigot and began the flow of documents from her financial institutions when Amy Scott was still on her accounts. A superficial look told them her aunt had almost immediately began to skim money from River's trust fund after she was named guardian. The expenses for the cost of the care of the fourteen-year-old were excessive, but not so evident that any of the transactions had been questioned by her bank or the courts. River didn't take an interest in her finances until she started her search for a college.

While drawing circles in a mound of ketchup with a french fry, River admitted that once she taken over the financial end of things, something had teased in the back of her mind that it had cost more to raise her than it did to live on her own. She'd ignored the feeling.

"I didn't look any further than the balance on the accounts when I accessed them. Maybe I was subconsciously afraid of what I'd find," she admitted. "Why did

Aunt Amy wait? Why wait until last year to start her assault?"

"Did she ask you for money recently?" Kevin asked.

"No. And I didn't offer any. I didn't know she needed it."

"You don't know she *needed* it," Kevin said. "Maybe she just *wanted* it."

Kevin regretted the statement as River's eyes pooled with unshed tears. Her aunt wanted her dead—because she wanted money more than she loved her niece.

"I'm sorry," he said as she knuckled away tears.

"I wish you'd all stop saying you're sorry. I don't want anyone's pity," she snapped.

"River…"

"Can we go now?" She reached for her purse. "People are watching and I'm tired of being a star in a freak show." She slid out of the booth and headed for the door.

"Tread lightly," Troy warned, staring after River. "She's not in a good place right now."

"Hang in there," Colt said, adding his support.

River was waiting by the car when he stepped out into the cool air. She said nothing as he popped the locks, then buckled herself in. Something told him now was not the time for conversation.

Colt and Troy headed back to the resort while Kevin drove River to the cabin. She was quiet, staring out the passenger window at the long shadows cast by the setting sun. They had one last night together in North Carolina. Tomorrow they'd be heading back to Florida. At least he assumed River would be joining them on the flight back. She'd brought a minimal change of clothing with her and a small part of the current project she was working on when they'd left Sanibel.

When they pulled up to the cabin, River let herself out

and into her home. She shrugged off her jacket, hung it on the hook near the door.

"Are you upset with me?" He'd been mentally running through what he'd said and if any one of his comments could have wounded her.

"You?" she asked, her eyes widening in surprise. "No. I'm angry at myself. I've elected to live a solitary life. Maybe if I'd been more involved with Aunt Amy, I wouldn't have missed the signs. Still, how could she be so cruel as to pull the Engleharts into her personal mission to obtain my finances? That goes beyond greed. It's mental terrorism. What sort of person does that? What sort of person kills a decent man for the sole purpose of luring me home? I don't understand any of this. How much of this is my fault?" She gulped air. "It hurts. God, it hurts so much."

Kevin pulled her into his arms. He continued to hold her as she soaked his shirt. She deserved to fill buckets with tears. Kevin personally wanted to kick the shit out of her aunt. The Engleharts were evil, mentally ill bastards. Roxbury could be dumb as a rock for all he knew. Amy, on the other hand, was greedy, cold, calculating and cruel.

Eventually, River's well ran dry. She took a deep breath, exhaled and stepped back. A gentle smile graced her face. The bloodshot eyes tore at his gut, but the smile soothed it.

"You okay?"

"Better." She brushed her hand over the damp spot on his shirt. "Sorry."

"Saves me a wash," he joked, making her smile grow wider.

"Let me crank up the heat," she said.

"I'll take care of it," he offered, turning her toward the

bedroom. "Why don't you get comfortable. It's been a long day."

He was glad to see a ghost of a smile still on her face as she stepped into the bathroom. He knew a good cry was cathartic. There were times on the battlefield he certainly felt like crying, but being a medic, he needed to project an air of confidence. He didn't want his patients to lose hope. Many nights, lying in the darkness, he would sometimes hear sobbing coming from another tent or bunker. It was hell. You didn't get through hell unscathed. Had his comrades who'd set their emotions free fared better than those who'd kept them in check?

Grabbing a few logs from the woodpile out back, Kevin started a fire. The crackling of the burning wood gave off a soothing sound. By the time River returned to the cabin from Sanibel, it should be warm enough that the fireplace wouldn't be needed. He was making assumptions again. Turning away from the mesmerizing flames, he noted the bathroom door was open, but the bedroom door was closed.

He stepped into the room and smiled. A candle flickered on the bedside table. River was in bed, the covers tucked under her bare arms. She was waiting for him.

42

———

*R*iver slipped out of bed early the next morning. She started a pot of coffee, then headed for the bathroom. Kevin joined her as she was rinsing her hair. It was a tight fit, but they didn't need much space between them.

She left him to finish his shower, grabbed a cup of coffee and started packing her things. She needed to head back to Sanibel. While she'd brought a portion of her current project with her, she required more shells to finish the mask. The vendors had promised to locate what she needed. There was also the task of getting the condo ready for rental.

The bathroom door opened, a puff of steam escaping as it did. The rooms were so close, it was hard to miss it.

"You're coming back with us?" Kevin asked from the doorway. He leaned against the jamb, a towel wrapped around his waist.

"I assumed it would be okay if I hitched a ride with y'all," she said. "I've got to finish this mask. By the time I get it done, I'll be free to set the condo up with the management company to rent."

There was a slight tilt of his head and a narrowing of his eyes.

"What? Did you think I was staying on the island?" She ignored the gnawing feeling and continued to pack up the box. "Besides, I'll be needed here for the investigation and trial."

"Why don't you spend some time on Sanibel? You won't be needed back here for a while and they conduct telephone interviews all the time. You have friends there, you know?" Kevin pulled up to his full height.

"They're your friends, Kevin. Not mine. They're special people to whom I owe a great deal." She'd lost so much—too many people in her life. Getting close to others would just mean more loss. He'd never understand.

"You don't owe them a damn thing," he said. Turning his back on her, he snapped the towel from his waist.

"What's your problem?" she asked, quickly turning her attention away from his backside. Why was he angry?

"I'm not the one with the problem." He threw his duffel on the bed, pulled out some clothes and began to dress.

"Excuse me?" Now she was getting angry.

"This place means more to you than anything, doesn't it?" He stopped buttoning his shirt to stare at her.

"You know it does."

"More than that?" He pointed to the bed.

River stared at the rumpled sheets and bunched up blanket. She given herself entirely to him last night. She'd known it would be their last night together. Apparently, he'd just put the pieces together himself.

"Why?" he asked. "Why are you coming back here to live your life alone?"

"This is my home." She bit her bottom lip to keep it from trembling. Her home was a major part of it. What he didn't understand was that being alone was preferable to losing anyone else. She'd believed she'd lost all she had to lose when her family was murdered. Then she lost Dan. Her aunt might as well be dead. Kevin would be deploying. He'd be gone for months, assuming he came back at all.

Then there was the issue of his friends. If she stayed on Sanibel, Cat, Josie, and Shayne would never leave her alone. They'd work on her until she was part of something else, something else she could lose—friendships.

"You don't have to give this place up, but you don't have to be tied to it, either."

"I belong here," she said, lowering her head until only his large feet were visible. She wouldn't look him in the eye. She couldn't bear to see the hurt.

"I thought you and I had something together. Didn't these last few weeks mean anything to you?"

Everything. It had meant everything and if parting hurt this much, she wasn't strong enough to survive his deployments. She might never see him again. It was better to make the break now than when he was halfway across the world. That would be cruel. There was no hope for them. She'd always be afraid of losing him, one way or another.

At first it had simply been sex. Damn good sex, but she fell for him. She hadn't known what it was like to be in love until she'd met Kevin. A voice in the back of her head had been warning her against it. She hadn't been listening. But now she listened as it lectured her. If you love someone, you will lose them. If she told him the truth, he'd try to convince her otherwise.

"I'm sorry, Kevin. I can't be what you want me to be."

It was time to cut the cord. "I'll find my own way back to Sanibel. Give your friends my thanks."

"You give it to them yourself. I'm not your errand boy." He zipped his duffel bag shut and slung it over his shoulder. "You deserve an Oscar. You had me fooled. I thought you were strong, but you're still a frightened little girl. You hang on to this place and your past. If that's all you want out of life, fine. I want more."

The door slammed followed by the sound of the car pulling away. It would only hurt for a while, she promised herself as she dropped to the floor. Curled up on the area rug, she cried. It was the right decision. Kevin was right. He deserved better. He deserved someone stronger— someone who wasn't afraid to take a chance.

43

River had been right on one point; the ladies of Sanibel did not give up. When she hadn't been on the plane when it landed in Fort Myers, the calls started. She'd let each one go to voice mail. Surprisingly, none of the messages berated her for what she'd done to Kevin. Instead, Cat, Shayne, and Josie all called to check on her.

To avoid any accidental meetings, she'd snuck back onto the island in the middle of the night a few days after Kevin had stormed from her cabin. Her visit to Sanibel was brief. She packed her clothes and tools and dumped the food from the condo. On her way out of town, she stopped by the postal store to pick up the shells she'd had shipped to her by the vendors on the island.

Her plan to make the unit available for seasonal rentals, never materialized. She'd had every intention of contacting the management company, but she continually pushed the task aside. Why?

Instead of dealing with the question, she'd work to exhaustion each day hoping to fall into bed, too tired to think. No matter how many times she'd washed the sheets, she imagined Kevin's scent as she wrestled with the covers each night. The idea of getting rid of both the sheets and the bed came to her as she lay awake one night, but she'd earned the torment. Punishment for breaking a kind, loving heart. Sleepless nights were a small penance to pay.

After a month of avoiding calls and various threats to show up unannounced, River texted Shayne to assure her she was okay, and they had no reason to worry—even though it wasn't near the truth. She was miserable. Her single text to Shayne didn't end the ongoing, but friendly, assaults by the three women. River had miscalculated again. Cracking that door open with a response had been interpreted as an invitation to walk through it. Eventually, she broke down and began to answer the texts from Cat and Josie, too. The texts morphed into phone calls. River shouldn't have answered but they'd been subtly dropping bits and pieces about Kevin. Those little bits of information lifted her from her consistent melancholy existence.

She succeeded in making a point to never ask about him. There would have been a full court press if she showed interest in him. There was nothing wrong being concerned about his well-being. Right? His team was in South America. The group on Sanibel communicated with him regularly via email and an occasional phone call. There was no mention of him missing her—which pinched at her heart a bit. He shouldn't care for her or how she was doing. She'd wanted him out of her life. The question was why she tortured herself hoping for bits and pieces of information on how he was doing and when he would be home safe.

As the weather began to cool, the women added a bigger weapon to their arsenal—Gib. The charmer contacted her regularly, trying to coax her down to the warmer weather. Admittedly, North Carolina winters were dreary which added to her mood, but she couldn't go back to Sanibel. Kevin should be stateside soon, if he wasn't already. What were the chances she'd run into him when he visited his friends? She wouldn't be able to hide her emotions. She'd set him free. He deserved better—someone who would make him happy.

A week before Christmas, she received a text from Gib which simply said "SURPRISE!" What surprise? She groaned at the knock on the door. A sigh escaped as she peeked through the window curtain. Gib was standing on her front porch, cupping his hands and blowing a warm breath into them. She'd forgotten his stunning looks. His thick, blond hair was secured at the base of his neck and hung over the collar of his windbreaker. The ruby stud in his ear, didn't sparkle in the overcast light as it did in the warm sunshine. What the hell was he doing here?

"C'mon on, River," he shouted. "Open up. Have pity on this Florida boy. I'm freezing out here."

Opening the door, she ushered him in. "Serves you right for showing up, especially without notice."

He walked past her and straight to the fireplace, rubbing his hands over the hearth.

"I come all this way to wish you a Merry Christmas and all you do is lecture me?" His glance went past her, then circled the room. "Where are your holiday decorations?"

"I don't do Christmas," she said. "I'm alone here. What's the point?"

"Because it brings you joy." Those wolf gray eyes narrowed at her.

Joy. It was a fleeting emotion.

Gib moved away from the fireplace and stood in front of her. "Why can't you be happy?" he asked, as he pulled her into a warm embrace. "You deserve to be, you know?"

Her shoulders dropped. She'd chosen her path. It was too late to change it.

"Is that why you're here? To lecture me. I've done enough self-lecturing to last a lifetime." Moving over to the fireplace where Gib had stood, she cocked her head in his direction. "I don't understand why you all care." It was the first time she'd voiced the question out loud. It sounded selfish.

"Because you're part of our family. You became a member when you and Kevin fell for each other."

"I kinda screwed that up, didn't I? I think I've nullified my honorary family membership." She wanted to kick him out. The subject hurt.

"You're still in love with him. You can't hide it—not from any of us," he said, joining her.

"I never told anyone that."

"You didn't have to. You can't get anything by us. The women are pretty damn astute, and I can tell by the look in your eyes where your heart is. Why don't you come back with me?"

She closed her eyes and asked the obvious. "Is Kevin there?"

"No. I guarantee you he is not."

"Will he be?"

"Stop running from things you can't see," Gib said. "We want you with us for the holidays."

She knew he was right. Running wasn't making her happy. Isolation no longer gave her comfort. She was simply existing. Nothing more.

"I assume you have access to your friend's sleek private jet?"

"Waiting at the airport."

"God, you're persuasive. I imagine there aren't many women that say no to you."

He just grinned.

"Let me change clothes and throw a few things together. Do you know how to kill a fire?" she asked, pointing to the fireplace.

"I think I can figure it out. If not, I'll Google it."

River rolled her eyes as she headed to the bedroom. She'd make sure the fire was out before they left. Grabbing some of her lighter clothing, and other things she would need for a couple of days, she stuffed them in an overnight case. Butterflies fluttered in her stomach. Was she hoping to see Kevin or afraid that she would? What would she say if he showed up?

There was no time to think of an answer. Gib's spot in front of the fireplace had been taken over by the man who visited her dreams when she was able to sleep. Her eyes fixed, her thoughts spinning, she couldn't speak. Damn Gib.

"Hey." Wasn't that profound?

"Hey," he answered…and then smiled.

He reached out and gathered her into his arms. She rested her head on his chest and inhaled the scent she hadn't been able to forget.

"You should hate me," she mumbled against his shirt.

"I could never hate you. I was angry. I left without trying to make things right between us. That's no way to leave someone you love."

"I hurt you. You had a right to be angry—and I don't think I was in any state of mind to get on the same page with you. I was messed up pretty bad back then."

"It took me a while to open my eyes and figure that out." He continued to stroke her hair.

She pushed back from him. "You love me? You said you love me."

"I did—and I do."

"I didn't want to love you," she admitted. "I didn't want to lose anyone else, but the minute you walked out that door, I'd lost you. Pushing you away didn't stop the hurt." She lowered her lashes, once again determined not to cry.

"River. Don't."

His palms cradled her cheeks as he tilted her head up. The kiss was warm and comforting. Oh, God. He tasted like home. As he began to deepen the kiss, she stepped back.

"How'd you know I didn't hook up with anyone else while you were deployed?"

He smiled. "The same way you knew I was safe."

"Cat, Josie and Shayne," she said with certainty.

His smiled widened.

"What if I had found someone else?" She returned the grin.

"Seriously?" he laughed. "I'd have been notified. Taken leave and dealt with the interloper. Now, where were we?"

A horn blared out front.

"Oh, shit. I forgot Gib was outside." He reached for her bag. "We'll finish this tonight."

She was grinning as she stepped out into the cold.

EPILOGUE

$\mathcal{S}$ummer, North Carolina Mountains

THEY EXCHANGED VOWS next to the birdbath in the butterfly garden. Kevin had known when he proposed that the wedding would take place where River was closest to her family. The dress was casual. The ceremony informal. The cabin had initially been intended as a place to relax and enjoy the natural setting. A place to love and to laugh. River wanted it to return to those happy times. She would continue to honor and remember her family—and one day, hopefully, bring children back here to play as she and her brother had.

The entire gang came up from Sanibel. River had also invited Dan's son, Jacob, and Sheriff Chamblee. Both men had kept tabs on her after she'd returned to the cabin last year. They'd become part of River's growing circle of friends.

After a two-week honeymoon in the cabin, they'd be

returning to Florida. The condo would be home base. Kevin would be starting work at a nearby hospital as an ER nurse. He'd also be volunteering at the island's free clinic where many of the workers on the island, who barely made a living wage, sought medical treatment.

Orders for River's unique masks were pouring in after her jeweled creation made its debut in a music video. She had an extensive wait list. She hadn't brought any work with her this trip, though. His plans were to keep her busy in other ways while enjoying the solitude of the mountains. These mountains had saved her life. Perhaps the two of them would create a new one together.

As River recited the vows she'd written, those ice blue eyes gazed into his. There were tears again, but he didn't fret over them this time. Her smile telegraphed her joy. He planned to spend the rest of his life making her happy.

ACKNOWLEDGMENTS

I never had an English or Literary teacher who wasn't a nun. The Sisters of The Little Flower and St. Thomas Aquinas HS taught me to love reading and encouraged creativity. I'm not sure how they'd feel about romantic suspense, but they planted a seed. It took a long time but that seed finally blossomed. So, a shout out to all the teachers who plant the seeds and grow gardens of writers.

A huge thank you to Sue-Ellen Welfonder , a USA Today Bestselling author. I am lucky to know her. She is one of my biggest cheerleaders and has given freely of her time and expertise. I'm still at the keyboard because of her.

The absolutely amazing cover is the artwork of Elizabeth Turner Stokes of estokescreative.com. I am so honored this skilled illustrator took the time for a wet-behind-the-ears Indie author. She has the uncanny ability to see what the author has envisioned. I have no doubt I drive her to drink—and that I owe her more than a few of them.

There are, as usual, too many others to thank. Books are not the sole result of a writer searching for the right words and a plot that will hold your interest. It's the result of family, friends and others who step in and give the author support, ideas, critiques and answer research questions. You know who you are, and I thank you for all your help. A special shout to Dr. Grace who took time out of her busy schedule to answer questions.

And, finally, to all of you who read my stories and leave reviews. They are, quite frankly, the biggest boost you can give any writer. Please take the time to review this and other writers' efforts so that we may continue to entertain you.

ABOUT THE AUTHOR

ABOUT THE AUTHOR

C. F. Francis is a native Floridian who loves mystery, suspense and romance. Her favorite pastimes are reading (of course) and traveling. Her diverse background includes working in law, insurance, tourism and a stint with the Florida Legislature's Organized Crime Committee. She is honored to have friends who have served in the Special Forces and Military Intelligence, who have generously shared their expertise when asked. Ms. Francis lives in Southwest Florida near the areas where her novels take place.

If you enjoyed this story, please consider leaving a review on BookBub, Goodreads or your retailer's site.

You can follow C. F. Francis at:

www.cffrancis.com

ALSO BY C. F. FRANCIS

Sanctuary Island

Lovers Key

Explosive Touch

www.ingramcontent.com/pod-product-compliance
Lightning Source LLC
Chambersburg PA
CBHW031932110726
47902CB00001B/138